T0154246

Pascal Garnier
Pascal Garnier was born in Paris in 1949. The prize-winning author of more than sixty books, he remains a leading figure in contemporary French literature, in the tradition of Georges Simenon. He died in 2010.

Emily Boyce
Emily Boyce is in-house translator and editor at Gallic Books.

Jane Aitken
Jane Aitken is a publisher and translator.

Melanie Florence
Melanie Florence teaches at the University of Oxford and translates from the French.

'Wonderful . . . Properly noir' Ian Rankin

'Garnier plunges you into a bizarre, overheated world, seething death, writing, fictions and philosophy. He's a trippy, sleazy, sly and classy read' A. L. Kennedy

'Horribly funny . . . appalling and bracing in equal measure. Masterful' John Banville

'Ennui, dislocation, alienation, estrangement – these are the colours on Garnier's palette. His books are out there on their own: short, jagged and exhilarating' Stanley Donwood

'The combination of sudden violence, surreal touches and bone-dry humour have led to Garnier's work being compared with the films of Tarantino and the Coen brothers' *Sunday Times*

'Deliciously dark . . . painfully funny' *New York Times*

'A mixture of Albert Camus and JG Ballard' *Financial Times*

'A brilliant exercise in grim and gripping irony; makes you grin as well as wince' *Sunday Telegraph*

'A master of the surreal noir thriller – Luis Buñuel meets Georges Simenon' *Times Literary Supplement*

'Tense, strange, disconcerting and slyly funny' *Sunday Times*

'Combines a sense of the surreal with a ruthless wit' *The Observer*

'Devastating and brilliant' *Sunday Times*

'Bleak, often funny and never predictable' *The Observer*

The Eskimo Solution
Low Heights
Too Close to the Edge

Pascal Garnier

A Gallic Book

The Eskimo Solution
First published in France as *La Solution Esquimau* by Zulma
© Zulma, 2006

English translation copyright © Gallic Books, 2016
First published in Great Britain in 2016 by Gallic Books

Low Heights
First published in France as *Les Hauts du Bas* by Zulma
© Zulma, 2003

English translation copyright © Gallic Books, 2017
First published in Great Britain in 2017 by Gallic Books

Too Close to the Edge
First published in France as *Trop près du bord* by Zulma
© Zulma, 2010

English translation copyright © Gallic Books, 2016
First published in Great Britain in 2016 by Gallic Books

ISBN 978-1-910477-60-1

Typeset in Fournier MT by Gallic Books
Printed in the UK by CPI (CR0 4YY)

The Eskimo Solution

1

Louis had slept on the bottom bunk in the children's room. He was surrounded by soft-toy monsters and a fire engine dug into his back. Somewhere outside a drill ripped into a pavement; it must be daytime. Louis turned over and curled up, knees under his chin, hands between his thighs, nose squashed under a downy pink dinosaur smelling of dribble and curdled milk.

Why had they rowed the previous evening? ... Oh, yes! It was because Alice wanted to be cremated whilst he wanted to be buried. For Alice, with her straightforward common sense, it was crystal clear. First of all, cremation was less expensive; secondly, it was cleaner; thirdly, it avoided uselessly occupying ground (think what could be built instead of the Thiais cemetery, for example!); and fourthly, her somewhat romantic conclusion was that she would like her ashes to be scattered off the coast of Kalymnos (where they had spent their last holiday) from the bow of a beautiful white boat.

He had interrupted her a bit abruptly. First of all, when you're dead you don't give a flying fuck about the burial costs; secondly, we already tip enough muck into the sea; thirdly, cemeteries are much more pleasant to wander through than dormitory towns; and fourthly, given the progress of science, it's entirely possible that one day we'll be able to recreate life from skeletons, whereas a handful of ashes thrown in the sea, well … He'd accompanied the last point with an obscene gesture.

And who was going to pay for his fucking burial? Was it not enough that he sponged off everyone while he was alive, did it have to continue after his death? Such egotism! Would he like chrysanthemums every Hallowe'en as well?

Of course he wanted chrysanthemums! And trees filled with birds, and cats everywhere! Wasn't she the one who went into raptures over the mossy old gravestones in the Père-Lachaise? That one where the stone had split under pressure from a growing laurel tree?

OK, so why didn't he put money aside to pay for his old moss-covered gravestone? Why was that, then?

Here we go, money, it's always about money …

After that all he remembered was a sordid slide into a petty domestic squabble and the harsh realities backed up with numbers that she threw in his face. He didn't have the ammunition to argue with Alice about money, so he had risen from the table, saying, 'If that's the way you feel, I just won't die. That'll be cheaper, won't it?'

And that was really what he had in mind. It was a conviction rooted deep inside him: he would never die.

But that certainty had been severely shaken this year; four of his friends had died. Obviously, as he was forty, he had encountered death before, but this was different. Before it had always either been old people – an uncle, an aunt – or acquaintances who weren't expected to live long, or if they were young, accidents, mostly car accidents, and the deaths seemed normal. But the last four had been people like him, going to all the same kinds of places, enjoying the same books, music and films. Their deaths had not been sudden; they had had time to get used to the idea, living with it for months, discussing it calmly, as you might discuss money problems, work problems or problems in your relationship. And it was that attitude of rational acceptance that had thrown Louis. People like him (not exactly like him now they were dead) had accepted the unacceptable. Four in one year.

As for the others …

Every day at the same time I go up to my study, read over these pages and ask myself, 'What's the point of writing a story I already know off by heart?' I've explained it to so many people that the tiresome formality of putting it down on paper is about as exciting to me as opening the TV guide to discover *The Longest Day* showing on every channel. In an ideal world I'd sell the story as it is, in its raw state, to someone who had some enthusiasm for writing it. Or who didn't, but would write it for me all the same. Not that it's a bad story, far from it. Madame Beck, my editor, is the only one to have expressed any reservations. I had a hell of a time winning her over.

'It's the story of a man in his forties called Louis, who's a nice guy but skint, and kills his mother for the inheritance.'

Madame Beck's harsh-sounding name suits her down to the ground. After a long, sharp intake of breath, she replied.

'Not exactly original.'

'Wait a minute, let me go on. It's a very modest inheritance – but that's beside the point. Since everything goes to plan, no trouble with the law or anything, he starts killing the parents of friends in need. Of course, he doesn't tell them what he's doing – it's his little secret, pure charity. He's an anonymous benefactor, if you like.'

Madame Beck lowered her head in despair.

'Why don't you carry on writing for children? Your kids' books are doing well …'

'This is a kids' book! He's a really nice guy! He loves his mother, loves his friends, his friends' parents, he loves everyone, but these are tough times for all of us, aren't they? He kills people's parents the way Eskimos leave their elders on a patch of ice because … it's natural, ecologically sound, a lot more humane and far more economical than endlessly prolonging their suffering in a dismal nursing home. Besides, he'll hardly be doing them harm; he'll do the job carefully, every crime professionally planned and tailored to the person like a Club Med holiday. Plus there's nothing to stop us giving him his comeuppance at the end. I could have him murdered by the twenty-something son he hasn't seen for years, who's got in with a bad crowd. Or have him fall prey to a random act of violence, a mugging on the métro gone wrong, something like that … What do you think?'

Two hours later, Madame Beck was reluctantly handing me a cheque, barely able to look at me.

With that meagre advance, I've been able to rent a cottage by the sea from a painter friend of mine, where I've spent the past two months yawning so hard I've almost dislocated my jaw.

'I wake up in the morning with my mouth wide open. My teeth are oily: I'd be better off brushing them before bed, but I can never bring myself to do it.' These words of Emmanuel Bove's, the opening line of his novel *My Friends*, sum up my state of mind exactly. I put aside my typewriter – already thick with dust – and tackle tasks more suited to my skills: washing up, a bit of housework, starting a shopping list, bread, ham, butter, eggs … I don't mind chores; they stop me beating a permanent retreat to my bed. Plus, routines are a useful way of preparing for the hereafter. Then I head to the beach, whatever the weather.

Today, it's glorious, a picture-postcard sky, framed by the

inevitable seagulls. The beach is very close to where I'm staying – a five-minute walk straight down Rue de la Mer. It's always a surprise to see that mass of green jelly at the end of the road and the no-entry sign sticking up like a big fat lollipop on the horizon. You find yourself leaning forward as you walk, head down against the wind that stands guard along the front. There's something minty about the cold. You can clearly see the chimneys of Le Havre and the tankers waiting their turn at Passage d'Entifer.

When you are mute, or almost mute, certain words explode inside your head like fireworks: ENTIFER. Or even: TOOTHBRUSH. I never speak to anyone, only the woman in the tobacconist's on Rue de la Mer.

'Good morning, Madame ... How are you today, Madame?'

Like the sea, she's up and down – she lives above her shop and is never seen anywhere else.

There are two people on the beach. As they approach the waves, they stop and ponder whether to turn left or right. In the end they part ways, one sticking out her chest and grabbing an armful of sunshine, the other spinning on the spot, flapping the wings of her coat. She stumbles into the foam and re-emerges, knees held high. I can put up with happy people, from a distance.

I never walk far along the beach.

Yes, when I was first here, I went exploring, clambering over rocks and craggy outcrops, coming back exhausted, my pockets filled with pebbles, shells, bits of wood. Now I prefer to sit on the bench for old people. There are none of them here at this time of year – it's too cold. For a brief moment, I enjoy the exhilarating feeling of being right where I should be, a feeling made all the sweeter by my knowing exactly where I'm headed: back to humanity with a thud.

Here comes the 'thug'! I know him by his lumbering gait; he walks as if pushing an invisible wheelbarrow. Shaved head, face like a suitcase that's been dragged around the world, hands like feet and feet that make furrows in the ground, whether sand, concrete or tarmac. The man has a permanent black eye or a hand in plaster – they say he's always getting into fights. And yet everyone accepts him, puts up with him. I, on the other hand, am terrified of him. If it was up to me, he'd have been locked up long ago, or simply eliminated. He forces me to get up and walk further. But further is too far for me. I decide to head back along the beach.

I love trampling on shells; I imagine they're my editor's glasses. There's no one left now that the two people have gone, and the thug with them. I suddenly feel so alone it's as if I'm invisible. The sky shrinks back above my head like burnt skin. The silence bores into my ears. I'd give anything to be anywhere but here.

As for the others (the ones who weren't dead, not yet) they were like him, living flat on their stomachs in hastily built trenches, keeping watch for the snipers that were decimating their ranks. Reaching their forties was starting to feel like the path to the emergency exit.

Louis would happily spend the day in the children's room, crammed into the little bed like a vegetable in a crate. When he was little, he used to spend hours like that, in a state of boredom. No one should believe that good children sitting quietly are gentle dreamers, inhabiting marvellous worlds. No, they're just bored. Although the boredom of childhood is of a different quality, a sort of opium. Later on, it's hard to recall that feeling. Tedium has replaced boredom. The row with Alice yesterday evening, or rather its consequences, were part of the tedium.

Suddenly the little room was suffocating; the pleasant gloom had become a black cocoon pressing in on him. Louis jumped out of bed, pulled back the curtains and opened the window. He was hit by the light and the hammering of the pneumatic drill. He closed his eyes, grimacing, and staggered back to the little bed. There was a note stuck under the bedside lamp. Alice's writing.

'If you could be gone by the time I get back, that would be good.'

Of course, he had been expecting this for a long time, but why now? That stupid argument must have been the last straw. As if he cared what happened to him after his death! Now he was going to have to move out.

The impact of the sparrow against the glass of the half-open window made no more noise than a rubber ball bouncing on a carpet. Yet this little collision radiated like an electric charge through Louis from his chest to his groin. All his childhood fears were contained in that little ball of grey feathers, tiny bones and quivering flesh now trapped inside the room by the curtain. Outside, the insistent thrumming of the drill was the counterpoint to the noise of the bird's panicked beak against the window.

'Go away!'

The bird froze in front of the window, framed by the white sky like a bad painting. Louis closed his eyes, hoping the sparrow would escape by itself, but the tapping of the beak started up again, shattering the silence. All he needed to do was lift the curtain and open the window wide but Louis could not bear the idea of even the briefest physical contact with the idiot bird. He would need a long stick, a fishing rod, for example. What if the bird, in freeing itself, flew into his face? Birds always got in your face, like cats and spider webs.

A breath of air briefly lifted the white net curtain. Enough to allow the sparrow to propel itself through the beckoning gap. But it was a very young bird, to whom no one had ever explained the difference between inside and outside. And so instead of flying off it began to twirl about like a demented wind-up toy between the four walls of the little bedroom. Exhausted and terrorised, it came to rest wide-eyed on the corner of the wardrobe. The smell of fear turned the atmosphere of the room into a toxic, unbreathable acid. Then another draught arrived to waft the curtain. The bird spotted the white rectangle and recognised its territory, the great outdoors with no corners and no obstacles that stretched from never to nowhere. Ecstatic, it flung itself at the opening. It was halfway out when the window banged shut, cleaving it in two.

Open-mouthed, Louis watched as grey feathers floated to the carpet. Just then the phone rang.

'Hello? Yes, it's me. Good morning, Richard. No, I haven't forgotten I owe you money. Yes, I know, but ... everything's a bit tight at the moment ... Listen, Richard, I can't talk to you now, a bird has just been decapitated in front of me ... No, it's not another of my excuses! I swear, it's shaken me up. Why don't we get together later, shall we say 12.30? ... Where? Brasserie Printemps, under the dome ... And why not? ... Yes, yes, I insist, it's a beautiful place. Excellent, see you soon.'

Why did I call him Louis? After the old French coin, because of his money worries? I must have been pissed when I came up with that. I get silly when I've had a drink, start playing around with words. Louis doesn't suit him. He needs a younger, more contemporary name. Like the guy at the other end of the bar, for example – what's his name? ... I can hear it from the mouth of the landlord serving him: Jean-Yves. I can't imagine calling my hero Jean-Yves for 200 pages.

Though I can't claim to have done much to serve the greater good today, I'm still feeling quite pleased with my efforts. My word count is hardly spectacular, but it's not a bad show for two hours' work. The bird incident was what got me back in the swing of it. When I opened my eyes this morning, I noticed that one of the panes in my bedroom window was broken and a fluffy white feather was caught in the Z-shaped crack. I don't remember hearing anything, but I'm sleeping deeply at the moment. Whatever it was, it could only be a sign, an invitation to pick up my quill. I could have written more but Hélène rang. Wants to take me on a three-day trip to England. I'll be glad to see Hélène, but why England? What's wrong with meeting up here?

After the phone call, I went back to the beach to watch the sun go down. The footprints in the sand are an odd reminder of all the people who've pounded up and down the beach, whom you'll never see. The sun was taking for ever to disappear, so I left before the show was over. On the way home, I stopped at a café for a half. I wasn't thirsty; I just needed some human company, to nestle among the other beasts in the stable. Plenty of people go out in their slippers here. The guy next to me's wearing a pair. He's a giant with tiny feet. Size 38 or 39, no bigger. I can't take my eyes off them. I've seen him around town several times but never noticed how small his feet were. I'd never caught the name of the café either, so I ask. They tell me it doesn't have one. Once upon a time the owner was called 'Bouin'. But it's changed hands several times since then. These days, you just go 'to the café' or 'to the tobacconist's', depending on what you need.

Staring into space as I wait for my pasta water to boil, I remember Hélène's phone call. Why on earth did I agree to this ridiculous trip?

'So, what d'you think? Good idea, isn't it?'

'Why don't we just chill out here for a couple of days instead?'

'No, thanks. I've seen enough of that place; it's a miserable hole.'

'But I've got work to do. I'm already pushed …'

'Exactly. What difference is a day or two going to make? If you're that worried, you could take the typewriter with you and work at the hotel. It's three days, not a voyage to the ends of the earth!'

'Three days in England isn't the same as three days here.'

'What are you on about?'

'I know what travelling's like! You cram so much into every day that it feels like two days in one.'

'For goodness' sake, you're such a homebody!'

'No, I'm not. I travel all the time, just not from place to place.'

'Don't you want to see me?'

'Of course I do. That's got nothing to do with it …'

After that, I continued to hear her voice but not the words. A bewitching melody was playing through the little holes in the phone in an unfamiliar and sweet-sounding language. I said yes. Then she hung up.

Now I'm really in the shit. She's coming to pick me up in two days' time. Two days is nothing – she may as well have said, 'I'll be there in two hours.' I'm looking at everything around me as if for the last time. I'll have to speak, and in English to boot! We'll get lost and have to ask for directions. I can ask for directions in English; I just won't understand the reply. That's not going to get me very far! We'll have to drive on the left, courting death at every crossroads. Hélène's obsession with avoiding all the places 'other people' go will mean she insists on experiencing the dingiest pubs, where I'll sit wincing while sailors drunk on beer make eyes at her. We'll have to lug heavy bags from one hotel to another in the pouring rain. I'll be among people in their natural habitat. Come to think of it, I'm in the same situation as

Louis, forced to do things against my will because of the choice a woman has made. Suddenly I'm feeling a lot more warmly towards Louis. Telephone!

'Christophe, how are things?'

'Well, to be honest …'

'Is it Nane? What's happened?'

'No, she's fine – well, there's no change. It's not that, or not just that. I dunno. The kids, work, money, time passing, a bit of everything. I've been thinking of you by the sea, all that fresh air … If I could find the time, I'd really like to come and visit.'

'That would be great, only I'm going away the day after tomorrow.'

'Oh, really? Where?'

'To England, with Hélène.'

'Oh, nice! You'll have to tell me all about it. Right, I'll let you get on. I've got to dash over to Nane's place, doctor's coming round. Bon voyage, you jammy git!'

Hardly! True, next to his problems, mine seem on the mild side. His ex-wife Nane is dying in a studio flat somewhere in the sixteenth arrondissement of Paris. Nane was as beautiful as a Sunday, as a day with no purpose, kind, intelligent, perfect. One morning, she walked out of the door without even saying goodbye, leaving Christophe to bring up two kids on his own. He never tried understand, but carried on loving her as he always had done, like an ox faithfully pulling its plough. Fifteen years went by with no news of her, and then a year ago he bumped into her by chance. She's ill – very ill. He's been looking after her ever since, as Nane's mother ought to have done if only she wasn't a self-obsessed monster. All that woman has done for her daughter is allow her to rent one of the studios she owns in Paris – at an extortionate price – purely because it would have been a headache to have left her on the streets. If only Louis existed in real life.

11

But he doesn't, and Nane is so exhausted that the inheritance would be no use to her anyway. Would he even get there in time?

I should have suggested Christophe and the kids come and spend a few days here. I thought about it, but I didn't do it. Faced with such an outpouring of sadness, I backed away. Hélène would call that selfishness. I disagree. I simply have a great deal of respect for other people's privacy, in good times and bad.

2

Just before jumping on the bus, Louis saw a well-known actor in the street, although he couldn't remember his name. He looked smaller than when he was on screen. Days when things like this happened weren't like other days. On the bus, he sat opposite a little old couple, both sleepy, one with their head on the other's shoulder. They were like two little old cigarette butts stubbed out on the seat. They gave off the smell of beef stew and waxed parquet. It was as if they were at home at siesta time. Louis was overwhelmed by a wave of emotion, which almost made him feel sick. It was more than tenderness; he was overcome with love for this adorable couple. It was ridiculous, for two stops he struggled to contain his sobs. Then the man gently shook the woman awake; his wedding ring caught the only ray of sunshine that day. A skinny little man took their place. He was carrying an enormous lampshade that he laid on his knees. Louis could only see his eyes and the top of his bald pate. He looked like a thing, an unusual, detachable object. When he left, two young people took his place. Louis hated them immediately. Especially the man. He looked as boring as all the hardware he had just bought at the DIY store, things for cutting, sanding, screwing, measuring, tightening and loosening. For each item he took out of the plastic bag, he read the instructions all the way through, in a low voice like a depressed vicar. The flat-chested blonde who was with him nodded as she listened, dull-eyed and slack-jawed. Their weekends must be a blast!

Under the plane trees, dead leaves glued to the pavement by the rain resembled pamphlets warning of the end of the world. Just before he reached Printemps, a knot in the crowd forced him to slow down. There was a figure, just visible between the legs of the passers-by. It was stretched out on the ground. One trouser leg was rucked up, revealing a pale, almost blue calf and a brown sock rolled down at the ankle of a shoeless foot. The shoe, an old one, was a little further along. A corpse! In newspaper photos of crimes or accidents, the victim had always lost a shoe. Instinctively, Louis looked up at the buildings on the street. The sniper had vanished.

As he pushed open the door of the department store, he was greeted by a gust of warm air and ladies' perfume which made his head spin. He was instantly horrified at the thought of any physical contact. Feeling bodies brush against his, he had the sensation he was paddling barefoot through slime, sinking into an obscene swarming mass, taking part in a disgusting orgy. He could imagine grubby underwear, soft white flesh, damp body hair, the sickening smell of sweat and saliva.

He felt a bit better when he reached the dome of Brasserie Printemps. The enormous umbrella of light caught the hubbub of conversation and the clinking of cutlery. He quickly spotted Richard, but didn't show himself. It was absolutely delicious to watch him playing nervously with his knife while looking at his watch or casting a mournful eye over the menu that was almost entirely composed of salads and desserts. He stood out amongst the prim and proper matrons and their grand-daughters daubed with banana split.

I won't go and meet him. Anyway, I can't give him his money back. I have nothing to give him as security except a brilliant horoscope for the coming month. I'll leave him stewing there.

A kind of short sigh followed by a thud caused him to turn round. One of the grandmothers at a table near him had just collapsed, her head in her plate of crudités. There was grated carrot in her hair, and a round of cucumber clung to her right cheekbone. By her chair a newspaper with a screaming head-line: AGEING SOON TO BE A THING OF THE PAST! No, there certainly wasn't any sign of the barrel of a rifle with telescopic sight under that shower of fragmented light filtering through the stained-glass panes of the glass roof. The shot could have come from any one of the facets of the giant kaleidoscope.

Louis ran out of the store and walked straight ahead for a long time. Then he sat on a bench, in a large park, the Tuileries, or maybe it was the Luxembourg Gardens. Out-of-work dads recognised each other from afar. There were dozens of them drifting along the avenues, one child clinging to their back like a wart, another dragging its feet in the dust while holding on to their father's hand. The dads greeted each other with a weary little conspiratorial smile: 'Welcome to the club.'

There was one beside Louis. He had his eye on a little girl who was sticking her fingers into a drain cover. They were still the fingers of a newborn, soft and pink like shelled prawns. She was burbling incomprehensible sounds full of wet syl-lables: *pleu, bleu, mleu*. Her brother, barely any older, was pedalling like a demon round and round the bench on a red tricycle. Other Michelin men, bundled up in their winter garments, threw handfuls of gravel, wooden lorries, spades and rakes at each other. Any object became a projectile in their hands. An hour spent in their company would drive you completely mad. Louis was not unhappy in his state of stupe-faction; he was no longer aware of the cold or of the strident cries. Far in the distance gardeners made little piles of leaves, which they then gathered into one large heap. He would like that work, simple and monotonous.

The little girl nearby began to shriek. One of her fingers was caught in the grille. Things like that were always happening to children – life is full of holes and there are so many little fingers. The father got down on all fours, trying to moisten the child's finger with his spit, murmuring reassurance to her. The child was screaming so much she was turning blue. Women came over to proffer idiotic advice to the poor father, now red with shame.

'You should have used soap.'

'You think I come to the park with my pockets full of bars of soap?'

He was envisaging having to pull out the grille and carry it still attached to his daughter's arm, but the little finger finally came free with a popping sound. The gathering dispersed, disappointed. They had been hoping for the fire brigade. The father stuck a biscuit into his daughter's dribbling snotty mouth and hastily gathered up the strange assortment of items that children must always have with them – a disgustingly grimy fluffy rabbit, a broken toy car, a retractable transistor aerial, a single roller skate. Had he missed anything? Yes, the little brother, who was pedalling at top speed towards the open gates to the street where huge menacing buses passed, hungry for little boys on red tricycles.

'Quentin! Come back here immediately!'

We're all children of children. This unfathomable thought kept Louis going until nightfall, until the time when everyone goes home.

It's time to go to the beach, but I'm staying put. My throat's a bit sore and I've a slight temperature – excuse enough to slack off for the rest of the day. Goes without saying it's this England business that's knocked me for six. With a bit of effort, it seems to me I could be properly ill by the time Hélène arrives. I open the window, unbutton my shirt collar and fill my lungs with the icy air, heavy with moisture off the sea. There – now all I need to do is slip under the duvet fully dressed and spend the whole day sweating, while dulling my brain with German soap operas and game shows. All being well, I should hit between 38 and 39 by the end of the night.

Watching Inspector Derrick's adventures only serves to give me a stiff neck. I'm better off staring at the wallpaper. I lose myself for a good while in the intricate faded flower pattern on the walls, when suddenly I get the strongest sense that Nane has died, right this very moment – puff! – like a light bulb blowing. All at once, the babbling in my head fades, to be replaced by a surprisingly clear memory of Nane's last birthday. We were celebrating in the ridiculous studio her mother put her in, on the fourth floor of a modern building in the sixteenth arrondissement. The decor and furnishings are all her mother's doing. The place is dripping with gold fixtures and walls of sky blue and pink. Every room is fitted with carpet, right up to the loo seats. Nane has never been allowed to change a thing. But what does a bit of fussy decor matter to her when she's dying anyway? She's made do with pinning a few postcards above her bed and sticking some flowers in a vase – no more than you'd expect to see in a hospital room. She has set up home in her mother's place the way a hermit crab moves into another mollusc's shell. A bed with a TV facing it. She lives off her own death, self-sufficient. Just as Hélène feared, Nane had 'made herself pretty'. Lipstick and eyeliner only emphasised the sorry state of her poor face. There was Hélène, Christophe and me. We'd just had a glass of champagne. Nane was about to blow out the thirty-nine candles on her cake. It was too much for her;

17

she couldn't breathe so we had to call an ambulance. Lying on the stretcher, her body under the blanket made no more of a mound than a closed umbrella.

I daren't call Christophe. I don't trust this sixth sense of mine. What if it's just my imagination trying to find an excuse not to go to England? Nane dying would blow the whole idea out of the water. It's possible to pray for things unconsciously and I wouldn't put it past myself to do so.

I'm eating leftovers of leftovers and half listening to the news on the radio when I hear a knock at the door. My first instinct is to find a weapon, but then I get a grip: it's only ten past seven – no one's killed at this time of night.

'Evening. I live next door. I'm sorry to—'

'Yes, I recognise you.'

'We don't like to intrude.'

'What can I do for you?'

'Well, see, the thing is … our daughter's going to be on telly this evening. *Going for Gold* – you know, the game show …'

'Yes.'

'Our TV's just stopped working, so we thought to ourselves, maybe the chap next door might … if we're not disturbing you … assuming you have a TV, that is?'

'Yes. I understand. Please, come in.'

'Oh, that's kind of you, ever so kind! … Arlette, come on, he says it's OK.'

Monsieur and Madame Vidal have invaded my solitude. We sit smiling idiotically at one another. They look like a pair of shiny new garden gnomes.

'The TV's upstairs. You'll have to excuse the mess.'

'Oh, don't mention it. It's us who should be apologising, barging in on you while you're having your supper.'

18

'No, no, I'd finished. Come on up – it's the first room on the left.'

I give the duvet a few whacks and sit my visitors on the edge of the single bed, twenty centimetres from the TV screen; the only way I can watch TV is sprawled on a bed. I feel as if I'm looking after two nicely behaved children.

'Ooh, it's starting!'

Since there's no room to sit next to them, I slide in behind them. Between Monsieur Vidal's shiny pate and the silver-blue lichen sprouting from his wife's head, the TV presenter's unappealing face appears, swiftly followed by those of the contestants wearing nervous or slightly crazed expressions. Among them is Nadine, twenty-seven, a teacher from Rouen, who takes the opportunity to say hello to her students as well as her parents, who have no doubt tuned in to watch her.

'There she is! That's our daughter. Gosh, doesn't she look awful!'

'Must be the nerves! You know how shy she is …'

Arlette's hand nestles inside her husband's. I have the curious feeling I must be at their house. I daren't move, in case they notice me there. I wonder who Nadine takes after most, her father or mother? Nobody or everybody? In fact she most resembles the TV presenter, bloated as if by a phantom pregnancy, with a look on her face that says, 'I may be ugly, but I'm highly intelligent.' We'd hate one another at first sight if we were introduced. She looks a nasty piece of work. How could such a lovely pair of people produce someone with such an inflated ego? And lovely people they are, I'd bet my life on it. This is the first time I've seen them up close, but I've often spotted them coming back from the market or from a walk, arm in arm, never in a hurry, protected, as though living inside a bubble. I've so often imagined and envied the admirably empty, clean and tidy little life they lead together, just the two of them. Every time I have a row with Hélène, and we each go home to our separate houses for the sake of preserving our precious independence, I think of them. Tonight they're in my home, watching my TV; I could touch them; they belong to me and not to the stuck-up little madam on the TV screen. I want them to adopt me, right now, this instant! I'd be a very good son to them, and what's more, I live just next door. I could ask them to talk to Hélène, to stop the trip from going ahead …

'… contains theobromine. Once the seed has been roasted and ground, it is used to make a drink …'

'Cocoa!'

Father and daughter say the magic word in unison, a split second before the time is up.

'Cocoa! That's the right answer! And that makes you today's CHAMPION!'

For a moment the bedroom flutters with the sound of beating wings as my two angels spring to their feet, clapping their hands. Part of me begrudges that stiff little princess her victory, but it has clearly made the two old things very happy.

'It's not just because she's our daughter – you have to admit she was the best. Ever since she was little she's always been able to learn whatever she wanted, and she retains it all, doesn't she, Arlette?'

'Oh, yes! She's always been very hard-working as well. It's not enough to be clever, you have to put the time in too! Besides, they don't give a teaching degree to just anyone, do they?'

'No, of course not! Right, I think this calls for a drink. You'll have a glass of something, won't you? Ah, go on!'

They won't stop droning on about their daughter – what about me, huh? We head downstairs. I run three glasses under the tap and open a bottle of Chablis.

'You've got a lovely place here. All these pretty things and pictures; it's very arty. What do you do for a living?'

'It's not my house. I'm renting it from a friend of mine who's a painter. I write books.'

'Oh, right …!'

I wait for the 'Oh, right!' to come back down to earth, having been blown out into the stratosphere to make way for a toast to Nadine's starry future.

'To Nadine! Yum … Nice wine, isn't it, Arlette?'

'Very nice! Well, we had you down as being in the film business. We thought we'd seen famous people coming in here. We just happened to notice, you understand! We haven't been spying on you.'

'Of course not. It's true, several of my friends are actors.'

'Aha! See, Louis? I was right!'

'Sorry, your name's Louis?'

'That's right. Why?'

'No reason. It's a nice name.'

'Oh, I dunno. Have to be called something, after all. And your name is?'

'Pierre.'

'Pierre's nice too. If we'd had a son, we'd have called him Pierre, wouldn't we, Arlette?'

'Yes, Pierre or Bruno. But we had Nadine.'

I offer them another drink. Louis accepts; Arlette covers her glass with her hand. Louis talks about the job he did before he retired, working on the railways. I hear him, but I'm not listening. I'm trying to find my features in his face and, of course, I succeed. The resemblance is actually quite striking. I wonder how Arlette has failed to notice.

'Anyway, enough about me, we've kept you long enough already …'

'Yes, my husband does like to talk! … Why don't you come for lunch with us tomorrow? It's market day. Do you like fish?'

'The thing is … yes, OK, I'd love to.'

'We'll see you tomorrow, then, Pierre! Thanks again!'

Why did I lie about my name? His really is Louis though …

3

Louis's mother took all her medication for the week in one go on Monday morning so that she could be sure she wouldn't forget. That was her best day of the week. She laughed at anything and nothing, spent an hour staring at the pattern on her waxed tablecloth, moved her knick-knacks about and invariably ended up embarking on a complicated recipe for which she only possessed a fraction of the ingredients. At eight o'clock, she collapsed in a heap for at least twelve hours.

Louis could smell it from the end of the corridor, something overpowering that caramelised his nostrils and covered his face like a leather mask. The radio and the TV were both blaring. His mother, curled up on the sofa, reminded him of a box of spilled matches. She had the bones of a bird that jutted out at all angles from under her black dress. A tuft of mauve hair indicated her head. Louis turned the volume of the television down, switched off the radio and went into the kitchen, holding his breath, his hand held out towards the cooker knob. Two fossilised pork chops lay on the bottom of a pan coated with burnt chocolate. On the side a cookery book was open at page 104, 'Cocoa chicken'. Louis opened the fridge and unearthed a slice of ham, a yoghurt and an apple and returned to the sitting room. Before eating, he propped his mother up with cushions, arranged a pillow under her head and laid a rug over her legs. He really liked watching television with her, especially when she was asleep. It was a programme made by Mr Average for Mr Average about Mr Average. Louis didn't bother to try another channel. He watched the television, not what was on. Exactly like in the street, or anywhere. What was happening in front of his eyes was only a pretext to let his imagination wander. It could be anything or anyone.

Sometimes he would follow someone in the street until he got fed up. The last time had been at Gare de Lyon, a woman with a parcel. She had led him as far as Melun. It must have been about one o'clock and the train was half full. Louis had sat a few seats away from the woman so that he could watch her without her noticing. About fifty, a bony head and torso, but plumper from the waist down. She was reading a magazine, *Modern Woman*, her elbows resting on the parcel on her lap. The parcel was so well wrapped that it looked fake: brown paper perfectly folded, string taut and knotted into an elegant but solid bow, the name of the recipient written in beautiful block capitals (M— something or other).

The buildings got smaller the further they went from Paris: tower blocks, then four-storey buildings, single houses and finally a cemetery, just before the beetroot fields. Very soon, the same sequence repeated itself but in the opposite direction as they approached Melun.

Melun prison! The package! The woman was going to visit someone in jail. A son? Or a husband more likely. She wasn't the kind of woman to have children. Melun was for long sentences. How many years had she been making this journey? How many times a week? There was something at once sad and comic in this image of the frumpy woman with the words 'modern woman' in her hands. What on earth could the bloke have done to end up in prison? Killed for money? To give it to this woman? At Melun, Louis had let the 'modern woman' disappear into the crowd. He understood at once that Melun was a dismal town, flat and useless. He had drunk coffee as he waited for the next train back to Paris.

Louis's mother let out a little fart, very short, but loud. How much was she going to give him? A thousand francs, two thousand francs? She never refused to give him money, but she gave it sparingly, at little old lady pace, so that he didn't stray. Even when his father had been alive it had been like that. Benefiting from the invariable paternal siesta, she would take him aside in the dining room. Eight uncomfortable, immovable chairs stood round a table as solid as a catafalque. There was an enormous sideboard in which piles of plates slept peacefully except for the once or twice a year they were taken out. They practically never went into that room, except to polish the furniture, a ritual like going to put flowers on Grandmother's grave on All Saints' Day. The rare dinners they gave were always depressing affairs, with his father's colleagues or family members, a universe of adults as icy as the polished mahogany of the furniture. You had to behave well, which meant you couldn't do anything you wanted to do. The moment his parents opened the glass doors hung with lace curtains that separated the dining room from the sitting room, they were no longer the same people. They assumed a stiff bearing and spoke in low tones as if they were in a museum. They didn't like going into the dining room either; they much preferred the kitchen, but that was how it was – grown-ups had obligations, work and dining rooms. It was because of little things like that that Louis had refused to grow up, and at forty, he wasn't about to change his mind.

'Louis, are you listening to me?'

'Yes, Maman.'

'I already gave you a thousand francs for your car insurance, and that was only two weeks ago. I'm going to give you another thousand but after that I can't give you any more. We have to have the garage door redone, you know, and that will cost an arm and a leg.'

'I told you, I'll pay you back!'

'Shh! Your father's next door. I would give it to you if I could, you know that; it's just … at the moment …'

Louis had not been ashamed of asking them for money. They had money, not much, but more than he had. His mother's face had been barely visible in the gloom. It was only when she had moved her head that there was a reflection off her glasses. They never put the light on until it was completely dark, either in winter or in summer. Not because they were miserly but out of respect for the memory of an era in which thrift was as much a virtue as a necessity. Louis's mother had opened the sideboard and removed some notes from an imitation-lizard-skin box. That was where she hid her meagre savings. Everyone had known it, but no one ever mentioned it. Like the dining room, his father's siesta or the tardy lighting up, it had been part of their little habits as tightly woven together as the twigs of a nest.

'Put that in your pocket, and don't tell your father.'

'Of course I won't. Thank you, Maman.'

On the other side of the partition, Louis's father had known perfectly well what was going on between mother and son and it was fine by him. It was part of their game. Louis had crammed the notes hastily into his pocket, which his mother disapproved of; you were supposed to fold notes neatly in two and keep them in your wallet.

'Right, Maman, I must run now – I'm going to be stuck in traffic. Say goodbye to Papa for me.'

At the end of the road, the entire house was framed in his rear-view mirror. If you had turned it upside down it would have begun snowing.

Something very strange was happening on television. His mother's date of birth had just appeared on the screen: 7/10/21. Louis turned the volume up.

'If anyone born on 7 October 1921 is watching, they should telephone us because they have just won this superb caravan!'

A sort of square igloo shiny with chrome filled the screen: WC, shower, folding double bed, electric hob, oven, fridge ...

Louis's eyes widened, like a child in front of a big Christmas toy. He wanted that caravan, he wanted it all for himself. That was where he wanted to live and nowhere else. A brand-new life in a brand-new caravan. It was obvious to him that destiny had made this programme just for him. And that wasn't all. He wanted everything else as well, everything his mother owned, her meagre savings, the house, her life.

The roll of cling film lying on the table was not there by coincidence. There were no more coincidences, just the last pieces of a puzzle all fitting together perfectly. That was why his mother was turning over, offering her face to the film of plastic Louis was preparing to press over it.

'Now you are brand new as well, shining and without a wrinkle. This is not going to hurt you any more than the day you gave birth to me. You're giving me life for a second time.'

There was barely a sound, a soft breeze rustling leaves and fingers opening and closing. The old woman, packaged like a supermarket chicken, had just died without making a fuss.

For a second Louis remembered the lady with the parcel on the train, and her husband in jail in Melun. But that wasn't going to happen to him; this was just a family affair, just something between him and his mother. It was nothing to do with anyone else. A little sooner, a little later ... for his mother it changed nothing and for him it changed everything. A new life was beginning, a proper life, the life of an orphan.

4

To tell the truth, I don't care that the Vidals are stupid, boring and not especially nice. At the beginning of lunch it bothered me a bit, then I got my head down and focused on the grub and the plonk. I stuffed myself like a goose for foie gras, until they once again seemed beautiful, radiant, unique, the perfect couple. I could tell that my ebullience was causing a few raised eyebrows, but, after all, arty types are always a bit zany. Still, they seemed pleased to see me go after the Calvados coffees.

I love napping on the beach, sheltered from the wind, leaning back against the jetty, my feet buried in the sand, hands in my jacket pockets, face to the sun. Slow explosions of red, green and yellow behind my closed eyelids. When I was little, I used to love pressing my eyes or staring at light bulbs to make fireworks go off inside my head. Arlette used the most marvellous expression when talking about a friend of theirs with a drink problem: 'His face has been completely defaced by alcohol.' She comes out with a lot of things like that. It must have been partially aimed at Louis, who was starting to go glassy-eyed after the aperitifs. She stopped him showing me the scar from his operation. 'Not while we're eating!'

Three horses gallop by in the distance, down at the water's edge. I hear their hooves on the hard sand, slightly out of sync. That's how I've been feeling since this morning – just marginally out of step, slightly missing something. It's not an unpleasant feeling – halfway between spectator and tourist.

This morning, Louis – my Louis – killed his mother. So that's one thing ticked off. I've deflowered him. No sooner had I turned off the typewriter than Hélène rang; the England trip is on hold. (What a shame!) Problems at the newspaper, problems with her daughter, problems as far as the eye can see.

'Sorry, darling. Poor you. Is there anything I can do to help?'

'No, love. It's as if everyone made a pact to be a total pain yesterday. Nat went off on one! I don't know what's up with her at the moment.'

'She's sixteen.'

'Yeah, well, it's no fun. She's buggered off God knows where. If you hear anything from her, will you—'

'Of course, if she rings I'll let you know straight away.'

Poor Hélène, at the mercy of 'other people'. If only you'd listen to me ... We could shut ourselves up here for ever. We'd never go to England, we'd never go further than the beach and we'd see nobody, except the Vidals from time to time. They're really nice, you know; you don't have to try to be clever around them. We'd eat, we'd make love, we'd sleep fused together like Siamese twins. War and peace, summer and winter would come and go around us and we wouldn't notice. It would all be the same to us. What the hell do 'other people' have to do with anything? Remember the time we stayed in bed for forty-eight hours? Wasn't it wonderful?

'But we can't spend our whole lives in bed! What would we live off?'

We'd take a leaf out of my Louis's book, wouldn't we? Remember after the famous birthday party at Nane's, after we'd taken Christophe home? In the car, you said, 'What I find really upsetting is that she'll never get the chance to enjoy a share of her bitch mother's money. She could at least have travelled in the last year, done the things she's always wanted to do ...'

'It's been years since Nane wanted to do anything. It's like she's living the same day over and over again.'

'Maybe, but it still leaves a bitter taste. When I look at all these old codgers who have more time and money than they know what to do with ... My father gets a new car every two years – he only uses it once a month. My mother's always on the lookout for a new coffee machine – she's already got seven. Can you imagine? Seven!'

'You'll inherit.'

'Yeah, right! They're rock solid. Not that I'm wishing them dead, but—'

'But it's like our pensions – we'll be half dead ourselves by the time we get them.'

'Exactly. What about you? Don't you think you'd make better use of your mother's money than she does?'

'No question.'

'So it's only when you no longer want anything that you get to do whatever you like? It's a joke!'

'I can never retire anyway – I'll just have to live off my fame and fortune. As for you, if you're relying on Nat and her friends to pay for you, things are not looking good. Our best hope is for an epidemic to wipe out the old people this winter.'

'They've all been vaccinated.'

We sat in silence after that, torn between feelings of guilt for having parricidal thoughts and dreams of inheritance. It was a struggle to get out of the car; the night sky looked like a huge empty black hole, or a box of ether-soaked cotton wool for killing kittens. The next day was when we stayed in bed for two days.

I've run out of cigarettes. It's starting to get chilly; the wind has changed. I've kept my evening plans to a minimum: a yoghurt and then bed. All of a sudden I feel exhausted, tiredness weighing on me like a great damp coat. Quick pit stop at the nameless café, where I hear it's going to rain tomorrow. I count my steps as I walk back to the house. I stop at 341; there's someone crouching outside my door.

'Nathalie? … What on earth are you doing here?'

'Just popped over to say hi. Is it a bad time?'

'Of course not. Come in.'

A gust of icy wind seizes the chance to come inside the house with us. I have a devil of a time trying to shut the door.

'Louis! Haven't seen you for ages! You haven't really changed. A bit fatter maybe.'

'A little, yes. Hello, Solange, you're looking good.'

'If you say it fast enough! But there you go, you can't make something new from old bones.'

Louis thought otherwise. He smiled at the mother of his first wife, Agnès. A voice from inside the house put an end to this embarrassing exchange.

'Bring him in, Solange! You can't just stand there in the doorway!'

'Yes, of course. Come in, Louis! Oh! Gladioli – you shouldn't have! Thank you, Louis.'

Nothing had changed, although now the furniture, the walls and Agnès's parents themselves were coated in a fine film of dust. It had been years since he'd set foot in this house, ten years, maybe more. Raymond, probably reluctantly, turned off the television and poured glasses of Ricard. Solange was twirling about with the gladioli, arranging them in a shaped crystal vase brought back from a trip to Hungary.

'Cheers, Louis!'

'To your good health.'

'Raymond! These drinks are really strong!'

'So what? That's exactly what a reunion like this calls for.'

'Condolences for your mother, Louis – Agnès told us. How old was she?'

'Sixty-six or sixty-seven, I'm not quite sure.'

'Oh!'

Louis saw they were subtracting their age from his mother's and noting with horror the tiny difference. Then …

'You know, we were really surprised to get your call the other evening, after such a long time.'

'I'm sure you were. It just occurred to me, after speaking to Agnès. Time passes so quickly.'

'It does, but nothing much happens in all that time, at least not to us. Just our daily routine. Can I get you another? Come on, just one more.'

That had been last week. From the window of his caravan, Louis watched the barges sliding along the Seine. He had parked his caravan in the Bois de Boulogne campsite. It was very quiet at this time of year. He had been here for two months, since just after his mother's funeral. He hadn't worried about her death for a moment. Everyone knew the state of her heart and how she took her medication all in one go. He was feeling good, as he had felt every day of the past two months. He wanted to communicate his happiness to other people. To let them know happiness was possible and it was important to believe in it. So he had opened his address book at 'A' and picked up the telephone. The first two 'A's had been out, but Agnès answered.

At first everything had gone well for Agnès but as time passed nothing was right any more. Jacques, the man she had been living with for seven years, had just lost his job, and hers wasn't going well either. Fred, the son she'd had with Louis twenty-two years ago, was nothing but a worry. She didn't know where he was, Holland, or England, but he was certainly caught up in some scam involving drugs. Hardly surprising, since Louis had never bothered doing anything for him. Well, anyway. The other two children though, the boy and girl she'd had with Jacques (and whose names Louis could never remember) were turning out fine. If only they had a bit of money, they would buy a van and go and sell *frites* and waffles far away from Paris, in those places where people are always on holiday; it would be a great life, but ...

Louis had listened all the way through to this stallholder's dream and then had ended the conversation, promising to send Agnès a cheque. He'd felt quite emotional after he'd hung up. He knew Jacques, a decent sort who loved Agnès as he himself would have liked to love her, but had never managed to. It pained him to hear that they had worries. The cheque he would send them would obviously not be enough to satisfy their desire for escape, but there was another way he could demonstrate his generosity. Just above Agnès's number was the number for her parents. There are phone numbers you keep without knowing why, and then one day, you do know.

Halfway through the butter-rich meal, Louis was already feeling very full. He had to make a superhuman effort to follow the meanderings of the conversation, particularly when Solange was speaking. Raymond mainly contented himself with filling the gaps in the conversation with shrugs and meaningful nods of the head. All the stories were about the misfortunes of people Louis didn't know, or barely knew, but whom death or illness briefly brought to life.

'Yes, you do! You must remember Jean, "le grand Jeannot" we always called him! He was at your wedding. He was the one who did an impression of a dwarf by putting his jacket

34

on the wrong way round and his hands in his shoes ... Well, anyway, he's dead.'

And so on and so forth, like the report of a naval battle: 'Le grand Jeannot, sunk!' Retirement had been fatal for them. They were slowly shrivelling like two cheese rinds under a glass cover, deaf to everything that happened outside their own four walls. They were adrift on their own ever-diminishing ice floe.

'Don't get me wrong, we like Jacques, but he's too nice – people are always taking advantage of him. We help them where we can, but we're not Rothschild's bank! A little more coffee?'

Louis hardly spoke. Sometimes he corrected a date, or a detail about a memory from the time he had been their son-in-law. Gradually the conversation began to dry up and he could feel their embarrassment. They had always found him intimidating. Even when he had been with Agnès they had been reserved around him. They were wondering what he was here for. Louis would have liked to stroke them like two puppies in a basket.

'Right, I'd better be going. I've already taken up enough of your time.'

'Not at all! Come back and see us again from time to time. We've really enjoyed it, haven't we, Raymond?'

Raymond acquiesced with a nod of the head, which he used to glance at his watch. It was all right, he wasn't going to miss the beginning of his television serial. As he took his leave on the porch, Louis checked that the spare key was still in its place in the pot of geraniums. That was where it had been when Agnès still lived with them. No, nothing had changed.

5

The clothes I've been wearing for more than ten days lie scattered around my feet like shed skin: shapeless tracksuit bottoms, trainers missing their laces, an old paint-spattered jumper. OK, I've got a bit of a belly, but I have nice legs and hands. Hmm. Ish. Besides, everyone looks a bit of a twat standing butt naked in front of the mirror. My God, it feels so good to lie down when you're tired, to piss when you need to, to eat when you're hungry and drink when you're thirsty. It's things like this which really sell life to you, whatever the price. It's strange to hear sounds being made around the house by someone other than me. I've put Nathalie on the sofa in the study and already I'm regretting it. She's bound to sleep in until midday and I'll get no work done tomorrow morning. When I stay over at Hélène's, I like hearing them nattering in the bathroom before bed. From the bed, I picture them in front of the mirror, making faces or twisting their hair, knife-sharp fingernails unleashed on the slightest pimple. The wall between us and the muffling effect of the various objects they hold between their teeth as they talk (grips, tweezers, hair bands) stop me overhearing their secrets, but I sometimes catch the odd word:

'Nicolas? I finished with him a month ago!'

'No, not that pot, it's mine! It's not good for your skin anyway.'

Meanwhile I lie there with my arms under my head, smiling up at the ceiling, happy as a bean sprouting between two layers of moist cotton wool.

At the dinner table earlier, Nat told me she would only be staying a day or two, just long enough to calm down a bit. Things are not going at all well with her mother.

'She's a pain in the arse at the moment. You can't say anything to her. I don't know what's up with her.'

'She's forty.'

'Yeah, well, it's no fun.'

I've heard that somewhere else. And it's not just her mother; it's school, exams, what's the point? Life's shit, may as well just get used to it. Then there's AIDS, and being bored of the company of people her own age, and old people too. Basically she's fed up, so she's come to see the sea.

I made her eggs with a few leftover lentils. She wiped the plate clean.

'Is there really nothing for dessert?'

'No. I've been working all day; I haven't had a chance to go to the shops. Depression obviously hasn't taken away your appetite.'

'No, it's the opposite. I eat ten times more.'

She's smoked all my fags, drunk I don't know how many coffees and never stops talking, sentence after sentence, cigarette after cigarette, throwing in literary quotations she may or may not have understood, all of them heavy with yearning for death above all else.

'Nathalie, look at yourself. You're like a Sicilian widow, all in black. How do you think—'

'It's the fashion.'

'I thought you didn't want to be like everyone else?'

'I wasn't talking about clothes.'

She still has an adolescent's fat nose which she hides by brushing her hair over her face. She still smells of sour milk. It's weird to see her here without her mother.

'Right, sweetie pie. I'm wiped out. You can sleep on the sofa in the study tonight. I'll sort you out a bed tomorrow. I can't face getting all the sheets and blankets out now. Is that all right?'

Yeah, yeah, whatever. She wasn't tired anyway; she was going to read.

'Oh, by the way, did Maman call?'

'Yes.'

'If she rings again, don't tell her I'm here.'

'You're asking a bit too much, now! You know perfectly well she'll be worrying.'

'Well, don't call her tonight anyway.'

'Fine. You can call her tomorrow.'

'We'll see. Don't you find her a pain in the arse sometimes?'

'No more than anybody else. Don't you think you can be a pain too?'

'That's different. She's the adult, it's up to her to be understanding.'

'Let's talk about it tomorrow.'

Tomorrow is such a handy thing. Everything you haven't done, everything you plan to do, tomorrow! That must be the most disconcerting thing about death – no more tomorrows. Other than when she gets it into her head to take me to England, Hélène is not too much of a pain in the arse. Apart from when we go to the supermarket: she's always realising she's forgotten something when we're already at the checkout. She'll leave me there on my own with a trolleyful of stuff, a queue of people fuming behind me and the cashier losing patience. When she eventually returns with that pack of cotton buds she absolutely couldn't do without, she'll take all the time in the world meticulously organising our purchases in bags before poring over the receipt line by line, and heaven forbid there's a mistake! She's a pain in the arse then, that's for sure. And when she decides she wants to have sex

38

outdoors. I hate it: the pebbles, the insects, the sand and especially the excruciating feeling you might be being watched. There's nowhere more overpopulated than a quiet little spot.

Those are the only things we argue about. And they're probably what I'd miss most if we broke up. Earlier, Nathalie asked why we don't live together. I gave her the same answer she gave me about the clothes: 'It's the fashion.' It was supposed to be a clever quip, but the more I think about it, the more it seems to me that there's no other reason.

What's she doing? She's put some music on! An incessant beat is making the flowery wallpaper quiver. You can only hear the bass, like the blood pulsing inside a rotten tooth. I could bang on the wall, but I can't help immediately picturing myself in a long nightshirt, holding a broom in my hand. I could get up and tell her to turn it down a bit. I could, but I won't. I don't want to see her on the sofa, cheek in hand, a book open in front of her, bare arm hugging the curve of her hip, looking at me as if she's the one standing and I'm lying down.

6

I slept really badly. Was it the meal at the Vidals'? Nathalie's arrival? One guest and suddenly the house is overrun. I'm struggling to put my thoughts in order. I need to move; I can't decide if I'm coming or going. As predicted, it's 10.30 and there are no signs of life from Nathalie. I've missed my date with Louis and I'm pissed off. Her mother may be a pain in the arse, but at least she gets up at a reasonable hour. What now?

'Good morning, Madame Vidal.'

'Call me Arlette! I've made too much beef bourguignon and I wondered if ... Oh, sorry, I didn't realise you had company.'

Nathalie appears doing her best baby doll impression, wearing a long T-shirt, yawning and stretching, her hair all over the place.

'Morning!'

Arlette seems disappointed. She looks as though she might take the Tupperware back off me, but it's too late.

'If I'd known, I'd have given you enough for two.'

'I'm sure there'll be plenty, Madame Arlette. This is Nathalie, my girlfriend's daughter ...'

'Oh, lovely, hello, Mademoiselle. Right, I must dash. See you soon.'

You hear, Loulou? His girlfriend's daughter! Arty people aren't just a bit zany, they've no morals either! That's what Madame Vidal will be telling her husband.

Nathalie scratches her bum and screws her nose up at the brownish-yellow substance inside the box.

'What's in there?'

'Beef bourguignon.'

'Yuck!'

'It's not for breakfast. I've bought you some jam and fresh bread.'

'You've been shopping already?'

'It's almost eleven. Right, I'd better get to work. Will you be all right by yourself?'

'Yep. Look at you, all smart today. You've shaved and everything.'

'I got changed, so what? See you later.'

'I don't understand, they were always so careful, especially with the gas.'

Agnès's hand trembled as she raised her glass of kir. Mourning really didn't suit her. Death is always a bit contagious. Louis hadn't expected her to be dancing a polka, but all the same, he felt she was taking it too far. 'You know, when you get older, you sometimes forget. What's so stupid is that it was caused by the bell ringing.'

'I'm sorry?'

'The postman ringing the bell, the explosion. It's a shame about the house.'

'Oh, yes, the house. Yes, but we're still going to sell it, somehow or other. I just can't take it in. I'm an orphan.'

'So am I! It comes to everyone sooner or later.'

'Yes, but both at the same time!'

'Perhaps it's better like that. They were together until the very end. Imagine your mother all on her own ... or even worse, your father ...'

41

'Yes, OK, but they were in good health, happy ...'

'For how long? Think about Jacques, your children, you. You're going to be able to buy your van selling *frites*; you're going to be able to escape, live how you want. I'm sure that would make them happy. In a way, it's their last gift to you.'

'Of course, of course. And you, how is it in your caravan?'

'Yes, very good. It feels like living on a boat that doesn't go anywhere. It's fun. How is Fred?'

'I hardly saw him at the funeral. He looked like an unmade bed. I'm afraid that no one can do anything for him any more. Do you think about it sometimes?'

'Yes, obviously. I've never known how to act with children – I'm a bit too like a child myself; I understand them too well to be a good father and I'm too old to be their friend. He's right not to love me, it's understandable.'

'Doesn't it bother you?'

'Yes, it does, but I'm sure we'll see each other one day, and that will be the day I'll be able to help him, to redeem myself in a way. I've always thought that.'

'You're very easy on yourself, as usual. What if he dies before you? It's perfectly possible, you know.'

'Then I won't get away with it.'

Louis was bored with the conversation. He was disappointed. Disappointed that he had failed in his work (although how could he have predicted that the postman's ring would make part of the house explode? The carbon monoxide from the boiler whose flame he had blown out at night should have been enough). Disappointed also by Agnès's reaction, which he had hoped would be more ... well, positive. But in any case, time was a healer, and in the end she and Jacques would accept their happiness. It was a first attempt, so certain little errors were inevitable. And some things are unforeseeable.

42

But it was a shame – Raymond and Solange had been sleeping like babies when he'd left them. They must already have been dead when the explosion happened. Apart from the shock, the postman had only suffered some little scratches on his face. The next time, Louis would try to avoid this kind of hitch. At the next table, a couple their age were talking about a Monsieur Milien. They kept repeating the name.

'I said to him: Monsieur Milien, you may be the head of department but that does not give you the right to tell me how to bring up my son. He had nothing to say to that!'

'Milien is a jerk. So did he give you your money?'

'Yes, but he didn't really have a choice.'

Louis would have liked to see this Monsieur Milien. Just see him, that's all.

'Agnès, I've got to go, I have a meeting. I've enjoyed this. Stay strong. You'll see, everything will work out. Kiss Jacques and the kids for me.'

As he left her in the bleak café, Louis felt like someone who's abandoned his dog on the motorway. It's not easy to learn to give without receiving. April is a tiring month. You never know how to dress – coat or light jacket? – you're too hot, too cold ... but it's pretty. Louis felt he was growing a halo.

7

I won't trust modern technology until it's 100 per cent reliable, which is yet to be the case. My typewriter has packed up – it's gone mad, thrown the tabulation all over the place, messed up the line spacing, basically added to the general disarray. I have to try to remind myself that machines are supposed to be at the service of men, though cracking the whip isn't likely to fix a typewriter. I don't get on well with machines, I don't know why – it's a curse. There's not a coffee machine that doesn't spurt in my face, a car that doesn't belch at my approach, a remote control that doesn't leap out of my hands to remind me of my age, the Stone Age. In the old days, the worst that could happen was your ink pot might tip over. Now, on a Monday at the beach in Normandy, where am I supposed to find someone to repair a typewriter?

'It's ready.'

What's ready? … Oh, yes, I'd forgotten, there's someone in my house. What a weird smell! … Nathalie's dream of no longer being Nathalie suits her.

'I've made you a Chinese thing. Rice with your neighbour's leftovers. What do you think?'

'It's … a bit strange, but it smells nice.'

'Is something wrong?'

'My typewriter's packed up … Jesus, it's hot!'

'I put some chilli in it. It's meant to give you a hard-on.'

'Why would you want to give me a hard-on?'

'I dunno, I thought that's what men needed.'

'Not all the time.'

'I've done a dessert. Crème fraîche with raspberry jam.'

I wolf down the spicy nursery food, every so often glancing at her over the bowl. The house isn't cold, but even so, walking around the house in a vest …

'Aren't you cold, dressed like that?'

'No. Do you think I should be putting my thermals on?'

When she smiles, all her teeth show, little porcelain miniatures that remind me of my grandmother's coffee set. I lower my eyes, and they settle on her breasts. The image of my grandmother's china vanishes, giving way to an uncertain no man's land I daren't venture into.

'Mmm. That was delicious! We could pop down to the beach if you feel like it.'

'Have you seen the weather? It's pissing down.'

'Quite right. I hadn't noticed.'

I can't think of much else to suggest besides the beach. I persevere, because of that uncertain no man's land.

'With a good raincoat on … It'll get the blood pumping.'

'Off you go, then, but I'm going to stay here and watch TV. *Inspector Derrick* will be on in a minute. I love falling asleep in front of it.'

'I think I'll call a place in Trouville about hiring a typewriter.'

'OK. I'll bring you a coffee.'

I hit the jackpot with the first number I ring. They've more typewriters than they know what to do with. If I pop in around four o'clock, I can take my pick. This is disconcerting, not to say disappointing. I had allowed myself to think I might have to spend a few days doing enjoyably little. Never mind. We can still make the most of the next two hours with a pillow under our heads and the TV at our feet. Nathalie brings the coffee; all that's missing is a little white apron and a Portuguese accent.

'Careful, it's hot! … Can I get under the duvet? I'm cold.'

'If you like, but why don't you just put a jumper on?'

'The duvet's better.'

She slid in like an eel, forcing me to the very edge of the bed.

'Why are you all the way over there? You'll fall out and break something.'

'No, no. I'm fine. Ah, here we go, it's starting.'

'Better off here than getting soaked on the beach, aren't we?'

'Yes, but shush or you'll have no idea what's going on.'

'Yeah, right! It's always the same on *Inspector Derrick*. The murderer's always the wife. She kills her husband because he's been cheating on her with a younger woman. Just wait – he'll explain it all at the end over a beer.'

'Why do you bother watching it, then, if you know what's going to happen?'

'Children only ever like one story. You've been writing them long enough, you should know. Why don't you take your shoes off?'

'Because this way, if there's a fire, I'm ready to go. Now, are you going to let me watch it?'

'OK, OK! Grumpy old fart …'

Nathalie's asleep well before Derrick solves the crime. It was indeed the wife who did it. Nathalie's head weighs more heavily on my shoulder than I'd imagined. Her hair smells clean and new. I daren't move a muscle, for fear of waking her, waking myself. A delicious state of torpor. I remember those first dates at the cinema, the heat of the other person radiating in the darkness, your head spinning until you forgot where you were, the actors on screen doing exactly what you wished you were doing. Fingers edging closer together on the arm of the chair, millimetre by millimetre … Wait, what am I thinking? Slowly, slowly, I pull myself free, slide a pillow under her head where my shoulder had been, and tiptoe out of the room.

'Oh, Hélène's in a meeting, is she? … No, there's no message. I'll call back later. Thanks, bye.'

8

Richard always ate like a pig, but today he was really stuffing himself.

'I was amazed to get your call. I had stopped believing I would ever get a cheque from you. I was angry, you know, but more about you standing me up in that bloody Printemps dome than about the money. You kept me hanging about with all those old bags and their grated carrot and Vichy water! You bastard!'

'I'm sorry, it was the day my mother died.'

'Never mind. So just like that you're suddenly loaded?'

'Well, a bit more comfortable, yes.'

'So you've suddenly acquired some principles? You're paying your debts. You're weird. In your place, I'd have fucked off. Actually, you've always been a bit—'

'A bit what?'

'I don't know, a bit like a Martian. Don't you want your *museau vinaigrette*?'

'No, go for it.'

'Thanks, I love that stuff. Listen, your call was great timing. I don't care about your cheque. But instead, you could do me a huge favour. I've promised to take Micheline and the kids to Deauville next weekend. But ... but I've a new secretary, as appetising as a leg of lamb on a fresh tablecloth, if you get my meaning?'

Richard glanced at Louis, and his glance was not appetising; his eyes were yellowish and bloodshot.

'You want me to be your alibi?'

'You've got it! I can't use the work crisis excuse again, I've used it too often. Micheline's always had a soft spot for you. Losers, they always turn her on. Anyway, if you help me out, you won't just be freeing me up, you'll also make me look like a devoted old friend. I win on all counts. If you agree, I'll tear up your cheque, OK?'

'OK, but keep the cheque.'

Richard stopped chewing, his fork in the air.

'I don't get it; you're even more bizarre than I thought. OK, whatever you want. I don't care either way. So we're agreed?'

Louis had woken up with a vile taste in his mouth that morning, and memories of a dream about Agnès, rape, blood, things that stuck in his mind like a morsel of veal stuck in a hollow tooth. He felt sticky with grime that no soap could wash away. It was because of that nausea that he had phoned Richard. Ever since he was a young child, Richard had always been his yardstick for disgust, a reference. At twelve, Richard was already a great big lecherous fool of a degenerate who always dragged him into his sordid affairs, from which Louis emerged humiliated and ashamed but curiously purified. These descents into sordidness were like a sort of redemption for him. Louis had ordered the same food as Richard. To eat like him was to start eating him.

'You didn't reply.'

'Yes, yes, I'll do it.'

All through the *îles flottantes*, Richard reeled off salacious stories about his clients, his mistresses, his friends' wives. His world was one long gang bang, unending fornication. Louis wasn't listening, he was watching, fascinated, as Richard's lips twisted like two slugs as they greedily took in the food. There was something of the abyss about that mouth in action; it was like watching a mysterious black hole.

'What about your son – is he still injecting?'

'Yes, he still is, I think.'

'You're not saying much, don't you care?'

'There aren't many opportunities for young people at the moment.'

'Hmm … if one of my kids tried that, I'd put him back on track with a boot up the arse. But it's not my business. So, shall we go? Leave it, I'll pay.'

They were on the platform and just as the métro emerged from the tunnel, Louis thought of Richard's children. A shove with his shoulder and Richard was no more than a signature at the bottom of a will. Louis was already far away down the corridor leading to another line when the crowd reacted. He smiled as he reflected that his cheque for five thousand francs would go to the children of the great fat pig, even if they didn't need it.

9

Good riddance to that prick Richard. I can't stand people I'm indebted to, and I had the urge to hurt somebody. I dashed off those last few pages in a bad-tempered scrawl but I feel no better for it. I need to get out.

'Nathalie! Do you want to come with me to Trouville?'

'Can we eat out?'

'If you like, but we have to go now.'

Through the windscreen, the rain is turning the landscape into a child's daubed painting, all the colours mixed up to make a pooey grey-brown. The horizon has gone, the sky's dripping from top to bottom and the town is reduced to a puddle.

'Drop me off at Prisu. I feel like buying myself something from the supermarket, any old thing.'

'OK. Let's meet at Les Vapeurs.'

The guy has rented me a little Canon, guaranteed to make very little noise, and so responsive you need only blow on the keys to get them working. The exact opposite of what I like – I'm going to really miss the Kalashnikov rat-a-tat of my old tank. I've been waiting at Les Vapeurs for half an hour. I'm not a fan of the place, but it's a bit like a Paris bistro, and since Nathalie doesn't like anywhere but Paris, she should approve. Here she is at last, beaming as if the tooth fairy's just been.

'What are you drinking? I'll have the same.'

The bitter taste of the Picon bière gets the thumbs down from

Nathalie. She rummages inside a plastic bag and pulls out a little pair of lacy knickers which she holds over the lower half of her face like an exotic dancer.

'Cute, aren't they? I got the bra to match.'

'Put that away, Nathalie.'

'Why, are you embarrassed?'

'No. You're being silly, trying to get a reaction.'

'Fine! ... Ugh. This Picon bière stuff really is foul.'

'You should have ordered a grenadine. Where do you want to eat?'

'Dunno, wherever's most expensive. That place we went with Maman – you know, the up-its-own-arse one.'

Toile de Jouy on the walls, crushed velvet seats, seafood platters and obsequious waiters to whom I find myself presenting Nathalie as my daughter. It's the first time this has happened and it feels slightly humiliating. Nat wants wine and so that's what we drink, and if she wanted to go and look around Honfleur, we'd do that too. The part of me that keeps the other part on a tight leash, the part that is aware of the appalling banality of the situation, gradually cuts it some slack, worn down by such stupidity. So, with my neck collared and eyes red, I trip over my leash, start talking about my book, how Louis eludes me, does things I wasn't expecting, kills people his own age ...

'All this stuff about your book is going right over my head. If I ever get married, it'll be to someone with a proper job.'

'What's a proper job, then?'

'I dunno ... lumberjack, architect, plumber ... Shall we get out of here?'

We head back to the car with a fishy aftertaste in our mouths and an incredible urge to giggle. The gingery moon looks like a cigarette burn in an orphan's cape. The scent of escape hangs in the evening air. An English couple ask us the way to Ouistreham.

I don't think they understand my directions. By the time we get home, I've shaken off the leash completely. There's the dregs of a bottle of white wine and half a bottle of Negrita. I'm determined to keep going until the small hours, but I proceed timorously, using Louis as my shield.

'Do you have to keep going on about that loser? Why don't you put some music on instead?'

My collection consists of a few old scratched records, the sound scarred, as if the tracks had been recorded in front of a wood fire. I pick the top one off the pile and place it on the turntable. I watch it spin, arms lolling by my sides like a village idiot.

'Shall we dance?'

'I can't dance.'

'It's a slow number – it's designed for people who can't dance.'

I must look as stupid as a seagull prancing on sand. I say as much to Nathalie and she tells me to shut my gob. Without my gob, I'm nothing. I let myself go like a floppy puppet, feeling my ears turn as red as a tobacconist's sign. The armful of youth I am holding against my body is bringing a flood of long-forgotten memories to the surface. I enjoy the moment all the more for knowing I'll regret it bitterly tomorrow morning. A last-ditch burst of morality saves me just in the nick of time. I pull myself free, stagger over to the sink and run my head under the tap, which looms like the guillotine.

'Right, Nathalie. I think it would be better if I went to bed.'

'Better than what?'

'It would just be better. Look, I may be pissed, but come on, the spice, the snuggles, the frilly underwear, the slow dances … Don't you think I can see it coming a mile off? If you've got a score to settle with your mother, just ring her.'

'Oh, calm down! Leave my mother out of it.'

'That's exactly what I'm trying to do.'

'Yeah, right! You're too scared to sleep with me, that's all.'

'Nat, you're really getting on my nerves. I'll do what I want, thank you very much. Besides, I've got a beer belly, I stink of Negrita, and … and afterwards? Have you even stopped to think about the consequences?'

'No, I'm sixteen. Anyway, for fuck's sake, it's not exactly complicated! What if I fancy guys with beer bellies who stink of Negrita? And what if—'

The telephone stops her short. It's Christophe telling me Nane has died.

10

A little white Scottie had just run under the bench where Alice and Louis were sitting. It was a bench the little dog knew well; it was just the right height for scratching its back. A little further away, on the road, a woman of a certain age in the beige mourning of the modern woman called the dog in a deep voice, 'Rimsky!' Behind her were two ponds, two twinkling mirrors, only slightly wrinkled by the skimming flight of the ducks. Alice and Louis watched the little dog as it bounded off to join its mistress. Neither of them said so, but they were both thinking that this was just like three years ago when they had just met each other. There had followed three or four months of a happiness as round and smooth as a boiled egg, like the two ponds they often visited, that gave them the vertiginous impression of eternity. It was the beginning of summer. Alice's children had been despatched to their grandparents. Louis had just spent an appalling winter living with his mother. Then the clouds had lifted. By a happy coincidence he had found himself acting as intermediary in a property transaction and had earned himself thirty thousand francs whilst barely lifting a finger. A very happy period, in which he had felt invincible.

'I still don't understand it! You disappear completely for six months. Then yesterday you call up as if nothing has happened!'

Louis tapped his shoes together to get the dust off. 'It was never the right moment.'

'The right moment? We'd lived together for three years! You just disappeared from one day to the next, as if you no longer existed, all your things still in the house, the children asking where you were ... It was as if you were dead!'

'My mother died; I had a lot to organise ... It wasn't the right time.'

'But now, it's the time to reappear? You come and go in people's lives as you please.'

'You told me to leave. Don't you remember your little note?'

'Oh, please, it's not as if it was the first time. We row, we separate for a couple of days so that we can cool off and then ... Well, anyway, what are you going to do now?'

'I've written you a cheque.'

'I don't give a stuff about your cheque! It's us I'm talking about.'

'But you said you were in the shit at the moment.'

'I've been in the shit for years and years as you well know. I don't care!'

'You're wrong, it's important – you should care.'

'And that's coming from you? Have you fallen on your head, Louis, or is it the inheritance from your mother that's made you blow a fuse? The old bat is doing you as much harm dead as she did when she was alive.'

Louis got up from the bench and took a few steps towards the pond. There were ducks, moorhens, catfish, frogs and turtles. There didn't use to be when they came before. The turtles were new. They climbed on top of each other, like mussels, then kept still, their heads up to the sun.

'Are your parents in Kalymnos at the moment?'

Louis turned round but the reflection of the sun from the

pool of mercury behind him prevented Alice from seeing his expression. Even when she put her hand up to shade her eyes, she could only see him as a dark shadow.

'Yes, like every year, why?'

'Oh, nothing. I was looking at the turtles; they reminded me of your parents.'

'Thanks very much! Don't stand on the edge of the water, it's blinding me. I can't see you – it's like speaking to a ghost.'

Louis came back and sat down beside her. He could have asked her for news of the children, or complimented her on her new haircut, or reminisced about the time they used to come here, but he didn't. All the sentences he prepared in his head seemed to him to ring hollow and died before they crossed his lips. It wasn't just an impression; she *was* talking to a ghost haunting a well-known landscape. He wasn't talking, he was reciting. A role learned by heart, without conviction, and the more he became aware of this, the more he felt himself shrinking, fading, crumpling up like an old tissue. He didn't dare look at her for fear of seeing two large tears forming on her lashes. Her face would be scrunched up, her mouth drawn down and her lower lip would be trembling almost imperceptibly. She would look ugly and a bit ridiculous, like everyone does when they cry. And there wasn't anything else she could do other than cry.

A group of children charged down one of the paths, shrieking. It was like a bag of balls tipping over. Two teachers puffed after them like two seals. 'No, don't go so close to the edge!'

A dozen little round white tykes lined up in front of Alice and Louis. 'Look at all the tadpoles! And the swimming tortoise! M'sieur, come and see the tortoise swimming!'

The arrival of the children provided a distraction for Alice and Louis, allowing them to relax a little. Louis stood up, massaging his stiff neck. Alice sniffled, looking for a handkerchief in her bag. Her voice was croaky when she said, 'There are turtles in the pond?'

'Yup, loads of them.'

'There didn't use to be. Turtles live a long time, don't they?'

'Very.'

One of the children, flat on his stomach at the edge of the water, had just caught one. He got to his feet, brandishing it over his head, and ran off, chased by the other kids.

'I caught one! I caught one!'

One of the teachers set off in pursuit.

'Stéphane!!! Put that back in the water immediately!'

Just before the teacher reached him, the kid threw the turtle as hard as he could into the water, like a stone. For one moment there was a commotion in the reeds. The moorhens and ducks fled the turtle bomb in a flurry of wings. The teacher slapped Stéphane, the children dispersed and the water closed around the flying turtle. Very quickly, it was as if nothing had happened. There was dead calm.

'Water is crazy; you can't make holes in it. If you threw an atomic bomb in, a quarter of an hour later, there would be nothing, barely a ripple.'

Louis wasn't certain he had spoken out loud. He said, articulating clearly, 'Strange day for that turtle.'

'Not only for that turtle.'

He had anticipated that response as if everything had been preordained, like a moment ago, before the arrival of the children. It was exasperating, that feeling of being nothing but an interpreter of a scene that was taking place elsewhere. Alice rose, putting her bag over her shoulder.

'Let's go, Louis. I want to go home. I expected something else. I find this painful.'

Louis wanted to reply 'Me too', but it wouldn't have been true. It was the absence of pain that worried him. From far off, they could have been mistaken for a couple of old people.

After leaving her at Gare Saint-Lazare with a weak smile, Louis went into the nearest travel agent. The girl who sold him the ticket for Greece had lank hair, circles under her eyes and bad skin, a skin that bruised easily – poor circulation. He would have liked to know her parents.

11

Sometimes I wish I was dead or, better still, that I had never existed. I had an awful night filled with corpses hanging above my head like hams. And then this morning I remembered I had to get the corrections for one of my kids' books in the post today. This one little chore suddenly seemed like the perfect opportunity to rejoin the land of the living. My salvation lay at the post office. I entered the building as if stepping inside a church (or more likely a mosque – I was losing my religion after all). There were three people ahead of me. An old man like origami, folded into eight, and two younger old women gossiping in low voices.

'… and that's exactly what I told her.'

'You didn't?'

'I did!'

'You mean you said—'

'What I just told you, right to her face!'

'Blimey, you're a one …'

What could the old tart have said, and to whom? Something nasty, no doubt. She had clearly been saying spiteful things all her life – they had twisted her mouth into a kind of harelip. There was plenty of other stuff in my upturned dustbin of a head that could have done with clearing up, but I simply had to have the answer.

'What did you say to her?'

The pair of grannies looked at me as if I had just spat in their faces.

'Are you having a laugh? ... Mind your own business! Really. It's got nothing to do with you!'

'Yes, it has! I might know the person you've been saying horrible things about.'

'But ... I didn't say anything horrible! What's the matter with you? You should see a doctor!'

'Fine, I'm not going to push it, but it wouldn't have cost you much to tell me, would it?'

'That's enough! Leave us alone!'

I shrugged. Let her keep her little secrets. Nothing else happened after that; the talk turned to purely postal matters. The two old ladies looked daggers at me as they left, screwing their fingers into their temples.

The post office having failed to deliver the serenity I'd been counting on, with my head spinning I try again by having a second breakfast and taking a second shower. I try to tell myself things are looking up. Nat's still asleep, or dozing, tangled up in the bedclothes. I'm glad; I don't know what I could think to say to her. I didn't know what to say to Christophe either when he told me Nane had died. I could have answered, 'You poor thing, I'm sorry; maybe it's for the best. Do you want me to come over? Do you want to come here? Is there anything I can do?' All I said was, 'Oh', followed by a silence that seemed to go on for ever. Christophe put an end to the exchange of sighs, saying he'd call me tomorrow; he needed to rest. I mumbled something incomprehensible and Christophe hung up. Nat raised an inquisitive eyebrow.

'Nane died.'

'Shit ... Do you want a coffee?'

She was filtering it when the phone rang again. It was Hélène.

'Nane died.'

'I know. Christophe just called.'

I couldn't take in what Hélène was saying. My brain had become so slow, it struggled to process every single word. Nat was sulking, having realised it was her mother on the other end of the line.

'Hello?'

'Yes, I'm here.'

'You weren't saying anything. I thought we'd been cut off.'

'No, I'm listening.'

'Is there someone with you?' (Silence.)

'No, why?'

'I don't know. I just got that impression.'

'No, it's the kettle; I put some water on to boil. Sorry, I'm just a bit stunned.'

'Me too, even though we were expecting it. OK, I'll let you get on. Shall I call tomorrow? Oh, by the way, you haven't heard anything from Nat, have you?'

'No, nothing.'

'That girl, she can be such a pain in the arse when she wants to be! Still, I'm not going to get the police on her back. Let me know if …'

'Promise. Speak tomorrow.'

I've lied a lot in my life, and come off none the worse for it, but this time I struggled to swallow my first mouthful of coffee. Nothing seemed to want to go in or out. Like a millstone around my neck, this enormous lie was going to drag me into the void, that is, into an endless succession of bigger and bigger lies, weighing on me more and more heavily.

Nat was perfect. I expected nothing, she gave nothing. After this second phone call, she threw her head back and blew out an invisible puff of smoke. 'Right, shall we go to bed, then? That'll do for today.' She put the mugs in the sink and gave the table a wipe. If you didn't look too closely, you could mistake this for a normal house with normal people in it. 'You' could; I couldn't. There was nothing normal about the way her rump wiggled its way upstairs, or her presence in my bedroom or her body under the sheets; still less my body, which did not feel like my own, and struck me as fairly unappealing.

'You know, if you've changed your mind, it's OK.'

I turned to face her. I wished I could say a word to her, 'the' word, the one you'd take with you to a desert island, the word before words, that would say everything and nothing all at once. It was silenced before it was said, an oblong speech bubble on the edge of her lips. I had never tasted her lips, only her cheek. It was enough to make me go back for another helping. I thought of all those people in war-torn countries with nothing to do after the curfew but make love. No electricity, no TV, no heating, just fucking, with the glorious energy of despair. But I was at war with no one but myself. The best part of me, or the least worst, had refused to enter the bedroom and stood scowling in the doorway as the other part of me tired itself out with weary embraces.

'Forget it, you've had too much to drink.'

I didn't try to persuade her otherwise or apologise. I simply made a mental note of the fact it was two in the morning and I had at least a few hours of sleep ahead of me, during which the rest of the world could crumble for all I cared.

Sadly, the world did not crumble, and here it is again in the guise of Arlette Vidal, whose shadow I can see through the curtain. Knock, knock …

'Morning! Here, I've brought a pot of jam for our young friend – it's home-made! They love sweet stuff at her age.' (Circular glance over my shoulder in search of evidence of debauchery.) 'Listen, we've just had a new TV delivered, but Louis can't seem to tune the thing. He's not very technical, and on top of that he's a bit off colour this morning. I don't suppose you'd be able to pop round and have a look?'

It's that or stare into my breakfast bowl.

'I'll be round in two tics, Arlette.'

Louis does have an odd-looking complexion, a nasty pair of bags under his eyes and shortness of breath.

'Not feeling too great, are we, Monsieur Vidal?'

'Oh, it's nothing, bit of a chest infection. It's this sodding television that's really not right. We can't make head nor tail of it – it's all written in American.'

After a good fifteen minutes, I manage to get a steady picture and show the local news in glorious Technicolor. The Vidals are happy, channel-hopping like mad things with the remote control.

'We didn't have one with the old set. Now we'll never have to stand up!'

Louis's spluttering with joy – who cares about the chest infection, he doesn't have to stand up. If only I could spend the day here with them, sitting in front of the new TV and nibbling sponge fingers. The three notes of the doorbell chime along with the news theme tune. Arlette gets up and trots over to the door like a wind-up toy.

'It's your step-daughter … what's her name again?'

'Nathalie.'

She's waiting on the doorstep, dishevelled, red-eyed, wrapped up in my parka.

'Your friend Christophe has just arrived.'

'Christophe! Excuse me, Madame Vidal. See you later.'

'OK, see you later.'

Nat utters a vague 'M'dame' which goes rolling into the gutter between an apple core and a crumpled packet of Winstons.

'Man, it stinks of cabbage in there! Smells of old people.'

'Has Christophe been here long?'

'Half an hour. I was waiting for you to turn up – I didn't know where you were. He's got a weird look about him, your mate, as if the lights are on but no one's home.'

12

Alice's parents' boat was anchored some way out from the coast. It was a huge effort to reach it and he was completely exhausted. His thigh muscles wouldn't stop trembling. Watching other people glide past in their pedaloes, you would never guess how heavy those things were. The reflection of the midday sun on the crests of the waves was unbearable. Even though he wore dark glasses, all Louis could see was incandescent white. He had never liked the sun and the sun had never liked him. He hated this island and the people on it, imbecile islanders and grotesque tourists. For a week now, he had been burning his nose, his shoulders, his thighs, in close proximity to the holidaymakers who were dazed by day, hysterical by night. It had been a week of humiliations patiently borne because of the focal point – the white boat belonging to Alice's parents.

Louis felt his heartbeat return to normal and his leg muscles finally relax. The only sounds were the lapping of the water that was as clear as in a travel advertisement, and the laughter of the people picnicking on the rocks, on the beach, or in other boats. Louis stood up and placed both hands on the shell of the enormous white egg that was swaying gently. Someone had just tossed melon skins off the bridge. He watched them float away like little gondolas. Alice's parents had finished lunch. Now they would move to the front of the boat. That was their routine every day. Louis had been watching them since he'd arrived. At eight o'clock, they left the port of Pothia and went to anchor a few inlets away for the day. Of course, Louis also knew their house, as pretty as a postcard, blue and white, with flowers exactly where they should be and a stunning view across the bay, very isolated. It could have taken place there, but Louis thought the boat was better. Alice and he had had such a good time in that house, barely a year ago. But the boat, on the other hand, he had never liked. He had been out on it once or twice in the beginning, to charm Alice's father, but as that had never worked, he had quickly found good reasons not to set foot on it again. Why had that man never liked him? Louis didn't mind him, even though he thought him an absolute cretin. It's perfectly possible to like morons; they also need affection, in fact more than most ... But Louis had no money and Alice's father could accept nothing from a poor man, not even friendship; it just wasn't done. It would probably be more difficult to kill someone who didn't like you.

Noiselessly, he tied his pedalo to the rope ladder and climbed the rungs one by one. His damp feet left little haloes on the wood, which the heat immediately erased. The two old people were taking their siesta under the blue awning. They looked like two smoked chickens. There was a smell of Ambre Solaire, salt and melon. The rocking of the boat was imperceptible but even so it made him seasick, or maybe it was that music, a salsa, coming from a boat in the distance. Louis was less than two metres from them, but he hadn't given any thought as to how he was going to kill them. He'd forgotten, which was stupid; he couldn't really explain it. He hadn't brought a bludgeon, or a rope, or a knife or a gun. He'd only got as far as working out how he would get near them, as if his mere presence could kill them. Suddenly Alice's mother sat up. A fly was caught in her hair. As she shooed it away, she saw Louis over her dark glasses. Curiously, no sound escaped her. She put her hand over her naked breasts, two poor flaccid, wrinkled things. Her husband beside her had not moved. He was asleep, his arm across his eyes. Louis tried an embarrassed little smile.

'Louis? What are you doing here?'

Louis put a finger to his lips and signalled to her to come with him. Alice's mother hesitated a moment, wrapped herself in a towel, rose and followed him to the back of the boat.

'Is Alice with you? Why didn't you tel—'

'Let's go down to the cabin. Come on, please.'

It was unbearably hot. Alice's mother stopped at the foot of the stairs to adjust her towel.

'Louis, are you going to explain what's going on?'

Louis looked desperately round him; there were kitchen knives and bottles. The most anodyne of objects could become a weapon. That large cushion, for example.

'Louis, what are you doing? Lou—'

He rushed at her, threw her down on the bunk, the cushion jammed over her face. One by one the old lady's false nails broke against Louis's shoulders without doing him the slightest damage. The almost naked body struggling under his gave him an incredible erection. He leaned with all his weight on the cushion. This lasted until a large red cloud burst in his head and in his swimming trunks, then everything went soft, damp and sticky. With a last jerk, the old woman knocked a table lamp to the floor where it shattered.

'Éliane? Éliane, what's going on?'

Louis dived into the dark corner at the foot of the stairs and seized a bottle by its neck. The hurried footsteps on the bridge above his head made his heart stand still. Alice's father appeared, bald head first, then his shoulders, covered in long grey hair. Louis hit him with all his strength, closing his eyes. The old man let out a raucous cry and fell to his knees, his hands on his head, covered in blood. He moaned like a child. Louis hit him with the bottle again, but the hands were like a helmet. The man was curled up on the floor kicking his feet. It was impossible to get his hands away from his head as he kicked. Blood had made everything slippery. And it was so narrow! Louis felt as if he were fighting in a cupboard; he couldn't raise his arm high enough to deliver a fatal blow to the old man who was letting out strangled cries. He let the bottle fall and squeezed the old man's throat, feeling the tendons and soft skin rolling under his fingers. Finally his mouth opened, with its displaced dentures, and his eyes bulged in terror, the corneas a bluish white. It was over. Louis couldn't unclench his hands. They stayed in the shape of the man's neck as he sat on the edge of the bunk and placed them on his thighs. He felt as if his head had been under the large bell of Notre Dame. All this blood, viscous, everywhere on his body; he wanted to cry, like a newborn. But instead of that, he urinated, without even getting up, and if his guts hadn't been all knotted up, he would have defecated as well.

In life, everything hinged on a matter of seconds; the merest millimetre could make the difference between success and failure.

13

'It was over in the space of a second. I didn't even think about it. She was a metre from the window. It all happened in one movement: I took her by the waist, as if to make her dance, and threw her out of the window, not maliciously, but as if she was a thing, a dead plant.'

As he tells me his story, Christophe knits his brow, like a child struggling in class.

'It was so easy ... one second she was there and the next she was gone from the room, gone from life, and I'd only had to move her a metre ...'

'Then what?'

'Then, nothing. I went downstairs, saw her body at the bottom of the building lying almost in the shape of a swastika, arms and legs all over the place. I got into my car and drove away.'

'And you didn't see anybody? ... Nobody saw you? ... She didn't scream?'

'No, I don't think so. I didn't even hear her body hit the pavement. Everything was quiet, or at least it seemed so ... This is going to sound really clichéd, but it was as if I was dreaming. Even afterwards, when I took the kids round to my parents', even in the car on the way here, even now talking to you. I can't be sure I'm really here.'

No wonder. I'm even beginning to doubt this peaceful Normandy beach is real. What a funny place to come to tell me you've just defenestrated your mother-in-law … The plus side of all this is that Christophe's problems make mine pale into insignificance. Imagine Hélène turning up or my dear editor calling to chase me about something – before they even had a chance to start berating me, I'd tell them something to shut them up: 'Sorry, my friend has just murdered his mother-in-law.' That's right, the tall, kind-eyed gentleman sitting beside me and getting his arse damp on the wet sand is a murderer, a real one! This is in a whole different league from Louis's crimes, gory or otherwise, crimes on paper, petty offences that leave only ink on your hands. As for Christophe, he really killed the old bird, bish, bash, bosh, just like he said: a little dance step and off she goes, straight out of the window! … I feel like a little kid beside him. Why spend all this time trying to think up stories? I want him to tell me his, over and over, in more and more detail.

'But why … I mean, did she say something to you? Were you planning to do it when you went over there?'

'No, I just wanted to talk to her about Nane's childhood, see some pictures of her when she was little. She said it was late, that I should call tomorrow.'

'The old bitch!'

'No, why? She looked tired; she didn't say it in a nasty way. She lit a cigarette and turned towards the open window.'

'She had her back to you?'

'Yes. She adjusted her dressing gown and shivered, choking back a sob, moving awkwardly. It's true it wasn't warm, but the window was wide open. I realised she was the one taking her leave, not me. It was like chucking away a fag end, she was so light … Have you seen that seagull?'

'Which one?'

'The big grey one. It's only got one leg.'

'You think?'

'Yes, just the one.'

The big grey bird hobbles at a distance from the others. As soon as it tries to approach the group, they all start pecking it and ruffling their feathers to drive it away. The sky behind them looks like the closing credits of a film.

'So what are you going to do now? Turn yourself in? Run off to Rio?'

'I don't know, I haven't thought about it yet. I'm a bit afraid of the police. Which isn't the way it should be, really.'

'Take your time. You can stay here as long as you like.'

'Thanks. How come Hélène's not here?'

'Work problems in Paris.'

'She was asking me the other day if I'd seen Nat.'

'Shall we go back? I'm freezing my balls off out here.'

'Yes … Do you remember last year, with the kids? We had a laugh, didn't we? You made such a mess of the barbecue …'

'Yes, we had a laugh. Come on, it's cold.'

Christophe stretches out his long limbs, taps his shoes together to get the sand off. The sun has left a huge bruise on the sky.

'Hey, look at that! A nautilus! I've never found one as good as that here.'

Christophe shows me a magnificent fossil, much nicer than any I've collected nearby. The hanged man gets all the luck.

We get home to find Nathalie giggling on the phone.

'OK, David, see you tomorrow.' She says 'bye' in English, then hangs up. 'That was my boyfriend David, from Rouen. I'm going to see him tomorrow. I got pizzas – fancy some?'

This David sounds like a right little shit.

14

The hardest thing was getting the blood out from under his nails. There were still a few traces under his left thumbnail and the nail of the little finger on his right hand. The rest had dissolved in the infinite memory of the Mediterranean. Louis didn't remember a thing, just a vague headache, that's all. He worked patiently at the little brown stain under his left thumbnail with the corner of a cigarette packet. He had nothing else to do as he waited for the plane to take him back to Paris. All around him suntanned tourists milled about in flip-flops and frayed Bermudas. The airport resembled a works canteen. At a neighbouring table a group of French people were swapping anecdotes, which they would rehash in the winter when they looked back nostalgically on their holidays. Someone said, 'Apparently it was fourteen degrees in Paris this morning!' A disappointed clamour followed that announcement. Louis hoped it would be raining when they arrived, a little drizzle, normal weather. He wanted to get back to his caravan and not see anyone for a while, at least no one he knew. Alice would probably telephone him; he wouldn't answer. He did not wish to hear about the horrific, incomprehensible death of her parents. You die as you live; the choice is made a long time ago, just as you choose to come out of one belly instead of another. The important thing was that they were dead, that Alice would now inherit, that she would be sheltered from hardship and that it was he, Louis, who had gifted her this radiant and unexpected future. But, God, the old bloke put up a fight! Louis's fingers tensed at the memory of Alice's father's dry, sinewy neck.

'Would you like a nail file?'

'Excuse me?'

'You'll never manage with your piece of card. Here ...'

A woman of indeterminate age (forty-five? seventy?) held out a pocket nail file between two coral-polished nails.

'Thanks. It's rust; it won't come off.'

'I know what that's like – I ruined a brand-new pair of trousers on the boat, the first day I wore them! It's awful, rust, and yet, it's very beautiful. Do you sail?'

'No, not often. This is from the balcony rail at my hotel. There, it's gone, thank you.'

The particle of dried blood drifted down to the floor, dust to dust. At the other end of the waiting area, an employee was vacuuming. Louis and the lady watched him for a moment, then they caught each other's eye. They smiled at one another. A thousand little wrinkles appeared around the lady's eyes.

'That's where everything ends up, in a vacuum-cleaner bag.'

Louis wasn't quite sure that was what she had said, but that's what he heard. He made a vague hand gesture that could have meant anything and lit a cigarette. He was embarrassed by the woman, but attracted at the same time. Everything she said seemed to have a double meaning. She was contradictory – old but at the same time young, like two overlaid images.

'Could I have one?'

'Yes, of course! How rude of me ...'

As he bent forward to give her a light, Louis received a waft of violet perfume full in the face. The woman barely had any cleavage, but it was touching. Somewhere inside the skin sagging around that neck there was a young girl. Because she wore a grey silk turban, it was impossible to tell what colour her hair was. Judging by her eyebrows, it was black. But could you accept the evidence of such well-drawn eyebrows?

'I gave up smoking yesterday.'

'Well done!'

'It was easy – it's just a question of will-power.'

They both laughed, and relaxed. Louis, especially, felt less tense. Good vibrations wove themselves around them.

'Where were you staying?'

'Kalymnos.'

'So was I! Funny that we didn't bump into each other.'

'I wasn't there for long.'

They then exchanged banalities, as you do with strangers. 'I used to have a little dog called Fidji ... I had an absolutely awful Christmas ... Lille is a very pleasant city ... I don't like going to the cinema, I prefer watching television ... During the war, I was living in Le Var, I was twelve ...' etc.

Passengers for flight 605 to Paris ...

'Ah, that's us!'

Of course, by the most enormous coincidence they found themselves seated beside each other.

'I'm Marion.'

'Louis, so pleased to meet you.'

They fastened their seat belts. The plane took off. The ground was marbled with white clouds. The sea was now no more than a pond. Marion's hands were like old silk and she wore three rings, but no wedding band.

'Do you have children, Marion?'

'Children? Goodness me, no, I never married. Why?'

'Oh, no reason.'

74

15

'It's funny – the way you're talking about it, anyone would think you were jealous of him.'

'Me, jealous of Christophe?'

'Yes, you; it's like you're wishing it was you in the shit instead of him.'

I had to turn to face the wall, muttering, 'Don't be stupid, I've got enough shit of my own to deal with.' But the truth is, Nathalie's right. I'd never admit it, but I've always been jealous of Christophe. From when we were very little, when we played football together and he was the goalie. I'd have liked to go in goal – no way, I was far too small. I can see him now, after school, on the patch of wasteland that we used as our pitch for everything. He'd put his jacket down, count four steps and then drop his satchel. He was totally at home between the goalposts; nothing got past him. He had gloves too. Later, I envied the love he shared with Nane, the pain he felt when she left him, the way he cared for his children, his exemplary approach to Nane's illness, the crap shoes he bought at André and yes, of course, the glorious act he had just committed. He lives, I bluff; he's a magician, I'm a con artist; he touches, I manipulate. I can't think about him without comparing myself to him. The fact of the matter is he has always put the spotlight on my own mediocrity. It doesn't stop me loving him; in fact it's probably why I do.

In the end, we just had to get on and do it, Nat and me. So

many awkward moments! Faced with such firm flesh, breasts and buttocks as hard as tennis balls, it was like having a blank page put in front of me, and scrawling all over it. I felt as if I was putting on a new item of clothing; I'm used to squidgier skins, more practised and therefore more practicable. She must have been taken aback at my shyness. What had she expected?

I didn't even hear her leave this morning. She left a note on the bedside light: 'I'll call you tonight x.' Her mother leaves me notes everywhere too. 'See you tonight xxx. Don't forget to pick up the dry cleaning xxx. There's an escalope in the fridge xxx.'

Downstairs, Christophe is moving pots around. I'll wait as long as I can before going down, until half past maybe. Someone's knocking at the door … Christophe goes to answer it … I bet it's Arlette … What did I tell you! … They're talking but I can't hear what they're saying … Christophe's coming up the stairs …

'Are you awake?'

'Ugh … yes.'

'It's your neighbour. She wants to speak to you.'

'Sod that.'

'I think it's important.'

I can tell he's smelled Nathalie's perfume. I get out of bed, blushing. He looks at me like a guy who's just walked into the ladies' toilets. Arlette's waiting for me on the doorstep. She has a raincoat on her back and a ridiculous transparent plastic thing over her shampooed-and-set hair. It's raining.

'I'm sorry to bother you, but it's Louis. The doctor came and I have to go and get some medicine. I'm afraid to leave him by himself, so if you could stay with him just while I nip to the chemist's …'

Everything is trembling as she speaks, her cheeks, the tight curls of her hair, the raindrops along the edge of her hood. She looks like a stump of candle wax.

'Of course, Madame Vidal. I'll just put an anorak on.'

On the pavement, I ask her what the doctor said.

'Oh, you know what doctors are like! They use all these words no one understands, but I could see from his face that it was bad.'

Death is yellow, and smells of vanilla. I got a great whiff of it as I entered Louis's room. I'd like a pair of pyjamas like his, blue-and-white-striped flannelette ones with a darker blue edging around the collar and cuffs. I can't bring myself to look at the murky puddles of his eyes. His mouth sends out a few bubbles of soapy washing-up water and his chicken-skin hands quiver before resting flat against the sheet. I have no idea what to say to him: 'Feeling a bit poorly, are we, Monsieur Vidal?' Or 'Hey, Loulou, how's it hanging?' I make do with smiling like a plaster saint.

'Righto, I'll leave you boys to it … I shan't be long. Are you sure you don't want anything, Louis dear? … No, all right then, I'll be off. See you soon.'

She chokes back a sob as she leaves the room. I pull up a chair and sit beside the bed. Louis looks as if he's struggling to place me. He doesn't look afraid, just surprised by everything.

'Lovely pair of pyjamas you've got there, Monsieur Vidal.'

His mouth flares open like an old hen's arsehole, but very little comes out, so he follows up by trying to point at something over my left shoulder. I turn round to look. There's the window hung with two lace curtains depicting two peacocks facing one another. Nothing else but the raindrops zigzagging across the window panes.

'Awful weather! Not a good day for a walk.'

This is clearly not the answer he was looking for. Louis keeps pointing to the window with his trembling finger. I stand up and part the curtains.

'Oh! Look, it's my house! … Funny seeing it from here – it doesn't look like the same house at all.'

The bathroom light is on – Christophe must be having his shower. What's he thinking? Has he come to a decision? Is he disappointed in me for sleeping with Nathalie? … Maybe he's just looking for a towel. Either way, it won't occur to him for a second that I'm watching him from a dying man's window. Louis has completely forgotten I'm here; he's staring open-mouthed at a corner of the mahogany chest of drawers. It must be an extraordinary piece of furniture to merit such close attention. The poor old thing won't get to enjoy his new TV for long. Another one who thought himself immortal. And he'd have been right, until yesterday, or the day before. He could buy himself a TV, plan to invite his daughter to come for Easter, think about having a word with the idiot plumber who did a shoddy job of fixing his boiler, consider having a look round the shops in Caen with Arlette on Saturday … That's over now; time is standing still for him.

Funnily enough, I found a few words written on the back of the note Nat left me this morning: 'Next Sunday, Louis went to …' – something I must have scribbled down for my book. I have no idea where 'my' Louis was supposed to go, or had gone, but the clash of future and past in the sentence gave me the impression of seeing double. Like Monsieur Vidal, I felt as if I was on standby, not in the past, future or present. The present is where other people are. Nat, who's bounding along the platform at Rouen station to throw herself into the arms of a cocky little blond boy; Hélène, who's biting her nails and drinking coffee amid a sea of printed papers; Christophe, drying his hair and wondering whether or not to hand himself in to the police; Madame Vidal, loading her shopping basket with bottles and tubes of medicine as expensive as they are pointless … I return to my seat. If you're going to be nowhere, you may as well do it sitting down. But I don't stay there long. Arlette pushes the door open, smiling weakly, shrouded in a wet mist.

'I wasn't too long, was I? There was a queue at the chemist's but Monsieur Langlois let me go first. I got you a piece of calves' liver; you can eat that on its own … What? What do you want?'

Monsieur Vidal is pointing at the window again, opening and closing his mouth like a fish.

'You want me to turn the heating up? … There you go.'

While Madame Vidal turns the knob on the radiator beneath the window, Monsieur Vidal looks at me with disgust as if to say, 'See, muggins, it wasn't that hard, was it?'

'Right, Madame Vidal, Louis, I'd better be off …'

'Of course. I'll see you out.'

Before opening the front door:

'So, how does he seem to you?'

'Oh, you know, I'm no doctor. He's obviously tired, but … this weather doesn't help, sunny one day, horrible the next. It wears you down.'

She doesn't seem entirely satisfied with my diagnosis. Still, I could hardly reply, 'If he was a used car, he'd be unsellable.'

'Anyway, if you need anything, don't hesitate.'

'That's kind of you. I've called my daughter. She'll be here on Sunday; she can't come any sooner.'

Arlette can see from the way I'm dancing from one foot to the other that I'm itching to leave, and I escape out of the door as the first gust of wind blows in. Halfway between the Vidals' house and mine, I stop and take a detour towards the café without a name. I feel like a beer and a cigarette. By the time I arrive I'm as damp and smelly as a mouldy old sponge. The couple who own the place are the only people there. I drink two halves in quick succession. The owner tells his wife he should have taken the opportunity to repaint the shutters last weekend. She doesn't respond; she's hunched over the needlepoint she's working on, depicting the head of a German shepherd. He should have spoken to me about it – I bet I'd have loads to say on the subject of his shutters. I feel as though I could talk convincingly on any topic. I down a third half and walk back up Rue de la Mer, now as washed out as an old theatre set.

Christophe is doing last night's washing-up. I give him a brief account of my visit to the old couple next door, and ask him if he's all right. Yes, he slept better than ever and is all the calmer for it. Hélène rang – she's around until lunchtime. And then Madame Beck called about urgent corrections on a book. He's thinking of going for a quick stroll down to the beach. Yes, even in this weather. He needs some air; he won't be gone long. For a moment I wonder if I should go with him, but he doesn't look like a man who's about to go and drown himself; still, those I know who've done so didn't look as if they would either. As long as he's not dead, a living person is still a living person, in the same way a criminal is still an innocent man a split second before committing his crime. I take advantage of Christophe's absence to do my telephone duties. The 'please hold' message that comes ahead of Hélène's voice annoys me even more than usual.

'Oh, it's you. Is everything OK?'

'Yes, as good as can be expected.'

'What's going on with Christophe? He said he'd done something stupid.'

'He killed Nane's mother.'

'WHAT?'

'He threw her out of the window.'

Silence. 'I don't know what to say … What's he going to do?'

'No idea. He's gone for a walk on the beach.'

Silence. 'Do you want me to come over?'

'It wouldn't change anything. I mean, it might be better if it's just the two of us, me and him.'

'Yes, I understand … I can't believe it … What about you, what do you think about it all?'

'Nothing.'

'What do you mean, nothing? Haven't you told him to hand himself in? He's got mitigating circumstances after all! You should give him some advice, tell him to—'

'Listen, Hélène, it's his decision. I'm just trying to look after him. What more can I do?'

'But the longer he leaves it, the worse it will look for him!'

'Maybe ... I'll talk to him when he gets back. I'll let you know.'

'Yes ... What a crazy business! ... And how are you taking it all?'

'Oh, you know, so-so.'

'OK, well, I've got a meeting in five minutes ... Oh, no news of Nat?'

'Er, yes, she phoned and said she's in Rouen with a friend, David – ring any bells?'

'Yes, he was at school with her last year. Did she say when she's planning on coming home?'

'No, she said she was thinking of coming here tomorrow.'

'And you said yes? ... With Christophe there?'

'He's not a professional killer.'

'That's not what I meant. If you'd rather I didn't come, I don't see why you'd want Nat there.'

'Well, you know, I didn't really think about it. I've got other things on my mind. She'll stay over and I'll send her off the next morning. Anyway, there's nothing to say she won't change her mind in the meantime.'

'Yes, knowing her ... OK, I'd better go. Love you, take care of yourself. Give me a call tonight.'

How far away she seems ... ever further away. I could have been in England with her now; there would have been no Nat, no Christophe, no Vidals. There's no place to hide.

16

Marion lived in an artist's studio in the eighteenth arrondissement, in an artists' commune inhabited by people like her who were not artists. Everything in it was white, including the cat. It was the third time since they'd returned from Greece that Louis had come to see her. He already had his allotted place – the right-hand seat of the white fake-leather sofa opposite the window diffusing a light that was ... white. It was four o'clock and they were drinking a deliciously cold rosé champagne. The day was heavy, so the air in the studio was stultifying. The rare breaths of air were like blasts from a hairdryer. There were crowds of people in the street, all still in holiday mode. In the bus on the way, girls pulled their skirts up to their thighs and fanned themselves with magazines. They were like ripe figs. The men, with their leaden complexions, their shirts sticking to them and their ties pulled sideways, sat looking vacant, their mouths open. People seemed to pass for no obvious reason from a state of torpor to feverish agitation, akin to hysteria. When he arrived at Marion's you could have wrung him out, like a mop.

They were at that delicious stage in their relationship when they told each other everything without ever giving anything away, as you do when you meet a stranger on the train. You allow yourself to lie by adding an element of truth, or tell the truth with a few lies thrown in, lying having the indisputable superiority of being infinitely adaptable.

'You were a teacher? That must have been terrible!'

'It was! Look ...'

Marion put a pair of spectacles on the end of her nose and stared at Louis severely.

'What did you teach the children? Was it things like "I before E except after C"?'

'Yes, and worse!'

'It's criminal to put things like that in children's heads.'

'We're there to make them into adults; we wipe out child-hood.'

'I never liked school. I always found it humiliating to be made to learn things I didn't know.'

Marion took the spectacles off and poured two more glasses of champagne. She was still very tanned. Even in winter she would look as if she were on holiday. Louis tried to imagine her a few years younger. He preferred her as she was, wearing her wrinkles like family jewels.

'Even in glasses, I can't see you as a schoolteacher.'

'Yet I was one and I didn't wear glasses then. Does that disappoint you?'

'Is that why you never had any children?'

'Perhaps.'

They drank in silence. The purring of the cat spiralled up and back down again. Louis stood up. 'Excuse me.'

The walls of the loo were covered with exotic postcards of the sea, beaches or coconut palms. Louis took one down. On the back: 'Dear Marion, this is the view from our hotel. Paris is no more than a bad memory. Thinking of you often, lots of love, Chantal and Bob.'

In a week, or maybe a month, Marion would tell him about Chantal and Bob. He felt as if he'd known them for ever. Inch by inch Louis was installing himself in Marion's life and felt comfortable there. He wanted to bask in it like the white cat in the pool of light by the window. They hadn't yet made love. That would come, probably, but for now it was of no importance. And perhaps it never would be.

What was more certain was that they would sleep in each other's arms.

Louis had been evasive about his past, offering snippets about his childhood, crumbs of his existence, peppered with some fairy tales. When Marion wanted to know more, he lied, he made up a life, to please her. He had spent too much time living with women he had not been able to satisfy while he was with them. Now they were financially secure thanks to him, he could retire with no sense of guilt. Marion had a few years on him; she could teach him how to live as a pensioner. He would have moved straight from childhood to retirement without stopping at adulthood, which he was quite proud of. He and Marion would visit little provincial museums, watch daytime television, go on bateaux mouches, have Chantal and Bob over, cure their little colds, their little injuries with little attentions and gifts. That little life was the height of his ambition. Louis had been born for old age, he had always known that.

In an hour he would be meeting Alice, probably for the last time. She had just returned from Greece where her parents had been buried. She was the one who had called him, she needed to speak to him. He couldn't see what she had to say to him, unless it was thank you, but obviously she wouldn't do that because she didn't know and would never know that she owed her providential inheritance to him. In any case, no one was overjoyed at the death of their parents, at least not immediately, especially when they had been killed in a hideous, inexplicable crime. He would see Alice one last time and Marion would replace Alice, as Alice had replaced Agnès, because everyone was replaceable, discardable, just like him. Louis buttoned himself up and checked to make sure he hadn't left any drops around the toilet. Everything was so clean here.

In the main room, Marion was on all fours playing with the cat.

'I have to go out, Marion, I have a meeting at six o'clock. But before I go, I wanted to ask you if you'll marry me?'

'Marry you? What on earth for?'

'I don't know, I think it would be good.'

'It's very unexpected. Do you love me?'

'I could. I'll call you tomorrow. Would you like to take a trip on a bateau mouche if the weather's good?'

He wanted to say to her, 'Alice! Alice! Look how happy everyone around you is. They're coming out of the cinema, or else they're on their way in. They all have parents, maybe are parents themselves. They're all mortal, but they don't know it yet, they're just happy to be here, to laugh while they can. You feel like an orphan now, but you're finally going to be yourself, without owing anyone anything. Perhaps that's what you don't like?'

Alice was very beautiful, much more beautiful than the last time he'd seen her by the ponds. She was wearing clothes he didn't recognise, chic, sober and brand new.

'That suit looks really good on you. Very smart.'

'You think so? I didn't have anything suitable to wear for the funeral.'

She blushed, instinctively turning to look at her reflection in the café window, one hand ruffling her hair. A quick smile, and then the mask of grief was back in place.

'So, what are you going to do now you are rich?'

'I don't know ... Buy a flat. You say that as if I'd just won the lottery. My parents are dead, for Christ's sake! Murdered!'

'I'm sorry, I—'

'No, it's my fault. It's just this is all so unbelievable; everything's happening so quickly! But what about you, what have you been up to recently? I tried to call you dozens of times – you were never there ... Aren't you going to ask me for news of the children?'

'Yes, yes, of course. How are they?'

'You don't give a stuff ... You don't care about anything; I don't know who you are any more. Is there still anything between us?'

Apart from a table and two empty glasses, Louis couldn't think of a single thing between them. He had never realised before how similar she was to Agnès.

'Have ... have you met someone else? That's it, there's someone else. Is there someone else?'

She was like someone knocking on the door of an empty house. Louis shrugged.

He thought back to that autumn. He had gone to meet Agnès at her dance class. He had known Alice for six months. The class was at the youth club in Colombes. He didn't normally go there, but this once, because it was his birthday and she had prepared a surprise for him, she had insisted that he was not to arrive at the house before her. Fred was a year old; he was staying with his grandparents. It was already dark, quite cold. Colombes station was like a rusty cage. The street that led to the youth club was a gloomy passageway in spite of the shops and neon lights, a Champs-Élysées for dwarfs. He had had to ask the way several times, having got lost in alleyways with ridiculously puffed-up names.

But he had still arrived early and been forced to watch the dire dance efforts of Agnès and her friends on their rubber mats. Seeing him leaning against a wall, she gave what was meant to be an elegant little wave, but was actually excruciating. She looked like a seal climbing out of water. The smell of chalk, hot rubber and feet made him feel nauseous. He had turned away. A badly printed poster announced the dates of various events: a singer from Languedoc, the Myrian Pichon ballet dancers, a table-tennis tournament, a production of *Ubu roi* and a judo competition. He heard the stamping of feet on the floor and the raucous voice of the teacher, 'Point your toes, point!'

In the train on the way back, everything seemed tired and poverty-stricken. Sometimes, as if by chance, Agnès's mouth sought Louis's, and, as if by chance, he avoided it. Then they were on the métro, the steps of the building, at the front door where Agnès said, 'Close your eyes! You can open them when I tell you to.' He would have liked never to open them because he knew what he would see: the kitchen table in the middle of the room, adorned with their sole tablecloth, three or four wilting carnations in a vase, two candles in front of two plates with serviettes, and, under his, a lighter or a pen. Behind his eyelids, all he could see was Alice, with whom he had spent the day. But he'd had to open his eyes and exclaim in delight, 'Oh! A lighter!'

As he stood at the window, glass in hand, listening to Agnès busying herself in the kitchen, he spotted that ageless-seeming woman that everyone called Maria on the other side of the courtyard. She had been struck down with an incurable illness; a port-wine stain covered three-quarters of her face, ending in a pool under her chin. It was monstrous. She was brushing her hair, slowly, with coquettish gestures, arranging a curl here and there, carefree and terribly beautiful.

When Agnès came out of the kitchen, he couldn't explain why he was crying. The next morning he left.

17

'But it's spoken language, Madame Beck! Kids say, "I dunno, I'm gonna, I ain't" … In the text, maybe, but not in the dialogue … Fine, look, Madame Beck, take them all out. Just send me my cheque, that's all I ask … That's right. Now excuse me, but I've got a whole heap of corpses to get back to … Of course, Madame Beck. Goodbye, Madame Beck.'

My editor's whinging voice has left the telephone all sticky. It was coming through the little holes in the handset like meat from a butcher's mincer. Very unsavoury. Christophe returned from the beach shrouded in mist while Madame Beck was breaking my balls with her idiot grammar. He looked like a baby who'd just had a bath. He brought back a bottle of Burgundy and a good slab of brawn.

'What's up?'

'Just the editor saying "na-na-na-na-na". They're like nits – harmless but irritating. You all right?'

'Yes. The wind outside's incredible. Makes you want to fly a kite. Fancy a snack?'

He opens the bottle and we tuck into the brawn straight from the paper it's wrapped in, bearing a picture of a jolly little dancing pig in a hat waving a string of sausages: 'Charcuterie Bénoult, world-champion tripe and black pudding maker'. Still chewing, Christophe starts taking the shells and pebbles he's collected for the children from his pockets. He spreads them out on the table and puts them in size order. He tells me that when he was little, he used to love playing with his grandmother's button collection. There were buttons of every type, made of wood, horn, mother-of-pearl, leather, fabric … He would plunge his hands into the box like a pirate revelling in a chest of gold coins. Then he would put them in order, make families or armies of them. He'd spend hours at it. Do I remember his grandmother? Vaguely, built like a tank with a bun on top?

Yes! And she put loads of butter on our bread? That's the one! Christ, yes, she slathered it on thick! Fat's a symbol of wealth, for common people. For instance, she would always ask the butcher for fatty veal for her blanquette, because it had a better flavour. It's true there's nothing like a bit of fat in cold weather, and a glass of Burgundy too. The glasses are drained and refilled. Take the Eskimos, for example, they eat nothing but fat; they couldn't survive otherwise. Not silly, Eskimos.

The opportunity is too good to pass up – I seize it with both hands. No, the Eskimos are damn well not silly! After all, aren't they the ones who've found the best possible solution for getting their elderly off their hands? Sit them on a chunk of ice, give it a kick and off they go – bon voyage! Christophe thinks for a moment, holding the glass to his lips. He doesn't seem to entirely approve of my tale of old people drifting off on an ice floe, probably because of his grandma. He prefers the Native American formula whereby granddad leaves the tribe to go and die with dignity beneath a venerable pine tree at the top of a mountain. I point out that if we were to expect the same thing of ours, we'd probably draw a blank as the fucking doctors have made them practically immortal. He admits I'm right, but even so, back in the days we looked after our elderly, they lived with their children until the end. I go 'Ha ha ha!' as if I learned to laugh from a bad book. Their children! They can't even put up with each other, let alone with the elderly thrown in! No, I'm telling you the Eskimos have the cleanest answer. Also, this Sioux thing you're talking about, it's not a million miles from suicide, and that's frowned upon in our religions; with my system of not-quite-murder, you're sending them on a fast train to paradise. Am I right or am I right? Christophe shakes his head, looking doubtful. The wine makes me as pig-headed as a missionary. I won't drop it: Nane's mother had a place in hell with her name on it, but you sent her to heaven.

'Well, I obviously didn't put my back into it, since she fell down to earth again immediately.'

Christophe drains his glass and smiles.

'Wanna know what Grégoire told me the other day, when I picked him up from school? What do you get when a Chinaman jumps off the Eiffel Tower? … A chink in the pavement!'

I never get jokes, but I can't seem to resist this one. It feels so good to laugh for the sake of it, a favour we should do ourselves more often. I make a note: 'Don't forget to laugh over silly stuff.' I empty the last of the bottle into our glasses, two purple tears.

'Hey, if we're going to want another one, we should go now – the shops will soon be shut until four.'

'It's going to be one of those days, then, is it?'

'It may well be.'

Outside, the wind carries us to Coccinelle so that we barely need to walk. While we're paying for our two bottles (one would not have sufficed) at the till of the minimarket, I tell Christophe I am determined not to put up with any more crap in my life. Editors, money, girls, winter, sick to death of all of it! Every day could be summer if we wanted it to be – it's up to us; we could leave, skedaddle, get the hell out!

On the way home, holding the bottles under my arms, head down against the icy wind, I describe to him in great detail the pleasures of a game of pétanque under the plane trees: the blue shadows, the speckles of light on skin that smells of salt and sun, bare feet in sandals …

'I don't like sandals. They dig into your feet and make you look like an idiot.'

'OK, fine, no sandals. But think about it – smoking a nice fat spliff leaning against a cypress tree, the peppery smoke from the weed mingling with the fragrance of thyme and lavender …'

'A nice fat spliff – now you're talking …'

'I know a guy in Rouen. We could go later, if you like.'

The house smells of wet dog and toilets. It takes a monumental effort to remain standing.

'Shit! Are we really going to wait until our beards have grown down to our knees before we go and find our place in the sun? You have to ride the wave when you catch it. I know a little place in Greece where you can live for nothing; a bit of bread and cheese, a few figs …'

'Is there no way of turning the heating up? Even my teeth are cold.'

'No, it's on maximum, but don't worry, Granddad, let's make ourselves a nice poor man's soup with what's left in the house. Pour us a drink, would you.'

You have to keep your hands busy, get back in touch with your body, to avoid becoming trapped by the ice. I take a stock pot out of the cupboard and throw in everything I can lay my hands on: carrots, lentils, an old yellowed leek, some Gruyère, a handful of pasta. I have ten arms, ten legs; I spread myself star-shaped across all four corners of the kitchen. I've put on the uniform of Captain Ahab; the white whale is right here, in a corner of my head. Meanwhile, in Christophe's head there's nothing but weariness, with bars across it and little kids passing through oranges. Now's the time to be an artist, a real one, a shaman, to move aside and make room for him. There is no better way of getting a man to share his troubles than by talking about one's own. In this case, all I have to do is think about my first wife while peeling an onion.

'Do you remember Odile? Before we broke up, I heard her chatting to her friends on the phone, talking about us as if she was describing an incurable disease: things are going better ... things are much the same ... things are getting worse ... She knew I was listening – our place was so small ... Afterwards she would hang up with a sigh, cracking her knuckles because she knew I couldn't stand it. I'd tell her, "You're squeaking like a new shoe" ... It went on like that for more than a year. We didn't think we'd ever get over it. I bumped into her six months ago. She was doing fine, and so was I. People are pretty solid, really, aren't they?'

'I'd say more soluble.'

'OK, soluble, then. Have you finished with the carrots?'

'I can't do it. They're all floppy.'

Jesus, he's a tough nut to crack! I can't squeeze the slightest tear out of him. I turn the screw, tell him about the little girl on the news, clutching a beam and slowly becoming mired in a river of mud. Then I go on to the stories my mother told me to send me to sleep, the fire at the Bazar de la Charité, the raft of the *Medusa* and the absurd death, three years later, of one of the sole survivors, the shipwright Corréard, who drowned in a puddle, pissed, on his way home from a country dance. And the *Titanic*! Ah, the *Titanic*! ... And that toothache I had last year! In agony for an entire Sunday, I was! Ooh, I can still feel it now ... Awful!

'So anyway, this soup of yours ...'

'What about it?'

'I can't smell anything.'

No wonder – I've forgotten to put the gas on underneath it.

'Look, it's not worth crying about. It doesn't matter.'

Oh, but it does! I can't even make a nice hot soup for my old friend the murderer who's dying of cold. I break down, unable to speak, hanging off the edge of my chair as if teetering on the edge of the world, my feet swinging in the void.

Out of the corner of my red eye, peering between the now empty bottles, I watch my Christophe suck in all the air in the room, stand up straight and become once again what he has always been, Saint Christopher carrying the little children who are afraid of getting their feet wet.

'Right, come on, we're going to Rouen to get some weed. A bit of fresh air will do us good. I'm not cold any more; everything's fine.'

I've worked my magic, but at a price.

'All right, I'll puke and then we can go.'

We take Christophe's car, an Opel as solid and reliable as him, although the seats are a little on the firm side. He takes the wheel – he's always handled his drink better than me. What's the point of drinking if not to get drunk? Plus I like being ferried around by other people. The windscreen wipers are slightly out of time with the music coming from the radio, a Dalida song: 'He had just turned eighteen, he was beautiful like a child, strong like a man ...' It's making my head throb. I don't mind; I need a head-ache the way a blind man needs his dog. The world outside the car is like my soup, uncooked brown mush. A few times, as we pass a police station, Christophe slows down to peer in before speeding up again.

'Do you want to hand yourself in?'

'No, I'm just looking.'

'What if we didn't stop at Rouen?'

'Then we wouldn't smoke a spliff.'

'And what if we said to hell with the spliff and all the rest of it? What if we just kept on driving?'

'Since the Earth's round, we'd end up back where we started.'

'Jesus, you're annoying sometimes! What I mean is, if we never stopped, never ever.'

'Then we'd be dead.'

'Do you think you can be dead without knowing it?'

'And you say I'm annoying? How the hell should I know? I just want to smoke a spliff, that's all.'

We're in Rouen because that's what the sign says, plus there's a cathedral and the Gros Horloge – if it wasn't for them, we could be in any European city: same town centre with the same pedestrianised streets, same little cobblestones laid like fish scales, same tubs filled with anaemic privet, same branches of Chevignon, same jeans shops, same croissant stands, same guitar strummers, same accordion players, same red-nosed clowns following you and mimicking your movements. Nowheresville. We've been wandering around for an hour; I'm lost, as lost as lost can be. Funnily enough, the last (and only) time I came to this dealer was three years ago, on a day as fuzzy as this one.

'It's definitely next to a bakery. You'll laugh, but this is exactly like last time. I came with a friend. We had a joint, then two, then three, and then, on the stroke of one in the morning, I had the urge to take a stroll around town. I went out, had a nose around, my head filled with the city stars, till my calves couldn't take any more. Only, I'd forgotten to take his address. Imagine, in November, at two in the morning, not a rat on the streets. And even if there had been someone, what could I have said? Do you know Horatio, the guy who sells weed and lives by a bakery? Hours I spent circling around this fucking town until eventually I found him by accident.'

'I'd just like to point out that this is the third time we've passed this branch of André. We're going round in circles.'

'It's next to a bakery …'

'There are bakeries everywhere! Come on, let's get something warm to drink; it's starting to rain.'

Through the opaque windows of the café, the road is morphing into an aquarium, clouded by the violet ink of the falling night. My Viandox tastes like a wet rag. I leave it to cool down while I watch the passers-by skip between puddles of shadow and neon, hunched over, holding newspapers open over their heads. They look like sandflies. Christophe is reading the menu – written in white paint on the window – backwards, when I catch sight of Nat, in a fit of laughter, walking by on the arm of a comma-shaped man, probably David.

'Doesn't steak hachis have an "S" on the end?'

'Why the hell should I care?'

Nat, all wet, like a kitten that's fallen into the bathtub, Nat laughing, Nat happy, without me. No matter how I try to tell myself that there's nothing extraordinary about bumping into her like this, that the centre of Rouen isn't that big and all the ghosts in the world have the right to walk there, I feel a horrible sense of unease coming over me, the sensation of turning up at a family party without having been invited.

'What's the matter? You've gone all pale.'

'Huh? Nothing, nothing, I thought I saw someone but it wasn't him. Doesn't this Viandox stink? Or maybe it's my hands; they do smell sometimes.'

'It just smells a bit damp. You know, I don't give a shit about the weed. If you want, we can just go home.'

'No! We are not going home!'

'It's almost eight. Where do you think we can go? Something's up with you all of a sudden.'

'I don't know, but we can't go home, ever. I don't want any more of this Viandox. I want a Picon bière instead.'

'Fine, fine, we'll get a Picon bière. Waiter?'

After the Picon bière, which perked me up a bit, we got back on the road, but we didn't go home. I would rather have dropped dead. We bought some beer from a corner shop that smelled of cat piss and rancid Gruyère. Christophe took a road heading towards the sea. I felt better. Everything was behind us again. I felt as if I had just avoided something terrible. J. J. Cale was on the radio. We joined in with the chorus together: 'Cocaine!' I wriggled about in my chair trying to find something to write with in my pocket. I was thinking of Louis; I had a brilliant idea. By the time I had found a scrap of paper, it had gone, evaporated. It was a shopping list: bread, sugar, washing powder, chocolate. The last word, oil, had been crossed out. Hélène had already bought some. On the other side, I wrote, 'In six months, Louis had put on six kilos.'

18

In six months, Louis had put on six kilos and been on two aeroplanes. One to Munich, the other to Copenhagen. Marion had been dying to go to those two cities. Louis would have preferred to stay put, but how could he come up with a good reason for not wanting to go to either Munich or Copenhagen when he had nothing else to do and he and Marion were newly married? Anyway, now that all the cities in the world looked alike, travelling wasn't too bad because it didn't really feel like travelling. There were the same pedestrianised streets in the centre, the same fashions, the same exasperating music everywhere – the same everything everywhere. Except that Marion, like all tourists, did not want to be taken for a tourist, which meant interminable traipsing around rancid suburbs looking for a 'typical' little hotel or a 'charming' caff whilst lugging enormous suitcases. Having said that, the exhausting excursions didn't last more than a week and the rest of the time was spent developing photos of the mini-adventures and sticking them into an album before going back to the travel agent to fetch stacks of new brochures.

'Listen to this: "Enjoy the ultimate Royal Scotland experi-ence. The most luxurious train in the world takes you on an unforgettable journey with views of the beautiful lochs and mountains of the Highlands. Also included are private visits to gardens, stately homes and mysterious castles with commentary from an experienced guide." What do you think of that?'

'That sounds good. Is it expensive?'

'About twenty thousand francs. Not bad.'

'We'll have to see.'

Twenty thousand francs! That was about all he had left in his account. Marion thought that Louis was not rich exactly, but comfortably off. He had been spending at the same rate as Marion, that of a relatively well-off retiree. He didn't have another mother or father he could kill off. It was a bit of a concern.

'I'm going out to buy the TV guide. Is there anything else you need?'

Once in the street, that street that he didn't like and that didn't like him, he repeated, 'I'm going out to buy the TV guide. Is there anything else you need?' several times in a row. How many sentences like that had he uttered in his life? Had he expressed anything else? And was there anything else to express? If you learned those words in all the languages in the world, you would be able to manage in any situation.

When he bought the TV guide, he also bought a French–German dictionary to learn his magic phrase. German, because he knew how to say it in English, and the French–German dictionary was on sale. In Munich, he had once wished he'd known some German. He and Marion were walking in the Englischer Garten, a sort of Bois de Boulogne in the heart of the city, full of bicycles, dogs, and Germans in shorts or dressed like punks. They took a little walk there every day before embarking on the inescapable trips to museums in the afternoon. By the lake, a little boy had passed close by them, walking a dog on a leash (although perhaps it was the dog leading the child – it was a huge dog, completely white). A flight of ducks? A sudden movement of Marion's? Something frightened the dog and his leash became wrapped round Marion's ankles, so that she, the animal and the child who held obstinately to the leather strap ended up in the black waters of the lake. The ducks were quacking, the dog was barking, his enormous mouth wide open, Marion was shouting, 'Louis! Louis!' and curiously the child was yelling 'Taxi! Taxi!' (It was only later that Louis learned that was the dog's name.) Louis didn't fancy saving any of them. In fact, he would happily have sunk them with stones, so unbearable was their shouting. Of course, lots of people suddenly appeared from goodness knows where. Two young men had already thrown themselves into the water. The lake was not deep, but it was full of mud. They got Marion and the child out covered in sludge but the dog had made it difficult for the rescuers and it took a while to save him. While this was going on, the people on the bank, an elderly couple wearing matching jogging suits, a young woman with a twin buggy, and a handful of punks with red coxcombs, had bombarded him with questions to which he had replied by throwing his hands up: *Nix sprachen deutsch*. He would have liked to explain to them that, contrary to appearances, he had done what he could, that is, nothing. The life he was leading now that he wasn't murdering anyone any more was boring beyond belief, and, no doubt to make up for the monotony of his days, had offered him this little spectacle that was more comic than tragic. That was the reason he hadn't moved, just as you don't climb on stage to stop Juliet from poisoning herself. But the only things he knew how to say in German were *Nix sprachen deutsch, helles bier, dunkles bier, lam, schwein, rint, links, rechts* and *gut morgen*.

As she got out of the lake, dripping from head to foot, all Marion had said was, 'Why?' Why had she been knocked into a Munich lake by a dog called Taxi, or why had Louis watched her from the bank without doing anything? But, in fact, it was a more general why, encompassing an infinity of other much more profound and essential questions, a universal why, meaning 'Why me?'

Up until that point, Louis had always considered Marion to be as eternal and inevitable as spring following winter, or as the desire to drink a lovely cold beer follows a long visit to a museum. He thought that by her side he would benefit from the same status, but this tiny fault had just given rise to a doubt. Marion was submersible and could ask herself pathetic questions like 'Why me?'

Every week when he went out to buy the TV guide, Louis treated himself to a minced-meat pie at the charcuterie next to the newsagent. They were so good, even cold. As he walked along, munching his pie, Louis opened the German–French dictionary at random. *Apfel* – apple, *Hase* – hare, *Schwere* – gravity, *Schwerpunkt* – centre of gravity. That's how he could have answered Marion's why beside the lake: *Schwerpunkt*, instead of brushing in vain at her clothes caked in mud.

Marion was preparing rabbit in a foil parcel when he returned. It smelled of mustard and tarragon.

'You put the blue vase down so that it was balanced on the fridge door. So when I opened the fridge, it fell on the floor.'

'*Schwerpunkt*.'

'What?'

'Nothing.'

101

19

Christophe is bent over his plate. Sitting opposite him, it's my face that I can see above his shoulders in the mirror behind the banquette. I look like a Corsican bandit. On escapades like this, I begin to look scruffy at an alarming rate. Time hits me like a ten-ton truck. The restaurant is practically empty; we had a hard time persuading them to serve us. In the car, I'd had the strongest craving for fried fish with white wine. There wasn't any. We had beef tournedos with a glass of red. Even though the place is called La Marine. There are sextants, compasses, telescopes, bits of rigging hanging all over the walls, but no fish on the menu. I'm disappointed. When men are unhappy, they think only of drinking and becoming sailors. I feel like going to sleep, like being cradled, but refuse to admit it.

'Why are you smiling?'

'No reason. I feel relieved.'

'Have you made a decision?'

'Yes.'

'You're going to hand yourself in, aren't you?'

'Yes.'

'I knew it! But shit, we could leave, cross the border; we can get false papers, you could send for your kids, start a brand-new life! I'm here for you, damn it! I can help you! … Why hand yourself in? Who for?'

'It's time to face facts, mate. Can you see me playing Jean Valjean with a false beard? It's a lot simpler than that.'

'Right, then. Coffee and the bill! Bish, bash, bosh, it's over!'

'This is real life! I'm not the hero of one of your fucking books! I'm not a hero of anything.'

'How do you know? You've never tried. Anyway, what do I care? Go on, you go and spend ten years behind bars making espadrilles. I'm gonna keep this going.'

'Don't be so ridiculous. I'm the one on the run, not you!'

'How would you know? You think you're the only one running away from something?'

The broom, passed expertly between our legs, brings an end to the debate.

Outside, the night unravels in trails of cloud, a few paltry stars flickering between them. I piss against the car in one long hard stream. My hands are old, my dick is old, the Opel is old and Christophe, who's waiting for me at the wheel, the oldest of them all. I collapse into the seat beside him.

'OK, here's what I think we should do. We go and watch the sun come up at Étretat – you know, where we used to take the kids, where the cliff looks like a slice of cake. And then … and then day will have dawned.'

I just shrug my shoulders. The truth is, I couldn't care less. My bladder must be directly connected to my brain. When I emptied it, I completely emptied my head, heart and the marrow of my bones. I am a kind of tube, open at both ends, incapable of taking the slightest initiative.

The car smells of plastic, mints and a full ashtray. It's like being at the prow of a boat, the trees either side of the road fringed with grey foam in the beam of the headlights. It's so nice to follow someone who knows where he's going. I should have shadowed him since nursery school; I needn't have been me or worn myself out becoming me. The road, the night, the music, how could it all come to an end? I have the firm conviction that I was destined to live for ever.

I must have fallen asleep for quite a while. The car slows down and turns down a track. There are no more trees, just an expanse of grass flattened by the weight of the sky, heavy with static clouds. There's nothing at the end of it, and I find this nothingness more and more oppressive as the car moves towards it, slowly, even more slowly, and then stops. A fixed image. Total silence. Christophe stretches his limbs, still holding the steering wheel.

'The end of the road, the end of the night.'

His serene smile, his calm assurance, the extreme banality of what he has just said annoy me immensely.

'The end of nothing at all, that's right. Now where are we? I don't like this place; let's get out of here.'

'We've been here dozens of times. Don't be an idiot, come on. The sun's going to come up. It's amazing from the top of the cliff.'

He opens his door and the void rushes into the car with the noise of a turbine. I see him walk a few metres beyond the bonnet, bent double, the two flaps of his raincoat plastered against his legs. Here we are, then; the sun will rise, our hero will receive the absolution of the raging elements and then bish, bash, bosh, off he'll go to hand himself in at the police station and it's over: violins, the end, credits roll. Or even fucking stupider: he says goodbye to me, smiling, and throws himself into the abyss like an angel, disappearing between two clouds. I bash my fist against the dashboard. The glove box opens, spewing out an old rag and a pair of glasses missing a lens. What a lousy ending, what a terrible script! I force myself out of my shell, ready to scream, 'Come on, then, Christophe. Do you really have nothing more original for me?' ... but the wind pushes the words back down my throat the minute I open my mouth. If I didn't keep both hands on the door handle, it would be me getting blown away. I throw myself down on all fours, fingernails digging into the ground. From the cliff edge, Christophe turns and motions to me to join him.

'I can't! I'm scared of heights!'

The wind bats a few words back to me: 'Come! … lovely! … sea!'

'No! … you come back! … to leave!'

He doesn't want to know. He keeps beckoning to me, with his back to the void. The idiot's going to hurt himself if he keeps waving his arms about like that. I creep towards him like an animal, screwing up my eyes, the wind grasping my face like the five fingers of an enormous hand.

'Christophe, for fuck's sake, let's go!'

'Come on, the sun's coming up, it's amazing! Give me your hand.'

So what? It comes up every fucking day. I'm cold and I've got vertigo. My fingernails dig into his wrist. He drags me to the edge, to the place where hope has almost gone, where all that's left is a sorry tuft of grass to which I cling for dear life.

'Well, isn't it wonderful?'

I only open one eye, which is more than enough. Nothing about it looks wonderful to me, only terrifying: rocks like jagged teeth, an inconceivably great drop, a pack of raging waves, pure horror under a scornful sky, vaguely tinted with a milky cloud. Paralysed by fear, I can do nothing but keep staring into the chaos. My brow is drawn downwards as if by a magnet and there below I see my body in pieces, arms and legs strewn about on the rocks. I hear a voice inside me say, 'You have never been the owner of your body, merely the tenant.' It's the voice of a witch offering a shiny red apple. A cry comes back in response, the cry of the beast within me refusing point-blank to heed the call of the abyss.

I close my eyes and leap backwards. My hand jerks out of Christophe's grasp. I seem to hear a sound like the crack of a whip or the whistling of a bullet, something narrowly missing me. I don't try to work it out, I roll through the grass. The only thought in my head is the need to get away from this hole, as far away as possible. I'll never be far enough away. Keep rolling, rolling …

20

The little girl was sitting on the edge of the white sofa. She'd perched Marion's glasses on the end of her nose and was holding the Gospel according to Saint Thomas open at page twenty-five, the page Marion had left it open at. Louis was watching her from the other end of the sofa. She was five years old and she was bored. Her name was Mylène and she was the daughter of Marion's niece. Marion had left him to look after her for the afternoon while she went shopping. Louis had played with her non-stop and read her three little books, laborious stratagems that had dragged him painfully towards three o'clock in the afternoon. Now they were both as bored as each other and a silence that almost made you want to cry reigned in the big white room. The little girl forgot about Louis. She was playing at being Marion, imitating the way she took her glasses off and put them on again. She was saying in her baby voice, 'Hasn't there been a phone call for me today?'

Louis remembered a day spent with a parrot. He had been at the house of people he hardly knew in Belgium, a huge house stranded in the middle of muddy fields. For a reason he now couldn't remember he had been left alone in the house with the parrot, a large grey bird with a red tail. He had been immersed in Maeterlinck's *The Life of the Bee* when the noise of a cork popping out of a bottle made him jump. Then came the scraping of curtains along a curtain rail and the voice of the master of the house, recognisable by his heavy Flemish accent, then the voice of his wife, high-pitched like clinking ice cubes, and finally the dog barking, all imitated to perfection. It was unbelievably realistic, especially the master and mistress of the house. At first, Louis had been amused but as it went on he became a little uncomfortable. He felt as if he were invisible and eavesdropping on private conversations, and even as if he were witnessing an intimate domestic scene. And all by dribs and drabs, interspersed with the *pop!* of corks which seemed to indicate that his hosts were fond of a drink. In front of him, they were courteous – a little distant, stiff even – but the parrot, possibly because it thought it was alone (Louis wasn't moving in his hidden corner of the room), had just given away what went on behind closed doors. It felt indecent to witness. Louis had spent the rest of the day in his bedroom on the first floor.

He had a similar feeling of indecency as he watched the little girl imitating Marion. And curiously, as with the parrot and his owners, the girl delighted in mimicking Marion's most ridiculous flaws, tics and obsessions. For a while now he himself had started to see her only as a caricature. He had had to admit to her that he had run out of money. She hadn't made any comment; in fact she had told him not to worry about it, that she had enough for both of them. But ever since, her behaviour towards him had changed. Not a lot, just enough to nag at Louis like a loose tooth. She sought his opinion less often, telephoned her friends more, imposed her choice of television programme on him. The other day he had groaned when she had asked him whether he would prefer to be buried or cremated. He had replied that he didn't mind, that death was a story for the living and that he was going to buy the bread.

The little girl was fed up with playing at being Marion and

was beginning to play about a little too close to the crystal carafes and other fragile knick-knacks that Marion had brought back from her interminable trips. The white cat had immediately picked up on the change in the child's behaviour and had gone to hide under the dresser. Louis was going to have to stir himself into action.

'Mylène, it's nearly four o'clock. Would you like a cake?'

It was strange to walk along holding the hand of a little girl, keeping to her pace. He felt awkward, at once proud but shy, vulnerable but powerful. The child was taking advantage of this by wanting everything she saw: a red motorbike, a multi-coloured feather, balls, sweets. It was like having a dog on a leash that would suddenly stop in its tracks.

'That! ... I want that!'

Louis felt sick when he saw what the plump little figure was pointing at. He had completely forgotten the fair that had been set up on the other side of the boulevard. Or he would, of course, have taken the other road. For as long as he could remember he had had a horror of fairs, circuses and in general of anything where fun was obligatory. The rare memories he had of fairs comprised nothing but drunken soldiers, obese women, terrifying dwarfs, which automatically triggered a violent feeling of nausea.

'But your cake? Don't you want it any more?'

'Nooo! Want roundabouts!'

Two solutions: he could pick Mylène up, kicking and screaming, and force his way through the crowd like a child catcher and attach her to a chair when they got home, or he could give in and let himself be dragged to the fair like a lamb to the slaughter.

He had to negotiate forcefully with a little red-haired boy for the driving seat of an ambulance. Now Mylène was going round and round, fading and disappearing in a whirlwind of light. Slyly, nausea was taking hold of Louis. He breathed slowly and deeply. He must not look at the roundabout, anything but the roundabout, the sky for example ... But his glance fell on the big wheel which, seen from this angle, seemed to be coming straight at him. Everywhere he tried to rest his eyes, it was all rods, gears and pistons coming to crush him. The stale smell of *frites*, waffles and toffee apples was the final straw. He had to sit down immediately or he would have collapsed in the dust amongst the fag ends, chewing gum, tickets, candyfloss sticks and crushed Coke cans. Over there, between two stalls, he thought he could make out a sort of drum, a red affair about buttock height. In spite of the crowd, he would get to that red thing, he had to. Once he was sitting on it, he closed his eyes. Three seconds more and he would have fallen over. An icy sweat broke out on his forehead and his legs wouldn't stop trembling.

'Louis?'

Louis half opened one eye. Agnès's head appeared in close-up wearing a ridiculous white cap. 'Agnès?'

'Louis! What are you doing here? Is everything OK? Are you ill?'

She was wearing a large white apron and Swedish clogs, also white. Even her face was white, as if floured. Perhaps her nurse-like appearance was reassuring because Louis was gradually recovering.

'I had a little turn. Fairs and me, you know ... But what are you doing here?'

'I'm working! You've just had the vapours beside my van!'

'The *frites* van?'

'Yes! Come and say hello to Jacques. I can't get over this, it's been ages ... Guess who I saw just now?'

'Who?'

'Your son, our son.'

'Fred?'

'Yes. I haven't seen him since my parents' funeral. So much for blood ties!'

For a fraction of a second, Louis could only see red as if all the other colours had disappeared, as if it was the only colour in the world.

'Come and have a glass of water. You don't look right.'

'No, no, I'm fine. But I'm with a little girl – she's over there on the roundabout.'

'Go and get her. I'll give her a waffle with lots of whipped cream on top.'

While Mylène was covering herself in cream, Jacques and Agnès insisted on giving Louis the tour of the van, as if it were a gastronomic restaurant. It was a wonderful business! The coast in the summer, the mountains in winter and all the little extras, like here. But how was he doing? Was that his daughter? Had he put on a little weight? But his grey hair suited him. Louis replied with idiotic little laughs, squashed into a corner of the van with Mylène. Jacques and Agnès continued to serve *crêpes*, *gaufres* and *frites*, all the while bombarding him with questions. He felt like a marionette in a cardboard puppet theatre. The people reaching over for their orders looked at him as if he were the bearded lady, just another attraction.

'We're thinking of expanding; we'd like to get another van, a bigger one like you get in Belgium. Food sells, you know. You can't go wrong.'

'That's true. I'm happy for you. Right, I'd better take the little one back to her mother. Mothers worry easily.'

Agnès rolled her eyes. 'What, now you're concerned about mothers? You really have changed. A few years ago, you'd have had to be forced to take your son to the fair.'

'Agnès ...'

'Don't worry, Jacques, Louis doesn't mind and, anyway, it's all in the past, isn't it, Louis? By the way, if you want to see your son, he's coming here about nine o'clock.'

Marion was eating an apple and flicking through the television guide. Louis was clearing the table.

'There's a documentary about Sri Lanka on France 2 at 8.30. My friend Fanchon went there last year; she thought it was amazing. I saw her photos, it—'

The tap running in the sink muffled Marion's voice. Louis couldn't decide – the fair or not the fair? Should he see his son – or not?

He could go or not go, what did it matter? It was as if there were another question behind that question, but he didn't know what it was. Since he had come home he had wrestled with that question mark like a trout on a hook, and his indecision was contaminating his every act. 'Should I do the washing-up – or not? Should I take a piss – or not? Should I scratch my nose – or not?' It was maddening.

'Louis, what are you doing?'

'I'm going to the fair.'

'What?'

It had just slipped out without him having the time to think about it, as if he were a ventriloquist's dummy and another voice had spoken for him.

'I'm going to the fair on the boulevard.'

'I thought you hated fairs!'

'I thought that too.'

'But when you went with Mylène this afternoon, you discovered you actually love them?'

'Possibly. It brought back memories.'

'Memories? I didn't even know you had a past to have memories of – you never talk about it. Do you want me to come with you?'

'I'd prefer to go on my own if you don't have any objection.'

'Why would I have an objection? It's just a bit odd. You don't look like someone who's going to the fair.'

'What do I look like?'

'Like a kid who's done something wrong, or who's about to. But in any case, don't forget your keys. I'm whacked – I don't even know if I'll make it to the end of my programme.'

'I won't be late.'

Marion went upstairs. The programme started. Louis put on his coat, hesitated by Marion's bag, then opened it and took out two 500-franc notes which he crammed into his wallet. The white cat watched him the whole time until he closed the door behind him.

The night air had the same effect on him as a damp cloth on his forehead. He could breathe again. He remembered his mother's perfume, Soir de Paris, thick, blue, in a shaped glass bottle, like an enormous precious stone. She would put one drop, no more, behind each ear, when she went out in the evening with her husband. They looked good together, like a married couple in a play. Louis would have liked them to be like that every day. Unfortunately they rarely were – only for a wedding anniversary or when his father received a promotion. The rest of the time they were just ordinary mortals.

A body was a stupid thing. All it needed was food and sleep, and on it went, just like any vehicle. But who was really driving it? As Louis got nearer to his destination, the music and smells of the fair became more and more invasive, attracting him like an insect caught in the U-bend of a basin. Yet something in him slowed his steps. He had nothing more to say to Jacques and

Agnès, and not much more to say to his son. He would slip him two 500-franc notes, that was all. But he could also just give them to Agnès and go home to bed.

The ephemeral town of lights and giddiness started on the other side of the boulevard. It seemed to take for ever for the lights to turn from green to red. He couldn't fathom why he was in such a hurry to get across. A group of youths beside him were horsing about hurling insults at each other. He didn't understand a word they were saying. He crossed the boulevard in their wake as if for protection.

The fair was not the same at night. Louis didn't know where he was. He had left the group of young people in front of the big wheel. Some of them wanted to go on it, some of them didn't. He wandered about looking for Agnès's van. He was dazzled, his ears assaulted by shouts and the sharp crack of rifle shots. It wasn't the nausea of this afternoon that now took hold of him, it was more like an inebriation, quite over-powering like his mother's Soir de Paris. It was only by chance that he stumbled on Agnès's van. Fred had not arrived yet. He could either wait for him there or have a go on the big wheel; a friend of Agnès's was running it. You could see the whole of Paris from there – it was fantastic. Well, why not? Normally, Louis would have categorically refused, but normally he wouldn't even have been here. And the intoxication he still felt seemed to protect him – he wasn't afraid of anything any more; he was watched over not by a guardian angel but rather by a well-muscled bodyguard. Everything seemed fun, everything sparkled, everything seemed appealing. He felt honoured and behaved accordingly, interested by everything around him. He settled down in the gondola of the big wheel like a king, arms ready to bless the crowd. He rose. The wind was stronger, colder. Soon the fair was nothing but a stream

114

of lava running between the trees. The gondola swayed gently each time the wheel stopped. The sky seemed closer than the ground. 'I have never been more alone. And curiously, it doesn't bother me at all. I'm not frightened of solitude any more because I'm the only one who counts, because the others don't exist, they're only there for effect.' In the gondola in front, actually below, the young man had succeeded in kissing the girl. Their kiss must have tasted of soda. They were snuggled into each other. They could have been anywhere. But they were here. A gust of wind blew the girl's scarf off. She gave a cry, putting her hand on her hair. They both burst out laughing. Everyone on the roundabout watched the zigzagging flight of the red scarf.

The exit led him down another path, behind the big wheel, opposite a tombola festooned with blue monkey cuddly toys. Louis had an urgent need to piss, which had come over him on the last turn of the wheel. He had to get behind the stalls in order to find a suitably dark spot. The urgency of the situation made him immediately dart between two stalls. A profound ecstasy spread through him as he relieved himself against the wooden fence. 'I'm exactly where I should be; I could only be here. I can almost say I recognise this place, as clearly as if someone had described it to me a fraction of a second before I got here. Someone is guiding my actions, imperceptibly anticipating them. I am a proxy for somebody else.'

A violent shove in the back propelled him against the rough planks he was pissing against. His teeth, lips and nose all split against the wood. Without understanding how, he was on the ground. Blows rained down on his body. He tried to protect himself, one hand on his head, the other on his penis which was still outside his flies. There were several people hitting him. He could only see their legs and feet, which seemed to increase in number as the pain worsened. The toe of a boot sliced off his ear, the music from the nearest merry-go-round rushed into the wound and bored into his brain. Hands were turning him over, rootling in his pockets. No one was watching over him any more. Between half-closed eyes he could make out two figures in a ray of green light.

'A thousand big ones.'

'Toss the wallet.'

'Wait ... I want to know what this bastard's name is ...'

'Chuck it, Fred, and let's get out of here!'

'Yeah, yeah, I actually don't give a shit who he is.'

Louis's wallet landed right beside his head. The two figures disappeared round the corner of the stall. Louis could no longer move. The machine was out of order. He was in pain but that wasn't what worried him, it was the pocket of ink that had just exploded in his stomach and was filling him with night. 'I'm leaking, gently deflating ... I'm dying ... I went to the fair with a little girl called Mylène and as a result, I'm dying ... right here in the grass ...'

Close by two dogs were copulating conscientiously. They stopped for an instant, when a gurgle escaped the mouth of the man stretched out near the dustbins, then they resumed, their tongues hanging out, gazing at the moon.

21

There. Louis's back in his ink pot. I turn off the typewriter, put down my glasses, rub the sides of my nose, pick up a cigarette but don't light it. I hold the manuscript in my hand, reassured by the weight of the thing. Because this story has become a thing, a matter of so many grams. I thought Louis was going to unmask me when he said, 'Someone is guiding my actions ...' He could have slipped away from me, away from himself. I can hear Hélène moving furniture around downstairs. She told me she was going to give the place a big clean-up this morning. Hélène always does as she says.

I only stopped rolling through the grass when I touched the wheel of the car. I lay there, flat on my stomach, for a long while, filling my lungs with the smell of petrol and the warm engine, and then I lifted my head. It was light, only just, but enough to establish that Christophe was no longer standing on the edge of the cliff. I shouted his name twice, three times, simply because that's what you do in those situations, but I had already realised what had happened. I knew exactly what I would see if I peered over the edge: a body lying broken on the rocks like an old alarm clock, a body that wasn't mine. The whooshing of air I had sensed as I threw myself backwards had been Christophe being sucked into the void. My moving backwards must have thrown him off balance and ...

Sitting there on the grass open-mouthed, the enormous consequences of my panic struck me full in the face. The sky had been reduced to one huge zero, round and smooth. I think I stammered, 'It wasn't me,' or else, 'It wasn't my fault.' Then fear, or an instinct of self-preservation – whatever you want to call it – took over. I didn't even check to make sure that Christophe really was at the foot of the cliff – what would have been the point? I was about to take the car, but once I got behind the wheel, I reconsidered. Why complicate the simplest of stories? 'A man in a state of shock over the death of his wife kills his mother-in-law and goes to the coast to commit suicide.'

A few lines in the local paper, no more. I wiped down the steering wheel, the bottles, the seats, the handle of my door. I walked to the village like an automaton, seeing nothing, feeling nothing, my legs stiff, the wind in my back. I waited there a good hour and a half for the bus to come. There was a café open – I could have gone in for a coffee but I didn't. I felt as conspicuous as if I was painted red. I got on the bus without thinking. A girl came and sat next to me. I could hear the *bzzzz bzzzz* of her Walkman right in my ear. She moved her left foot to the beat, oblivious to the fact her knee was rubbing against mine. She must have taken me for a suitcase, some package or other. I moved my leg. Snatches of the night's events came prowling around me; I waved them away like mosquitoes, sent them back one by one to the chaos they had emerged from. Later, tomorrow, but not now. The road hugged the coastline. I remembered those maps of France printed on transparent plastic; you had to trace the contours with the tip of a pencil: the receding hairline of Pas-de-Calais, the frowning eye of the Seine estuary, the wart of Cherbourg on the nose of Finistère, the pout of Gironde and the pointy chin of the Landes. I could have stayed on this bus all the way to Saint-Jean-de-Luz and never taken my eyes off the coast.

I got off at the church with tears in my eyes, my nerves and muscles tight as the strings of an instrument. It was market day.

The man I get my eggs and cheese from waved at me. I didn't stop. Nothing could have prevented me getting home. Having reached my front door, for one awful moment I couldn't find my keys. They had fallen inside the lining of my jacket. The first thing I did was clear the table of the previous day's leftovers, the paper the brawn had been wrapped in, the empty bottles and wine-stained glasses, the end crust of bread. I washed everything. Then I changed the sheets on the bed Christophe had slept in. I didn't want any trace of him left anywhere. Afterwards I took a shower and got changed. I went and tidied my study. I sat down in front of my typewriter and slipped a blank sheet into the carriage. There, nothing had happened; I had just got up and everything was fine and dandy. After a minute of staring like an idiot at the piece of paper, I began to feel dizzy. I filled in the empty space by typing meaningless words, among which AZERTY-UIOP came up often. I had to do something, anything, to escape the silence and stillness. I threw words onto paper like twigs onto a fire, to avoid freezing on the spot; two, three, four pages of pretending to write until I heard a knock at my door. I slid behind the curtain to see who it was. I immediately recognised the Vidals' daughter, the game-show champion. Beyond her, an ambulance was parked in the road behind a beige Renault 4. The girl tried again, took a couple of steps back to peer into my window. I stayed still; she shrugged, turned and left. Two male nurses emerged from the Vidals' place carrying a stretcher on which a body lay entirely covered by a grey blanket. They slid it into the back of the ambulance the way a baker slips a batch of bread into the oven. Madame Vidal appeared, clutching her daughter's arm, her face buried in a handkerchief. One of the nurses helped her into the ambulance while her daughter struggled to lock the gate. The ambulance drove off and the girl got into the Renault. I let the curtain fall back into place.

Hélène is humming to herself while she does the hoovering. She's happy to be here, to be doing the housework, to know that I'm in the study upstairs. She and Nat made up over the phone. They'll see each other back in Paris. She thinks I was right to persuade Christophe to go and hand himself in to the police; it was the sensible thing to do. As for my neighbour's death, it's sad but, at that age, it's only to be expected at some time or another … In short, as far as she's concerned, everything is back to normal, only she doesn't think I'm looking great. A week from now she'll have me right as rain, I can count on her. What she would like more than anything is for me to be done with that damned book. She hates it without having read it; when it's off my hands, we'll go to England, or somewhere else.

And the lake's skin will heal over without a scar.

Low Heights

*The best way to avoid getting lost
is not to know where you are going*
Jean-Jacques Schuhl

'Today's programme is all about stomach ulcers and with us in the studio we have Professor Chotard from ...'

Monsieur Lavenant clenched his fist in irritation, as if he were crumpling up an invisible sheet of paper.

'Will you change the station, Thérèse? Or even better, turn the radio off altogether.'

'There.'

The presenter's nasal voice was replaced by the roar of the engine. Monsieur Lavenant tugged at the seat belt, which was digging into his left shoulder.

'In any case, it's ridiculous to try to listen to the radio in these gorges – you know perfectly well it's impossible to pick anything up clearly.'

'It was you who asked me to turn it on, Monsieur.'

'Hmm, well ... We weren't in a gorge a minute ago.'

The river Aygues wound its way to the right of the road along the sheer rock. With the non-stop torrential rain of the past few days, its coffee-coloured water carried along dead branches which gathered in the rocky river bends like sets of pick-up sticks. Above the cliffs, birds bounced acrobatically on the taut blue trampoline of the sky. Nature was drying her sorrowful tears of the previous day. The car swerved.

'Look out, Thérèse!'

'That's what I'm doing, Monsieur. There was a big stone in the middle of the road. It's because of the storms.'

'You're driving too fast.'

'A minute ago you were criticising me for going too slowly.'

'A minute ago we were on a straight road. You drive too fast when you shouldn't, and too slowly when you need to accelerate. Anyway, in a car like this!'

'It may be old but it serves me well. And you too.'

'It stinks. It stinks of petrol and wet dog.'

'I've never had a dog.'

'You must have had one in the car, then. I may be gaga but I can still recognise the smell of damp dog!'

Thérèse gave up. Whatever he said, whatever he did, the old boy wouldn't succeed in spoiling the good mood she had been in since the moment she woke up. She felt serene, happy with the sort of happiness which hits you out of the blue.

'Why are you smiling?'

'No reason. The weather's fine.'

'The weather's fine ... Pah! In the desert it's fine the whole time – d'you think the Bedouin are laughing?'

'I don't know, Monsieur. I've never been there.'

'Well, I have, and believe me, there's no reason to smile. Slow down, Thérèse, we're coming to the tunnel!'

'I know, Monsieur. I know the road.'

'Exactly! That's why accidents happen. You know, you're confident, and then wham! Vigilance, Thérèse, vigilance, at all times. It only needs a second's lack of concentration ... Look there, what did I tell you? English bastard!'

Monsieur Lavenant's voice yelling through the open window was quickly swallowed up in the dark shadow of the tunnel, while the camper van which had almost clipped them disappeared in the rear-view mirror. At the exit, the sun striking a layer of rock made them blink. The geological strata formed swirls, folds of ochre, gold or incandescent white trimmed with the green fur of spindly oak trees, all their roots clinging on to the slightest toehold in the ground. The birth of the world could be read there, its bursts of energy, its hesitations, twists and turns, its centuries-long periods of stagnation and thunderous eruptions. Now and then, perfumed clouds of thyme or lavender wafted in, accompanied by the non-stop chirping of the crickets.

'What about …?'

'About?'

'I was going to say something silly, Monsieur.'

'Say it, then.'

'What about having a picnic after we've been to the market?'

'That's not silly, that's downright stupid! Have you been drinking, Thérèse? I've heard it all now! Picnic? Do you think you're on holiday or something?'

'I'm sorry, Monsieur.'

'A picnic! And then a little dip in the Aygues, and in the evening maybe a dance, under paper lanterns? You'd be better off looking where you're going. Here, switch the radio on again, we're out of the gorge. I'd rather listen to the world's bad news than your ramblings.'

'Very well, Monsieur.'

The first cherries were barely ripe, yet the market in Nyons was teeming like high summer. Space was limited and they had been forced to park well beyond the Pont Roman, which had, of course, only exacerbated Monsieur Lavenant's bad mood.

'Just look at that! English, Dutch, Germans, Belgians ... Do I go and do my shopping in their countries? No! You'd think we were still under the Occupation.'

'I could easily have done the shopping on my own; you didn't have to come.'

'That's right, you'd like me to stay shut up in my hole like a rat. I do still have the right to go out, you know.'

'Why don't you wait for me nice and quietly on the café terrace with your newspaper and a cold drink?'

'That's exactly what I had in mind. But don't dawdle like last time. It doesn't take three hours to buy a kilo of tomatoes. Have you got the list?'

'I have. See you later, Monsieur.'

'And don't let anyone rip you off, we're not tourists.'

Seated at a small table in the shade of a blue-and-white-striped awning, he watched Thérèse go off, basket in hand, and melt into the brightly coloured crowd. As soon as she was out of sight he felt a vague anxiety, a sense of having been abandoned. He shrugged his shoulders and curtly ordered a pastis from the waitress who was bustling among the tables like a frantic insect.

Thérèse allowed herself to be carried along by the wave of passers-by, intoxicated by the infinite variety of colours, scents and sounds, as if at the heart of a giant kaleidoscope. Bodies scantily dressed in the lightest of fabrics rubbed against hers and she experienced the same giddiness as she had at dances in her youth. She desired everything, and everything was there. After the gloomy days counted off like rosary beads in Monsieur Lavenant's joyless house, this was a sort of resurrection and she made the most of it, every pore straining for the tiniest atom of life. She criss-crossed Place du Docteur Bourdongle, enclosed by arcades whose violet shadows suggested stolen kisses, filling her basket with tomatoes, peppers, aubergines, basil, fromage frais, piping-hot bread. She tasted an olive here, a crouton dripping with virgin oil there, a slice of saucisson, a spoonful of honey …

As she made her way back, having come to the end of her shopping list, she stopped short in front of a stall selling hats, dozens and dozens of hats …

GREAT DEALS!
FREE! We will clear your attic, cellar or whole house … 500F plus paid for German helmets, uniforms, other historical memorabilia, Resistance, militia, US …
PRIV. INDIVID. SEEKS OLD MILITARY objects, from flintlocks to caplocks, matchlocks, percussion caps, trigger guards, various barrel bands, even in poor condition …

Monsieur Lavenant pushed his newspaper away and stared mournfully at his empty pastis glass. In theory he wasn't allowed more, but since sucking the ice cube, all he could think of was having another. There was something indecent about feeling so good, and everything in him rebelled at the idea of calling the waitress again. Yet he was dying to. He would have to make up his mind before Thérèse came back. He glanced at his watch but as he didn't know how long he'd been there, he was none the wiser. The sight of the crippled hand to which his watch was attached decided it for him. It was scrawny and hooked, like a bird of prey's talon, the hand of an Egyptian mummy, of use to him now only as a paper-weight to stop the newspaper from blowing in the breeze.

'The state I'm in already ... Fuck it! I can do what I want.' Immediately, his right arm shot up and the crow in a white blouse and black skirt replaced his empty glass with a new one which he half emptied in order to fool Thérèse, before becoming engrossed once more in the indescribable experience of reading the classifieds.

BULTEX SOFA BED, new, yellow. 1300 F.
WIN BIG ON THE HORSES! 70% success rate for our tip with good odds. WATCH THIS SPACE FOR RELIABLE INFO!
HORSE MANURE TO GIVE AWAY.
TWO THOUSAND-LITRE SEPTIC TANKS.
BRIDAL GOWN, size 38 + veil and tiara. 1000 F.

For a moment he saw it floating before him, a wispy cloud of white muslin. Deep in his wizened heart, something came loose. How long was it since he'd just let go, stretched out on the grass and watched the clouds go by? Years ...

'There now, I wasn't too long, was I?' Thérèse's voice jolted him back to reality.

'What have you got on your head?'

'A hat.'

'A hat!'

'Well, you're wearing one.'

'It's different for me. I can't tolerate the sun. My hat is … useful.'

'Well, mine is a hat that I like.'

It was a small straw hat with a wide brim which cast a veil of shadow over her shiny, slightly puffy face. Her violet eyes, the only beautiful thing about her, were sparkling with mischief, almost impudence. Monsieur Lavenant tried unsuccessfully to find something to say to make her lower them, but could only snigger and look away.

'At the end of the day, you're the one wearing it. Now, what have you brought for the picnic?'

'The picnic?'

'Yes, the picnic. Have you lost your wits or something?'

'I thought that …'

'You thought that … You thought … I've changed my mind, that's all. I'm entitled to do that, aren't I?'

'Oh, it doesn't bother me. Quite the reverse; it's such lovely weather. We've got all we need: melon, tomatoes, cheese and an excellent ham.'

Paying for his drinks, he couldn't hide the fact that he'd had two pastis and she raised her eyebrows indulgently.

'Yes, I've drunk two pastis; it won't kill me.'

Monsieur Lavenant decided they should take the Défilé de Trente Pas and look for a place to stop on the way to the Lescou Pass where the air was cooler. The road was very narrow and winding. Thérèse drove carefully, sounding her horn at every bend since it was impossible to see round them. The walls of rock were so close together that it felt like being a bookmark between the pages of an ancient tome exuding a strong smell of mould. It was very impressive but slightly anxiety-provoking. The dense vegetation screened the river below, whose presence was suggested only by a guttural roar, an uninterrupted chant. Neither of them uttered a word until they were out of the gorge, and as one they sighed with relief when the little car came onto the road to the pass. The sun was sounding a fanfare and the clumps of trees were thinning out the higher they climbed. Their stomachs rumbled meaningfully and, quite independently, Thérèse to the left and Monsieur Lavenant to the right, they scoured the horizon for a favourable picnic spot.

'Take that little one on the right! There, right away!'

Having missed it, Thérèse reversed and turned onto the track. It led to a not very attractive ruin without the slightest patch of shade. The view of the valley was magnificent but all they could think of was the Drummond family murders or something else sinister and tragic. Despite the hunger gnawing at them, they turned round. A little further on, a side road led them straight to a farm, out of which shot a large hound, fangs bared, slavering all over its chops and howling blue murder. Once more they had to turn back. Monsieur Lavenant was bright red, his jaw clenched in a silent fury which crept through him like poison.

'Are you trying to make us die of hunger or something? It's just like you to do something like this!'

'You were the one who was set on coming here. You know the area, apparently.'

'It's changed! Everything changes the whole time. How do you expect me to know where we are? Anyway, you drive too fast so obviously we're going to miss the best places. We passed dozens as we came out of the ravine.'

'You wanted to go higher up because of the air.'

'So it's my fault now! Was I the one who had this stupid picnic idea? I loathe picnics. You always end up next to a rubbish tip, being eaten alive by insects, sitting on a pile of stones, with greasy hands and warm drinks – that's if there's not some local halfwit hiding in the bushes waiting to cut your throat during your siesta.'

'Let's go home, then.'

'Yes. We *will* go home, we've wasted enough time.'

Each of them had retreated into a palpable sulk when, at the entrance to a hamlet, they noticed a tiny chapel in a hollow, with a small meadow in front of it, shaded by three magnificent lime trees. A stream meandered along the bottom of the field. Thérèse braked and gave Monsieur Lavenant a questioning look.

'We've come this far, we might as well have a go.'

Thérèse parked the car in the shade of one of the big trees. The new-cut grass gave off a smell of hay which mingled with the pollen from the limes. Not one fly, not one mosquito. The serenity of the modest chapel with its lime-washed façade surmounted by a silent bell banished all dark thoughts. It was paradise as conceived by a six-year-old. In spite of all his bad faith Monsieur Lavenant had to give in.

'Take a seat under that tree where it's nice and flat. I'll see to everything.'

The bark of the tree trunk seemed more comfortable than the velvet of his armchair. He put his crippled hand between his thighs, and removed his hat with the other. A breath of wind caressed the skin on the top of his head, ruffling the few hairs which crowned it like swansdown, and then swooped down the open neck of his shirt. In the far distance a cock was crowing, and a dog barked in response. He closed his eyes and opened his mouth, since he had nothing better to do. Little by little the rapid pulsing of blood in his veins slowed to match the peaceful rhythm of the lime tree's sap, which he could feel circulating at his back, from the nape of his neck to his waist. *C'est un trou de verdure qui mousse de rayons* … He would really have liked to remember the poem … *C'est un trou de verdure* …

131

'There, it's ready!'

Thérèse was smiling, cheeks flushed, hat tilted back, kneeling down, like the little girl she must once have been, proud of her dolls' tea set. In the absence of a plate, the melon slices, ham and cheese were set out on their wrappers. There was even a bottle of rosé, cooling inside a towel she had soaked in the stream.

'If I'd known, I'd have brought glasses, plates and cutlery ...'

Something Monsieur Lavenant hadn't felt since ... maybe the end of the world, caught in his throat, prickled his nose and brought deliciously salty water to his eyes.

They made a good meal of the melon, ham, tomatoes and cheese she spread on slices of crusty bread, like canapés, using a small knife she always carried in the glove box. The wine was barely chilled, but they drank half of it straight from the bottle like savages. Monsieur Lavenant got carried away, describing the gourmet meals he'd had in some of the world's top restaurants. Thérèse loved food and he remembered that he used to as well. Then, like a child falling asleep at the table, he stretched out, good arm beneath his head, and promptly began to snore.

Thérèse cleared away the leftovers, put the cork back in the bottle, gathered up the melon skins and the ham and cheese rinds and put them into a plastic bag, scattered the crumbs for the birds and lay down in her turn – but only once she'd given a satisfied glance at her hat. There are days like that.

The day was at its hottest when Monsieur Lavenant opened his eyes. He stretched, yawning like a lion. If his right arm obeyed orders, the left remained stubbornly bent, like an iron hook. He had had this disability for a year now and was relatively used to it but it still astonished him sometimes when he woke up. He lay flat again. The play of sunlight through the lime's foliage marbled his skin blue and gold. If Cécile had still been alive and there next to him, he would probably have made love to her. She would have feigned sleep and put up with it, with a groan. But Cécile had died suddenly of cancer almost ten years ago. He had never accepted being left behind, just as certain blind people will never get used to sightlessness. He had been angry with her and, out of spite, had thrown himself into his business with the merciless efficiency of the most ruthless predator. It wasn't for the money, as he was more than comfortably off, but in order to anaesthetise himself, wear himself out, cause himself pain as others do pleasure, until that evening in September when an episode in a grand Lyon restaurant had forced him to pack it all in. He had felt a rush of hot air to his face, his legs gave way beneath him and his reflection disappeared from the spotless tiles above the urinals. His last thought was of his flies, which he hadn't had time to do up.

After his stay in hospital, and on his doctor's advice, he had decided to leave his apartment and office in Lyon and to move into the house at Rémuzat which had been in his wife's family and where he had set foot only once or twice. That was as good as anywhere else. Since his state of health made nursing care necessary he had recruited Thérèse through a specialist agency. In two months' time this odd couple would have been together for a year and he had no idea how long this might last, the future not being on his agenda any more.

A lime blossom, a tiny helicopter, came to land on his chest. He hadn't drunk much but his mouth was as 'caramelised' as after a heavy night. Propping himself up on one elbow, he downed what was left in the bottle of Evian, which a ray of sun had heated almost to boiling point.

Thérèse was sleeping with her mouth open and her red hair (white in places) plastered to her forehead. Her hat had left a red mark on her skin. A few drops of sweat were visible under her arms. Her dress was rucked up in the brazenness of sleep, exposing soft white calves lined with blue veins which made him think of certain artisan sausages he had a taste for. She was neither beautiful nor ugly, simply robust. Aside from her professional references he knew nothing about her except that she was Alsatian, from Colmar. It was as if he were seeing her for the first time, seeing her as something more than a medical aid, and it disturbed him. One of Thérèse's knees was marked by a crescent-shaped scar, some childhood accident, a fall from a bicycle perhaps … Without thinking, he went to stroke it, but at that moment Thérèse opened one eye and he put his hand down again, turning red.

'I'm sorry, I think I fell asleep …'

She sat up, tugging her dress down over her knees and tidying her hair. A few blades of grass were sticking out of it, like pins. Once again she was smiling. The low neckline of her dress revealed a beige bra strap, more suggestive of a hernia bandage than of sexy underwear.

'Perhaps we ought to be thinking of getting back, it's nearly four o'clock.'

'We ought to, yes.'

'What a lovely place, though … Imagine, some people actually live here …'

A quarter of an hour later, the car started bumping gently along the track. Before they came to the road, Monsieur Lavenant met Thérèse's gaze in the rear-view mirror. A tear hung on her eyelashes.

'Thérèse, are you crying?'

She sniffed, wiped the corner of her eye with the back of her hand, and shifted into first gear.

'No, it's nothing, Monsieur.'

'Yes, you are, you're crying. What's wrong?'

'I'm fifty-two today, Monsieur. It's my birthday. Silly, isn't it?'

FOR FARMHOUSE RESTORATION, Apt area, seek couple as caretakers, no family ties, motivated, stable, gd health. M 40–55 gen. builder for outside work, F to look after well-appointed house, no visitors allowed. Furnished accommodation + salary, to start 08/01. Send CV + salary expectations.

ICE-CREAM SELLER WANTED, Male, Ruoms area, for summer season.

The other advertisements disappeared under the salad leaves Thérèse was rinsing. Even if these household tasks – cooking, washing, cleaning – were not high on her list of duties, they were nevertheless the ones she liked best. She had her nursing diploma, of course, but very early on, after two or three years of hospital work, she had chosen to practise her profession in a way that let her move around. Maybe it was the result of her childhood as an orphan, hopping from foster family to hostel as if over stepping stones, until in the end the only place she felt at home was in other people's houses. Twenty-five years of spending weeks, months, even years with her 'clients' had given her a quite remarkable capacity to adapt. A split second in the kitchen and she would know where the vegetable peeler was, what sort of coffee maker they used and whether or not they skimped on cleaning products, or, in the living room, what wasn't to be moved in any circumstances, ornaments, rugs, the way the curtains hung or, in the bedroom, a very specific manner of arranging the pillows, all these little habits which mean that no interior is anything like another, although they may at first sight appear to be identical.

She loved living like a chameleon – an actor, even – absorbing other people's lives to the point that she adopted their smells, their tics, their expressions and their accents, and then, overnight, wiping all that away to begin again elsewhere, as a hermit crab changes shells. Alone in a place of her own, she would have self-destructed within five seconds, vanished into thin air, to be remembered as vaguely as the date of a battle in a history book. It had already happened to her once, between two jobs, and it had left her with the painful apprehension an insomniac feels at nightfall. So she had travelled a lot but only within metropolitan France. Naturally, at the start of her career the idea of joining a humanitarian mission had crossed her mind. Reading *It is Midnight, Dr Schweitzer*, about a fellow Alsatian, had something to do with it. But the far away was really too far and the infinite too much of a prison. She felt freer within stable, well-defined borders. Moreover, for her, exoticism was less a matter of geography than of human nature, and she knew that even if she lived to be a hundred she would never manage to see all of it.

Before Monsieur Lavenant she had only agreed to look after women. It wasn't that she feared for her virtue, she could take care of herself, but, never having attracted the attention of men, she no longer paid them any heed. They had always ignored her, except one drunk, once, at the end of a dance. It had been over with as quickly as you remove a bottle top with your teeth. She hadn't been hurt, physically, but the disappointment she had felt, lying on a bale of straw with the man vomiting at her back, had extinguished her most ardent dreams for good.

And so she had spent her whole life among women, usually

widows and a few elderly spinsters, from the sweetest to the most cantankerous. Many of them had died in her arms.

If she had accepted the job at Monsieur Lavenant's it was because, although she felt much more vigorous than many a man in his fifties, her age was becoming a handicap, as if old age demanded that its final moments be attended by a grace which she cruelly lacked. At all events, Thérèse was no longer really concerned about human gender, male or female. In her eyes they all belonged to the same company of the infirm, of angels almost.

Nonetheless she was a little discomfited on meeting Monsieur Lavenant for the first time. Instead of the doddering old man described to her by the agency, she found herself confronted by a good-looking, upright man, one with a crippled arm it was true, but tall, slim and elegant. In spite of his coldness and peremptory tone she had immediately perceived his weak spot, a secret wound inside, where he had taken refuge like a hunted animal. She had accepted the conditions of the contract – modest salary, remote house in a small village in the Provencal Drôme region, almost no days off – and recalled how he had seemed surprised, even disappointed, at not having to wrangle with her, certainly hoping for a refusal. That had been in Lyon, in a cold, austere panelled office, one, however, which he visibly had no desire to leave.

Since they had been sharing this house, no more cheerful than the Lyon office, he had done all he could to make himself disagreeable, but the more he persisted in this attitude, the more Thérèse took a malicious pleasure in receiving the blows with the unshakable indifference of a padded wall. This was neither sadism nor masochism on her part; she was simply convinced that one of these days she would succeed in bringing him out of his hole. Thérèse was as pugnacious as a pike fisherman, and this was a catch she was not going to let go. Yesterday after the picnic she had scored a point.

Thérèse took a salad shaker out of the cupboard, one of those previously used for collecting snails, made out of woven metal wire. Everything was old here, a family house where nothing had been changed except for the washing machine and central heating. She heaped the leaves in the shaker and went to drain them on the doorstep. The drops raining from the salad made dark galaxies on the already warm stone flags. Above the Rocher du Caire, whose outline resembling an Indian chief was silhouetted against the washed-out sky, a dozen wild vultures were circling before swooping down further into the valley. Shepherds must have put out a ewe's carcass for them. She came back to the sink, put the fresh curly lettuce leaves into a salad bowl and, before starting on anything else, touched her earrings with a smile, two little green stones which a blushing Monsieur Lavenant had given her for her birthday the evening before.

Monsieur Lavenant drank the lukewarm dregs of his bowl of coffee, used the side of his hand to sweep the scattered breadcrumbs into a little heap on the table, and then gazed at it. The noise of the motorised cultivator starting up came in through the open window and made him jump. He hurried to close it, railing against his idiot of a neighbour. The farting noises from the countless pieces of machinery the man used every day of the week, including Sunday, were becoming intolerable. People in the country spend their time in strange ways. They dig holes, fill in others, put up walls made of very heavy stones, lug enormous beams about in order to build the frames of sizeable buildings which they never finish, divert watercourses, sand, saw, twist and untwist pieces of scrap metal, cut down trees, knock in posts, heap their gardens with the carcasses of old Renault 4s, sometimes turning them into henhouses, with the result that their properties look like rubbish tips, breakers' yards. The more arduous and risky the work, the happier they are. They can't stop wearing themselves out, baking their skin in the sun, as if the way to save their souls is by the total exhaustion of their bodies. Everything they build is ugly, as are the materials they use: corrugated iron, asbestos cement, plastic sheeting, old tyres. They don't give a stuff about the birdsong or the sunsets. Nature, for them, is merely a source of income from which they scarcely profit. All this was going to end badly. One day Monsieur Lavenant was going to kill his neighbour.

This murderous prospect livened him up. He had slept badly and since waking had felt listless, caught up in an uncharacteristic melancholy. One half of him resisted this mood but the other would gladly have given in to it, like his whim of the evening before. What had got into him that he had given Cécile's earrings to Thérèse? Two little emeralds set in gold, which he had brought back from Bangkok for her in ... Just like in films, to symbolise the passing of time, he saw the pages of a calendar flying off, but couldn't keep hold of a single one. They lay scattered in his memory, just so many days he had passed by without noticing. The feeling of emptiness made him suddenly dizzy and he had to sit down in his armchair, almost winded. 'Bloody hell! I *know* I've been to Bangkok! I'd swear it on my life.' Not that that was much of a guarantee any more. The more he tried to bolster himself with his memories, the more they dissolved into a pallid watercolour, drained of all significance. 'Silom Road, Chao Phraya River, Sathon Tai Road ...' Names, just names, which in being spoken were stripped of their meaning and only increased his doubt. He gave up on Thailand to concentrate on more elementary things. Once he had recited all his times tables he felt a degree of reassurance. His doctor had warned him about possible temporary after-effects of the stroke which should, however, not cause him alarm. It must be one of those.

Right, he had given Cécile's earrings to Thérèse because ... because he had felt sorry for her with her fifty-two years and her little straw hat, that was it, he'd felt sorry. And yet, deep down, he didn't think that was the right word. Unless ... unless it was himself he'd felt sorry for. Never had he been so acutely aware of the immense solitude in which he'd been steeped for years as he had yesterday outside the little chapel, beneath the lime tree. Without Thérèse there he might perhaps have died of it. By giving her this modest jewellery he had wanted to thank her, it was as silly as that. But how had she construed his gesture? As a cheap come-on? A weakness on his part? And why had he insisted on grilling the chops in the fireplace, preparing the fire himself with his one hand, opening a bottle of champagne and talking nonsense about his life and his travels … He was drunk, that was it. He was drunk and had let himself get swept up in the stupidest sentimentalities. Until they'd parted, almost reluctantly, in front of the dying fire. He'd all but kissed her before going up to bed. He was angry with himself now, yes, he was angry all right! That morning he'd done everything he could to avoid her, just a grumpy 'good morning' before having his breakfast. He hadn't looked at her but was sure she was smiling as she brought his coffee.

Closed window notwithstanding, the vroom of the motor grated on his nerves like a dentist's drill. He'd go and give him a piece of his mind, that moron! Couldn't you even have peace and quiet on a Sunday? But was it in fact Sunday?

'You shouldn't have lost your temper like that. It's not good for you and it achieves nothing.'

'Nothing? Can you still hear it? No, well, you see!'

'At this time he'll be having his lunch, like us.'

'That's something. Sometimes those louts forget to eat. Have you tipped the salt cellar into the salad or something?'

Monsieur Lavenant pushed his plate away, pulling a face. He was pale, and his right hand shook as he wiped his lips with his napkin. It wouldn't have taken much for him to burst into tears. He wasn't hungry. The altercation with his neighbour had spoiled his appetite. Naturally he hadn't been slow to tell him what was what, but the other man had retorted that, for one thing, he was at liberty to do what he liked in his own home and, for another, it wasn't Sunday but Wednesday and, during the week, not having the luxury of twiddling his thumbs like some people, he had every right to work.

Stuck on the other side of the low stone wall, Monsieur Lavenant had felt betrayed. He stood stock-still, open-mouthed, until the hulk disappeared, pushing a wheelbarrow filled with rubble. It wasn't Sunday … Time no longer belonged to him and he no longer belonged to time. A stream of bewildered protestations wedged in his throat like dead branches in the river Aygues in spate. He put his hand to his forehead, closing his eyes. A word was blinking in his head like a hazard light: SENILE. His knees started trembling as they had in front of the urinals just before his stroke. He went back up the steps to his house holding on to the rail, as stiff as a wooden puppet.

'Why didn't you tell me it wasn't Sunday?'

'Well, you never asked me. We went to the market yesterday, that's always a Tuesday.'

'Tuesday …'

Thérèse saw his expression darken, begin to turn nasty. Embarrassed, she got up and began clearing the table.

'Tuesday, Wednesday, Sunday, what does it matter? One day's as good as another. It's true my salad was too salty.'

Monsieur Lavenant had his coffee in the sitting room. The closed shutters cast stripes of light and shade around the room. The house suited him well, really; the internal walls were plastered and the sun was kept out. But the house, at least, had a memory. He grabbed the remote control and began playing with the buttons the way others play Russian roulette. Except that in this case there was a bullet in every chamber of the barrel. Each of the advertisements streaming by seemed to be addressed specially to him by some diabolical means: Norwich Union, life assurance, home lifts, denture fixative and featured actors he remembered when they were young and famous. This distressing *danse macabre* persisted after he had switched off the TV. On the convex screen was a reflection of his own image, a desiccated mummy huddled in an armchair streaked with light like an old negative. This was the last thing he saw before letting his chin drop onto his chest, overcome by a pitiless fatigue.

He woke up in the grip of a strong sensation, somewhere between pleasure and pain. He had the most enormous erection. A dark stain formed a sort of island shape on his left thigh.

'What the f—'

He stood up, legs apart like a child caught wetting his pants. It was the first time this had happened to him. Red-faced, he made a rush for the bathroom. On the stairs he ran into Thérèse, who was forced to press herself against the wall to let him go past.

'What's the matter?'

'Nothing, absolutely nothing.'

Bolting the door, he took off his trousers, switched on the hot tap and looked for the nail brush. With only one hand and in his febrile state, every action became hazardous. As he was preparing to scrub the fabric, he realised he was dealing not with urine but with sperm. A readily identifiable thin white film was drying on the borders of the stain. He had to sit down on the edge of the bathtub, torn between pride that he still had it in him and shame at having lost control. The touch of the icy enamel beneath his thighs made his hairs stand on end and again his penis grew hard.

'I've got an erection, for …! An erection and I'm ejaculating …'

It was as though an old piston were starting up again inside his head. What had got this old locomotive of a body going? What could he have been dreaming about?

'Monsieur, are you all right?'

'Fine, Thérèse. I've overheated, just need a shower.'

He ran it over his skin and found himself amazingly reinvigorated, as if the water gushing from the shower head were coming straight from the spring at Lourdes. While drying himself, he observed his body in the mirror. There were folds of skin on the bones of course, but he was still svelte and stood tall. He shrugged his shoulders at so much vanity, but flashed himself a smile anyway, before rolling his trousers and underpants into a ball in the laundry basket.

While he was in his room getting changed, he asked himself the name of the little prostitute in Bangkok, the one he'd found so exciting. Natcharee! Every prostitute in Bangkok was called Natcharee. Maybe he'd been dreaming about her. Either way, it tended to prove that his memory was as intact as his sexual potency, and that was all that mattered. The monotony of a life lived on the margins of the world and its realities explained his earlier confusion over dates. He wouldn't let himself be fooled again. The air flooding in through the open window of his room was scented with lavender and thyme. Above the Rocher du Caire a pair of vultures were majestically following the twists and turns of the rising warm air currents.

'Thérèse, what are you doing?'

'I was about to put a wash on.'

'Can't you put it off till later? What about going to watch the vultures at the Rocher?'

'But … Of course, I'd love to.'

'Why are you looking at me like that?'

'You're wearing your Sunday clothes.'

Once past the village of May, sitting atop a rocky peak, the road wound like a skein of wool between the cherry trees, their branches bowing under the weight of fruit. Monsieur Lavenant made

Thérèse stop so he could pick some, which he presented to her with the same smile as for the earrings the evening before. The cherries were crammed with black sunshine and one of them, bursting between Thérèse's teeth, made three red spots on her top.

They had to leave the car a good fifteen minutes from the birdwatching spot. An official sign indicated the point beyond which the track was accessible only in a 4 x 4. They set off on foot, wearing hats to protect them from the sun, which was on home territory here. Other than the occasional tumbledown sheep fold and two or three stunted oak trees there was nowhere to seek shade. Monsieur Lavenant was wearing his binoculars round his neck and Thérèse had a bottle of Evian in her bag. The fields of lavender were crackling with insects. Several hundred metres beyond the point where the pair had set off at a marching pace, Monsieur Lavenant stopped. Large beads of sweat were forming on his forehead and there was a certain stiffness in his foot arch.

The immensity of the sky seemed insufficient to fill the void which was making his lungs wheeze like a rusty accordion. Thérèse was already far ahead, driven by the pugnacity which never left her, no matter what she was doing. She turned round to see him sitting on a stone trying to get his breath back.

'All right?'

He nodded a 'yes' as no sound would come out of his parched lips. He took a few deep breaths of the burning air, bit the inside of his cheeks and then set off again. Thérèse had disappeared from sight now and for a split second he told himself he would never see her again, which made him speed up. He found her, bright red and out of breath, at the foot of the large wooden cross which dominated the cliff top. In a single gulp he drank half the bottle of water she held out to him.

The raptors nested on the cliff face, so that from where they were sitting at the edge of the rock they could watch them take off a few metres below their feet. They were impressive creatures, weighing nearly ten kilos and with a wing span of almost three metres. As their weight meant they couldn't propel themselves by flapping their wings, they would dive into the void with their wings almost still, and a few seconds later were only a tiny dark speck on the other side of the valley. Sometimes one of them flew so close above their heads that they could hear the wind whistling in its feathers. Since they ate only dead things, they were completely harmless, but their intimidating appearance – hooked beaks, fierce eyes and powerful talons – had led them to be hunted to extinction. Five or six years previously, a few pairs had been reintroduced to Les Baronnies massif. Some had readapted, others had not. The day after their release into the wild, one had been found on the roof of the baker's van, and another on the back of a bench in the square at Rémuzat. But many had recovered the memory of their wings and today there were a good thirty of them. The dead ewes that shepherds left out for them more than supplied their needs. With the ability to spot a carcass at more than three thousand metres, they would swoop down on it, and a quarter of an hour later there would be only a pile of bones.

Thérèse and Monsieur Lavenant were 'oohing' and 'aahing', squabbling over the binoculars like a couple of children watching the graceful acrobatics of kites. How heavy, awkward and clumsy they felt next to these soaring creatures, the secret of whose aerial grace resided in their obliviousness of their bodies.

As the sun grew lower, they heard distinct sounds rising from the valley floor – a dog barking, a moped engine, a child's laugh – but it was impossible to pinpoint where they came from. They were seeing what the gods see, which is to say, nothing in particular. Thérèse shivered with the ancient fear which grips humans' hearts at the end of the day.

'Perhaps we ought to be thinking about getting back?'

Monsieur Lavenant didn't reply immediately. His profile was not unlike that of the wild vultures. He waved his hand as if brushing away a fly, and agreed, getting to his feet. A sudden gust made them teeter as they stood upright again, and Thérèse's hat almost blew away. On the way back, which seemed unbelievably short compared to the outward path, they neither spoke nor looked at each other. Only their shadows, out in front, seemed to fall into step occasionally.

'I really wonder why I make dessert for you, you never eat any of it. Strawberries like that, it's a waste!'

It was such a simple phrase, perfectly ordinary, and yet so full of affection that Monsieur Lavenant gave a faint smile. In his head the huge birds he'd been watching still soared. They'd had dinner outside, in the patch of garden bordering the path to the little wood. It was balmy. Pipistrelles flitted among the branches so quickly that their presence was detectable only from the merest vibration in the air, heavy with the scent of the limes. Monsieur Lavenant was smoking a cigarette, savouring each puff as if it were his last. Strictly speaking, aside from the picnic, the row with his neighbour, the wet patch on his trousers and the vultures in flight, you couldn't say that anything out of the ordinary had happened in these past two days, and yet Monsieur Lavenant felt intensely alive, intoxicated by the sweet weariness of days lived to the full. Every detail took on its own particular significance; nothing was without some use – though what this new way of interpreting the everyday really meant, he could not say. He felt as if he'd come home after a long, long journey. It was like reading a book he'd had as a child, seeing an old film again, the subtle pleasure of conjugating the past in the present. Was it important to remember everything? The memory's capacity to absorb has its limits and one day you have to become selective. 'FREE! We will clear your attic, cellar or whole house …' Who hadn't dreamed of one day clearing the decks, of disappearing one fine morning or one filthy night with no baggage but the skin on his bones and the miserable handful of memories that hold it all together? Did he need all that junk one accumulates on the pretext that 'it might come in useful some day' and which, over time, rusts like so many saucepans? What should he keep from a day like today? The crash of the Tokyo stock market or the vultures' imperturbable flight? The answer was obvious.

The crunching of footsteps on the path made him jump. Two shapes appeared at the edge of the little wood, their pale garments creating an aura against the background of blue shadow. A short stout woman of indeterminate age, with eyes inordinately magnified by a pair of glasses with lenses as thick as jam jars, was approaching, holding by the hand a strange creature, a sort of human fingerling of a phosphorescent pallor, probably albino, who could nevertheless be identified as female by the dress she was wearing, which was made from the same beige and blue-sprigged fabric as the short lady's.

'Good evening, Monsieur.'

'Good evening.'

'What a beautiful evening, don't you think?'

'Very.'

The lady's face was unbelievably elastic. The smile she gave Monsieur Lavenant, despite the darkness, split her face from ear to ear like a gash to a watermelon. The impressive goggles sitting on her trumpet nose made her resemble an amphibian, the random result of a furtive coupling between an innocent young girl and a facetious toad. Other than the dress, the young girl accompanying her bore no family resemblance to her, except her strangeness. Even face on she seemed to be in profile, so thin and evanescent was her figure, shaped like a lengthy drip of candle wax.

'After all the rain we've had, it's good to have a breath of evening air.'

'That's true, it does you good.'

The stump of a woman looked up at the sky and immediately her immense glasses trapped the moon. It had risen, almost full, and cast a disturbing light through a reddish halo. Some anaemic stars were pecking around it.

'Might not last. We should enjoy it while we can, shouldn't we?'

'Tomorrow is another day.'

'You mustn't believe that, Monsieur. It's just the same one beginning over and over again.'

Monsieur Lavenant hadn't expected his banal comment to arouse such strong feeling in the short lady. She had grabbed hold of the garden gate with both hands so vehemently that it looked as if she was going to uproot it and go off with it. Confronted by the rubbery mask looming towards him, glasses daubed in moonlight, he shrank into his chair.

'You only live for a single day, Monsieur, just one! But it's the most beautiful one. I wish you good evening, Monsieur. Farewell.'

He saw them disappearing hand in hand at the corner of the road, leaving only a sort of echo of their presence. For a few seconds he wondered whether he might not have dreamed them, then went back indoors. Thérèse was just serving the lemon verbena tea.

'Thérèse, have you already come across the two women I've been talking to?'

'Which two women?'

'Two out for a walk. One tall, and one small with huge glasses. They had identical dresses, beige with blue flowers …'

'I wasn't watching, I was doing the washing-up. Why?'

'No reason. You must have heard me talking to someone though?'

'I confess I didn't, with the tap running and the noise of the dishes. Is it important?'

'No, we just exchanged a few words about the weather, that's all.'

'It's quite usual to have a little after-dinner walk when the weather's so fine. We ought to take advantage of it more often. Be careful, the tea's boiling hot.'

Monsieur Lavenant was having difficulty concentrating on his book. He read the same sentence for the tenth time and it still made no more sense to him than if it had been in Chinese. He saw, running through the pages like a watermark, sometimes the frog woman's face, sometimes that of the ectoplasm accompanying her. Uncertainty that they existed was bothering him like a wobbly tooth you wiggle with the tip of your tongue. He laid his book down open on his thigh and lit a cigarette, thinking to himself that it would take a lot more than a cup of lemon verbena tea to send him to sleep. Opposite him, wearing the cone of orangey light from the standard lamp as a hat, Thérèse sat, lips slightly parted, leafing through 1960s issues of *Paris Match*, which she must have dug out of the attic. There were trunks full of them, and also of *Ciné Revue*, *Elle* and other magazines Cécile had a liking for. An onlooker might have taken them for an old married couple. Had his wife not been dead, they would certainly have spent the evening in the same way. Cécile was beautiful, Thérèse was not, that was the only difference; that and the fact that today Cécile would be ten years older.

'Is it good?'

'I'm sorry?'

'The magazine, is it good?'

'Pfff … It's funny, it reminds me of my childhood: Martine Carol, Gina Lollobrigida, the Algerian war, the Peugeot 403, Saint-Tropez … It passes the time.'

'Are you bored here?'

'No more than elsewhere. It comes with the job.'

'Your work bores you?'

'That's not what I said. A little bit, sometimes, like everyone. That's normal.'

'I was never bored when I was working.'

'But you had worries.'

'True. But worries aren't the same as boredom. With worries, you always find a way of working things out, whereas with boredom it's another thing altogether.'

'You mean it's harder to work things out with yourself?'

'Yes. Obviously, with other people it's quite simple; they're always in the wrong, so you can argue, but when you're all alone, face to face with yourself in the mirror …'

'I understand. Personally, I'm never bored by boredom. Listen, without boredom, no prisoner would ever think of digging a tunnel several kilometres long with a teaspoon in order to escape. There'd have been no Christopher Columbus discovering America. On a much smaller scale, how would I ever have left Colmar if I hadn't been bored to death there?'

This whole jumble of words descended on Monsieur Lavenant like a summer downpour. He would never have suspected Thérèse could hold that many. Everyone, this evening, seemed to know better than him.

'Why don't you speak to me like that more often?'

'Because you don't ask me to. Because it's not very important, I suppose.'

'I was wrong.'

Maybe it was an effect of the light, but Thérèse was no longer quite Thérèse and Monsieur Lavenant was less and less Monsieur Lavenant. In the closeness of silence, each of them was shedding the faded trappings the years had gradually covered them in.

'You know, my name is Édouard.'

'I know.'

'Ah ... Perhaps you might call me Édouard instead of Monsieur.'

'If you wish. That's not a problem.'

'Good. It's easier, isn't it? It seems a little ... old-fashioned.'

Thérèse locked her lavender eyes on his until he had to look away. He was no longer accustomed to such trials of strength. Generally it was other people who lowered their eyes in front of him. He had forgotten just how delicious it is to lose one's head, to lay down one's heavy rusted armour at the other's feet. Wiping his hand over his face to get a grip on himself, between his fingers he caught a glimpse of Thérèse's shoulder, her mouth and a lock of hair that lay across her brow. The desire rising in him could not be blamed on the lemon verbena tea.

'Maybe we should go to bed.'

'Together?'

Édouard felt a shiver run through him from head to toe, a seismic shock he didn't even try to contain.

'I'm an old man, you know.'

'You are a man and you need tenderness; I'm a woman, past my youth, and I need some too. I'm sorry, I don't know what came over me ...'

Édouard held her close while, sniffing, she took hold of the tray.

'I'd be honoured, Thérèse, very honoured. Leave all that.'

They exchanged an awkward kiss, trembling so much that their teeth knocked together, and that made them laugh.

With his fingertips Monsieur Lavenant felt around for Thérèse's body. Nothing was left of her but her imprint on the crumpled sheet and one hair forming an initial on the pillow. It had to be very early nonetheless, as dawn was only just breaking. Invisible birds were chattering in the trees. He pulled the cover back up over his shoulders because there was still a touch of the night's chill in the air. He listened out but could hear no sound from either the bathroom or the kitchen. He was a little disappointed. He would have liked to surprise her sleeping. They hadn't made love but the tenderness they'd felt falling asleep in each other's arms was worth any number of orgasms. He was amazed that he didn't feel guilty, like he had every time he'd slept with women other than his wife. It was because this was in no way comparable. It wasn't about satisfying a sexual need, which in any case generally provided him with only mediocre satisfaction. He wasn't sleepy any more. An excitement like that of a child on Christmas morning bounced him out of bed. He wanted coffee, bread and jam, and to throw himself headlong into any activity whatsoever. He wanted to live.

Passing Thérèse's room, he heard the bed squeak. This morning he would be the one to prepare the breakfast.

Obviously, with only one arm, the whole business took some time and the results were somewhat haphazard. Thérèse appeared just as he swore at a stubborn jam-jar lid.

'What on earth are you doing?'

'The damn lid's stuck.'

'Never mind. Give it here or you'll do something silly.'

Usually when he came downstairs in the morning, he would find Thérèse washed and dressed, and well into her day's activities. Today she still bore the stigmata of sleep: ruffled hair, sticky eyelashes and pillow stripes scarifying her right cheek.

Grumpily, she took the jar out of his hands and urged him to go and sit down. She was the one who poured the coffee and spread the bread, without a word or a look.

'Good morning anyway!'

'Huh?'

'I said, good morning anyway.'

'Good morning.'

'What's the matter?'

'Nothing. It's just I don't think it's sensible for you to get involved with cooking. You could have been scalded or cut yourself. And anyway it's my job.'

'Why didn't you stay in my room?'

'Because I'm not used to sleeping with someone else.'

'Do I snore?'

'It's not that – though, yes, you do snore. Listen, let's be honest with each other. I'm not after your money. I'm very fond of you but you mustn't think … We got carried away yesterday evening. I don't regret it but we mustn't make a habit of it or …'

'Or what?'

'It wouldn't be the same.'

'So?'

'So? I wouldn't be me any longer, and you wouldn't be you. Besides, nothing happened, so let's leave it there. It's better that way. Why are you smiling?'

'You've got a coffee moustache at the corners of your mouth.'

'Very clever.'

Thérèse wiped her lips with her napkin. Her eyes were brimming with tears as she got to her feet. Édouard caught hold of her wrist before she could escape.

'Listen to me, Thérèse. I'm not trying to make you play the part of the priest's housekeeper. I feel comfortable with you and I believe you feel the same way. It's as simple as that. Whether we have a sexual relationship or not isn't important, you know, at my age … What matters is that for the first time in long years, I don't feel alone any more; that's to say I'm no longer the centre of a shrunken world, and humbly I feel able to give you that same gift, because although I know almost nothing about you, one thing I'm sure of is that you are much more familiar with this solitude than I am. There's no obligation on your part or mine; you can go on sleeping in your own room; we can continue to call each other "vous", but from now on, whatever you may do, there is a Thérèse and Édouard.'

With a squeeze of her fingers he let go of her hand, sensing that Thérèse was about to dissolve into tears and that she wanted to be alone to unburden herself of the pressure filling her chest.

Towards nine o'clock the sky had grown dark, leaden with thick banks of cloud like a herd of elephants. The electricity in the air made it impossible to stay in one place for five minutes. Monsieur Lavenant and Thérèse had done nothing but meet each other coming and going like two demented clockwork toys. The atmosphere was stifling; the air piled up in the lungs like a wad of grey cotton wool. Then on the dot of eleven a violent storm broke, the rain streaming down hastily shut windows. Noses pressed to the window panes, Thérèse and Édouard jumped in unison at each lightning flash that preceded the din of thunder. Édouard counted the seconds, one, two, three, four … between the brilliant flashes and dull thuds which made the house shake.

'That one wasn't far away, four kilometres at the most. Above May, perhaps. It can't be much fun over there.'

The herd of elephants disappeared as it had come, leaving behind only a hammering noise on the eardrums, and a swollen sky above Rémuzat. A spider's web fringed with raindrops at the corner of the gutter glimmered like a diamond necklace.

'That might be enough, don't you think?'

'Yes … No, wait, that one too, it's a giant.'

After the morning's storm, Édouard had taken it into his head to go and look for snails by the roadside. They'd collected far too many, more than they'd ever be able to eat, according to Thérèse, who with a sinking heart was contemplating the laborious preparation of the gastropods that lay ahead. But Édouard kept discovering ever bigger ones, with the result that the dozens were multiplying.

'Édouard, it's a waste. We're never going to be able to eat all those.'

'You're right. But it's such a long time since I went snailing … I must have been a young boy, I suppose.'

They set off peacefully for home, Édouard tickling the grasses on the verge with his walking stick, Thérèse carrying the slimy basket. The hot, humid earth was exhaling heady perfumes.

'When we get there, we'll purge the creatures and then go into town.'

'To Nyons? What for?'

'I need to buy a typewriter.'

'Ah.'

'And a ream of paper. There's no better age to write your memoirs than when you're losing your memory. Come on, let's go faster.'

On arriving back from Nyons, their arms full of a brand-new typewriter, two reams of paper (Monsieur Lavenant had so many memories) and some carbon paper, they had the pleasure of discovering the kitchen overrun by freedom-loving snails. The lid of the pail in which they'd been imprisoned along with two generous handfuls of coarse salt had not withstood the pressure from the escapees. They were everywhere. Some were bravely setting off up the north face of the fridge, while others, sensing where their career was to end, were clinging to the glass door of the oven, but most were just wandering around completely lost on the tiles, in total disarray. Streams of sticky slime were coming over the top of the pail and drying in silvery patches here and there. It took longer to catch and return them to their container than it had to collect them in the grass. While a grumbling Thérèse took

158

a cloth to the floor, Édouard carefully unwrapped his work instrument, put on his glasses and began to give the instructions his most serious attention. At almost midnight, the table on which the machine took pride of place was surrounded by a sort of snowdrift of balls of crumpled paper with YYWW OOOOOOO ffff §§§§ … … +++++ … … nnnnn … … %%%%% or /////
printed on them. More than once Monsieur Lavenant had come very close to slinging the thing out of the window, having first crushed it with an iron. But thanks to Thérèse's cool head, they had finally managed to get it to tabulate correctly and produce more or less legible type.

'There now, we've done it.'

'Yes, but you must admit it's ridiculously complicated. I had a manual Olivetti for years and it never let me down.'

'It's the modern world. Just look at all the things you can do with this one: delete, save, make corrections …'

'But I'm not asking all that of the modern world. I'm quite capable of doing corrections myself, I'm not an invalid … OK, it's a figure of speech … Goodness, with all this we haven't had any dinner.'

After the frugal meal, Édouard went upstairs to clean his teeth and put on his pyjamas, before stretching out on his bed in the dark, eyes wide open in spite of his fatigue. He hadn't dared ask Thérèse to join him, hoping she would do so of her own accord. Listening out, he could hear water running in the bathroom, and the washing process seemed interminable. Although he tried to stop himself falling asleep, his eyelids drooped inexorably and he yawned like a wild beast. He barely felt her slip between the sheets beside him and plant a very gentle kiss on his cheek.

'My name is Édouard Lavenant. I'll be seventy-five next October. I spent the night with my nurse. It was very …' There followed a list of adjectives such as pleasant, nice, reassuring, tender, touching, all crossed out. The rest of the page was covered in scribbles, the kind doodled in biro during a telephone conversation. From his long years of existence, that was all he remembered and it dated from the evening before. There was no need to be put out by this, beginnings are always difficult. Monsieur Lavenant stretched in his chair and consulted his watch. Two hours of work, that wasn't too bad. He had taken the infernal machine up to his room where it was quieter. It looked good on the small desk, with the white pages adorning the carriage. A bunch of impeccably sharpened pencils stood alongside the dictionary, which was next to an ashtray already overflowing with cigarette ends. A real writer's table. He yawned so wide he could have dislocated his jaw.

Too late to bed. Out of practice. Too nervy. Strange dreams where he was travelling in a narrow lift that never arrived at either the top or the bottom floor. Not nightmarish, merely boring. It was only in the early hours that he had been able to enjoy completely undisturbed sleep, and when he opened his eyes, Thérèse was no longer there. But that didn't matter, as he was sure she had spent the night with him. A whole night. The proof being that she had left her dressing gown and slippers at the end of the bed. He who had decided to immerse himself in the past was now interested in nothing but the present. Right, that was enough for the first day's work. He needed to stretch his legs, and thanks to sitting on that chair he had backache and wanted to pee. In short, he had every incentive to be elsewhere.

'Making progress?'

'Gently does it. You don't just dive into that sort of enterprise, you have to think; it takes time.'

'A bit like the snails, then. That's five times I've rinsed them and there's still loads of slime! That was a great idea you had there.'

'I'll see to the *court bouillon*.'

'No, leave it, it's fine. I'll manage better on my own.'

Behind the grumpy front, Thérèse was smiling, while her reddened hands were moving the shells in the stream of water. Édouard went over and awkwardly stroked her hair. She turned in amazement and he put his hand down again, blushing.

'I'm going to buy cigarettes. Do you need anything?'

'Butter, please. I'm worried about having enough.'

Aside from the buzzing of the flies and the inevitable sputtering of a machine somewhere in the distance, there was no noise in the village. In spite of the tinted lenses in his spectacles, the contrast between areas of light and shadow was painful on the eyes. Monsieur Lavenant felt as if he were moving in an old silent home movie with a jumping black-and-white picture, random changes of speed and occasional white flashes where the film had melted, eaten away by a luminous leprosy.

As he went through the narrow streets, the ground-floor shutters seemed to half open to allow a split-second glimpse of a Goyaesque figure looming out of the darkness. A cat jumped down from a wall and crossed the road, glaring at him with blazing eyes, before taking up another strategic position. He was forced to step over a horribly fat dog, as dirty as a pig, which was slumped in the middle of the pavement, snoring. Apart from these two mammals he didn't meet a living soul until he reached the tobacconist's. The cool breath of a fan caressed his face as soon as he had passed the curtain of multicoloured strips which kept flies out of the shop. During the two or three minutes before the tobacconist's leisurely appearance, Monsieur Lavenant, like a child in Ali Baba's cave, was seized by an overwhelming desire to treat himself to something, anything – a postcard, a ball, a badminton set, a fishing rod.

Back on the pavement, with his cigarettes in his pocket and his fishing rod under his arm, he felt a strange mixture of pride and shame. If he'd wanted to go in for the sport seriously, he could have bought himself a decidedly more sophisticated piece of equipment. He'd tried his hand at it, salmon in Scotland, big fish in the Pacific, but no, it was this rod, this child's bamboo cane with its cheap little reel, its line, and its two-coloured float in a neat plastic packet which had taken his fancy. It was more than likely that he'd never use it, but so what? It had brought him pleasure and, drunk on his own daring, he sat down on the café terrace in the completely deserted square and ordered a barley water.

'Are you going fishing?'

'No, it's a present for my grandson. How much do I owe you?'

'The same as usual; my prices haven't changed.'

What was that supposed to mean, 'the same as usual'? It was the first time he'd set foot in the place. There was some mistake, the chap had confused him with a regular. Plus, why were the waiter and the tobacconist as alike as two peas in a pod? The same stocky build, same steel wool on the cheeks, same shifty look ... Brothers, no doubt. In such a small village it's not unusual to see members of the same family running different businesses ... Monsieur Lavenant chased away his question marks with a large gulp of barley water. The ice cube banging against his teeth was like hitting an iceberg. He must have been seven or eight when he'd first gone fishing, with his uncle, Bernard ... No, not Bernard, Roland, yes, Roland! Or maybe Martial? A fat man, at any rate, who laughed all the time and whom his mother thought vulgar. Édouard had kept his eyes on his float the whole day without catching a single fish. When he went for a pee, he'd looked over his shoulder and seen his uncle hooking a roach to the end of his fishing line. 'Édouard, come quickly! You've got a bite.'

Not only had that not brought him pleasure, he'd felt humiliated by it. That evening he hadn't touched the fried fish.

Monsieur Lavenant mopped his brow with his handkerchief. He could still see the scene clearly and yet he could have sworn that this memory didn't belong to him. He was no longer as certain as all that of having been fishing with an uncle, Bernard, Roland or Martial, nor of having gone fishing in Scotland or the Pacific, nor whether he'd drunk barley water on this terrace before ... Apart from the fishing rod, whose bamboo pole he was clutching in his fist so tightly it might break, he was no longer sure of anything.

In front of him, without his noticing, a group of boules players had magically sprung up in the square. The boules knocked into one another and laughter erupted: 'Oh, Daniel, you're not even trying.' On the benches in the shade old women were quietly knitting new rows in long-running quarrels. A little boy was going round and round in circles on his tricycle. They all bore a striking family resemblance to the tobacconist and waiter. Monsieur Lavenant wondered whether his left arm hadn't perhaps contaminated the rest of him, he had so much difficulty getting up from his chair. As stiffly as Pinocchio he crossed the square and vanished into the maze of narrow streets. The butter, he had to get some butter ... But where was the minimarket? Where was he himself, come to that? And why did he have to get butter?

And why did his mother find his uncle vulgar? And why was this fishing rod under his arm? He had to lean against a wall, tears in his eyes, lungs choked by a cry which couldn't escape, a cry which came from far, far away, from the very pit of his stomach ...

'Good day, Monsieur. Enjoying your walk?' The woman with the rubber mask turned her unfathomable gaze on him. Two steps behind her stood the gangling young woman, pale as a shadow on a negative.

'It's stupid, I can't find my way …'

'It's not a very big place!'

'I know, but a few months ago I had a stroke … an illness …
I don't know …'

'Don't worry, we'll walk you home. Give me your arm.'

The touch of the woman's skin on his own chilled him. It felt
like marble. The tall girl walked along behind them like a faithful
spaniel, without blinking once.

'I'm sorry, this is the first time …'

'It happens to us all … Don't worry, we're only five minutes
from your house. Are you a fisherman?'

'No, no, it's for … a child.'

'He'll like it, I'm sure. All children love fishing, even if they
generally hate fish. Children are a bit cruel. I knew a charming
one, who ripped off …'

Monsieur Lavenant didn't understand a word of what the
woman was saying. His body was now nothing more than a sack
stuffed with cotton wool, incapable of the slightest initiative. Not
until he saw the familiar steps concertinaing up to his doorstep
did Monsieur Lavenant recover his wits.

'I'm most grateful to you for accompanying me. May I offer
you a cold drink?'

'That's very kind of you but we have to get back. Another
time. Good evening, Monsieur.'

'Good evening, Mesdames.'

He watched them as far as the street corner, where they de-
materialised in the rays of the setting sun.

'What on earth have you been up to, then? It's almost three hours
since you left. And what about the butter?'

'I'm sorry, I couldn't find the minimarket. Really sorry.'

'It doesn't matter, but I was worried … What's that?'

'A fishing rod.'

'Are you taking up fishing?'

'I don't think so. It's a child's one.'

Thérèse watched as he laid the rod on the table and slumped into a chair. The expression 'shadow of his former self' suggested itself to her immediately.

He seemed to be sitting just to one side of his body, like a transfer applied by a shaky hand.

'I haven't put them back in their shells.'

'I'm sorry?'

'The snails, I didn't put them back in their shells – I've done little ramekins. It's less work, and easier for you to eat.'

'Good idea, Thérèse.'

'And it tastes just as good.'

Monsieur Lavenant hadn't so much as poked his nose outside the door for three days, and was communicating only in monosyllables – yes, no – completely haphazardly. Occasionally his words hit the mark, but more often than not they didn't, which had a way of really exasperating Thérèse. 'Look, I'd prefer it if you didn't say anything at all!' He was scarcely more voluble at his keyboard. While waiting for 'it' to come, he would try on words like hats, in upper and lower case, dipping into the dictionary at random in the vain hope of finding one which would be the key to his sealed-off memory. None existed, however, for the simple reason that his past didn't interest him in the least. Everything in it was drab, faded, without colour or scent. He had come to the conclusion that any life at all was worth more than his. Even the best moments were coated with that obstinate dust which inspires you not to take up a pen but to resort to clearing the attic. He wanted nothing other than to be reborn, virgin, nothing behind him, nothing ahead, to learn everything afresh. He had noticed that if you typed the same word all over a whole page, that word ended up losing its meaning completely. Only an empty wrapper was left, which could be filled with some completely different sense. PIANO, PIANO, PIANO, PI-A-NO, PI-A-NO! The repeated experiment plunged him into a state of strange exaltation. Today he had just wrung the life out of the word PUGNACIOUS and derived the serene satisfaction of having done his duty. It was exhausting work, and a real marathon, when you considered that the Petit Larousse contained 58,900 common nouns. But the game was worth the candle; when he had unlearned everything he would be entitled to a completely new life.

Switching off the typewriter, he laid the PUGNACIOUS page on top of the PIANO one. He stood up, rubbing his back. Thérèse's nightdress cascaded over the back of the chair. He noted CASCADE on a pad, in pencil. That was tomorrow's word.

'Édouard? ... Monsieur Lavenant?'

'Yes?'

'Someone's here asking for you.'

Thérèse was waiting for him at the foot of the stairs, frowning.

'It's a gentleman.'

'What does he want?'

'He says it's personal.'

'Oh.'

'He's waiting in the sitting room.'

As in a doctor's waiting room, when Édouard came in, the man put the magazine he was flicking through down on the coffee table, got to his feet and held out his hand. He must have been around forty, tall, slim and well turned out.

'Jean-Baptiste Lorieux.'

'To what do I owe the pleasure?'

'The name Lorieux doesn't ring any bells?'

'Lorieux? No, I don't think so.'

'That doesn't surprise me. I'm Sylvie Lorieux's son ...'

'That doesn't mean anything to me either.'

'I understand. We're going back about forty years. Sylvie Lorieux was your secretary at that time.'

Monsieur Lavenant narrowed his gaze. The man's face was strangely familiar but he couldn't see the slightest trace of a Sylvie Lorieux coming through.

'Don't rack your brains, I'll explain. I'm a communications consultant and by the greatest coincidence I found myself working for your firm in Lyon. My mother often spoke about you. For a long time I was in two minds about meeting you, then … well, here I am.'

'I don't quite grasp the purpose of your visit.'

'I'm your son.'

When it was hot, Sylvie Lorieux used to put her hair up in a chignon, held in place by a pencil. She was a pretty girl, gentle, discreet. They had spent only one night together, during a business trip to Brussels. A simple one-night stand. Some months later she had left her job. He no longer remembered the reason. He'd missed her as she was very competent. Sylvie Lorieux.

'Sit down. How is your mother?'

'She died. Four years ago.'

'Oh, I'm sorry. Have you known for long that …'

'Yes. Since I was old enough to understand.'

'And you never tried to contact me?'

'Yes, once. I must have been sixteen or seventeen. I phoned. It was your wife who answered. I hung up.'

'Were you living in Lyon?'

'No, Paris.'

The silence uniting the two men was short-lived. The merciless neighbour had just started up one of his diabolical machines. As Monsieur Lavenant got up to shut the window, Thérèse knocked on the door.

'I have to go out for some shopping – you don't need anything, do you?'

'No, thank you, Thérèse.'

She stayed for a moment, surreptitiously giving him a questioning look, and then, receiving no sign from him, closed the door behind her, but not before she'd given the stranger a dark stare. Monsieur Lavenant sat down in his armchair again, lighting a cigarette to give himself time to think of something to say.

'I find it a little hard to believe you. The relationship I had with your mother – can it really be called a relationship? – was extremely short.'

'I know, she told me. Once is enough though. That being so, she never blamed you for anything. I think she was really very much in love with you. There was your wife, however. She chose to leave the scene.'

'She never married?'

'No. The odd boyfriend. I never felt she missed the past. She had good memories of you. I believe she had quite a happy life.'

'You … Were you ever in need?'

'I wanted for nothing.'

'Not even a father?'

'To be honest, no. Well, sometimes, maybe. Most of my friends were fighting with theirs. It doesn't make you wish for one.'

'So why did you want to meet me after all this time?'

'In Lyon I discovered that you'd been seriously ill. I think I would have regretted not having known you.'

Monsieur Lavenant gave a bitter little laugh.

'Sorry, but I've already made my will, and anyway, as you can see, apart from this crippled arm I'm in the best of health.'

'I *knew* you'd think of that. You're mistaken. I make a very good living, I don't need money.'

'Come on! You'd be the only one, then. I'm warning you, I'll categorically refuse to take any test of my supposed paternity.'

'You've got it wrong. As I've already said, it's not a question of that. I needed to see you, the way one needs to look at oneself in a mirror, to follow a river upstream to its source.'

'Very poetic, I'm sure, but you've happened on a stagnant pool.

What do you expect me to do with a son at my age? Bounce you up and down on my knee?'

'I'm sorry. You're right, I'm on the wrong track. I'm sorry for disturbing you.'

Jean-Baptiste stood up, hesitated, then held out his hand to Édouard. It was a hand as honest and wholesome as a slice of bread.

'Oh, sit down, for heaven's sake! I'm not sending you away. You parachute in like this, without a word of warning ... Are you going back up to Lyon?'

'No, I'm on my way to Avignon. That's why I made the detour. I have a meeting tomorrow, in the early afternoon.'

'So you're free for the day?'

'Yes.'

'Then you'll stay to lunch. I won't take no for an answer.'

When Thérèse came back from shopping, Édouard introduced Jean-Baptiste as an employee of his firm, and she seemed relieved. During the meal they talked work, percentages, profits and losses, things Thérèse didn't understand but which in a way reassured her. When this Monsieur Lorieux had turned up that morning, she had been struck at once by his family resemblance to Édouard and, without really knowing why, had thought it augured badly. Now she was cross with herself for her misgivings. The man was most polite, calm, something of a dreamer. Édouard seemed pleased to have met him. In contrast to the previous days, he was talkative, full of a verve which took years off him. Even so, that resemblance ... She left them to have coffee in the garden and went off to attend to other tasks.

The shadow of the lime tree cast a myriad of ever-changing patterns on the white tablecloth. A bee prowled round the sugar bowl. Édouard and Jean-Baptiste had started talking about business only to put Thérèse off the scent. At present they didn't really know what to say to each other, both of them afraid of lapsing into the worst banalities.

'Do you like fishing?'

'Sorry?'

'Angling, do you like it?'

'I don't know. I've never tried. I've always lived in a city.'

'Not even on holiday though?'

'No. It never appealed. Do you fish?'

'Once upon a time. Do you feel like it?'

'Now?'

'Yes, why not? There are fish in the Aygues. I bought a rod yesterday. Why not sleep here tonight? With an early start you'll have plenty of time to get to Avignon for the early afternoon.'

'Why not? I have to admit I wasn't expecting that, but ...'

'Did I expect to have a son?'

The stone was red-hot in the place Édouard had chosen, a two- to three-metre overhang above a pool just after a little waterfall. He had discovered the spot during a walk; you could see fish the size of your hand swimming back and forth in the clear water. After explaining to Jean-Baptiste how to prepare his line, he had sat slightly further back, where the branches of a willow formed a shelter. His son had square shoulders; his white shirt was so dazzling in the sun that Édouard had to pull the brim of his hat down over his eyes.

'If someone had told me this morning that I'd be going fishing with my father ...'

'If we knew everything about the future, the present wouldn't be worth a jot. Are you married?'

'Yes.'

'Children?'

'Two. Richard's nine and Noémie turns six next month.'

'So I'm a grandfather?'

'You certainly are.'

'Have you told them about me?'

'No, and my wife doesn't know either.'

'Will you tell them?'

'I don't know. What do you think?'

'Don't turn round. Keep your eyes on your float ... You should do what you want. It makes no difference to me. I'm not family-minded. What's your wife's name?'

'Nelly.'

'So, all in all, you're a happy man?'

'You could say that. What are those birds up above the mountain? Buzzards?'

'No, vultures.'

'Vultures, here?'

'Yes, griffon vultures.'

'I'm out fishing with my son. I have a daughter-in-law called Nelly and two grandchildren. It's grotesque! Children steal your past in order to make their own present from it; they take you apart like an old alarm clock and leave you in bits. Vultures at least have the decency to wait until their prey is dead before they rip it to pieces. Secondary tumours, that's what they are, reproducing themselves ad infinitum. I didn't want to leave anything behind me, not a thing! What do you have to do to finally be at peace? To stop dragging the past around like a ball and chain? I was just beginning to feel lighter, then this idiot fetches up with his healthy looks, his good intentions and his nice little family. He can go to hell!'

His hand tightened around a large stone, as smooth and round as an egg.

'That's it! I've got one! What do I do now?'

Monsieur Lavenant let go of the pebble. Jean-Baptiste was wrestling with his line, at the end of which wriggled a gleaming fish.

'Well, you unhook it and throw it back into the water. They're inedible, these fish, packed full of bones.'

Jean-Baptiste had gone to fetch his bag from the car, carrying the fishing rod – a gift from Monsieur Lavenant – under his arm. Thérèse was in the garden reading, feet up on a chair. Seeing Édouard coming, she lowered her dress, which she had hitched halfway up her thighs.

'Has Monsieur Lorieux left?'

'He's gone to fetch his things. He'll have dinner with us and spend the night here.'

'Oh?'

'Yes. What's so surprising in that? There's no hotel here. He's leaving for Avignon early tomorrow morning.'

'Oh, it doesn't bother me, it's just that I have to get a room ready for him and change my menu. I think he's a very likeable young man, very well brought up. It's unbelievable how much he resembles you; he's like you as a young man.'

'What do you know about it? You never knew me when I was young.'

'I'm imagining …'

'Well, you imagine wrong. I wasn't at all like that. I'm going to take a shower.'

With a towel round his waist, Édouard faced himself in the bathroom mirror. 'No, I wasn't at all like that. No one thought I was likeable. I was already a dried-up old stick. I didn't look like my father, short and stout with such dull eyes. I've always suspected my mother must have been unfaithful to him, even if

173

she would never admit it to me. It's better to be no one's son than just anybody's.'

Slowly the steam turned the mirror opaque and Monsieur Lavenant was relieved to be back in the limbo he should never have left.

Thérèse had been behaving flirtatiously all evening. She and Jean-Baptiste seemed to get along extremely well. He had done his military service near Strasbourg and knew Alsace like the back of his hand. Monsieur Lavenant thought her ridiculous in the lilac dress he had never seen her wearing before. He felt sidelined, relegated to the rank of aged relation whom people respect, admittedly, while keeping a surreptitious eye on his wine and cigarette consumption. Thérèse and Jean-Baptiste had just discovered something else they had in common, besides Alsace. They had the same birthday. Wasn't that amazing? They'd just missed spending their birthday together! Monsieur Lavenant insisted on cracking open a bottle of champagne, even though the other two didn't see the need.

'Yes, yes! It's not every day you have something to celebrate. I'll go down to the cellar.'

Édouard sat on a packing case, staring at the naked forty-watt light bulb hanging from the vaulted ceiling. There was a smell of humus, mushrooms, the dark. So that was where he'd be spending eternity, while the others danced on his head, eating, drinking, making love, laughing in honour of that bitch, life. How could all that continue without him? There was still too much light in this crypt. Wielding the bottle like a club, he smashed the bulb. Groping his way, he dragged himself up the slippery steps and out of the cellar, like one of the living dead in a horror film.

Thérèse had cleared the table. Her cheeks were flushed, her eyes shining. With his back to them, Jean-Baptiste was holding both window panes wide open, breathing in the blue pigment of

174

the night. On the ground his shadow made the shape of a large cross.

'Well now, where were you? You've been ages.'

'The cellar light's not working.'

They drank to the health of who knows what, health itself perhaps, before Thérèse disappeared, leaving father and son face to face.

'Thérèse is a very warm person. She seems very fond of you.'

'She's competent.'

'No more than that?'

'That's all I want from her.'

Jean-Baptiste bent his head, then brought it up again immediately, with a serious look on his face.

'Are you angry with me for coming?'

'Tomorrow you'll have gone.'

'I don't understand you. One minute you're open, the next closed up, and I never know which side of the door I'm on.'

'Who's asking you to understand me? Am I trying to understand you? Anyway, what is there to understand? You wanted to see me, you've seen me, job done.'

Jean-Baptiste drained his glass and put it on the coffee table, damp-eyed.

'You're harsh, and it's taking a lot of effort to be like that. I'm sorry for you.'

'Oh, please. I haven't asked for anything from you. And why should I deserve pity more than you? My life has been what it's been; it's as good as any other. I shall leave it with remorse, perhaps, but without regrets. Yours is just beginning, a little grub of a life that you're feeding with your illusions of a man in his prime. What a load of shit! No matter what you achieve – success in society, a happy family – it will all blow up in your face just as it does for the most heinous criminal. No, Monsieur Lorieux,

I am not to be pitied, any more than any other human being.'

'How black your view of the world is.'

'If you think white is preferable then go and live on the ice fields. Everything's white over there – the igloos, the bears, the polar nights! There's no one there any more; even the Eskimos have cleared off.'

'I wouldn't like to be like you at the end of my life.'

'There's no danger of that happening to you. Right, I think we've said all we had to say. I'm tired, I'm going to bed. Has Thérèse shown you your room?'

'Yes. We won't see each other again, then?'

'I don't see the need.'

'I'd have liked to do something for you.'

'The harm's been done, thanks. Goodnight.'

Monsieur Lavenant had had a bad night. Around four in the morning a cat fight had broken out on the roof of the shed next to his bedroom window. Starting off with threatening growls, it had turned into a stampede that set the old Roman tiles rattling, and culminated in an explosion of shrill miaowing which had reduced what remained of the night to tatters. He hadn't been able to shut his eyes again until almost six, and then only to marinate in a feverish half-sleep which had exhausted him more than if he'd stayed awake. It took him some time to clear his head of the shredded remnants of his dreams.

Entering the kitchen, he was astonished to see Jean-Baptiste busy washing his hands in the sink, motor oil up to his elbows.

'You're still here?'

'My car's broken down. I've just spent an hour trying to get it started, but no joy.'

'Oh.'

Édouard turned his back and poured himself a bowl of coffee. He didn't want his son to see the secret satisfaction on his face. Not because of his engine problems but because he was still there. He couldn't have said why.

'May I use your phone to call a mechanic?'

'Yes, but round here the mechanics are more often off fishing or hunting than in their garage. Worth a try though!'

He gestured towards the phone with his chin and began sipping his coffee, eyes level with the curved rim of the bowl. Without appearing to, he pricked up his ears.

'What, three at the earliest? Well, give me the address of one of your colleagues. Oh … well, in that case … Yes, I'll manage somehow, thanks.'

While Jean-Baptiste suffered defeat after defeat with the car mechanics, a broad smile was spreading across Édouard's face. Naturally his mouth reverted to its usual downward curve when his son came and sat down opposite him, chewing his thumbnail.

'You couldn't make it up! They all have urgent breakdowns.'

'What did I tell you? A little coffee?'

'Yes, please.'

'I think you might not make your meeting in Avignon.'

'My meeting? Oh, yes. To tell you the truth, I haven't got a meeting in Avignon.'

'What?'

'No. My wife's taken the children to her parents' for a few days. I took advantage of the break to come and see you.'

'So you're not in a hurry?'

'Not especially.'

'Do you often tell lies, Monsieur Lorieux?'

'Of course not! I needed a pretext, that's all.'

'Butter me a piece of bread, would you? I can't manage it with one hand.'

Édouard was taking a mischievous delight in the situation. Jean-Baptiste was really just a big kid caught with his finger in the jam jar.

'Not too much honey! Just a spoonful or else it gets everywhere. Thank you. Isn't Thérèse here?'

'She's gone to the market. We had breakfast together.'

'What do you think you'll do?'

'What do you expect me to do? Wait three hours for the

mechanic to get here. I'll go for a walk. Is there a good restaurant here?'

'No. There are two, both equally appalling.'

'Oh, well, too bad. I'll make do.'

Monsieur Lavenant lit a cigarette and voluptuously blew smoke towards the ceiling.

'Do you know how to make rings?' he asked.

'Sorry?'

'Smoke rings. Can you blow them?'

'No. I've never tried.'

'You should start now; it takes a while. Make your mouth into an "O" and let a little smoke come through; keep it there for a moment until it's quite dense and then send it out in short bursts with your glottis, raising your chin like so.'

A series of blueish rings issued from Édouard's lips and hovered for a while before dispersing as they hit the ceiling beams.

'Amazing, isn't it?'

'Very impressive.'

'It works better with cigars; almost perfect rings. I used to be quite an attraction at the end of a meal. What about whistling with your fingers, can you do that?'

'I ... I don't think so.'

'Whatever did your mother teach you? Place your thumb and index finger in the corners of your mouth, there, like so. Bend your tongue back as if you were about to swallow it and then blow ... Harder! Again!'

Jean-Baptiste was turning bright red but all that came out of his mouth was a damp hissing sound. Meanwhile opposite him Édouard was producing a range of shrill sounds which would have made many a young rascal green with envy. It was like a wildlife documentary, the old blackbird teaching his fledgling son to warble. Just at that moment Thérèse opened the door.

'What on earth's going on here? I could hear you all the way down the street! You're still here, Monsieur Lorieux?'

For an instant both men froze, fingers in their mouths, before Monsieur Lavenant stood up, taut as a bow.

'Monsieur Lorieux's car's broken down. I was teaching him to whistle. He'll be having lunch with us. I'm going up for my shower.'

The mechanic let the bonnet drop and wiped his hands on an oily rag, shaking his head.

'Very strange ... In theory a bit like that never goes ...'

'Is it bad?'

'No, but I haven't got the part. I'll need to get it sent from Lyon.'

'Will it take long?'

'Well ... Five o'clock now. If I order it straight away, I'll have it for tomorrow afternoon. By the time it's fitted ... tomorrow evening, maybe?'

Unable to make up his mind, Jean-Baptiste rubbed his chin, eyeing his car as if it were a UFO. Behind him Monsieur Lavenant was growing impatient.

'You've got no choice. Leave your car to this gentleman here and let that be an end to it. You're in for another night at our house, that's all. Isn't that so, Thérèse?'

'Monsieur Lavenant's right, there's nothing else for it.'

'I'm so embarrassed ...'

'Oh, come on, no fuss, please. You'll have your car back tomorrow, no need to make a big thing of it. Let's go home. There's no point in standing here.'

Jean-Baptiste handed over his keys to the mechanic and all three of them started for home. If the son seemed upset, the father was visibly in an excellent mood. Between the two, Thérèse didn't know which attitude she should adopt.

'Come on, no need for that face. You've your whole life ahead of you – that's what you said, isn't it? Look, I'll buy you an aperitif.'

Thérèse was startled. 'But it's barely five o'clock.'

Thérèse had a strawberry and vanilla ice cream, Jean-Baptiste a beer and Monsieur Lavenant a *perroquet* because the lurid green cocktail suited his mood so well. In the square, the shadows of the plane trees made large mauve patches like continents on the dusty ground. According to a changeless ritual, the same scene was played out every day at the same time with the same actors: the boules players in their shorts, caps and old shoes, the old women gossiping on a bench amid the murmur of bees, and the little kid pedalling his tricycle like a maniac. Monsieur Lavenant gave a little laugh.

'Have you noticed?'

'What?'

'They all look alike, the old women, the boules players, the kid, the café owner. All from the same family.'

'Do you think so?'

'Of course, Thérèse. You can't miss it. Isn't that right, Lorieux?'

'It hadn't struck me, but now …'

'It's obvious! They've all come from one stock, the mechanic as well; that nose, those ears …'

'The mechanic had an Italian accent.'

'So? What does that prove? His father's second or third wife might have been Italian. Besides, you're annoying me, Thérèse, questioning everything all the time! If I say they're all from one family it's because I have good reason for it. If there's one thing I know about, it's family!'

'No need to get on your high horse. It's nothing to me whether they belong to the same family or not.'

'Obviously. You wouldn't know what that is; you've never had one.'

Thérèse's periwinkle gaze clouded and she turned away. Édouard drained his glass as if he wanted to swallow the nasty little words again. 'I'm sorry, Thérèse. I don't know what came over me. Besides, I've never been one for family. That gregarious need to be part of a whole has always been intolerable to me. We are born alone, we die alone and in between we act as if we're not. Oh, Lorieux, the vultures! Look how they soar ...'

A dozen raptors were initialling the sky with their wing tips above the Rocher du Caire. They didn't know how to laugh or cry, didn't wonder about birth or death, they just ate, slept, reproduced but above all they soared.

'Lorieux, how would you like to go and see them at closer quarters tomorrow morning? I've got excellent binoculars. It really is something to see, I assure you.'

'I'd love to.'

'Will you take us up there tomorrow morning, Thérèse?'

'Of course.'

'Perfect. Tell me, Lorieux, do you play boules?'

'It has been known, but I'm no expert.'

'I'll buy some straight away. I wonder why I didn't think of it earlier; it's one of the only sports I can play. The tobacconist nearby sells them. I'll be right back. We'll have a game tonight in the street, before dinner.'

Monsieur Lavenant leaped up and disappeared round the corner of the square, leaving Thérèse and Jean-Baptiste a little disconcerted.

'Is he often like this?'

'No, not really. For the last week he's been acting strangely. I think he's happy that you're here. He's behaving like a young man. With me, his life's a bit monotonous. Sometimes he's clumsy but it's because he's not used to it.'

'Used to what?'

'Being happy, I think.'

The boules were sold in pairs in a woven leather bag or in sixes in a wooden case with a jack and a square of chamois leather. They gleamed, nickel-plated and incised with different patterns, in their casket lined with midnight-blue velvet. They were like rare pearls. Édouard felt the weight of one before delicately putting it back.

'I'll take them. They're suitable, I mean, the weight ...'

'I'll say so! Monsieur Drisse, our local champion, never uses anything else. He's won three trophies with them so that just shows you.'

Édouard left the tobacconist's to the tinkling of the little bell which marked customers' entrances and exits. Just at that moment a ray of sun striking the windscreen of a passing car dazzled him so much that he almost lost his balance. When he opened his eyes, everything was white, incandescent, motionless, as if turned to glass. The noises he could hear were no longer identifiable, compressed into one block of sound. He was suddenly overcome by a feeling of extreme loneliness, survivor's anguish. 'There's no one left. There's never been anyone ... except me.' Death seemed a thousand times preferable to this prison existence. The boules weighed a ton. He took one step and then another, not to go anywhere as there was nowhere to go in this arid desert, but simply to start moving again.

'Is something wrong, Monsieur? Not well again?'

Édouard put his hand up to shade his eyes. Before him stood the two women, backs to the light, under the shadow of an enormous umbrella.

'Where are the others?'

'The others? People, you mean? Over there, of course, outside the café as usual.'

'Oh. For a moment I felt I was alone in the world, a sort of survivor. It was awful ...'

'I know what you mean. That often happens to me; I'm an insomniac. Not being able to shut your eyes when everything around you is sleeping is a terrible trial. But don't worry, everyone's just where they should be. You've bought boules! They're lovely … For the child again?'

'Um, yes.'

'You're spoiling him. That's what children are for. Look at that one, pedalling his tricycle like a little racing driver. Isn't he sweet?'

For a few seconds they watched the little boy as he whirled around, head down, nose to the handlebars of his little trike, raising clouds of white dust.

'Pity they have to grow up. Well, we've got things to do. Have a good day, Monsieur.'

They vanished as they had appeared, in an overexposed patch of light.

Édouard had to make a great effort to hide his emotion when he found Jean-Baptiste and Thérèse again on the café terrace.

'Is something wrong?'

'No, I'm fine.'

'If you want me to make a meal worthy of the name we really need to go now.'

No sooner had they stood up than there was a squeal of brakes from the main road, followed by an almost imperceptible thud which nevertheless froze everyone in a silent scream. The driver of the articulated lorry leaped down from his cab and rushed over to the body of the child, whose mangled tricycle lay there, one of its wheels still spinning. As if everything were being sucked out of the square, the boules players, the old women, the café owner and everyone rushed to the crash site. Only Édouard, Thérèse and Jean-Baptiste hung back. Someone said, 'It was bound to happen.'

Thérèse claimed to have a letter to write, in order to leave the two men alone in the garden. The night was balmy, lacquered. From her seat at the little desk she couldn't see them but through the window she could hear their voices clearly, rising with the drifts of cigarette smoke. She had realised that they were linked by more than just a professional relationship but she couldn't have said what. Besides, she didn't want to discover the secret. Far from feeling excluded by their complicity she felt quite touched at seeing them circling round each other with the awkwardness of two young puppies, Édouard twice as eccentric and Jean-Baptiste mired in his shyness. Sometimes when the two of them got lost in mutual incomprehension, she was the one they turned to, seeking a reliable mooring in her presence. Aware of her role as go-between, she would calm them with just a word or a smile. She felt useful, and that was enough for her.

Not having anyone to write to, she naturally began her letter with 'My dear Thérèse ...' then, pen poised in mid-air, allowed herself to be lulled by the murmur from the garden.

'Have you any photos of your children?'

'No.'

'But that's the done thing. All fathers have photos of their children in their wallets.'

'Not me.'

'Nor of your wife?'

'Nor of her.'

'That's a shame. I'd have liked to see them. Do they look like you?'

'Who?'

'Your children!'

'Oh ... I don't know. People say they do. For that you'd have to know what kind of face I have.'

'Mine, according to Thérèse.'

'It's hard with small children, they change all the time. Between taking the photo and getting it developed, they're already different.'

'And your wife, what's she like?'

'Oh, well, blonde, average height, brown eyes ...'

'You don't seem to be madly in love with her.'

'What makes you say that?'

'You're giving me an identikit description. What about your job? Do you like it?'

'I get good results, I think I'm quite competent.'

'A charmed life, all in all?'

'Do you turn into a pain in the arse at this time every night?'

'Ah, finally some bad language! A hint of rebellion and of sincerity. I'd given up hope of that. Shall I tell you something? You've no children, any more than you've a wife, and what's more, you don't work for my company. Don't deny it. I phoned my offices the day you got here. Not known at this address. You've lied to me all along except about one thing. I'm sure you're my son.'

Thérèse spat out the little bits of plastic from the ballpoint she had been chewing. The silence that followed this revelation made the darkness turn pale.

'What have you come here for?'

'I came out of prison a week ago. Maman died while I was inside. I didn't know where to go. I went by your offices and they told me where you were.'

186

'But why all these lies?'

'I wanted you to like me.'

'You've succeeded there! And what got you into prison?'

'Fraud. I worked for the Banque Nationale de Paris. I got five years.'

'I'm wondering whether I should believe you. In the end, I couldn't care less. Lie for lie, I prefer that one to the pathetic little life that was supposed to win me over. Have you any more nice surprises like that up your sleeve?'

'No, that's all.'

'Pity, it was just starting to get exciting! And what is it you expect from me? A word of apology? Power of attorney over my bank account?'

'Nothing. Nothing at all, I swear to you.'

'So things are fine as they are?'

'I'm really stuck. I haven't any friends or family. My whole life revolved around Maman. We were a sort of couple, like two shipwreck survivors on a desert island. She was always ill. My work suffered ... but I wanted to make her comfortable at the end of her life, beside the sea, far away from the lousy one-bedroom flat where we lived in Batignolles. I wanted to give her some fresh air before she died. Fresh air, do you see?'

'Please, spare me the violins. It might make them cry in the stalls, but not here. You're a failure. Full stop, end of. Tomorrow, in memory of your mother, if you haven't cut my throat between now and then, I'll write you a cheque and you can go and get yourself hanged elsewhere.'

'But I don't care about your sodding money! Don't you under-stand anything? What have you got inside that cage of bones, under all that wrinkled skin? Old bastard!'

'Little prick!'

Monsieur Lavenant didn't recognise Thérèse's voice when she

187

shouted 'ÉDOUARD!' It seemed to come from deep inside himself, an echo that stopped him in his tracks as he was about to slap his son.

'Édouard, get up here immediately!'

He looked at his hand as if it belonged to someone else and let his arm fall, while Jean-Baptiste looked straight into his eyes, pale, lip trembling. A light came on in one of his neighbour's windows and the silhouette of a man with a bare chest appeared, like a shadow puppet.

'Stop that racket!'

Édouard gave a shrug and went up the steps to the door. Jean-Baptiste lit a cigarette and disappeared into the shrubbery.

Thérèse was standing on the doorstep, unbending as justice, and looking daggers at Édouard.

'How dare you shout at me like that in front of a stranger?'

'A stranger? I heard everything. You're hateful. From tomorrow you'll do without my services. I'm leaving you.'

'Why? What have I done to you?'

'To me? Nothing. But it's shameful to see a father humiliate his son like that.'

'My son, my son … a liar, a crook, a thief! Two days ago I didn't even know he existed. You think someone becomes a father in forty-eight hours?'

'That's not the point, he's a human being. You can see the poor man's completely lost.'

'Is that my fault? I'm not responsible for the pitiful state he's in.'

'You are a little, actually. He needs help and you're content to just throw him a bone. Don't tell me you don't feel anything at all …'

'A burning desire to show him the door with my foot up his backside, that's what I feel!'

'You're lying. You're as lost as he is. Anyone would think you're ashamed to take him in your arms.'

'You're totally mad. You read too many women's magazines. Paternal instinct, blood of my blood! It's all nonsense!'

'But look at yourself. You've changed since he's been here; you never take your eyes off him, as if you're looking for yourself in him.'

'For a mirror, one could do better. He's pathetic, a failure. And anyway, why are you interfering in the first place? What gives you the right to judge me?'

'I'm not judging you, I feel sorry for you. He may be a failure, as you say, but he's young, he still has his chances, while you ...'

'What about me?'

'You must have made a mess of things in your life in order to have become what you are. Too bad. It's a waste.'

Thérèse turned on her heel and disappeared. Monsieur Lavenant felt an enormous weight descend on his shoulders. He was short of air like newborns who suffocate between two sobs. Anger and confusion created uncontrollable turbulence in his head. He felt like a boxer alone in a ring with no one to fight but himself. He looked around for something to break – it didn't matter what. He was about to grab the lamp on the little desk when he caught sight of the letter beginning 'My dear Thérèse ...' All that emptiness, all that blank space that followed made him dizzy, forcing him to sit down. He couldn't take his eyes off the pure white page splashed with light from the lamp. Automatically, his right hand took hold of the pen: 'Well, yes, I have been a father for two days. I have a child but he is an orphan ...'

When Thérèse and Jean-Baptiste came back they found him asleep, forehead resting on the desk, and the page completely filled with his small handwriting.

My dear Thérèse ...

Well, yes, I have been a father for two days. I have a child but he is an orphan. It's rather unusual ... but that's how it is. It has had the same effect on me as learning of my own death. He looks like me, it appears; personally I don't see it – he's much too young and I wouldn't wish that on him anyway. What would the world do with another Édouard Lavenant?

You know how old I am, my dear Thérèse. Who knows better than you my physical and mental decrepitude? I'm a wreck, aren't I? You may understand what it's like for me to feel this old wrinkled prune of a heart beat again in my hollow chest. I'm afraid of this new life; it's as though I had to start everything again from the beginning, question everything again, tear down the citadel of certainties in which I have taken refuge for so long. What an irony of fate to see the past resurface just as my memory is emptying like a basin of stale water. Thanks to you, I was gradually learning to accept this state of affairs serenely, aspiring to nothing more now than to live hour by hour, minute by minute, second by second. Old people, like lovers, are alone in the world, which is to say, profoundly egotistical. They need to be understood, they are fragile; with the slightest draught their bones shatter like glass. Everything is too strong for them, the cold, the heat; they protect themselves from life while they wait for death.

And then suddenly this vision of youth standing before me like a phantom … Recognising this son meant looking myself in the face, and that is something which, through cowardice, I have always refused to do. With all the strength I have left I have fought against this unfamiliar emotion which has gripped me since Jean-Baptiste's arrival. Everything for which I reproached him was really addressed to myself. Now I surrender. I lower the arm which I raised against him and offer him my hand. I don't care what he may or may not have done, good or bad. Jean-Baptiste was born two days ago and that is all that matters. And in any case which of us has greater need of the other?

My dear Thérèse, will you help me in this task by assuming the place which falls to you at the core of this odd family? I wish it with all my heart.

Yours, Édouard

Jean-Baptiste handed the letter to Thérèse without meeting her gaze. The sheet was trembling in his hand. Thérèse folded it up carefully and slipped it into her pocket. After putting Monsieur Lavenant to bed they had each gone back to their own room but, unable to sleep, had met again in the early hours in the kitchen, where the remnants of night still stagnated.

'A little coffee?'

'Yes, please.'

It was a day like any other except that it seemed to be setting in for eternity. Jean-Baptiste tilted his head back and gave his neck a rub.

'I think I'll go for a walk. I need to stretch my legs.'

When he had gone out, Thérèse set about removing all traces

of the evening before, emptying the ashtrays, washing up, cleaning the floor – exorcism by housework. She felt no tiredness; floor cloth, broom and duster flew in her hands and her feet scarcely touched the floor. She made a mental note that the walls could do with a good lick of paint and it would be nice to change the sun-bleached curtains in the living room. Yellow perhaps, that would be more cheerful. Then in a short pause she dreamed of the little blue dress she had thought about buying on her last trip to the market. For lunch she would make a Swiss chard gratin, yes, a nice chard gratin with béchamel sauce. Édouard was wild about it. A mouse moving along the skirting board stopped just opposite her, staring at her with its little round eyes. Thérèse just shook her duster and the creature vanished into a tiny hole behind the sink.

Édouard had been awake for some time but couldn't manage to drag himself out of bed. Or rather he didn't want to. He didn't regret the letter he had written but dreaded coming face to face with Thérèse and Jean-Baptiste, which was unavoidable. Never had he felt this exposed, this unprotected; so much so that he thought he wouldn't ever get up, speak, eat or laugh again. The effort he'd had to put into writing those few sentences had drained him of all substance. Opening his eyes, he had been amazed that he was still alive. It was rather like a failed suicide. While he knew that this unpleasant sense of vulnerability was only the result of his wounded pride, he had enough of it left to refuse a complete surrender. His last trump cards lay in his age and the precariousness of his mental health. That was why he had let himself be carried like a parcel the previous evening when he could perfectly well have gone upstairs to bed on his own. After what he considered an exemplary *mea culpa*, the least they could do was be concerned about his condition, cosset him, do him justice and homage. Otherwise, of what possible use was redemption?

But his overfull bladder compelled him to get up, slip on his dressing gown and make a rush for the toilet. No sooner had he got back into bed than there was a knock on the door and, without waiting for a reply, Thérèse appeared with the breakfast tray. The beatific smile on her face exasperated him in the extreme.

'I heard you going to the toilet and thought you'd like to have your breakfast in bed.'

His only answer was to turn his face to the wall.

'It's a fine day, a little wind but the weather's good. Shall I open the shutters? All right, I'll leave you, then. Have you remembered we were going to see the vultures at the Rocher du Caire? The weather's ideal; it would be good to be there by about eleven. Édouard, are you listening to me? Édouard? Stop being so childish. No one's cross with you, quite the reverse. Don't spoil everything. Jean-Baptiste himself fetched the croissants; they're freshly baked. We'll wait for you. It's only half past nine, take your time. I'm so proud of you. What you did was very brave, worthy of a true father.'

Left on his own, Édouard pushed back the covers and punched open the shutters with his fist. The daylight was like a pail of water full in the face. 'It was very brave, worthy of a true father … I'll say!' He wolfed down both croissants, drank his coffee in one go, showered and took an absolute age to get dressed, as if he were going out on a date. When he appeared before Thérèse and Jean-Baptiste he was wearing a pearl-grey pinstripe suit, a soft panama hat and was wreathed in clouds of vetiver.

'Well, what are we waiting for?'

This theatrical entrance left the other two speechless. All he needed now was a cane, which he naturally found in the umbrella stand, a metal-tipped walking stick with a handle shaped like a bulldog. He twirled it a few times, as if trying out the balance of a sword, then leaned on it, legs crossed and arching his eyebrows. He wasn't lacking in style but his bad night had given him a waxy complexion. He was like a waxwork from the Musée Grevin on a day off.

'Well, then, are we off?'

'Of course.'

Édouard refused to get into the front of the car. 'At my age one sits in the back, leaving the risks to those with their whole lives ahead of them.' Thérèse drove carefully. Édouard talked constantly, about everything and nothing, like those who are uncomfortable with silence. It was only once they'd parked the car at the end of the little path and gone a hundred metres or so that the verbal diarrhoea stopped for lack of breath. Thérèse went in front, and Jean-Baptiste made clumsy attempts to match his stride to his father's.

'Are you all right?'

'Of course I'm all right!'

'You can lean on my arm if you like.'

'I have more trust in my stick. I'm fine I tell you, son.'

'Can I call you Papa?'

'Might as well. Tell me, what are you good at?'

'Well, er … not much. I studied accountancy.'

'And we've seen where that got you. Haven't you got a passion for something … I don't know, model-making, travel, water-colours?'

'I studied astrology in prison. I know how to do a birth chart.'

'That's a lot of good to us! An astrologer!'

'I'm not as stupid as all that, I'm a fast learner. Look.'

Jean-Baptiste stopped, stuck two fingers in his mouth and filled his lungs. He produced such a piercing whistle that a long way ahead, even with the wind against him, Thérèse turned round.

'Not bad.'

'I practised this morning. With the smoke rings I'm not quite there yet.'

'A whistling astrologer … It's a start. Go on, give me your arm and take my stick – it's more of a nuisance to me.'

Thérèse had arrived at the top well before them. She had always been proud of her legs, not for their shapeliness but because they were strong and reliable, like a team of Percheron horses. They had never let her down. Leaning against the big wooden cross, shading her eyes with one hand, she followed the slow progress of father and son, arm in arm, on the path. From time to time they would pause. Édouard was holding his hat on and would nod his head as if affirming something. Jean-Baptiste signalled his agreement in the same way. Without knowing what they were talking about she sensed the two of them were getting along extremely well. Her heart was pounding in her chest, less from the physical effort than because she was certain she had finally attained the happiness she had been waiting for all her life. She smiled as the wind played around her like a young dog, blowing her hair back onto her cheeks and forcing her to hold her skirt down with one hand. The wood of the cross vibrated at her back. She turned round, eyes filled with tears: 'Make this last for ever …'

'Something wrong, Thérèse? Do you feel dizzy?'

With their jacket tails flapping around them, the two men looked like birds about to take flight.

'No, it's the wind.'

'It's mighty strong, that's for sure. Oh, Jean-Baptiste, look, there they are!'

Two vultures launched themselves a few metres away, regal, their outspread wings sweeping through space, eyes fixed, hooked beaks parting the sky like the prow of a boat. Three others followed, as if from nowhere, scratching cabbalistic signs on the azure expanse. Jean-Baptiste spread out his arms, facing into the wind, leaning at a 45-degree angle, mouth open, eyes closed.

'I spent hours staring at the window of my cell. "All that blue for nothing," I'd think. Eventually I no longer saw the wire netting, the bars … For a moment I was free.'

The wind had gone mad, intoxicated by the birds. It was making them draw incredible arabesques as if it wanted to prove to us poor earthbound creatures the eternal supremacy of the void.

'Hey, my hat!'

The white panama spun on the cliff edge and lodged in the branches of a bush lower down. Jean-Baptiste rushed over.

'Leave it, Jean-Baptiste, it's too windy – let it go!'

'It's not too far; I can reach.'

Thérèse and Édouard clutched each other. Pressed against the rock, clinging on to the stump of a thorny bush with one hand, Jean-Baptiste inched his other arm towards the hat. He finally managed to catch the brim between two fingers, and looked up at Thérèse and Édouard with a radiant smile.

'Got it!'

At that moment the root gave way. His smile froze and an astonished expression flicked his eyes wide open. Jean-Baptiste toppled backwards, hat in hand, like a music-hall entertainer taking his bows. His body plummeted some hundred metres onto a vulture's eyrie, from which the terrified female flew up with the shrillest of cries. Thérèse fell to her knees, arms hanging by her sides. Her lips were moving but no sound came out. The raptors were wheeling, undecided, up above the corpse which the sky had delivered to their door.

'It's not right, leaving him up there.'

'Why? Would you prefer it if he turned into a sack of maggots six feet underground?'

'I'm not saying that, but it's not Christian.'

'Big deal! In many countries no one would be shocked. It's clean, useful and spiritually impeccable.'

'Don't you feel any sorrow, Édouard?'

'What difference does it make what I feel? It's not me I'm thinking of but him. All his life he tried to take off, but, maybe because he didn't spread his wings wide enough, he never could. A few brief forays outside his feathered nest, stolen hopes, nothing more. Now he's soaring, he's in every one of those birds churning the sky. I'm certain that at last he feels at home. I'd rather think of Jean-Baptiste as I watch them wheeling freely in the boundless sky than when I'm staring at an icy marble slab. Besides, I would never have gone there, I've got a horror of graveyards – they smell of rotting geraniums and you get dodgy people there.'

'Well, personally I'll never be able to look at the creatures ever again. And you'll be bringing trouble to your door; it's against the law not to declare someone's death! You can be sure that sooner or later his body will be found ... What's left of him, rather – his clothes, watch, papers ... They'll suspect you of killing him, because no reasonable person would act the way you are. We've got to go to the police station; there's still time.'

'Do you think so?'

'I'm absolutely sure of it. Trust me, Édouard.'

Édouard had to admit that Thérèse was right, but he baulked at the chore. They were going to have to explain the inexplicable, and he felt that was beyond him. He wasn't afraid, it was quite simply a nuisance.

'So we'll go, then?'

'Purely to please you.'

The gendarmerie was no bigger than a family-size box of matches, covered in ochre rendering and topped by a dishcloth of a flag in mauve, beige and pink. The two gendarmes manning it were fine, but seemingly as deaf as each other; everything had to be repeated three or four times. Out of cowardice, Édouard had opted to play the senile old man, and it was Thérèse who answered the questions. The typewriter didn't work very well and there was a smell of sweat and stale cigarettes.

'But why wait so long before coming to make your statement?'

'Monsieur Lavenant felt unwell. I had to attend to him.'

'It's five o'clock already. My men are going to have difficulty recovering the body ... We'll come and pick you up in the morning for the identification.'

From trying not to hear anything, Édouard had a buzzing in his ears when they left, as if on a plane coming in to land after a long flight. They walked home. As they passed the bakery, Thérèse stopped to buy bread. On the glass door was a notice announcing a Mass on Saturday at 10 a.m. in memory of little Ange Spitallieri who had been killed in a tricycle accident.

They had dinner early, barely touching their soup and exchanging no more than two or three words. It was still light when they went up to bed, exhausted but sure they wouldn't be able to fall asleep any time soon. After tossing and turning a thousand times, Édouard got up and opened the window wide. The dark spread like an ink stain in the room.

'What does it all mean, all this dark, all this time?'

The quick padded steps of a cat on the tiles answered him, only to be snatched away again by the thick, echoless silence.

'Édouard? Who are you talking to?'

'Who d'you think I'd be talking to? Nobody.'

He came back and stretched out next to her, shivering, incapable of formulating the slightest thought, not that he had any.

'Can you hear, Thérèse?'

'What?'

'All this nothing, this emptiness surrounding us ... I think we've been forgotten. Not a breath of wind, not a cat miaowing, not a rustling in the leaves ... People have abandoned the world; there's only us left.'

'I can hear your heart beating.'

'It's just habit. It's striking its anvil like an old workman who doesn't know how to do anything else.'

'And my heart, can you hear it?'

'Yes, it's answering mine. It doesn't know why it's beating either. It's beating because it's been told to beat. Thérèse, will you suck me off?'

Thérèse gave a start beneath the sheet, a sort of gagging, but her hand gripped Édouard's shoulder more tightly.

'I'm sorry, Édouard. I don't think I can. I've never done it. It's not that it disgusts me, it's just that ... I wouldn't know how to ...'

'Don't apologise, I understand. To tell you the truth I don't really feel like it. I can't get to sleep so I just thought that maybe ...'

'I can masturbate you if you want? I've already done that, to a man in the hospital. He had only a short time to live. The two of us struggled for quite a while. He didn't get there. I was doing my best though. No doubt I'm not cut out for that. He'd been very badly burnt and it was the only part of his body that had been spared. He stroked my hair and, beneath the bandages covering his face, he smiled at me. He died two days later.'

Monsieur Lavenant propped himself up on one elbow and felt for his cigarettes. In the glow from the lighter flame he saw the mass of Thérèse's red hair spread out on the pillow, a sepia pool, an armful of floppy seaweed.

'As soon as we're finished with all this, we'll go away.'

'Where to?'

'I don't know. Wherever you want; go away just for the sake of it. Here isn't there, and you're bound to get there one day or another. Do you want to go back to Alsace?'

'I don't know. I've no family there, no ties. It was so long ago ...'

'I said that off the top of my head, just to start us thinking; I could just as well have said Mont-Saint-Michel. What about abroad, does that appeal to you?'

'Isn't it a bit far?'

'That depends. Switzerland's next door. It's peaceful, Switzerland, and yet it's abroad.'

'Do you think I'd get used to it?'

'Of course, it's like here.'

'Then why go there?'

'Why? Why? Because it's like here only more expensive, that's why!'

'That's a stupid answer!'

'A stupid question deserves a stupid answer! You don't ask why people go to Switzerland, they just go, full stop, end of story.'

'No need to get angry! If that's what you want, we'll go to Switzerland.'

'My, oh, my ... It takes you an age to make a decision. You'll like it, you'll see; it's very clean, the climate's good for you and although the clocks are always right, time passes more slowly there than anywhere else in the world. All old people like Switzerland.'

'Do you consider me old?'

'No, but that'll come soon enough. You'll be grateful to me when you're old in Switzerland. Now we have to sleep.'

The dark was no longer as dark. With the decision, a door had opened a crack, and behind it a vague glimmer could be seen, the germ of a future.

'Thérèse, I love falling asleep in your arms ...'

The dawn had a muddy complexion. The sky was wondering about going off sick. It was a 'roll on bedtime' sort of a day. The two policemen from the previous afternoon seemed in a similar mood when they appeared at Monsieur Lavenant's door. As their van was too big to get along the narrow street, all four of them had to make their way back to it on foot, under the prurient eye of the neighbour spying on them from behind his curtains.

'Hey, Miriam, what did I say? Pretends to be a real gent, that one, and ends up flanked by policemen.'

Thérèse was white with shame as she got into the vehicle. Monsieur Lavenant just looked extremely weary. Two or three people on their way to empty their dustbins stared at them and whispered. Everyday people who today weren't everyday people any more. Édouard shrugged his shoulders.

'It's ridiculous, all this fuss and bother. We could have walked to the gendarmerie.'

'It's the rules, Monsieur.'

'Rules, bah!'

The garage adjacent to the police station, the place tyres were stored, was where Jean-Baptiste's body had been laid out, on a wooden board supported by two trestles. An ambulance was parked beside it. Two men in white coats stopped playing football with an old tennis ball when they arrived.

'We'll need to be quick as the ambulance has to get off to the morgue. It's not very savoury; the vultures didn't leave much. I don't know which of you …'

'Stay here, Thérèse, I'll go.'

The first thing Édouard noticed, even before the sheet was lifted, was that the loafer was missing from Jean-Baptiste's left foot.

The sock had been reduced to shreds of elastic thread at the ankle, and the foot to some bones held together by purplish tendons.

'Will you be all right?'

Édouard nodded his head. Of course he'd be all right. He had been born in Lyon, the home of the puppet Guignol – what was there to fear in a marionette without strings?

The teeth were immaculate and one of them, a gold molar, reflected the daylight's milky gleam. Jean-Baptiste was smiling because that's all a human being is left with once the skin and flesh are stripped away. All that remained of the eyes and nose – the tastiest morsels no doubt – were unfathomable cavities allowing you to imagine the vacuity of the skull, jaggedly split like a coconut shell and already orbited by a big fat fly. Lower down, the ribs protruded under the torn shirt and the entire entrails and internal organs had disappeared. A burst drum. The hands like small rusty tools were clutching nothingness. Two fingers were missing from the right hand and the thumb from the left. The rest was just shreds, leftovers from a banquet too soon interrupted by the rescuers' arrival. In spite of the products with which he had been sprayed, Jean-Baptiste was giving off a stench of flatulence.

'Do you recognise the victim?'

'The very image of his father.'

'What?'

'Sorry, yes, it's definitely him.'

The two men in white coats stowed Jean-Baptiste in the ambulance and Monsieur Lavenant, accompanied by the officer, rejoined Thérèse in the fetid offices of the gendarmerie. Once again it was necessary to go over the distressing banality of the previous day's events. They had to sign a statement and were asked to remain available to the authorities until the post-mortem. All these formalities were lengthy and boring; it was like being back at school. Monsieur Lavenant refused to let the police take them home.

'Thank you, you've done enough.'

They met no one on their way home, or else they didn't notice, each of them was so lost in their own thoughts. Édouard's naturally took him towards Switzerland. The page had been turned; soon he would no longer remember it. The next chapter opened with the Swiss flag, which had always made him think of an Elastoplast cross stuck over a red mouth. This symbol of mutism suited him perfectly. He had already left.

'Well?'

'Well what?'

'What was he like?'

'Dead.'

'Yes, but …'

'Dead like a dead man, out of his body. Only the shell of him was there.'

'You're speaking about him as if he were a thing!'

'Well, yes, a still life. There's no reason to be offended by it. Oh, it's raining … You didn't bring an umbrella, obviously. What were you thinking of, Thérèse?'

Despite hurrying they arrived home soaking wet. Édouard lit a fire and Thérèse made tea. It was barely eleven o'clock but you would have thought it was the evening. Édouard was delighted. If only every day could be this short. Twenty-four hours, that's far too many! Half would be enough, eight for sleeping, four for getting bored stiff. Twelve hours gone to waste when they could be useful to someone else, a poor man for example. What a gift that would be!

The log that Édouard was poking at in the fire had taken on the appearance of a bison's head, blowing jets of spitting flames out of every orifice: flaring nostrils, hollow eye sockets, misshapen ears. Paradoxically the more the piece of wood was consumed, the more alive it became. It was fascinating.

'Stop poking at that log, Édouard. You'll end up setting light to the house.'

'Bah, what does it matter, we're never coming back.'

'We can't leave nothing but ashes behind us.'

The button Thérèse was sewing on slipped out of her hands, rolled over the stone slabs, and settled again, spinning like a top between her feet, almost back where it had started. They had both followed its spiral course and were now staring at it, a mother-of-pearl button with four holes in it. It looked like the world's navel.

After several days the authorities had to acknowledge that Jean-Baptiste's death was simply the result of an accidental fall, even if the victim's dubious past and his uncertain relations with Monsieur Lavenant allowed some doubt to remain. At any rate the latter was now free to go wherever he wanted.

They left one morning, early. The previous day Thérèse had cleaned the house from top to bottom. No trace of their presence remained, and Thérèse was disturbed by this as she glanced round for the last time before closing the door. Who could have imagined that people had prepared snails and lit a fire in the grate here, that they had laughed, cried, loved and suffered ... The smell of the cleaning products had left a whiff of amnesia. Thérèse felt tears come to her eyes.

'What's wrong?'

'It's as if nothing had ever been ...'

'Well, yes, it's as if ... that's how it is. You wipe everything away and start again; life is a palimpsest. Oh, look where you're going, Thérèse, or you'll miss the step.'

'What shall I do with the keys?'

'I don't know ... Hang them on the nail under the beam. Whoever finds them can have them, the rust first and foremost.'

It had been agreed that they would spend a day or two in Lyon, just while Monsieur Lavenant sorted out some business. Thérèse's old car struggled and coughed its way along under the weight of luggage.

'First thing tomorrow we'll buy a new one. We can't go to Switzerland in an old jalopy like this, people would take us for gypsies.'

'She's still game! She's overloaded, that's all. I couldn't bear to see her go to the scrapyard.'

'We'll put her in my garage, then. She's earned her retirement, don't you think? What are you looking at in the mirror?'

'I thought I saw two women waving us off at the corner of the street.'

'One tall and one small?'

'Yes. Do you know them?'

'Vaguely. I've seen them go by.'

The sky was as white and opaque as a cinema screen. It seemed as if at any minute Charlie Chaplin would appear, twirling his cane, on the horizon of the motorway. Thérèse kept to the slow lane, huddled over the steering wheel, stoically putting up with the exhaust fumes from the lorries she couldn't bring herself to overtake. Every time she went under a bridge she would shut her eyes, her lips stammering out unintelligible prayers.

'Open your eyes, for God's sake! You'll have us off the road.'

'I can't help it, I hate the motorway, especially the bridges. There's always people on them looking at us.'

'So?'

'I'm scared they'll throw things at us.'

'That's ridiculous! What do you think they'd throw at us?'

'I don't know ... A bicycle, a log, stones ... It *has* happened.'

'I love travelling with you. It feels so safe. You can stop at the next service station; I urgently need to go.'

Hemmed in by two articulated lorries, Thérèse missed the first one. Édouard's bladder was at bursting point when they came to the second. He rushed into the toilets, the ones for disabled people which he found more spacious, and stayed there for some time. It was like the North Pole, a vast expanse of pristine tiling, from which seals, penguins and bears might be expected to appear.

Thérèse was waiting for him in front of the coffee machines. They each had a tomato consommé. In the nine hours since they had left, they had covered only about a hundred kilometres. Tousled kids, bright red in the face, were clamouring loudly for everything the service station had to offer them: cuddly monkeys, cakes, fizzy drinks, key rings, music cassettes, sandwiches, regional specialities, knives … To relax after long hours at the wheel, fathers were practising virtual steering on video screens. It was a strange, murky world, slightly resembling that of a Jacques Cousteau documentary. They left their cups still half full on some plastic mushrooms and took refuge in their car, certain of having narrowly escaped some sort of danger.

They took over four hours to reach the capital of the Gauls. Terrified by the traffic, Thérèse got lost a thousand times before – nerves in shreds and totally distraught – drawing up in front of Monsieur Lavenant's residence in Boulevard des Belges, a stone's throw from the sparkling gates of Parc de la Tête d'Or.

The apartment was immense, seven rooms, maybe more, stretching over almost five hundred square metres and with very high ceilings. Édouard showed Thérèse round at top speed before abandoning her in the drawing room while he shut himself in his study to make some urgent phone calls.

Perched gingerly on the edge of a sofa made of the thickest leather, Thérèse looked over the decor surrounding her. It was expensive, to be sure; each piece of furniture, every carpet and ornament had to be worth a small fortune, but this ostentatious luxury dripping with gold and satin was out of keeping with Monsieur Lavenant's character. It was hard to picture him moving around in this monstrous bonbonnière in which the sugared almond-coloured lampshade frills vied for first prize in the bad-taste stakes with the chantilly cream tie-backs for the fuchsia curtains. The plethora of objects in the display cases, on the occasional tables and on the shelves was enough to give you indigestion. In a vain attempt to find a moment's escape from the riot of bronze, porcelain and other biscuit ware, Thérèse's eyes lit on one of the countless terrible paintings staining the walls. Like the others it depicted a bunch of flowers, but the artist had larded it with so much red and blue that it had the same effect as an open abdomen spewing its steaming entrails. Thérèse found refuge only in contemplating a triangle of sky which gave the window a matt-white tint.

'Say what you like, people are not like us.'

So this was how other people lived. Well, so long as they liked it …

She got no further in her reflections. Édouard had joined her, a leather briefcase under his arm, bouncing with energy.

'Right, a car's coming for me. I've two or three matters to sort out. Make yourself at home. I'll be back around eight. I'll book a table at Orsi's, very nearby; that'll be simpler for this evening … Sorry?'

'I didn't say anything.'

'Oh, I thought … Right, well …'

Édouard seemed like a different person in these surroundings, smaller somehow. He was like one of those portraits of adolescents you find when leafing through a family album, awkward-looking, ill at ease.

'Cécile had terrible taste. See you this evening.'

When he returned shortly before eight o'clock, Thérèse was still in the same place. Only the now open window showed that she had moved. The sun was sinking behind Fourvière hill.

Édouard talked and talked, of things Thérèse understood absolutely nothing about: his business, his lawyer, figures. She wasn't listening to him in any case; all her attention was focused on the excellent *blanquette d'écrevisses au vin jaune* which she was savouring in tiny mouthfuls.

'It's atrocious, Thérèse, isn't it?'

'Sorry, what's atrocious?'

'My place, it's atrocious, don't you think?'

'I wouldn't say that. It's … big.'

'I'm going to throw all that out. Every day she would bring home some thing or other, some whatnot, so hideous that I always used to wonder where on earth would sell it.'

'You know, tastes and colours …'

'No! It wasn't that she had bad taste, she had none at all. She didn't respond to colours or flavours or … Take your *blanquette*, for example. You've savoured it. Well, she'd have swallowed it like a mess of tapioca. Imagine a bell with absolutely no resonance. She was extraordinary, unfathomably vacuous. It was no doubt to fill that void that she bought all that, to please me, maybe … Or to annoy me; I've never known which. On the other hand she could do impeccable imitations of farm animals.'

'Farm animals?'

'Yes, cows, cockerels, goats, sheep … You couldn't tell them from the real thing. She could have had a career in music hall. Animals would answer her, you know. She could hold a conversation with a duck for nearly forty minutes!'

'She loved animals.'

'I don't think so. It always ended in a row. They'd try to bite her and she'd hit them with a stick. She knew their languages, that was all. A pointless gift, like her beauty. She never made use of it. I got to wishing that she would cheat on me. She had many admirers. It never happened.'

Thérèse noticed something like a little wave in Édouard's look, with a mast in the distance, sinking beneath the foam.

'Is something wrong? You haven't touched your plate.'

'I'm fine. It's strange, I can't remember her face at all, only her voice …'

On leaving Orsi's, Édouard went in the opposite direction to the one from which they had arrived. Thérèse was surprised but, not knowing the city, followed him. After a good quarter of an hour (whereas they'd taken only five or six minutes to walk to the restaurant from Édouard's apartment) she asked him where they were going.

'I've no idea, I'm following you.'

'But we're going to your apartment!'

'Oh …'

'Your place, Boulevard des Belges.'

'Boulevard des Belges …'

'Don't you remember where you live?'

'No.'

'The big apartment that's … ugly.'

They had taken so many turnings down so many empty, identical streets that Thérèse now had no idea at all where they were. Luckily a passer-by pointed them in the right direction. They had gone a long way off course but Édouard seemed unconcerned. He let himself be guided by Thérèse with the serene confidence a blind man has in his dog. Finally she recognised the façade and the carriage entrance opposite the park gates. Access was by a numerical code.

'Seven, eight, nine, three.'

'You're sure?'

'Of course!'

Thérèse pressed the buttons without really believing him, yet the gate opened straight away.

'Are you making fun of me?'

'Why?'

'You don't know where you live but you can remember the code?'

'Get in quickly instead of asking stupid questions. It's starting to rain.'

Édouard was sitting in a chair, his morocco-leather briefcase flat on his knees. He was wearing a dark suit, white shirt, red tie and black shoes. There was a strong smell of aftershave emanating from him. Like a traveller on a station platform, he was waiting. For what? He would have found it very difficult to say. He knew only that he had to wait. Outside it was still dark. The 100 watts pouring from an imitation Venetian chandelier lit him cruelly but he seemed scarcely to notice. With age you become patient, giving time no more value than it deserves; you put it in your pocket with your handkerchief on top and take tiny sips of the present like a glass of port. Oh, yes, of course! It was coming back to him. He was waiting for his driver, who was to take him to Maître Billard, his lawyer's. Smiling, he tapped his briefcase. Everything was there, neatly arranged. Half of his possessions would go to Thérèse, the other half to Jean-Baptiste. The split seemed equitable. One person would be able to live out her days in peace and the other finally to embark on a life worthy of the name. You had to know how to wipe the slate clean. Which young man has never done anything stupid? Besides, there were mitigating circumstances. An orphan, a child who'd been given life without an instruction manual. He was entitled to a second chance. It was for him, Édouard Lavenant, to give him that and he felt great pride and a profound relief. No one would be able to reproach him for being a bad father, no one …

He thumped his fist on the table and a silver saucer flew across the room before landing, spinning, on the marble floor of the entranceway. The cymbal clash spread in concentric waves throughout the house.

Thérèse appeared, hair untidy, rubbing her eyes, one heavy breast escaping from her dressing gown, pulled on in a hurry.

'Whatever are you doing here?'

'Waiting for my driver. I've got an appointment with Maître Billard.'

'It's five o'clock in the morning!'

'Oh …'

'You need to go back to bed.'

'But I've been to sleep, I'm dressed …'

'It's too early, Édouard. Come on, I'll help you.'

Once undressed he'd fallen asleep again immediately. Thérèse, on the other hand, lying next to him, found it impossible to go back to sleep. She was suffocating in this house with its clutter of hostile objects which, every time she moved, immediately seemed to gather together to block her way. Unable to bear it any longer, she got up and opened the window wide, in desperate need of air. The fluffy foliage of the unnaturally green plane trees stretched, dripping, the whole length of the avenue. On the pavement opposite, two women hurried past, clutching an umbrella. The smaller of the two looked up at the window and for a split second her glasses captured the street lamp's gleam. Thérèse recoiled. She could have sworn the woman had given her a slight nod.

Thérèse was waiting for Édouard in one of those imposing bras-
series in Place Bellecour which make you feel as if you've gone
back a hundred years: lofty ceilings, over-ornate mouldings,
murals with pastoral scenes in pastel colours, gleaming brass,
polished wood, waiters with long white aprons and handlebar
moustaches. The clientele was in keeping. Beyond the window
the square with its brick-red ground made you think of an enormous tennis court, with the equestrian statue of Louis XIV as an
incongruous centrepiece. It would no doubt be hot today. Mist
was rising from the freshly watered pavements, with a smell of
hot damp cloth.

She had woken Édouard at eight o'clock. He had no memory of
having been awake earlier, but as he seemed in a particularly good
mood Thérèse hadn't mentioned it. After breakfast he had insisted
she accompany him, something she had gladly agreed to (any excuse
to get out of the house) while refusing to go up to the offices out of
decency. She wouldn't want people to think ...

All this seemed slightly mad, illogical, but Édouard's enthusiasm
was so infectious that she felt ready to follow him to the ends of the
earth, all the more so as this would probably be no further away
than Lake Geneva. She didn't care about the distance; for once she
was resolved to take a train that was going somewhere. Édouard
needed her, more today than yesterday perhaps.

She saw him go past the café so quickly she had no time to

217

knock on the window. Then he reappeared, going in the opposite direction in just as much of a hurry, talking to himself and shaking his head. Suddenly, instead of coming into the café, he crossed the road, paying no attention to the cars screeching to a halt in front of him, walked across the square and began going round and round the statue. Thérèse paid for her drink and rushed over to join him.

'Now, Thérèse, what have you been doing? Our plane leaves in two hours; we're cutting it fine.'

'Two hours? What about our luggage?'

'We'll buy everything once we're there. You've needed a new wardrobe since birth. Taxi!'

Satolas Airport had been rechristened Saint-Exupéry and no one had informed Monsieur Lavenant.

'Saint-Ex! What a name. Saint-Ex! Well, if that's progress …'

The car smelled of new plastic. An unidentifiable orange furry creature was bouncing on a length of elastic beneath the rear-view mirror.

'Couldn't you take that thing down, it's getting annoying …'

'No, M'sieur. It was a gift from my children.'

'Well, at least switch off the radio!'

'Yes, M'sieur.'

'Right, my secretary has booked us a hotel in Geneva. We'll hire a car locally and then we'll look for a chalet higher up in the mountains. Oh, Thérèse … Old age! That poor Billard is going completely gaga, yet he's ten years younger than me. I had to repeat things ten times for him and he kept replying, "Are you really sure, Édouard? Really sure?" It's terrible to see someone I've been friends with for thirty years in that state. But now everything's arranged. It was time Jean-Baptiste took over!'

'Jean-Baptiste?'

'Of course Jean-Baptiste. Until there's proof to the contrary, he's my only son!'

'But Édouard …'

'What?'

'Jean-Baptiste is dead!'

Édouard's face froze. His lower lip began to quiver and his eyes to blur. He turned his head towards the flat-roofed buildings with signboards on top which lined the road.

'Don't ever say that again, Thérèse.'

His good hand reached for Thérèse's and she took it. It was dry and cold, perhaps because of the air conditioning.

Thérèse had never travelled by plane. Airports were not like railway stations. Everything was cleaner, well looked after, hushed voices, a sort of hospital where people would just disappear without a trace, never die. Paradise was within arm's reach, no doubt because of the proximity of the sky. While waiting for Édouard, who had gone off somewhere, Thérèse watched the planes taking off for Bangkok, Rio de Janeiro, Toulouse, Milan, Lille, Strasbourg … The people you came across here weren't the same as those in the street. They smelled of elsewhere, wore different clothes, walked differently – more slowly, as if weightless. Here nothing was far away so you didn't hurry.

'Here, Thérèse, this is for you.'

Édouard was holding out a small bag embossed with the logo of a famous parfumier.

'You can open it on the plane. Let's hurry.'

Later, while Édouard was asleep with his head on her shoulder, she opened the package. It was a star-shaped bottle, filled with blue perfume. She sprayed a little on the back of her hand. It smelled of altitude, the blue sky above the clouds, a landscape she was discovering for the first time in her life.

'What are you doing, Thérèse?'

'Er … I'm making the bed.'

'You're making the bed. Would you like to do the washing-up as well, while you're about it? Let me remind you that we're in one of the most opulent hotels in Geneva.'

Thérèse blushed. She hadn't been able to resist. She liked making the bed in the morning and to tell the truth she wouldn't have objected to the washing-up either. Having been up since six, after washing and dressing as unobtrusively as possible she'd had nothing else to do, and ensconced herself on the balcony between two big ornamental vases, eventually feeling like one of them herself, until room service had arrived with breakfast.

'Leave it, I'll see to it. Monsieur is still asleep.'

The waiter, accustomed to fantasies of love affairs with servants, had given her a conspiratorial wink, which shocked her deeply.

'I'm sorry, Édouard. I can't just do nothing. It makes me feel …'

'Helpless?'

'A bit.'

'Wealth always does that to begin with, and then you get used to it.'

'I don't think I will.'

'Now put your jacket on, we're going out. You want things to do, you shall have them.'

The morning's shopping was a veritable Way of the Cross for Thérèse. They visited an incredible number of boutiques, each more luxurious than the last, and each time Thérèse came away more humiliated. As soon as she entered, even the most junior salesgirl would look her up and down, shooting her a contemptuous glance which made her even more gauche, stupid and inarticulate. She felt dirty, ugly and out of place, and if Édouard had not made all the decisions for her she would, from shame, have rushed to throw herself in the lake with a stone around her neck.

'Well, Thérèse, do you like this dress? Would you like to try another size?'

'No, no, it's fine.'

In the intimacy of the final fitting-room cubicle she dissolved into tears before her grotesque reflection. Never had she felt so miserable.

'Right, now you need a handbag. Hermès is just next door.'

'Please, Édouard, I'd like to go back to the hotel. I don't feel well.'

'Already? True, it's nearly one o'clock. Let's go for lunch. We still have the whole afternoon ahead of us.'

It was nice on the terrace. There was a cool breeze from the lake. The fillets of perch were excellent, the service impeccable, yet it was as if something like an imperceptible odour of putrefaction hung over this perfect world, accompanied by a worrying ticking sound. It was probably coming from Lake Geneva, the dull beat of an army on the march. It was as if all the clocks and all the watches had agreed to start an inexorable countdown which made you await with terror the imminent alarm bell announcing the attack.

'Dessert?'

'No! Thank you. Excuse me, Édouard, I don't feel very well. I'm going back to our room.'

'Do. I'll join you in a minute.'

Thérèse made her way unsteadily across the restaurant terrace, among the mummies with their clinking jewellery and shrill laughter, their skeletons jerking like miserable puppets. Their plasterwork make-up was flaking off, and underneath there was nothing, nothing but dry, white bone.

The room was littered with the packages Édouard had had delivered. It looked like Christmas gone wrong. She collapsed onto the bed and took refuge in sleep, her cheeks glazed with tears, the source of which she would have been unable to identify.

Tiny white yachts were racing one another on the blue waters of the lake, delicate angel feathers scattered by the whistle of a ferry as it returned to the landing stage. On the right, the proud water jet plumed over the city, lending an iridescence to the view of the mountains, but Monsieur Lavenant only had eyes for the magnificent pair of yellow Westons he had bought himself. Squeezed into the cane armchair on the balcony, legs outstretched, he banged them together. They reminded him of a pair of ducks. He would probably never wear them. They were simply beautiful, like Cécile … He had wanted her and he had got her, solely for the pleasure of snaffling her from the pack of suitors who trailed after her with their tongues hanging out. It was as stupid as that. Cécile was a two-way mirror through which he could enjoy the ever-recurring spectacle of others' covetousness, of the thousand and one base deeds motivated by the desire to possess what one hasn't got. If they had only known, poor things …

Monsieur Lavenant glanced over his shoulder. Thérèse was still asleep, one hand beneath her cheek, her presence confirmed by gentle snoring. It was reassuring.

'I could get some bread while I'm about it …' Édouard couldn't get the little phrase overheard in the street that morning out of his head. A man talking to himself outside a bakery. A phrase necessitating no metaphysical dissection, but which, unlike the many others one feels compelled to fill with sense, had the merit of saying what it meant. "I wasn't thinking of it, but since I have no bread left and I'm outside a bakery, I might as well get some bread." Contained in these simple words was all the good sense of humankind, which ensures we are still alive, standing, humble and irrefutable. The same good sense, no doubt, which had moved Thérèse to make the bed.

Make your bed and lie in it.

Ill-gotten gains profit no one.

Once a thief …

Slow and steady …

The pitcher goes to the well so often …

A never-ending list of ridiculous proverbs appeared before his eyes, like driving-school slides showing improbable scenarios.

'I've had it up to here with good sense! What the hell's she doing – is she dead or something?'

He flushed the loo several times without closing the door. Thérèse raised one eyelid, like a monitor lizard.

'What time is it?'

'Time to go for an ice cream.'

Her new natural-linen dress let the air through so deliciously that Thérèse blushed, as if she were out walking naked. By contrast, the too tight straps of her gold sandals were cruelly wounding her swollen feet. Édouard was wearing a suit that matched her dress and his yellow shoes captured the sun's rays beautifully. The two were like a team of horses. A couple of sickly-looking joggers in matching tracksuits ran past them, each on the verge of a heart attack.

'Have you noticed that old couples dress the same? Such a lack of taste!'

Quai Wilson, Quai du Mont-Blanc … To rest their feet, which were killing them though they didn't say anything to each other, they stopped for a moment in front of the statue of Empress Sissi, sited at the spot where she is supposed to have been stabbed by an Italian anarchist. Thérèse found it disappointing.

'She doesn't look like Romy Schneider.'

And in fact the unpleasant bronze sculpture was more reminiscent of the horrible bunches of gladioli people give their mothers-in-law at Sunday lunchtimes than of the legendary actress's graceful outline.

'Do you know, she didn't notice anything at the time, a punch at most. She and her lady-in-waiting got into the boat and it was only in the cabin that she knew she was mortally wounded. How many of us are in that same situation, believing they're still alive when they're dead? It's a mystery. One acts as if … And it works!'

They chose to have their ice cream at the Bains des Pâquis, a bathing place created by building out into the lake. Access was by a raised wooden walkway which gave you the impression of stepping onto the deck of a ship. The architecture of the rows of changing cubicles separated by duckboard pathways must have dated from the early twentieth century. It exuded an old-fashioned charm which the reggae music coming from the bar could not dispel.

The naked bodies of young Adonises glistening with sun-tan oil mingled uninhibitedly with the three-piece suits of respectable bankers, and mothers chasing after their shrieking offspring. Some were cruising, others having tea in the most civilised manner. Thérèse and Monsieur Lavenant took the table furthest from the bar, because of the music.

'This need for music all the time is crazy! It's everywhere: in shops, in the street, even in the hotel toilets! What's so frightening about silence?'

They ordered ice creams with exotic names, which turned out just to be scoops of vanilla and chocolate hidden under a layer of grated coconut. Opposite them, imperturbable, the water jet kept up its insolent ejaculation. Out of the corner of her eye, while she sucked her spoon, Thérèse stole furtive glimpses at the perfectly tanned youths brushing against each other suggestively, without eliciting the slightest disapproval from the worthy citizens.

'Honestly, really ...'

'Honestly what?'

'But ... See for yourself!'

'What is there to see?'

'Those youths there ... they're that way inclined ... In front of all those children. Honestly ...'

'What's it to you? At least that lot don't reproduce, that's something. Tomorrow we'll begin our search for a chalet to rent, as high up and remote as possible.'

'Oh, yes! I admit I feel out of place here. Édouard?'

'What?'

'There's a man looking at you very intently.'

'A man? Where?'

'Over there, leaning on the bar. It's funny ... he could be you ... He's coming over!'

Against the light Édouard could not make out the man's features, but the silhouette seemed familiar.

'Excuse me, are you by any chance Édouard Lavenant?'

Now the man was leaning over the table, his face appeared as plainly as his own reflection in a mirror. Except for the moustache, the close-cut hair, that sallow complexion and eyes with dark rings like two holes in an old pair of socks, this was his 'certified copy'.

'Jean!'

'Yes. Allow me to sit down – this is quite a shock. Forgive me, Madame, I haven't introduced myself. Jean Marissal, a very, very old friend of Édouard's. If I'd thought ...'

Thérèse had heard it said that everyone on earth has a double, but that two of them should be intimately acquainted seemed almost miraculous.

'How did you recognise me after so many years?'

'Oh, come, Édouard, how could I fail to recognise my own face?'

'Of course, that was stupid …'

It was when they had started their first year at the Lycée du Parc in Lyon that they had discovered this odd whim of nature. Although their surnames differed the teacher had seated them side by side like twins. Other than this incredible physical resemblance, however, they differed in every respect. Édouard came from what is known in Lyon as the hill that prays, Fourvières, and Jean from the hill that works, Croix-Rousse. Édouard was as reserved and studious a child as Jean was exuberant and mischievous, attracting attention from those around him wherever he went. Right from the start Édouard suffered horribly from the existence of his double, but Jean very quickly grasped the benefits to be gained from their extraordinary likeness. For over a year Édouard had, like Dr Jekyll, to put up with the dire consequences of Mr Hyde's misdeeds. It was during a science lesson where they were dissecting frogs that Édouard put an end to this unjust fate by gashing Jean's cheek with a scalpel. The punishment was severe but he accepted it unflinchingly, even with relief. Henceforth, no matter what happened, people would always be able to tell them apart. From that moment, Jean's attitude towards him changed radically, resulting not in a real friendship but in a sort of complicity which made them respect each other. They were nicknamed 'the Duellists'. Then when they reached adulthood life took them in different directions. Édouard carried on his father's business and Jean embarked on a career as an artist. They had never seen each other again. With the tip of his finger, Jean stroked his scar, almost invisible now, masked by wrinkles.

'I daren't count the years.'

'No point. What are you doing here?'

'It's a meeting place – as you can see. I lived in Morocco for a long time but the climate no longer suited my health. Since I work with galleries in Geneva, Basle and Lausanne, I settled here.'

'Are you still painting?'

'Let's say I exist now only by virtue of having existed. What about you? Are you here on business?'

'No, it's out of my hands now; that's the right expression for it!' Édouard raised his crippled arm, letting it fall back onto the table. 'A stroke, several months ago.'

'So you're here to convalesce, as it were.'

'You could say that.'

A young man with curly hair and eyes like a gazelle, dressed in a tight-fitting black T-shirt, laid his hand on Jean's shoulder and whispered a few words in his ear.

'No, not tonight, Mehdi. Another time. Yes, I'll call you. Where are you staying?'

'At the Bristol, but we won't be there for long. I'd like to rent a house far away from it all; I need quiet.'

'I know of some. I live right up in the mountains, half an hour from the city. Speaking of which, what are you doing this evening?'

'Nothing special.'

'Then why not come over? I've got a splendid view over the lake, and I'll bring you back after dinner. It will give me a chance to get to know Madame. You'll have to excuse us, this meeting was so unexpected ...'

'Not at all, I quite understand. We'd love to. What do you think, Édouard?'

'Why not?'

Thérèse had insisted on getting into the back, to give the two men a chance to reminisce, but neither of them seemed to want to take advantage of it. No doubt they needed some time to start up the time machine. The road looped round and sometimes your view plunged down to the mist-covered lake, sometimes your gaze came up against a phalanx of black pointed fir trees against a reddening sky.

The chalet was built on a rocky cliff, almost balancing on the top. A gap in the forest opened up a clear view over the lake; all that was visible of the opposite side were glimmering lights like fireflies, beyond which nothing else seemed real. Leaning on the balcony rail, Thérèse and Édouard silently drank in the peace of this majestic spectacle, which reminded them somewhat of the Rocher du Caire.

'This is exactly what we're looking for, a real eagle's nest.'

'You don't know how true that is. There are lots of them here. I spend hours watching them circling in the sky. Would you like a drink?'

Resinous scents wafted in through the wide-open picture window like incense. The living room where they drank champagne was vast and practically empty, minimally furnished with a table, sofa and, at the back of the room, a desk flanked by an armchair. Nothing on the walls, not one picture. The sole item of decoration was a sort of bronze wading bird some fifty centimetres tall, in a niche behind the sofa. It looked like a house someone was about to leave or had just moved into.

'It's a little bare but I love the space. I never have visitors. Before, I used to love objects. My house in Morocco was a veritable souk. I left everything behind. You change. With time, you prefer travelling light.'

'And it's easier to look after.'

'Exactly. You're quite right, Madame.'

Jean and Thérèse argued politely over who should make the

dinner, and Thérèse won. Wouldn't you expect two old friends to have some time on their own? But above all she felt an over-whelming need to be in a kitchen again, to handle pans, plates, cutlery and glasses, things she understood, which understood her and which she had missed dreadfully since their departure from Rémuzat. She had a connoisseur's appreciation for the cleanliness of the place, the simplicity and quality of the utensils and the practicality of the way things were arranged. It was surprising for a bachelor. Jean showed her where to find everything she might need and in less than five minutes she was going backwards and forwards between oven and fridge, as much at home as a goldfish in its bowl. She threw herself into making a rice salad with tuna.

It was a house like this that they needed, quiet, far away from everything, with, if possible, this magnificent view, which at every hour of the day would remind them of the peace and sweetness of life. She would furnish it differently, of course. You could bring a little more warmth to the pretty chalet: carpets, curtains, these little nothings which mean everything. Aside from his manner, which was rather precious for a man, Jean was a charming person, attentive, delicate. A little too much so. When he smiled, and he smiled often, there was an air of melancholy about him which made you want to throw yourself out of the window. Men on their own … If they could find a similar house somewhere nearby, Édouard and he would be able to see each other, exchange ideas, talk about the good old days. It would do them good … The sound of the timer dragged her from her daydreams; the eggs were done.

To be honest, Édouard was no keener than Jean was to bring up the good old days. What preoccupied them, though they didn't mention it even as they stole glances at each other, was not this chance present but their future, as brief as it was uncertain. Jean emptied the last of the bottle into their champagne glasses, before sliding a silver powder compact out of the coffee-table drawer.

'May I?'

It was filled with white powder. Using a razor blade, he made a line of it on the mirror on the inside of the lid and then inhaled it through a straw.

'Are you taking drugs?'

'I'm anaesthetising myself. Does that shock you?'

'No. At our age we all have our drugs.'

'Thérèse?'

'Thérèse isn't a drug.'

'Forgive me. She's charming, very ... unspoilt. From you, that astounds me. You were always keener on women who enhanced your worth.'

'Maybe I'm not worth much any more. You live here alone, then?'

'Solitary as a monk. When I have needs I go to the Bains des Pâquis, but that's less and less often now. I hadn't set foot there for six months. I was about to leave when I noticed you.'

'Aren't you afraid of problems?'

'What sort of problems? Oh, the powder, the boys? What do you think could happen to me now? Besides, this is Switzerland. If you have a bank account and make sure to cross at the crossing everything's allowed. Besides ... whatever I do I'm not risking a life sentence. You've seen the way I look, I'm already a condemned man. It's only a matter of days, hours ... I'm not even seeing my doctor any longer.'

'Are you frightened?'

'No, not really. It's a bit drawn out ...'

'And the painting?'

'I gave up a long time ago. You know, I've never been a great painter, an artist. I'm much too cowardly for that. Skilled

231

technically, no more than that; bogged down in formal beauty, and charm. I painted portraits my whole life without realising that, contrary to appearances, behind every man and every woman there was a human being. But tell me, what are you in search of here?'

'Another life.'

Jean's face lit up like a lantern and he started laughing, which almost choked him.

'Another life? Is that all? At your age, aren't you ashamed? Wasn't your own enough for you?'

'That wasn't my life. I'm firmly convinced it was a mistake. Anyway, I've hardly any of it left; I've erased it all. Apart from this arm, which I don't miss, I'm in excellent health and ready to start all over again.'

Jean appeared to be weighing him up like some curious object found in a junk shop.

'I believe you could ... Why not? You've no children?'

'What for?'

'True, what for? They're no use; people like us have no need to live on. And yet, sometimes, without intending to, you know, like with plants, you end up producing offshoots.'

'I've never had green fingers. I've killed artificial flowers before now.'

'You always were a dried-up old stick.'

'So? The desert's dry but that doesn't stop it being alive.'

'And going on and on for ever ... I know a bit about that, I've done it enough. All the same, Switzerland, for two old sods like us ...'

Jean's laughter was as false as his teeth. Between the two men was everything that separates the beginning from the end, an uncertain and illusive no man's land. Jean lay back on the sofa cushions, eyes closed and hands behind his head.

'One day – I must have been eighteen – my father asked me, "What are you going to do with your life?" I had no answer for him. And today if I ask myself what I've done with my life, I'm just as mute. What happened in the meantime?'

Dinner was light-hearted and convivial. In earlier days Jean had liked cooking. Thérèse and he exchanged recipes, tagine with prunes for *blanquette à l'ancienne*. The wine was excellent. Édouard rather overdid it so that by the cheese course he was beginning to nod into his plate. Only snatches of conversation reached him now, or even just words like *ksar*, *moucharabieh*, *medina* with which Jean spiced the stories of his travels. Occasionally, after a juicy anecdote, Thérèse's laugh made him jump before he sank back into the sweet torpor of a child who falls asleep at the table.

'Édouard? ... Édouard? I can't wake him. I'm embarrassed; he's not used to drinking so much.'

'Let him sleep, then. There's a guest room. You can spend the night here and I'll take you back tomorrow morning.'

'But what if he wakes up ... He'll be completely lost. Since his stroke his mind has gone blank at times ...'

'Don't worry about it. I'm an insomniac. You go to bed. I'll stay here beside him. When he wakes up I'll be with him.'

'That's very kind. It's awful, he won't accept ...'

'Being his age? Me neither. Don't worry about anything. The bedroom's at the end of the corridor, on the right, next to the bathroom. I've had a lovely evening.'

'So have I. Don't hesitate to ...'

'Goodnight.'

"'*Le héron au long bec emmanché d'un long cou …*" Well, Lavenant, I'm waiting for the next line – haven't you learned the text by heart? "The heron with a long beak …"'

Behind the sofa, the bronze bird was pointing its long sharp beak at Édouard. On each side its glass-paste eyes were peering into the darkness. Someone was murmuring at the other end of the room. Édouard propped himself up on one elbow. Jean was on the telephone, stooped over in the cone of light from a desk lamp.

'I can't speak louder, there's someone sleeping … No, it's not what you think. The past, nothing but the past. I'll tell you about it. What time did you say your plane was arriving on Wednesday? … Ten seventeen in the morning. I'll collect you … Did you find the catalogue at the Guggenheim Museum?'

Suddenly it was obvious to him. All that stood between Édouard and his new life was this alter ego, this ghostly double who was spluttering on the phone. By staring at him, he now saw Jean only as ectoplasm, a pallid shapeless form. There was no such thing as chance; matters were arranged with an implacable logic. Now he understood why Jean had led him here and why nature had made them both in the same mould. During dinner, Jean had, while speaking about his health, quoted a sentence: 'Death will catch me unawares, because I want it to.' Édouard grabbed the metal bird's feet and got up noiselessly.

234

He was in his stocking feet, something Thérèse had seen to, no doubt.

'Three years since we last met? ... Possibly ... I don't notice. Time stands still here; nothing ever happens ... Excuse me a second ... Édouard?'

The bird's beak went a good ten centimetres into Jean's forehead. He had the same incredulous expression as Jean-Baptiste when the root had come away in his hands before he toppled into the void. The receiver fell to the floor, emitting 'Hello's like the cries of a rat. Édouard crushed it with his heel. Jean's arms flailed about in the air before he fell backwards, taking the armchair with him. The wading bird embedded in his skull seemed to be slaking its thirst on the dark blood running from the wound. Édouard seized the cigarette which was burning away in the ashtray and took a long drag. It tasted of dust. It didn't take long for Thérèse to appear.

'What's going on? Oh, God!'

Hands clasped to her mouth, she fell to her knees in front of Jean's body, his legs still twitching convulsively. Édouard stood contemplating the scene reflected in the window. It was like one of those stupid depictions of the Descent from the Cross.

'What have you done?'

'It was suicide.'

'No! You've killed him. It's a crime!'

'Call it whatever you like.'

'You're insane! I'm calling the police.'

'The phone's not working.'

'But why? Why?'

'You couldn't understand. It's between him and me, a pact, an exchange. In any case he didn't have long to live.'

'But ... This isn't a natural death.'

'What does that mean, "natural death"? All deaths are natural or else it's death itself which isn't. Don't just stay there in front of that chair, shaking like a jelly! Do something ... well, I don't know what ... coffee, yes, make some coffee!'

Like an automaton she stood up and made her way to the kitchen. Édouard shrugged his shoulders. He was cold. As he went to fetch his jacket from the sofa he slipped on the pool of blood.

'Oh, it's disgusting! All that'll have to be cleaned up, do you hear me, Thérèse?'

The soil was loose at this spot in the garden, but despite all the strength in her arms it still took Thérèse almost two hours to dig a hole deep enough to lay Jean's body in.

'That should do, Thérèse. We'll bend him a little if need be. Get out of there – it's almost dawn.'

Somehow or other they managed to bundle their host into his last resting place and, after covering him with earth, planted various flowers, taken from their pots, here and there on top to form an attractive flower bed.

'It's as pretty as a roundabout. All it needs now is an old wine press.'

'I can't think how you still have the heart to laugh. What are we going to do now?'

'Move in, of course. We were looking for a house, we've found it. You like it, don't you?'

'That's not the point. Sooner or later someone's going to worry about Jean's disappearance.'

'But Jean hasn't disappeared. He's right here in front of you.'

'You're not going to tell me that …'

'Yes! Didn't he benefit from our amazing twinhood for a good part of my youth? It's my turn now. Believe me, I know him better than you do and he wouldn't hold this against me.'

'It's impossible!'

'No one's indispensable, you'll see. It's a second life I'm giving him. Put my jacket on, you'll catch a chill.'

The ribbons of mist were fraying on the tips of the pine trees. It was still too early to know whether it would be fine or not. What was certain was that a new day was dawning. A few skilful cuts from Thérèse's scissors and another man's face was appearing, with a towel knotted round his neck, in the bathroom mirror.

'The hair's fine but what about the moustache?'

'Let's say I shaved it off last night. It made me look old. Surely you're entitled to a change, aren't you? Or else I'll grow one.'

'And the scar?'

'A detail. Give me the razor.'

'Oh, no!'

'Give me the razor and clear off!'

What pain was there to fear since this face was no longer his own? With no hesitation and a steady hand Édouard gashed his cheek and indeed felt nothing but a sort of leaking, the hissing of a punctured tyre. Alcohol on the wound had the effect of an invigorating slap like the one they give new babies to give them a taste of life. Once he'd put a sticking plaster on, Édouard smiled at himself in the mirror.

'Bloody Jean, indestructible!'

Jean's style of dress was sporty but understated, clothes in good taste and of good quality. They might have been made to measure for Édouard except for the shoes: in contrast to him, Jean's left foot was bigger than the right. He struck some poses like a toreador in front of the wardrobe mirror then, satisfied, joined Thérèse.

'What do you think, then?'

'It's … It's truly amazing but …'

'But what?'

'The scar …'

'Yes?'

'You've got the wrong cheek.'

Mirrors are always playing tricks, but Édouard was unperturbed. Left, right, who would worry? For the moment other things were more pressing. They had to go to Geneva to retrieve their things from the hotel.

'Will you be able to drive this car?'

'It's an automatic; I don't know.'

'It's very simple: forward gear, reverse gear. Actually I should be able to manage it myself. Let me take the wheel.'

Thérèse wasn't entirely reassured but after a few kilometres she agreed that Édouard was acquitting himself very well. The gracefully negotiated bends followed one upon the other like the figures of an accomplished skater. The sun spread a gilded pollen in the air. There was a cassette in the car radio. Édouard pushed it in with the tip of his index finger. Berlioz's *Requiem* accompanied them in grand style right up to the Bristol.

Once the bill was paid and the luggage stowed in the boot, Édouard and Thérèse found themselves burdened with a completely new freedom. It was half past ten and the weather was glorious.

'What do you say to a drive along the lake? We could have lunch in Thonon or Évian.'

'If you like.'

There was little traffic, camper vans in the main, driven by retired couples in no hurry to arrive anywhere. On the left a signpost announced 'EXCENEVEX, MEDIEVAL TOWN OF FLOWERS'.

'Tempted, Thérèse?'

'Why not?'

All the car parks charged a fee, which made Édouard lose his temper. So they parked some distance from the centre in a place where it was free, near a campsite where elderly people plastered in sun lotion were getting some fresh air outside their caravans.

They found more of the same, only more suitably dressed, in the twisting narrow streets of the town. The women went into raptures over the window displays in the souvenir shops, while the men videoed the half-timbered balconies spewing torrents of geraniums. Every house was a business; everything was on sale: hand-knitted pullovers, sausages, cowbells, carved walking sticks, musical boxes shaped like chalets, handmade leather sandals, brightly coloured caps and T-shirts. The most unassuming little door claimed to be a '*crêperie*', a '*sandwicherie*', a '*friterie*' or an '*atelier d'art*'. The wrought-iron shop signs swung lazily in an asthmatic wind. As was proper, the visit to the town ended at the foot of a castle whose towers rose straight out of the lake. Happily there was no one at that spot. Thérèse and Édouard sat down on the flat polished stones which sloped down into the clear water. Ducks fluffed up their feathers, quacking. A woman dived off a yacht anchored a few metres out: 'Come on, Tony, it's lovely.' A silent aeroplane split the sky in two. In a room in the castle, someone was picking out notes on a piano, a clumsy approximation of a Chopin étude. Every sound ricocheted off the lake; the echo went on for ever. Thérèse seemed happy. Her gaze drifted over the smooth surface, far away, beyond the mountains in their turbans of wispy cloud.

'How peaceful it is …'

'Let's go and look for a restaurant, but not in this madhouse.'

'Édouard?'

'Yes?'

'What about having a picnic?'

They went to the shops in Thonon. The streets were heaving with a multicoloured and very noisy crowd, halfway between a village festival and a riot. Édouard had left the choice of menu to Thérèse. He was waiting for her in front of the delicatessen with a baguette under his arm, in the company of an ageless poodle with watery eyes. Pennants of various colours were strung across the street, flapping in the wind, and loudspeakers crackled unintelligible announcements between salsa tracks. Certain places are non-places and Thonon-les-Bains was one of them. Édouard was convinced that if he were to go round behind the façades of the houses he would find only wooden stays, like the ones used to support scenery on a film set. Ditto with the people who, from the front, couldn't be more than one centimetre deep. In October they must fold all that up, leaving Thonon no more than a name on the map. That said, Geneva and Lyon had made the same impression on him. Doubtless because he was no longer in the cast list for this bad film and was glad of it. He had only one desire, to get the hell out of there. In a gap in the crowd, his attention was caught by the shopfront of an outdated clothes shop: 'A. CARON, founded 1887'. Diagonally across the window was a banner with 'EVERYTHING MUST GO' written in red on a white background. Behind the sign, two headless mannequins, one tall and slim, the other small and stout, sported identical beige and blue sprigged dresses. The back of the shop was immersed in total darkness. Édouard couldn't help smiling when he recognised the two familiar figures, and touched his hat in greeting. Eventually Thérèse reappeared, hair all over the place, as if emerging from a gladiatorial combat.

'What a queue there was!'

'Let's get out of here.'

On their way out of the town, just past the Château Ripaille, they turned into a road at random. It led to the Gavot Plateau. The higher they climbed, the fewer houses there were and the easier it was to breathe. Just like locals, they went straight off along a little track lined with hazels which came out into an idyllic meadow argued over by sun and shadow. A wooden fence separated them from a field of piebald ponies, which ceased grazing to watch, wide-eyed, as the visitors sat down. After the bustle of the town, the infinitely peaceful sight of the animals charmed them. Édouard broke off a lump of bread and went over to the enclosure. A mare followed by her foal plodded over to meet him. Édouard stretched out his palm and stroked her nose. It felt hot and damp. A delicious smell of hay and leather was coming from her. The foal, like a bolster on top of two wobbly trestles, kept at a cautious distance. One by one the others came forward, as shy as they were intrigued. For a moment there was peace on earth, men, things and animals gathered together in the most perfect harmony. Édouard then made the mistake of throwing the piece of bread. Immediately the horses began fighting, biting one another, and of course the strongest came out on top.

'Load of idiots …'

'Édouard, it's ready!'

Thérèse was radiant, like a celluloid doll appearing out of a fake cabbage. She looked as if she had fallen out of the sky, her blue dress spread out like a parachute on the green grass. The shadow of the leaves gave her a little veil.

'You look magnificent, just like a Watteau. So, what's on the menu?'

The ponies had gone back to their grazing, as indifferent to them as they were to the rest of creation. Thérèse was brushing some crumbs off her lap. Édouard was lying on his back, picking his teeth with a blade of grass.

'Édouard?'

'Yes?'

'What are you thinking about?'

'Nothing. I'm looking for the ogre.'

'Ogre?'

'The one in children's puzzles. "The ogre is hiding in the tree. Can you find him?"'

'Have you found him?'

'There are so many.'

'Doesn't this remind you of something?'

'What, the ogres?'

'No, here, now ...'

'I give up.'

'The picnic at Nyons.'

'Oh, yes, indeed.'

'How far away that seems, another life. I don't really know where I am any more. I have the feeling of going from dream to nightmare with nothing in between.'

'The best way to avoid getting lost is not to know where you're going. I read that somewhere – it's true.'

'But ... Don't you feel any remorse?'

'No more than I feel regret. I'm alive and I'm sleepy.'

For some unknown reason the horses began to prance in the meadow, neighing. Édouard was already asleep, one arm covering his eyes. Thérèse stretched out next to him. A ladybird ventured onto her hand. 'Ladybird, will it be fine on Sunday?' The insect spread its glossy wings and flew away. It was Saturday.

It was quite beyond belief – how could strapping great lads like that flaunt themselves in that sort of outfit, striking poses that were downright ... Thérèse tried to find the appropriate adjective, then, having failed, shut the body-building magazine and put it back in the pile she'd taken it from. She knew that type of publication existed but she'd never had a look at one before. They didn't seem like Jean's sort of thing. Of course his slightly too fastidious manners, along with the place they had met him, left little doubt as to his tendencies, and she wasn't shocked. But 'that' was vulgar, just one step better than an advertisement for Boucherie Bernard. How can you tell with people? One side of the wall is always in the shade. She wondered what hers might be like, where her place in the shadow was and what vice might be lurking there. There were ten thousand or none at all. It was like when she was a little girl going to confession. She had been obliged to invent sins for herself, out of fear that if she had nothing to ask pardon for, people would suspect her of concealing horrors. Hatred and jealousy were foreign to her; she had never envied anybody anything, nor harmed anyone. She didn't consider herself a saint but it had to be admitted that the sum of her sins would not weigh very heavily in the scales at the Last Judgement. She wasn't proud of this, merely astonished. In this respect she wasn't exactly like everyone else, and had sometimes suffered for it, as if it were a sort of character flaw. That said, she was still complicit in a murder. Two days before, she'd been digging a grave in the dead of night and burying the body of a man she'd known for only a few hours. She was aware of this, without managing entirely to believe it. Life had resumed its course, as peaceful and serene as at Rémuzat before Jean-Baptiste's arrival. Only the scenery had changed; eagles had replaced vultures. It was nice on the balcony; it smelled of wood and hot pine resin.

'Well, Thérèse, getting a tan? Here's the mail – I ran into the postman.'

'The postman?'

'At the end of the track. It was "Bonjour, M'sieur Marissal. Lovely weather!" We talked about this and that. He's a very pleasant young man.'

'He didn't …'

'Not for one second. Let's see … Bank statement … advert … advert … and a body-building magazine. Nothing very interesting.'

'It's not right to open his mail.'

'Why not? He's got nothing to hide any more, neither the state of his bank account – which, by the way, seems satisfactory – nor his little foibles. And stop talking about him; you'll give me a split personality. I'm Jean Marissal and I'm even going to start painting again.'

'You?'

'Of course. At the end of his life Monet was painting with two stumps, and I've still got one good arm. The studio's never been used – there's not a spot of paint, nor the slightest whiff of turpentine. That poor Jean's latest canvases are painful to look at. Nothing but portraits of children – star pupils, not a hair out of place, absolutely perfect in their execution but quite devoid of emotion. An orphans' gallery! I can see why he stopped doing it altogether. Have you seen them?'

'No, I've not been downstairs.'

'Good God, Thérèse, own the place, fill the space. Get out of your kitchen and your laundry room, broaden your horizons!'

'I will, I'll go. What do you want for lunch?'

Édouard wondered which annoyed him more, the strands of air-dried beef stuck between two of his teeth or Thérèse's extraordinarily apathetic reaction to their new situation. What would it take before the umbilical cord keeping her on a leash from the larder to the balcony, from the balcony to the laundry, broke? Enough had happened since he'd taken her on: a son gobbled up by vultures, a significant inheritance, a brand-new wardrobe, a Swiss chalet rid of its owner ... Damn it! What was wrong with the fat cow? But no, even on tiptoe a dwarf is still a dwarf.

The tiny bit of meat exploded onto the balcony rail, as if shot out through a pea-shooter. Thérèse was sleeping peacefully, mouth half open, snoring gently, her chubby hands with their palms like cats' pads turned up to the sky on the lounger's armrests, her legs stretched out, feet turned inwards ... 'Fat cow,' he repeated through clenched teeth, but with all the candour of a child encountering a fat cow for the first time.

As he got up from the wicker chair he could not have said which of them creaked more. The sky was paved with clouds; there was no one up there any more. The great puppetmaster had let go of the strings. Even the trees were sagging.

The big empty room frightened him. The silence especially, nibbled by the mandibles of unidentifiable insects. In Switzerland time seems slow but it's just an illusion. An implacable stopwatch has it on a leash and every last second is counted, stored, recorded. There nothing is left to chance because chance has been bought as well. No risks are taken. Lake Geneva will never flood.

Édouard sat down behind the desk, drummed his fingers on

the green morocco-leather blotter and began opening the drawers. The first held nothing but boring paperwork – receipts, insurance policies, chequebooks – all of it in a total mess. Clearly Jean was no longer keeping on top of things, just letting them pile up. Most of the envelopes hadn't even been opened. The second contained a small nickel-plated 6.35-calibre revolver with a mother-of-pearl handle, and a dozen unremarkable photos, taken in Morocco no doubt – palm groves, ochre mud buildings, red sand dunes. Jean figured only in the last one, along with a tanned young blonde girl who was smiling broadly into the lens. She had her arm round Jean's waist and was resting her head on his shoulder. His arms were folded across his chest, and he stood stiff as a post, screwing up his eyes, grimacing. They seemed to be in the middle of nowhere, white ground and uniformly blue sky. The desert perhaps? The print had been torn and stuck together again with sticky tape. It must go back a number of years. Jean didn't yet have the look of a dead man. The third drawer was locked. Édouard forced it, using a paperknife in the shape of a salamander with the blade as its tail. Strangely all he found there was a bent paper clip. Evidently Jean had had a clear-out and wiped the slate clean where his past was concerned. Apart from Édouard's visit, he could no longer have been expecting much from life and had left the place in the state in which he had found it on moving in. Édouard was grateful for his consideration, which allowed him to assume Jean's identity without burdening himself with his memory. He then spent a good hour imitating his signature for no particular reason, the way you kill time in the dentist's waiting room by doing a crossword.

Thérèse woke up lying sideways, with sunburn on her left cheek. She had never in her life been drunk but this siesta gave her a vague idea of what a hangover might be like. It was because of that stupid dream in which she and Édouard were flushing eagles out of burrows, a dark labyrinth which smelled of soil and hen droppings. They were moving around on all fours, their mouths and nostrils full of feathers, their hands and knees crushing eggs which groaned. Édouard was going ahead of her like a furious mole: 'And another one!' Dreams were stupid, so stupid that you ended up believing them.

With furred-up mouth, unsteady on her feet, she took refuge in the kitchen and swallowed two big glasses of water one after the other. The clock said five. It was still too early to start cooking but she needed to occupy her hands in order to rid herself of her head. Not much was left in the fridge or cupboards – a few potatoes, some shallots, a pack of smoked herring. She plunged the potatoes into a pan of salted water, staring at it until it came to the boil. Then she chopped the shallots as finely as possible to make it take longer. As long as her hands were doing something, nothing could happen to her. What little good sense she still had lived in her ten reddened fingers with their broken nails. She didn't want to think about anything any more, anything at all. If Édouard had arrived unexpectedly she could have stuck the vegetable peeler into his throat without batting an eyelid. Frightened by this sudden upsurge of violence, she let go of the knife and collapsed onto a chair, arms hanging by her sides. 'I'm going mad as well now ...'

During his schooldays Édouard had many a time used his talents as a forger to get his schoolmates out of a jam – school reports, absence notes – always in return for a reward of course. Jean himself had called on his services. By now Édouard could imitate his signature with his eyes closed – a merely stylistic exercise, because in no way was he thinking of emptying the dead man's bank account. What would he have done with it? He was richer than him. It was a way of putting himself in the character's skin, unless it was the other way round ... Let's just say that they were currently proceeding hand in hand. He crumpled up the scribbled pages and threw them into the wastepaper basket. It was as he was straightening up again that his eye fell on the little silver box Jean had sniffed the powder from on their first evening. He opened it, licked the tip of his finger and tasted it. It was bitter, like all medicines. Closing it again, he automatically pocketed it before going downstairs to the studio.

As the house was built on the side of a hill, the studio, like the ground floor, benefited from a large picture window through which light poured in. An armchair, a sofa, a large Godin stove and an enormous studio easel that was like some medieval instrument of torture made up the furniture. Édouard pulled out one of the dozen canvases stacked with their faces to the wall, and placed it on the easel. It depicted someone near life-size, a young woman or a young man, you couldn't really tell, seen from behind, head turned, appearing to look over their shoulder. Édouard uncorked a bottle of turpentine and soaked a rag in it. At school he had always volunteered to clean the blackboard. Verb tables, divisions, multiplications, date and moral for the day would disappear as he wiped, and soon there remained on the black surface only a tangle of large figures of eight, dripping with milky water which dried in patches. Yesterday turned into tomorrow, a single day always starting afresh, eternity in the everyday. His arm had instinctively rediscovered this windscreen-wiper movement and little by little the adolescent face disappeared, making way for a strange landscape in which the colours ran together according to the fickle rules of chance. Édouard was triumphant, intoxicated by the solvent fumes and the certainty of having opened the door which had been shut in Jean's face.

'Form is limitation, poor old Jean, form is imitation! Vanity, nothing more! Outlines are confines, the sky has no angles! The body is unstable, that's why it's survived!'

Gripped by a frenzy worthy of Bernard Palissy burning his furniture as his wife looked on in terror, Édouard gave three or four other paintings the same treatment, before Thérèse arrived.

'What are you doing, all covered in paint? You're behaving like a madman!'

'Look, Thérèse, look! That's astonished you, eh?'

'That doesn't look like anything, all those daubings.'

'Exactly! Exactly.'

'You really have no respect for anything …'

'But you don't understand. It's the opposite – I'm carrying on his work, going where he was never able to go because he was so trammelled by his knowledge … I'm un-teaching him, that's it … Un-teaching him!'

'Lovely paintings like that … Right, go and wash your hands, it's ready.'

Thérèse's reaction in no way dented Édouard's morale. A good many artists before him had suffered the incomprehension of those around them. However, as he sat down to eat he reproached her for not cooking him something hot.

'Don't you like my herring salad?'

'I do, but I'd have preferred soup, a nice soup. You make such good ones.'

'For that I'd need something to make it with. There's nothing here but tinned food.'

'Tomorrow we'll go shopping. Speaking of which, what day is it?'

'Tuesday.'

'Then tomorrow's Wednesday … Wednesday … We've nothing planned for Wednesday?'

'What would we have planned?'

'I don't know … It seemed to me … Pah … I'd like a little more, please, I'm as hungry as a wolf. What's wrong now, Thérèse? You've got ever such a long face.'

'I can't do it!'

'Do what?'

'Get used to the idea that we're murderers!'

She collapsed sobbing on the edge of the table. Édouard was stunned. It was all so simple, so obvious …

'Come now, Thérèse, my dear …'

He stood up and took her in his arms, gently patting her on the shoulder.

'You're too emotional. Give yourself up to the great happiness we've been given.'

She put her arms round his waist, her head nestling against his stomach.

'If that were true, there's nothing I'd like better … Why did you do it?'

'You don't get something for nothing.'

'But you're not short of money – we could have rented a house.'

'This was the one, there wasn't any other one. I knew it as soon as I set foot here. And Jean knew that too.'

'What would you know about that?'

'I know because I am him. Now stop your moaning, enter into the game and play your part, for goodness' sake. You'll never have a better one. Stop looking over your shoulder, there's no one following you. You're like me and Jean, you have no past. Who's going to weep for us? You're giving us too much importance.'

The night was pitch-dark, an immense sky, like a cavern. Billions of stars speckled the picture window, indifferent to the unaccustomed sight of a hysterical old man daubing solvent onto warped canvases in the company of a woman flat out on a sofa, both of them bathed in a jelly of white light.

'You see, Thérèse, literature wasn't made for me – too complicated, too ambiguous, too many words, mere soap bubbles! Whereas painting, it's concrete, material, sensual, real! Am I right?'

Thérèse had no opinion on the subject, nor on any other. She was floating, her whole being absorbed by the supreme power of the white powder which Édouard had made her sniff.

'What is it?'

'A medicine. It's very good for what you've got. Close one nostril and breathe in very deeply.'

'Is this a drug?'

'Go on, for heaven's sake.'

Thérèse wasn't fooled but had succumbed to the powerful need to rid herself at all costs of the anguish which held her captive. It was like an atomic mushroom exploding in her head, an orgasm

252

which sent her off into unimaginable spheres from which she descended gently, as if with the aid of a parachute, to land, ecstatic, on this sofa as soft as a cushion filled with rose petals. She had administered morphine to terminally ill patients in the final stages and now she recalled how their faces were transformed, the pain slipping away, forming a kind of halo … Now she understood. Death was nothing, nor was life … But survival! Édouard had taken some as well but the product didn't have the same effect on him … He was gesticulating non-stop, arguing with himself as he rubbed the solvent-soaked rag over Jean's canvases and, she had to admit, allowed much richer forms and colours to come through than those originally depicted by the painting.

'Making a white rabbit come out of a hat, that's a conjuring trick; anyone can do that, but drawing a hat out of a white rabbit, that's real magic! Do you grasp the distinction, Thérèse?'

Thérèse couldn't have cared less. Her eyelids were growing heavy and she felt better than ever. The persistent smell of petrol proved that paradise was nothing but a huge garage, and on this certainty she sank voluptuously into the most perfect no man's land.

Édouard had taken hold of another canvas, which showed a young Adonis reclining at the foot of an oak tree. The rag went to work again but unlike the other paintings the bland image was hiding another: two ladies, standing, identically clothed in the same pale dress with a blue pattern, the smaller afflicted by a divergent squint and the other straight as a letter i with its dot disappearing under a vault of shade. Édouard burst out laughing: 'You're indefatigable! I wish you good evening, Mesdames. Make yourselves at home.'

Édouard could have slept for no more than a couple of hours yet he felt on top form, fresh as a daisy, with such an appetite for life.

Thérèse was still sleeping, rolled up in a cocoon of sheets and covers.

'Well now, Thérèse, wake up! It's almost ten o'clock. We've got shopping to do.'

On automatic pilot she took her shower, swallowed a bowl of coffee and, without knowing quite how, found herself at the steering wheel.

'I'm driving?'

'You've got to start. Imagine if something were to happen to me. I may be immortal but no one is proof against a bad cold. It's child's play, you'll see.'

And indeed, despite swerving a few times starting off, Thérèse soon felt as much at ease as on the sofa where she had spent the evening. She was not to exceed 60 kmh. The effects of the drug she'd taken the evening before were still there and her head lurched this way and that like a jar full of a thick, sweet liquid.

'How are you feeling?'

'Well, very well … A little woozy. But fine.'

'That stuff's amazing, isn't it?'

'Yes.'

'No wonder young people take drugs.'

They burst out laughing like a couple of kids hiding behind a curtain.

They made some random purchases in the village minimarket, where Monsieur Marissal was greeted very deferentially, which sent them into a new fit of uncontrollable giggles. Nothing was real, everything was allowed. On the way back they listened to the radio news. A footballer had just been bought by a club for some incredible sum, and a husband and father, unemployed and crippled with debt, had just wiped out his family before killing himself in a bungalow in the Pas-de-Calais region. A storm was expected in the evening, and traffic jams on roads out of Lyon. It was a perfect world.

Someone was waiting for them outside the door, a tall blonde girl who rushed towards them as soon as they had parked.

'Where have you been, Papa? You were supposed to collect me from the airport.'

Like two insects in amber, Thérèse and Édouard stared dumb-struck at the bizarre apparition framed by the car window. The girl must have been twenty-five or thirty years old, with clear skin and glossy hair, not unattractive, although her teeth seemed slightly too big for her mouth. Her features vaguely reminded Édouard of someone.

'I tried to call you but your phone's out of order.'

Édouard drew his hand over his face like an actor pulling on his mask. The girl, good God, the girl! In a split second he identified her: she was the one in the photo which had been torn and stuck together again, now a few years older.

'I'm sorry, my dear, I completely forgot. I worked all night. Have you been waiting long?'

'The taxi dropped me off half an hour ago. I was beginning to worry ...'

'I'm really sorry ... Thérèse, let me introduce my daughter ...'

The young woman got him out of an awkward situation by introducing herself, offering her hand through the window.

'Sharon.'

'Delighted to meet you. Go ahead, Monsieur Jean, I'll see to the shopping.'

Édouard dragged himself from the car and let himself be kissed on both cheeks.

'Have you shaved your moustache off? It makes you look younger. You seem on top form. So this is where you live? It's magnificent but, my God, it's isolated! The taxi driver had a hell of a time finding it. "Low Heights", what a funny name.'

'Did you have a good journey?'

'I almost missed the plane in New York thanks to Gladys. In the space of a week I only ever saw her in passing, then at the last moment she remembered I was there. But you know her …'

'Of course, yes.'

Édouard was getting flustered with the lock. He couldn't find the right key among the bunch.

'What's wrong with your arm? Have you hurt it?'

'Nothing. No, I … I had a stroke a few months ago. Paralysis of the left side. Everything's fine now except for this arm.'

'Why didn't you say anything?'

'Old people's stuff, no one's interested. I can manage, I tell you. There, go in.'

Immediately they were inside, a furious desire to shove the girl into the cupboard under the stairs and double-lock the bolt came into his head. CLICK CLACK! Jean's offspring out of the way; out of sight, out of mind the girl with the big teeth – good riddance! But she was already making her way into the sitting room.

'Lovely space! You must feel lost, all alone in here?'

'I'm not alone.'

'True. And who is Thérèse?'

'My nurse. To begin with I couldn't do much on my own. She still helps me a lot. Plus she's excellent company.'

'It's still strange for me to see you with a woman.'

'There was your mother, you know!'

'Gladys isn't a mother or a woman, you know that as well as I do.'

'Yes, all right. Do you want me to show you to your room? You'd no doubt like to freshen up.'

'I would, yes.'

In the kitchen Thérèse was weeping hot tears over a heap of thinly sliced onions.

'What are you making?'

'*Gratinée à l'oignon*. You wanted soup so I'm making soup.'

'But … that's a very good idea.'

'What is she doing?'

'Taking a shower.'

'I told you this would end badly.'

The blade of the knife rammed into the chopping board vibrated like a tuning fork. The tears reddening Thérèse's eyes were not just from peeling onions. Édouard shrugged his shoulders, fiddling with a packet of grated Gruyère.

'I can't help it if I've got a big family.'

Sharon gave the plastic shower curtain a sharp tug, heart pounding. Of course there was no old woman hiding behind it, brandishing a butcher's knife. She stuck her tongue out at her reflection in the mirror and rubbed herself vigorously, without, however, being able to banish the strange unease which had gripped her since she'd been reunited with her father. It was stupid but she didn't recognise him. It was him and yet not him. It wasn't to do with the absence of his moustache any more than with his disability, nor the fact that she hadn't seen him for almost three years. It was something else – the stiff, staccato way he moved and his voice which crunched words like glass. Maybe the stroke had changed him ... But when it came down to it, how well did she really know him anyway? In twenty-seven years of existence she had crossed paths with him only five or six times. Until she was eighteen Gladys had let her believe that he was dead. If it hadn't been for that fortuitous encounter at a private view at a New York gallery she would never have suspected his existence. He had been as surprised as she was since her bitch of a mother had never informed him of her birth. One month later, free of her mother's authority, she joined him in Morocco where he was living at that time. He hadn't been against her coming and had shown himself full of goodwill and consideration towards her, but she had quickly understood that there was no place for an eighteen-year-old girl in the life he was leading. The drugs and the young boys took up too much space. She hadn't resented him for it and had led her own life, while staying in regular contact with him by post or telephone, or by meeting up with him here or there, in London, Paris or Berlin, wherever fate brought them together. They had never spent more than four or five days together, just enough time to share superficial pleasures and take leave of each other awkwardly on a station platform or in an airport waiting area. Their relationship was difficult to define. Love had never had time to blossom but the sporadic meetings had ended up creating a tender complicity between them as if they shared a secret, though neither of them knew what that secret was. Perhaps it was just an irrepressible attraction to the void? She had known he was ill for several years, which was why he had left Morocco for Switzerland, but this stroke did not tally with the usual symptoms of the virus he had. Apart from the bent arm he appeared to be in perfect health. If that hag Gladys had not refused her the five thousand dollars she needed to open her interior design studio she would never have made the journey here, such was her fear of illness and death. Only the lease had to be signed in two days' time and this was her only option.

Having blasted her hair dry until she had restored its full bounce, she put on a T-shirt, a clean pair of jeans and some trainers and left her room, sticking her chest out like a boxer making for the ring.

Édouard was waiting for her on the balcony, a cardigan over his shoulders, at a low table with several bottles of alcohol lined up on it. He seemed older than he had just before.

'Here, the Guggenheim catalogue you asked me to get.'

'Thank you, Sharon. What will you have?'

'The usual.'

Édouard hesitated. There was Scotch, vodka and white Martini. He reached for the last.

'With an olive.'

'Of course, I haven't forgotten.'

He served her and began leafing through the catalogue.

'You've started working again, then? From what you'd told me, I thought there was no question of that.'

'Let's call it a relapse.'

'Will you show me?'

'If you like, but it's still at the sketch stage. To you, then!'

'To us! … What, are you drinking whisky now?'

'At my age you can't taste anything or else you like everything, which comes to the same thing.'

The clink of ice cubes answered the rumbling of the storm which was announcing its arrival by sending thick clouds scudding over the lake.

'Isn't Thérèse joining us for a drink?'

'She's coming. She's a little shy. We live like bears in a cave here. Do you like onion soup?'

'I'll never forget the one we ate together the last time we saw each other, at the Pied du Cochon in Les Halles in Paris. Do you remember?'

'Of course, what an evening!'

A blast of infernal heat made Thérèse take a step backwards when she opened the oven door. The layer of golden Gruyère was rising, letting out little jets of steam, each bowl like a mini volcano. On the table the apple and walnut salad sat alongside the cheese platter. All that was missing was the guests. Thérèse wiped her eyes with a corner of her apron, a ridiculous apron made to look like the torso of a woman wearing a bra and sexy knickers. There weren't any others. Thérèse could put off no longer the inevitable confrontation with the girl who had appeared from goodness knows where. She wasn't the one from whom a blunder was to be feared, because after all she wasn't supposed to know of Sharon's existence, but rather it was

Édouard. The high-wire act on which he had embarked, without even the flimsiest safety net, was making her panic. He reminded her of the tarot card, the Fool, depicting a vagabond with his head in the air and a meagre bundle on his shoulder, one foot poised over a void, and a dog hanging on his coat-tails. No matter how crafty or diabolically cool-headed he was, some day or other he would end up falling into the void, and this girl, this Sharon, was the void. That was visible in her excessively blue eyes, like two small bottomless lakes. For the first time in her life she felt hatred towards someone and was horrified by this. She jumped as if she'd been caught in the act of an evil thought when Édouard called her.

'Aren't you joining us for a drink, Thérèse?'

'No, thank you.'

'So it's ready, is it? Can we eat?'

'Er ... yes.'

The soup was scalding but delicious accompanied by an excellent white wine of which Édouard, to Thérèse's relief, partook in moderation. Contrary to her fears he was behaving like a worthy patriarch, sober and sparing in his words. As Thérèse was no more talkative than Édouard, the responsibility of making conversation fell on Sharon. Once the anecdotes about the crazy life people led in New York and treacherous attacks on a certain Gladys, her mother, were over, they learned that Sharon had been living in Munich for five years and was counting on opening an interior design studio there in the near future, with someone called Monica.

'Like I told you on the phone the other day, I've brought the file. You'll see, it's a gold mine! But we can talk about that later, can't we?'

'Whenever you like.'

Then, as nothing could top that, the conversation lapsed into more anodyne subjects like the weather forecast, the swift passage of time, the peaceful beauty of the Swiss landscape and, finally, the recipe for the onion soup. By coffee, absolute silence reigned over the cups and Édouard almost knocked his over by nodding off at the table.

'You'll have to forgive me, I need to rest for a little while. Wake me in an hour, Thérèse.'

'Of course, Éd— Monsieur Jean.'

To hide the confusion which was making her blush, Thérèse began clearing the table. Sharon did not appear to have noticed her slip. She was inspecting her chewed nails with a look of disgust.

'I've tried everything – lacquer, medication, therapy. I can't do anything about it; it's been like this ever since I was tiny.'

'You must have an anxious nature.'

'That's for sure. I wonder whether I get that from my mother or my father … While we're on the subject, Thérèse, how do you think my father is?'

'But … well. He's made a very good recovery. It's not out of the question that he might regain the use of his arm some day.'

'I didn't mean physically. Still, I have to admit I'm amazed to see him in such good health. AIDS doesn't usually regress like that.'

'AIDS?'

'You do know my father's HIV positive?'

'Yes, of course … But Monsieur Jean is someone of great courage, a real fighter.'

'That must have happened late in the day. The last time I spoke to him on the phone he seemed, well, resigned.'

'He has his ups and downs like everyone else.'

'No doubt. But even before he was ill I never saw him look like that, fierce, authoritarian. I don't know whether to be glad about it or frightened. It's as if he were possessed.'

'By who?'

'I don't know.'

'He's seriously ill; seriously ill people are always unpredictable.'

'Yes, I'm sure you're right. You know more about it than me. How long have you worked for him?'

'Nearly a year.'

'A year! Why has he never said anything to me about you?'

'I suppose he didn't want to worry you.'

'And he's never spoken about me to you?'

'Not in so many words. He's a very private man.'

'Very! But I'm bothering you with all my questions. I'm sorry, Thérèse, it's because I'm concerned about him.'

'That's only natural.'

'I think I'll have a short rest as well. See you later.'

Jean had AIDS! Of course, with the life he led, that emaciated body, the thin hair and the whole heap of medicines in the bathroom. Why hadn't Thérèse thought of it earlier? But she had never mixed with that kind of people. For her it was a young person's disease … And she didn't know any young people. She knew next to nothing about the disease, only what she'd heard on the TV and radio … Leprosy, the Black Death, she could have coped with them, but AIDS? How was she going to be able to answer Sharon's questions? Once she had rinsed the sink, Thérèse took off her rubber gloves and looked at her hands. They were redder perhaps than the young woman's, but in a better state. If her own nails were short it was because she cut them regularly every week for reasons of cleanliness. She had never bitten them, even at the most anxious moments of her life. She'd broken some, of course she had, scrubbing other people's toilets or scouring the bottoms of their saucepans, but she had never bitten them. They were strong, hard as horn. A pretty girl like that with such ugly hands, she must have been through some really tough times! She wasn't a bad kid, even if she did give herself airs, a little girl who'd put on her mother's high heels, that was all ... The concern she showed for her father was touching ... touching but really annoying.

Thérèse gripped the edge of the sink with both hands as if she wanted to pull it off.

'Oh, Édouard, lies are so complicated!'

The house whistled like an ageing lung. Outside, the wind prowled in search of cracks and already raindrops were splattering onto the picture window. Sharon had never liked mountains; they made her feel like listening to Wagner and she loathed Wagner. She disliked the house too, unless it was the other way round. All the empty, silent space was crushing her.

There was nothing in the desk drawers, nothing of interest except for the photo of herself and her father, torn and stuck together again, and a small women's pistol which she had put in her pocket after discovering in the wastepaper basket three crumpled pages covered in her father's signature, going progressively from the clumsiest to the most assured.

'Who are these people?'

The photo trembled in her hand. The rip was vertical as if someone had wanted to separate the two figures. Sharon had just turned eighteen and she was meeting her father for the second time. The snap had been taken the day after she arrived on the beach at Essaouira. A powerful wind was whipping up the sand, stinging her arms and legs like buckshot. As she huddled against her father for protection she had felt him stiffen. He said, 'I'm sorry,' in a strangled voice, the way people do when they bump into someone on the train. It had been Omar holding the camera, the son of the people who were renting the house to her father. She had been in love with him for the week of her visit. Unfortunately Omar preferred her father.

Sharon closed her eyes. Who was this man who was passing himself off as him? It was clear: in the photo the scar ran down the other cheek. It wasn't really fear that she felt, but a sort of stage fright. She found herself in the position of an actor who had been put on stage at the end of a play without knowing its denouement. No doubt she had a part to play in it, but which one? Murderer or victim?

It wouldn't be long now. The sky was chewing iron, sharpening its lightning bolts on the peaks of the mountains.

'Let it out, let it all out.'

At last his bladder let go and blissfully, eyes half closed, Édouard relieved himself before noticing, as he did up his flies, that he'd urinated on his wardrobe.

'Oh, shit! Well, if people keep changing the layout of the rooms all the time without telling me!'

Whose fault was it? Huh? Whose fault? That slattern Thérèse's, of course! You couldn't rely on her. Oh, she was very good at daydreaming in the kitchen. But when it came to informing him the toilet had been moved, she was useless! Useless! In any case, he didn't need anyone any more; he'd give her notice tomorrow and good riddance! Because he had work to do – he wasn't just an extra on this earth, he had a task to accomplish, something brilliant that had come to him in his sleep: the essence, get back to the essence of things … His previous night's work was just a preliminary; he had to rub, keep rubbing, right down to the canvas and beyond! And next … He could no longer remember but there was a next, he was sure of that …

He put on his yellow shoes without tying the laces and almost fell flat on his face on the staircase.

'Are you going through my drawers?'

'Oh, you're awake now? I was looking at our photo.'

'Which photo?'

'This one, at Essaouira.'

'Oh, yes. You haven't changed.'

'You have.'

'That's because old people age more quickly than young ones. That's nature, you can't do anything about it. I'm sorry, but I've got work … What's got into you?'

Sharon was aiming the little 6.35 at him.

'Who are you?'

'What d'you mean, who am I? Your damn fool of a father, that's who!'

Édouard and Sharon both jumped at the same moment. The lightning must have struck not far off. Édouard was the first to regain his composure.

'How much do you need?'

'You're not my father!'

'But what makes you think that?'

'The scar on your cheek, the three pages of practice signatures … And then your tone, your expression, the way you move, that energy! My father had AIDS, he was worn out. Damn it, I am his daughter, after all.'

'Oh, here we go, blood ties, family feeling, all nonsense. Enough, let's get this over with. You've come to get money out of me, that's the sole reason for your visit. Well, forget about the violins, how much do you want?'

'What have you done with him?'

'Aargh, she's so annoying! All right, then, he is dead, dead and buried. How much? You can double it.'

It was almost dark. Sharon put on the desk lamp. The pistol appeared fake in her hand, as harmless as a cigarette lighter. With her other hand she took a mobile phone out of her pocket.

'I'm calling the police.'

'We'll see. Do you think that thing's going to work round here in weather like this? He's dead, I tell you, stiff as a board and eaten by worms by now, like any self-respecting Christian. You've arrived too late, I'm afraid, but I can take his place very advantageously.'

'You killed him for his money?'

Édouard burst out laughing, slapping his thigh, and yet he didn't want to. Big Teeth was beginning to seriously rattle him He was going to squash her with the back of his hand like a gnat.

'Oh, my poor dear, I'm much richer than him. Go on, put that … thing down and we'll talk business. I'll leave you all his possessions and add half as much again for emotional collateral damage. How's that?'

'I don't know who you are but one thing I'm sure about is that you're utterly mad.'

'But your father was mad too. I knew him better than you did and for much longer. One father or another, for what you need him for, we won't quibble …'

'Murderer! I'm calling the police.'

They both screwed up their eyes as if looking into the flash in a photo booth. The lightning stopped time for just long enough to see Thérèse brandishing the bronze stork over Sharon's head.

'No! Don't do that, Thérèse!'

Édouard stretched out his arm, his hand open.

A gunshot rang out and Thérèse's menacing form vanished at the same time as the room sank into total darkness.

'The light, for God's sake, the light!'

Sharon's presence was evident now only from a poodle-like panting, which was answered by Thérèse's moans.

'Put the light on, damn it!'

'The power's gone.'

Édouard lit his cigarette lighter and got down on all fours beside Thérèse. She was lying on her back, eyes wide open, pink blood frothing at the corners of her mouth. The lighter flame was burning his fingers. He had to keep relighting it.

'There's a candle on the desk. Quick, give it to me!'

In the light from the flame, Thérèse appeared to be smiling: 'You were right, Édouard. It's not really that terrible … It happens so fast … I thought I was doing the right thing. I'm sorry about Sharon. I know you can't hear me, that my heart has stopped beating, that I'm dead. But I have no regrets, Édouard. I loved you, very much …'

'Is … is she dead?'

Édouard stood up, his face blank, devoid of all expression.

'When you shoot someone at point-blank range you have to envisage this kind of eventuality. You have just killed the most innocent of creatures.'

'But she was threatening me. It was self-defence!'

'Oh, please … This isn't the moment. Keep it for your lawyer and your judges. And put that gun down; you've done enough, don't you think?'

'No, you're going to kill me.'

'Are you completely stupid or something? What would I do with your body? I need your arms. There's a spade in the shed. They may not have known each other long but Thérèse and Jean seemed to get along well.'

'You're useless! Your omelette's foul. Thérèse had her faults but she never ruined an omelette. Besides, you're clumsy with everything. You managed to decapitate your father when you were digging the hole for Thérèse.'

'You're vile!'

'No. I like work done well. I've always been demanding with my employees, firm but fair.'

'I'm not your employee!'

'As good as. The choice is yours. Either I sign everything you want, the money's yours, and you can set up wherever you want, or we both get dragged into sordid legal proceedings. I would remind you that you have your whole life ahead of you and where I'm concerned my past has no future. Do you understand? I'll give you two hours to think about all that. The clock's ticking and your mobile is in your pocket. See you later.'

Édouard wasn't sleepy. It was nice walking among the pine trees. A subtle smell of mushrooms was coming from the undergrowth. A quilt of white mist still covered the lake. Édouard sat down on a rock. A bright-orange slug was nonchalantly moving among the bedewed blades of grass.

'You should have let me sort this business out on my own, Thérèse. I'd soon have got that kid to change her tune. I shall miss you. I already miss you.'

*

Sharon's bag was waiting in the hallway like an overweight dog. The taxi would be there any minute.

'You're really going to stay here?'

'Of course. I like it here. I liked it the moment I set foot in the place. This is my home. It's different for you, and it would be best if we never saw each other again. A regular cheque as we agreed, but nothing else.'

'Don't worry, I've no intention of coming back here.'

'Then all's well. Ah, there's your car.'

The Mercedes bumped along the track and drew up in front of them. The driver, a small stocky man with an exotic accent, greeted them and stowed the luggage in the boot while Édouard took Sharon in his arms.

'See you soon, my dear, take good care of yourself.'

'Murderer.'

'You too, you too ...'

The car turned round and disappeared behind the trees. Édouard rubbed his aching back and went to glance over the flower bed. Rhododendrons, maybe, or canna lilies? That would look classy ...

'Hello?'

'Monsieur Marissal?'

'Speaking.'

'I'm ringing about the advertisement, the live-in nurse.'

'Yes.'

'Well, I'm interested in it.'

'Do you have references?'

'Of course.'

'How old are you?'

'Forty-five.'

'That's very young.'

'Do you think so? Generally people find the opposite, that ...'

'It's not important. Aside from your professional skills can you cook, look after a house?'

'Certainly. I've already ...'

'And gardening?'

'I love the countryside; I spent my entire youth there.'

'The location is quite ... austere.'

'That doesn't frighten me. I don't like cities.'

'You know my conditions, no visits, one day off per week and ...'

'I know about them, they're fine and so is the salary.'

'What's your name?'

'Carmen.'

'You're Spanish?'

'No. My father loved opera.'

'When can you start?'

'Tomorrow.'

'Good, take a taxi. I'll expect you at eleven o'clock. Be on time, I hate waiting.'

'You can count on me. See you tomorrow, then. Goodbye.'

'See you tomorrow.'

Carmen, what a name! She'll be called Thérèse and that's that.

Then he went to make too generous a lunch, as if he were expecting a visit. From two ladies passing by, perhaps?

Too Close to the Edge

To Nathalie

Papa, papa...
Serge Gainsbourg

As the peeled potato fell into the pan of water, it made a loud *plop* which rebounded off the kitchen walls like a tennis ball. Holding the peeler still in her hand, Éliette paused to savour the moment; this – she was certain – was pure happiness.

Buffeted and battered by a year of uncontainable sobs, her heart had at last steadied itself like the green bubble in a spirit level. There was no particular reason for this new-found calm, or rather, there were a thousand: it was May, the rain was beating against the windows, there was baroque music playing on France Musique; she was making her first vegetable jardinière of the season (fresh peas, lettuce hearts, carrots, potatoes, turnips, spring onions, and not forgetting the lardons!); the Colette biography she had picked up the day before at Meysse library was propped open at page 48 on the living-room table; she wasn't expecting anyone, and no one was expecting her.

All these little things along with countless others meant that for the first time since Charles's death she did not feel lonely in the house by herself, but one and indivisible.

The France Musique presenter introduced the next programme in a voice which called to mind a priest with a pickled liver. Éliette opened her eyes and set to work on the last potato, challenging herself to peel it in one continuous length. Then she cut the carrots and turnips into perfectly evenly sized pieces, gave the lettuce a shake and plunged her hands into the colander of peas with a sigh of pleasure. The sensation of the little green marbles rolling between her fingers was as enjoyable now as it had been in childhood, when she helped Mémé Alice shell peas. It was the reward for her hard work.

Her grandmother's kitchen was like a women-only hammam. The windows were clouded by aromatic steam. Mémé Alice's gnarled arthritic fingers resembled moving tree roots as they sliced vegetables, trussed chickens and kneaded dough as soft and white as the flesh of her arms. There was no talking in Alice's kitchen, only singing. Edged with a thick layer of grey fluff, her upper lip quivered as she hummed 'Les Roses blanches', 'La Butte rouge' or 'Mon vieux Pataud'.

With her sizeable girth straining against the front pocket of a huge black apron, Mémé Alice strongly resembled the cast-iron stove which seemed to blaze constantly. Indeed, such was the affinity between the two that you almost wondered in whose belly her dishes had been baked, stewed or roasted as she brought them to the table, huffing and puffing like an old steam engine.

Despite the fact she now had three grandchildren of her own, Éliette would never be a Mémé Alice. The children called her Mamie – probably because she was not old or fat enough to be a Mémé, her hair not long enough to pin up in a taut bun like a cartoon elderly aunt. These days, old age was regarded as an insult, an ugly omen from which children should be shielded. It brought to mind visions of prolapse, support stockings and many other repulsive things besides, as hideous a prospect as death itself. Éliette was sixty-four.

She was one of those people who had always been and would remain attractive in a wholesome, obvious sort of way. She had never needed to give nature a helping hand. Just a touch of lipstick now and then when she and Charles went out of an evening, purely for the raspberry-flavoured kisses. Even the few wrinkles gathered around her eyes brought a new charm to her face. It was as though time had polished her with beeswax. Only Charles's passing had slightly dulled the sparkle in her eyes, and placed her smile in permanent parentheses.

The two of them had shared forty years of untarnished love before Charles was suddenly carried off by cancer two months before he was due to retire. They had already started packing for their move from the Parisian suburbs to this house in the Ardèche, where life was supposed to be a never-ending holiday.

They had bought the former silk farm thirty years earlier. Year after year, they had spent every spare moment doing it up to turn it into the haven of peace that sadly she alone now enjoyed. After Charles's death, Sylvie and Marc had tried to put her off going through with the move.

'It's madness, Maman. What are you going to do with yourself, stuck down there in the back of beyond? It's a nice place to go on holiday, but living there full-time is another story.'

'But I won't be on my own. The Jauberts are there!'

'The Jauberts! I mean, they're decent people and everything, but all they do is go on about tractors and frosts and their disappointing onion crop. And as far as neighbours go, that would be your lot. You haven't even got a driving licence and the nearest village is eight kilometres away. How are you going to do your shopping? On a bike?'

'Why not?'

'And what if you're ill?'

'I've got a telephone.'

'It's ridiculous, completely ridiculous!'

For a few months Éliette had been undecided, kicking about the flat in Boulogne with nothing on the horizon but the TV schedule and the possibility of a Sunday visit from her children and grandchildren. Then one day ...

'I'm selling Boulogne and moving to Saint-Vincent.'

Marc rolled his eyes and Sylvie, as usual, burst into floods of tears. Of course it was madness, but that was exactly what she was missing: a touch of madness to stop herself sinking into reason.

She moved house in late spring. For the first few months, Éliette quelled her doubts by indulging in an ever-increasing range of activities, some more productive than others: she repainted doors and shutters that didn't really need doing; planted vegetables and flowers, most of which died of boredom before they had even budded; set out to learn Italian on a tape recorder she never quite worked out how to use; spent considerable sums on subscriptions to lifestyle magazines – *Grow Your Own Veg, Sew Your Own Curtains, Learn to Love Yourself*, and so on; and started a diary, but never got beyond the first three pages. Then autumn came along.

Until this point, Marc and Sylvie had taken turns helping out with her screwball schemes, but they had their own lives, families and jobs to get back to, and at the beginning of September they both returned to Paris, leaving their mother in the care of the Jauberts, who lived on a farm two kilometres away.

Rose and Paul Jaubert were slightly younger than Éliette, but looked a good ten years older. Although on the face of it they did not have a great deal in common, thirty years as good neighbours had forged a true friendship which Charles's death and Éliette's permanent move to the silk farm had taken to a new level. The Jauberts now saw themselves as Éliette's protectors, an arrangement as well meaning as it was burdensome.

Almost every evening until late November, Éliette was obliged to join them at their Formica-topped kitchen table for a supper washed down with generous helpings of whatever happened to be on TV. It was almost impossible to wriggle out of these nightly invitations without causing offence. She eventually did so on the pretext of needing time alone to collect her thoughts, an excuse the Jauberts accepted without understanding, but which must have come as a relief to them as much as to her.

Thus Éliette had won the freedom not to watch TV but to listen to the radio, read or, most often, lie in bed for hours on end, stiff as a corpse, willing sleep to hurry up and come. At times like this, the Mogadon pills always had the last word. Not that she was complaining: there is nothing worse than having to share your solitude with other people. In any case, she still saw the Jauberts almost every day, especially Rose.

'Here, I brought you some soup, a bit of salad, some onions and courgettes. I'm going shopping; do you need anything?'

Éliette's fridge was constantly filled with vegetables that regularly ended up on the compost heap. No, she didn't need anything, or if she did, that would be the one time Rose stayed away. This was how the idea of a microcar came about. She had spotted a few of them on the winding roads near her home and envied the septuagenarian couples calmly crawling along at a snail's pace, unfazed by the honking horns and flashing headlights of furious motorists on the verge of shunting them into the ditch.

'For crying out loud! Those things should be banned! Honestly, I could go faster in my tractor!'

Éliette held her tongue while she and Paul overtook one on the way back from the market, but secretly she could picture herself at the wheel of one of those smart little motorised buggies. She thought about it during the day and dreamed of it at night, like a child longing for a big toy for Christmas. It took all her skills of persuasion to convince Paul to take her to a dealer.

'Éliette, why don't you just take your driving test? Then you could buy a real car. My cousin's selling his Renault 5, in perfect condition.'

'No, I'd be bound to fail.'

'But Rose took hers at forty-five!'

'Well, I'm sixty-four. And anyway, it's what I want.'

'But Éliette, it's not a car; it's a toy, and an expensive one at that!'

'Exactly, it's a toy I'm after.'

Thanks to Charles's pension and the sale of the flat, she could easily afford to indulge her whim. Paul reluctantly agreed to drive her to Montélimar, where she purchased a magnificent top-of-the-range cream Aixam. It took a little while to get used to driving it up the dirt track that led to her house, but after a few days she was able to go backwards and forwards, left and right without too much damage to the bumpers. Her first solo expedition (a round trip of about twenty kilometres) gave her as much of a thrill as if she had piloted a plane. Window down, hair blowing in the wind, she sang at the top of her lungs: '*Je n'ai besoin de personne en* Harley Davidson ...'

The vehicle had changed her life. To begin with, Rose had seemed put out, as if Éliette had taken a lover. But in the end everyone got used to the idea, and even laughed about it.

'Ah, there goes Éliette in her bubble car!'

Yet Madame de Bize was hardly in the first flush of youth. The lines on her face, hollowed by constant smiling, heralded the impending onset of her forties; her fulsome hips, whose immodest curves had once been celebrated by friends of both sexes, were becoming heavy ...

She was interrupted in her reading of the Colette biography by the sharp ring of the telephone. It was midday, so it could only be Sylvie. This was her regular slot. She called once a week from the office, just before going for lunch.

'Hello, Maman? It's Sylvie.'

'Hi, darling. How are you?'

'I'm all right, just knackered. Justine's got measles.'

'Poor little thing!'

'What's the betting she's going to pass it on to Antoine?'

'You did the same to me, you and your brother. Do you think you'll make it down for Whitsun?'

'Oh, yes. She'll be better by then.'

'Are you still planning to arrive on Friday?'

'That's the idea. Anyway, how are you?'

'Fine. I've just made myself my first vegetable jardinière of the season.'

'You lucky thing! Richard and the kids don't like veg. I'm jealous!'

'I'll make you one when you're here.'

'With lardons and crème fraîche?'

'Of course. And how are things with Richard's job?'

'Oh, you know what the property market's like at the moment … He's got a few things in the pipeline. He's been travelling a lot. Are you sure you're OK?'

'Absolutely! It's been stormy the last couple of days, but it's supposed to cheer up in time for the weekend. I'm reading Colette's biography and very much enjoying it. What about you? What are you reading?'

'Oh, I don't have time to read. When I'm not working or looking after the kids, doing the shopping …'

'I know, darling. We ought to retire when we're young and work when we're old.'

'You work all your life and then look what happened to Papa! Sorry, Maman. I'm just so stressed at the moment. I can't wait to see you and have some home comforts.'

'Don't you worry. I'll look after you and you can put your feet up. What about your brother? I haven't heard from him. Have you arranged things with him?'

'Oh, I never know what's going on with Marc. He always has all the time in the world. Everything's always hunky-dory. I've no idea how he does it. Actually, I do know: it's Sandra who does everything – the kid, the house – always with that vacant smile on her face. The perfect housewife!'

'Don't be unkind about your sister-in-law. She's very nice.'

'Very, and I think that's what annoys me most about her. She never lets that mask of domestic bliss slip. It's easy when you don't have a job.'

'That's not fair. Sandra's very ... traditional. Your brother earns a good living; she likes looking after the house. What's wrong with that?'

'You're right, yes. She's very traditional. Anyway, let's talk about something else. No issues with your little car?'

'None at all. It works like a dream!'

'Maman ... are you happy?'

'Of course I am, sweetheart!'

'I don't understand how you do it, living in the middle of nowhere. How does anyone manage to be happy in this lousy world? You know, just the other day ...'

Éliette was no longer listening. She loved her daughter, of course, but at this precise moment she could not care less about the little one's measles, or Richard's problems at work, or what Sylvie thought of her brother or sister-in-law or this lousy world.

'Sorry to interrupt you, darling, but I can smell something burning in the kitchen.'

'Oh, OK. We can talk about it another time. I'll call you if there's a problem, but we should be there on Friday evening.'

'Bye, love.'

Nothing was burning in the kitchen. There was just the re-assuring *blub-blub* of the jardinière simmering gently on the stove. Éliette pushed back a log which had slipped in the grate. The smouldering embers glowed like the ruby-red seeds of a ripe pomegranate. It was not cold, but the rain and the pleasure of reading by the hearth had given her the urge to light a fire. She returned to the sofa and let out a sigh.

Confinement breeds confinement. Though her isolation might at first have felt limiting, she soon realised she had no choice but to accept it, settle into it, even become comfortable with it, to the extent that the world beyond her four walls seemed like nothing but chores. Of course she loved her children and her children's children just as she might love the sky, the trees, the mountains, life in general – but after two days in their company she could no longer stand the sight of them. It was probably exactly the same for them. Eight hundred kilometres was a long way to travel to see her for Whitsun, even without counting the cost of the journey. There was a degree of obligation on both sides, but if the family had not come, she would no doubt have missed them. It was paradoxical, but that was the way it was. It had taken her a while to admit it to herself: she needed them, but after twenty-four hours couldn't wait for them to leave.

Tonight it would be Marc's turn to call and tell her which day he would be arriving, and tomorrow he would call again and say he would probably be later than expected, what with work ... She would grumble a little for the sake of form, but the truth was she didn't give two hoots.

All the minor irritations that had irked her for years now left her totally indifferent. What did it matter if there were nine people or five for dinner? She could always make an omelette, a salad ... The only thing that now differentiated her children from anyone else was the pang of emotion in her chest when they said goodbye. After all, what is a child but a kite you fly and then let go, for it to reappear among the clouds? She had read somewhere that we were all the children of children.

*

The jardinière was divine. As she munched her way through it, she felt like a rabbit grazing a veg patch. The nap that followed was equally delectable. By the time she woke up, the rain had stopped. A baby-blue sky extended as far as the eye could see. There was a smell of washing powder in the air, of sheets drying on the breeze. In the garden the bay leaves were fringed with water, each droplet holding a ray of sunshine within it. All around, the mountains were steaming, streaked ochre and purple and foaming minty green to freshen the wind's breath.

She asked herself if it might be an idea to undertake a commando mission to the supermarket in Montélimar today, rather than await the inevitable trolley gridlock at the end of the week. Without much deliberation, she told herself it would not. Her solitary way of life had made her overly wary of approaching a town of more than eighty inhabitants. But there was nothing in her fridge or cupboards that two couples and their children might want to eat after a long journey. One way or another she would have to make the trip, today or tomorrow.

It was only four o'clock, and it was no longer raining. Éliette decided to grin and bear it and went up to her room to change. She was ashamed at the sight of herself in the mirror of her wardrobe: shapeless woollen cardigan, baggy-kneed leggings, thick socks and grubby clogs. This was what country life looked like: a far cry from a Fragonard shepherdess frolicking on a swing in a flouncy dress. While nature was blossoming in a riot of colours and scents, she was slowly turning into a hideous caricature of the frumpiest pages of the La Redoute catalogue. While she had never been a slave to fashion, Éliette had always made an effort with her appearance. But with nobody to look nice for …

'You're letting yourself go, old girl. Take a look at yourself: you're like something off the compost heap!'

Earlier in the week, Rose had been extolling the benefits of the disgusting nylon overalls she wore day in, day out. 'They're just so practical! You wash them and half an hour later they're dry again. And even if you put a bit of weight on, they're so roomy!'

If her body had not rebelled in the face of such an outrage, Éliette could almost have been convinced. Stripped down to her bra and knickers, she began emptying her wardrobe in search of something decent to wear, holding various dresses, jumpers and blouses against her body, but all she saw reflected in the mirror was the sad face of a glove puppet poking out from behind a curtain. Tears welled in her eyes. One last shirt fell to the floor to join the pile of sloughed-off skins, each more tired and outdated than the last.

She cupped her breasts, turned sideways on and posed like a toreador, fluffing up her hair. Her chest was still firm, her stomach flat. Plenty of women half her age would envy a figure like hers. But what use was it to her, with no one around to touch it? Her body had become as pathetic as a bouquet of flowers left to wilt on a station platform by a jilted lover.

Even Rose, bulging out of her vile overalls like a saucisson d'Arles, was a thousand times more alluring than she was. Paul was a red-blooded man; they probably did 'it' every night … How long had it been since Éliette had made love? Since the beginning of Charles's illness. What was the point in still being slim and attractive and faithful to the memory of a man reduced to a stinking pile of bones at the bottom of a pit? What had she been trying to prove since becoming a widow? That it was possible to survive without sex? Who was she trying to fool?

A few weeks earlier, Paul had helped her put up a curtain pole in her bedroom. She had been standing on the stepladder hanging the curtain when her foot had slipped. Paul caught her by the waist and gently lowered her to the floor. For a few seconds, his hands had remained on her hips and their eyes had locked bizarrely.

She could not help but feel a little unsettled when she recalled that moment, as she had done several times.

It was like a fist inside her belly. Cursing that fat cow Rose and the rude health of her husband under her breath, she pulled on a black jumper, black trousers and a pair of flats the same colour.

Putting aside the storms of the last two days, spring had come remarkably early this year. Even at the beginning of the month, summer had been in the air. Éliette had rarely found nature so sensual: the merest blade of grass seemed swollen with sap, leaves undulated on the breeze, and every shrub appeared to quiver with a frenzy of animals mating in its midst, setting Éliette's senses firing. She was buzzing all the way to the supermarket, and on her arrival went straight to the freezer section. She kept her head down, convinced that every man in the shop was staring at her.

In the vegetable aisle, she blushed as it dawned on her she had filled her trolley with courgettes, aubergines, carrots, cucumbers and even an enormous long white turnip weighing nearly 300 grams, which she struggled to make herself see in a culinary light. It was stronger than she was; a kind of inflammation of her mind was slowly turning the supermarket into a sex shop. She found herself getting drunk on the potent cocktail of shame and desire. Having finished her food shopping, she was drawn to the clothing section where she picked up the sexiest underwear set Continent could offer, along with a pair of skinny jeans and two low-cut tops that even the boldest fashionistas in Montélimar would have deemed too risqué to wear.

As she unloaded her trolley, she avoided the gaze of the woman on the checkout, pulling her blonde hair over her forehead so that no one would see the word SEX branded across it. She stumbled weak-kneed out of the shop as if emerging from an orgy, piled the shameful evidence of her countless vices into the back of the microcar, and breathlessly set off home.

'You're totally loopy, you poor old thing! Totally loopy!'

She had never driven this fast before. She couldn't wait to get home, put all this food away in the fridge and find a home in the bottom of a cupboard for these clothes she would never wear.

So she had suffered a bit of an 'episode'; there was no need to make a drama out of it. She would laugh to herself about it later while finishing the leftover jardinière, having taken a Mogadon to overcome the ache in the small of her back, strangely pleasant though it was. She came off the main road at Meysse and took the little road along the River Lavezon. The river water was the colour of milky coffee. The poplars were bowing dangerously low and the sky was puffing out cheeks newly refilled with soot. In ten minutes the storm would break. She had just crossed the little bridge when the Aixam swerved, made a curious fart noise, zigzagged across the road and ended up on the verge.

'Shit! Shit! Double shit!'

It had never crossed her mind that she might get a puncture. Yet that was exactly what had happened to her front left wheel, barely two kilometres from home. Panicking, she got out and circled the vehicle, giving the tyres little kicks as mechanics do when trying to diagnose a problem. All this achieved was to make the little car quiver on the spot like a stubborn ass refusing to walk on. The first raindrop fell on her forehead as she was calling the heavens to come to her aid. The manual she retrieved from the glove compartment, hitherto untouched, was incomprehensible double-Dutch covered in pictures which bore no relation to anything she could recognise. Yes, she knew the jack and the spare wheel came into it somehow, but they were so well hidden!

It didn't occur to her to run back to the house, call Paul and ask him to give her a hand. Instead she contemplated suicide, for example by throwing herself into the muddy waters of the Lavezon. It was at that moment she saw him coming. A man, but not from round here. A man in a three-piece suit, jacket slung over his shoulder, briefcase in hand. A man who seemed to have come a long way judging by his heavy, steady gait and the hair slicked to his forehead. It was like a scene out of a Western: beneath a low sky, a stranger walks calmly towards his widescreen destiny.

'Problem?'

'I've got a flat ... I don't know how to use ... all this.'

The smile he shot her opened a hole inside her head.

'Mind if I take a look?'

He appeared to be in his forties, not very tall, not especially thickset, with a baby face. His shoes and trouser bottoms were covered in mud. As he set to work on the wheel, the rain began to drop like a portcullis. Éliette could not tear her eyes from his muscular back, which showed through his sodden shirt. He was finished in under ten minutes.

'There you go. Done.'

Standing face-to-face, streaming with water like two freshly landed fish, they burst out laughing. The sky no longer existed.

'Thanks. Can I give you a lift somewhere?'

'That would be great. I broke down myself, a few kilometres away. I was trying to find a phone.'

'I live just up the road. Hop in, quick.'

The windscreen wipers struggled to give some definition to the muted watercolour landscape. The Aixam skidded as it climbed the muddy track. Back at the house, after several trips back and forth to unload the boot, they stood breathless in the kitchen, droplets of water fringing their eyelashes.

'I'll get some towels. Goodness me, I need wringing out!'

They towelled their hair dry and took in the sight of one another: all fluffy and dishevelled, like chicks emerging from their shells. They cracked up again. Outside, thunder was rolling above the roof.

'Would you like some tea?'

'Please.'

Éliette was cack-handed, or all fingers and thumbs: she couldn't think where the cups lived, almost tipped over the kettle and banged into a chair while vainly trying to think of something witty to say.

'It's been pouring down like this for two solid days! It's because the last month has been so hot.'

'Probably.'

The water was taking an eternity to come to the boil. Everything was too slow, and yet she would have liked this moment to go on and on. Every now and then she threw a glance at the man sitting at the table, discovering him bit by bit as though piecing together a puzzle: the nervous long-fingered hands, the blue vein pulsating in his neck, the blond cowlick on his forehead, the brown eyes that seemed to be searching for something on the ceiling ...

'Are you from round here?'

'No ... I'm from Paris.'

... nice mouth, but bad teeth ...

'So your car broke down too?'

'Um ... yes. Must be something in the air today.'

... a deep voice which hesitated over every word, as if they all started with a capital letter. A little boy in a man's body, two opposites inhabiting the same skin. The kettle began to whistle.

'Here we are. It's ready!'

They drank their tea without saying a word. The patter of the rain filled the silence. From time to time their eyes met, they smiled shyly at one another and looked away.

'Nice place you've got here.'

'Yes, I like it. But it took an awful lot of time and effort to do it up. When we bought it, thirty years ago, it was a wreck. We were living in Paris at the time, in Boulogne. All our holidays were spent cementing, plastering ... We wanted to retire here. Sadly my husband died two years ago.'

'I'm sorry.'

'I decided to come and live here on my own. I have pictures of what it used to look like—'

Before Éliette could finish her sentence, the phone rang.

'Excuse me.'

'Of course.'

Why oh why had she ever had children? It could only be Marc. She went into the living room and answered the phone with irritation in her voice.

'Yes? Oh, it's you, Paul ... Yes, no. What's going on? ... What? ... Patrick! ... Oh, Paul, I'm so sorry ... and Rose? ... Of course ... of course ... I'll come right now, Paul ... Yes, see you very soon.'

Éliette returned to the kitchen, ashen.

The man noticed and instinctively rose from his chair.

'Bad news?'

'That was my neighbours. Their son has just been killed in a car accident ... I have to go round.'

'Of course. I'll go ...'

'No, don't. It's still raining and the next village is eight kilometres away. The phone's in the living room and there's a phone book underneath it. But I doubt you'll get anyone to come out at this time. Anyway, make yourself at home. There's wood by the fire if you want to dry off.'

'That's very kind of you ... I don't know what to say ...'

'What about "See you later"?'

'See you later.'

The truth was that beyond feeling sorry for Rose and Paul, Éliette was not especially upset to hear Patrick had died. She had never liked the kid. Even as a little boy he had been a nasty piece of work. Sylvie and Marc had hated him because he was always throwing stones at dogs, cats, chickens, people in general and especially his brother, despite being the younger by four years. Serge, unlike Patrick, was the very model of sweetness and sensitivity. He had left the farm as soon as he could and was now a teacher living somewhere near Grenoble. His family seldom saw him. It was Patrick who was the apple of his parents' eyes, despite the fact he openly despised them. But he was a good-looking lad with the gift of the gab, and had just passed his exams at the agricultural college in Pradel with flying colours. He would one day inherit the farm, since his brother wanted nothing to do with it.

Old Bob pulled half-heartedly at his chain and bared time-worn canines as Éliette parked outside the house. Paul opened the door to her. He had the face of a zombie, his eyes were red, and the breath from his wet mouth was thick with pastis.

'Ah, Éliette, Éliette …'

For the first time in the history of their friendship, he put his arms around her. He smelled of the sweat of misfortune. She felt as if she were falling from the ladder again, only this time he was the one leaning on her, and that changed everything. It took a little effort to extricate herself from the embrace.

'It's awful, awful ... We don't understand ...'

'Oh, Paul. You poor thing ... Where's Rose?'

'In the kitchen. I didn't know what to do. I'm sorry for dragging you out in this weather.'

'Please, don't mention it. What are friends for, after all?'

Éliette had apologised to everyone when Charles died too. People are always ashamed of the misery that has befallen them, as though it were an act of divine retribution for a long-forgotten sin of theirs. Walking unsteadily, Paul led her into the kitchen where Rose seemed to be dozing, rocking back and forth in her chair near the stove. When Éliette put her arms around her, Rose turned to show a face wrecked by tears, washed of all expression. Her flabby skin fell in folds, as trickles of wax on a candle stump.

'It's not even as if he was coming back from a knees-up! ... He wasn't even drunk! ... In broad daylight!'

'You let those tears out, Rosie. It'll do you good. I know how you feel, you know ...'

'I know you do.'

'I brought you something to take. Have this and put yourself to bed. Tomorrow, things will be a bit clearer. There's nothing else you can do.'

'Yes. We need to look after Paul. He's in pieces ...'

'Of course. Don't you worry.'

Paul sat slumped, shoulders hunched, elbows on the Formica table top, a bottle of pastis in front of him, despite the fact he usually barely touched the stuff. Éliette filled a glass with water from the tap and handed Rose a tablet.

'I'll take her up to bed and I'll be right back down, OK, Paul? Paul?'

'Huh? Yes, yes.'

Rose let herself be guided up to the bedroom, which was decorated in the most ghastly brown and orange flowery wallpaper. The blue satin quilt gave a kind of sigh when Rose fell onto it. A piece of boxwood fell off the crucifix above her head and went spinning onto the carpet.

'He did whatever he wanted. He came top in everything ... It's not fair, no, not fair ... Have to look after Paul. We're old ... We've become old all of a sudden.'

'Don't worry, I'm here. You need to sleep.'

'I'll never sleep again.'

'You will. Just let yourself go.'

In the mirrored wardrobe door, Éliette could see herself holding Rose's hand. Her neighbour's face was hidden behind her round belly; in the foreground was one bare foot and another with an old slipper hanging off the toes. The scene was dimly lit from above. This was where they made love, where the couple's children had been conceived ... The wedding photo on the bedside table seemed to come from another age, from a time when children died not in car accidents but in wars, or crushed between the jaws of some agricultural machine.

Rose was extremely house-proud. There was not a speck of dust or the merest cobweb to be seen, whereas Éliette collected them like the works of old masters. How did they have sex? From the front? From behind? It was ridiculous, but it was all she could think about. She tried to rid herself of these visions of copulation – all the more obscene in the circumstances – to bat them away like persistent flies. She felt Rose's hand go limp. She was asleep, mouth open and nostrils pinched. Éliette wriggled her hand free and tiptoed out of the room.

Paul had not moved an inch. He seemed to have become permanently embedded in the table edge and was staring straight ahead.

'She's asleep. It'll do her good. You should do the same, Paul.'

'Huh? Yes, yes.'

Éliette smelled something burning. The remains of a stew were turning to charcoal on the hob. She turned the heat off under the pan and came to sit across the table from Paul.

'How did it happen? Do you want to talk about it?'

'Happened around midday, the gendarmes say. They found him at two o'clock down the bottom of a ravine off the little road at Le Coiron – you know the one. Nice views but it's so narrow and wiggly. Someone had left a car parked on the road, right before a bend. Maybe Patrick was going too fast, but what was that driver thinking, leaving his motor in a place like that? The road's tight enough as it is! Even if he'd run out of petrol, even on a hill ... I don't know ... You'd push it or something, you'd get it off the road! He was trying to get round it ... He died instantly ... When we heard, I tried to call you, but you weren't in.'

'No, I was out shopping in Montélimar. Have you told Serge?'

'Yes, he'll be here tomorrow. What do we do now?'

'There's nothing you can do except go to bed and sleep next to Rose. She mustn't be left alone. You need to look after one another. All these dark thoughts going round in your head, they're not getting you anywhere.'

'You're right, of course ... You know, the strange thing is, the guy never came back for his car. The gendarmes called me earlier. They think it was stolen.'

'That is odd, yes.'

'Yes ... and what are all these kids doing, driving around like mad things? Five this year, just in our little patch! Last one was young Arlette, Robin the builder's daughter, remember? In November?'

'Yes, I remember.'

'They think they're untouchable! How many times did I tell him, "Patrick, you're better off getting there late than not getting there at all"? Might as well have been talking to a brick wall! He stopped listening to me a long time ago. Thought other people were a waste of space, his father especially. I gave that kid everything ... Would you like a bite to eat, Éliette? I've warmed up some leftover stew.'

'No, thank you. I've got someone waiting for me at home.'

'Oh, I didn't know. I ...'

'It's fine. Besides, I think your stew's burnt. I just took it off the heat. Can't you smell it?'

'No. Another time, then?'

'Of course. Do you want one of the pills I gave Rose?'

'No, thanks. I've got that.'

He indicated the half-empty bottle of pastis with his chin.

'Take care of yourself, Paul. It's no use letting yourself go. Remember you've got Rose to think of.'

'It's kind of you to have come, Éliette. At times like this you need your friends.'

'I was glad to help. You did the same for me when Charles died. And tomorrow, Serge will be here.'

'Yes ... but it's not the same with Serge, we don't speak the same language. Patrick and me, we were salt of the earth. We didn't need to chat ... I love Serge just as much ... only, I never feel totally comfortable around him.'

'He's just very different from his brother, that's all. I'm heading off now, Paul, so you should go to bed. If you need anything at all, just call. Either way, I'll pop in tomorrow morning.'

He nodded, but was no longer listening. His gaze was clouding over, his eyes turning the colour of pastis. Éliette patted his shoulder and left the kitchen.

Outside, the smell of thoroughly burnt food lingered in her nose and throat. The rain had stopped and a single star was twinkling above hills as rounded as Paul's back. Old Bob barely turned his head as Éliette passed him. The look in his eyes expressed something beyond weariness. Éliette started the car, and once the lemon-yellow light of the Jauberts' window had disappeared from her rear-view mirror, she broke into sobs. It wasn't only the Jauberts she was crying for, but Old Bob, the single star, the dark hills and herself. The tears flowed on and on like the swollen Lavezon river, washing away all her sadness. Paul and Rose were neither friends nor family, more like fellow passengers on an overnight train. They had nothing in common besides existing in the same space and time.

She had once read a definition of poetry as 'two words meeting for the first time'. There was an element of that in her relationship with her neighbours. It was so easy to love like-minded people, but when chance threw someone totally different in your path ... like the man awaiting her at home, whose name she didn't even know. What if he had gone? He might well have called a taxi. Éliette lifted her foot off the accelerator. The truth was she had spent the whole time at the Jauberts' thinking of him. That was probably why she had forced Rose to go to sleep and encouraged Paul to do the same. She had to some extent been trying to get shot of their sadness. And why not? Today was not just any day! Her heart was pounding in her chest as she put her foot back on the pedal. What if he had got hold of a mechanic? What if ...? She saw the light at the living-room window and let out a cry of joy. For the first time in so long, someone was waiting for her.

He was sitting by the hearth where a fire was blazing. He

straightened up when Éliette came in, as though caught doing something he shouldn't.

'You didn't get through to a garage, then?'

'Er ... no.'

'I'm not surprised – we're out in the sticks here. At least the rain's stopped. It's clearing up.'

'How are your friends?'

'He was their favourite son. I gave them some sleeping pills. Nothing else we can do. Such a terrible blow. But it happens all the time round here; people drive like lunatics; they're a law unto themselves. Every weekend, they roll out of the discos and it's carnage on the roads ... Listen, here's what I think you should do. It's too late to find a garage or hotel round here. I have plenty of spare rooms. Why don't you spend the night here and I'll take you to a garage tomorrow?'

'That's very kind of you, but you don't know me ...'

'Well then, introduce yourself!'

'Étienne Doilet.'

'Éliette Vélard. So, what do you say?'

'Well ... yes.'

'I'll warn you now: if you're a murderer, I have very little to lose, and there's nothing here worth stealing unless you count the walls. Are you hungry?'

'I think so.'

Éliette warmed up the leftover jardinière, cracked four eggs into a frying pan and opened a bottle of wine. The fluctuations of the weather served once again to fill the awkward silences. But after two glasses of wine, Éliette's tongue loosened and she began lauding the region to Étienne, who was a first-time visitor here.

'You know, the Le Coiron road – it's on my mind because that's where my neighbours' son had his accident – well, it's

300

magnificent! The landscape changes every couple of kilometres. On the plateau, you're right up in the mountains. It's glorious. Oh, by the way, there was a funny thing about Patrick's accident: someone had left their car in the middle of the road. Patrick was trying to get round it when he plunged into the ravine. And no one ever came back for the car. The gendarmes say it was stolen. Strange, isn't it?'

'Yes.'

'Well, anyway. Oh, I'll tell you another wonderful road: the one from Saint-Thomé to Gras. It follows the river and ... is something wrong?'

Étienne was making a strange face, as if he had just bitten into a lemon.

'No, no. I'm fine!'

'I'm boring you, playing the tour guide. I don't get out much!'

'Not at all, honestly. It's nice to hear someone talking so passionately about where they live.'

'Thank you. Hang on, where was it that you broke down?'

'Me? Um ... This is ridiculous, but I have to tell you the truth. I didn't break down.'

'Oh!'

'It's so stupid ... OK, I was in the car with my girlfriend and we had an argument. Things got heated; I told her to let me out and she did. Leaving me in the middle of nowhere ... Not clever, I know.'

Éliette burst out laughing. Étienne's cheeks were red and he hung his head like a little boy owning up to doing something silly.

'I'm sorry, Étienne. It's a nervous thing.'

'Don't apologise. It was such a childish thing to do, but I couldn't help it. I've never been in a situation like that before.'

'There's no need to be embarrassed about it. It's quite funny, really!'

'Can I smoke?'

'Go ahead.'

Smoking was not normally allowed at Éliette's house. Marc was asked to go and puff on his cigarette outside, and even then only on condition no butts were dropped in the garden. But this evening she was enjoying watching the smoke emerging from Étienne's nostrils like the genie from Aladdin's lamp.

'Where's the dog?'

'What dog?'

'It says "Beware of the dog" on the front door.'

'It's a deterrent; we've never had dogs. If anyone came to the door late in the evening, I'd shout, "Charles, keep hold of the dog!" ... It makes me feel safer. But no one ever does come. That's why I don't need a real dog.'

'Don't you get bored here?'

'You must be joking! I've no chance to be bored. Only today I've had a flat tyre, a death at the neighbours' and a stranger in my house! And it's like this every day!'

Étienne stubbed out his cigarette. When she smiled, Éliette looked like a teenager.

'Oh, I almost forgot: your son, Marc, called. I think he was a bit taken aback when I answered. I told him you were at your neighbours' ... He'll call again tomorrow.'

Marc's phone call brought Éliette back to a reality she would have preferred not to have to face that evening.

'Yes. I have a son and a daughter and three grandchildren. I'm a grandmother.'

'That's nice.'

'Why?'

'I don't know ... You have a family ... You're not on your own.'

'No, I'm not ... Goodness! It's almost midnight! I ought to have been in bed at least two hours ago. I'll show you your room.'

Out of the bedrooms Éliette offered him, Étienne chose Sylvie's. Whitewashed walls, film posters, amateur photos of twisted tree trunks and overexposed sunsets, an old teddy bear at the foot of the bed, a bunch of dried flowers in a stoneware pot, a few children's books, teen magazines, the odd splash of pink.

'If you get cold, there are extra blankets in the wardrobe.'

'Thanks. I think I'll sleep well.'

'Good. Right, then ... Good night.'

'Good night, Éliette.'

There's a man in my house, just the other side of that wall, in Sylvie's room. I can hear him coughing, getting undressed, slipping between the sheets. I don't feel like going to sleep; I won't take a Mogadon. I want to play it all back in my head, see him appearing at the bend in the little bridge, changing my tyre, driving home with me in the rain ... Then later, when I got home from the Jauberts' and found him waiting for me beside the hearth. Someone was waiting for me tonight, Charles ... I told him about us; maybe I should have said more about you ... He's not asleep; I can hear him turning in bed, see the light under his door ... I'm alive, Charles, I'm alive.

Éliette's nostrils quivered at the wafts of toast and fresh coffee. She opened first one eye and then the other, and sat bolt upright. *He's up already?* Yawning, she let her head fall back onto the pillow and stretched out as if trying to touch the walls either side of the bed. The alarm clock showed eight thirty. Slippers, dressing gown, despairing glance in the mirror.

Étienne was at the sink finishing last night's washing-up. The draining rack was sagging under a typically masculine pyramid of precariously balanced plates, glasses, cups and saucers.

'Morning.'

'Morning, Éliette. Sleep well?'

'Very well. You should have left all that; I'd have sorted it out later.'

'It's no trouble. I like washing up in the morning. It helps me clear my head. People shouldn't complain so much about household chores. I've made coffee, but maybe you'd prefer something else?'

'I'm more of a tea drinker, but it's fine. It's good to ring the changes.'

'I can make tea! I'll put the kettle on.'

'OK, then.'

Éliette sat on a chair, hands dangling between her thighs. The sun filtering through the part-closed shutters cast a ladder of light on the wall. It was strange to have had the role of hostess taken from her.

He had robbed her of her little morning habits. She missed the radio and felt vaguely awkward, as if she were in a hotel.

'I'm not used to being waited on.'

'It's not as bad as all that, you'll see. What do you use to strain your tea?'

'There's an infuser in the left-hand drawer.'

Steam rose from the tea and twirled around the piercing ray of sunlight reflected off the glazed surface of the bowls.

'Not easy finding your way around a new kitchen. I hope I haven't made too much of a mess of things.'

'No. Just the bowls. These ones are for soup.'

'I do apologise!'

'I suppose I can live with it, just this once.'

'Madame is too kind!'

They laughed. Étienne unfolded the napkin he had wrapped around the toast to keep it warm. For once, life seemed not to need an instruction manual.

'It'll be warm today. Look how the light's flooding in.'

'It's like being on holiday. We could have had breakfast outside ...'

'Let's do it!'

They sat and finished their bowls of tea on the enormous stone slab that served as the front step. The sun flowed into them like honey trickling deep into their bones. Eyes half closed, Éliette pointed out the features of her garden. It was surrounded by a drystone wall, surpassed in height only by a fig tree and a cypress. To the right, an old barn housed a long table and benches.

'That's my summer dining room. We've had some good times in there: barbecues in the evening with candles in glass holders, the children ... I have a telescope. On summer nights you can see the stars up close ...'

'It makes me think of houses in Morocco, the internal courtyards.

305

They smelled of jasmine, incense burning on the embers, fresh mint tea ... The drumbeats ... as if marking their rhythms on the taut skin of the moon. The stars twinkled, and the sound was like the copper jingles of a tambourine.'

'Are you a poet?'

'No, I'm just remembering.'

'Do you know Morocco well?'

'I was there for a while.'

'For work?'

'In a sense. Would you like another cup of tea?'

'No, thank you. I'll go and have a shower. Are you ... in a rush? I mean, for me to take you to Montélimar?'

'No, no. Take your time. I'm fine right here ...'

'In that case I'll leave you to your memories.'

Where would the world be without soap? Éliette sang as the water gushed out of the shower head onto her newly confident body. Étienne was clearly in no hurry to be leaving. It was lovely, what he had said about Morocco. What was he doing over there? And here? ... Perhaps they could get the barbecue out? ... He looked tired: why not suggest he stick around for a couple of days? The children were not coming until the weekend ... It could be a digression, a short aside in the long monologue her life had become.

Plans were building to a lather in her head and the toothpaste was foaming in her mouth when she heard shouts coming from the garden. She ran to the window. A taxi had parked outside the front door. A girl in her early twenties with a messy heap of dyed red hair, in black sunglasses, a T-shirt and ripped jeans, was marching towards Étienne, swinging her bag above her head. Before Étienne could scramble to his feet, the bag hit him full in the face, knocking him backwards.

306

'Fucking idiot! What have you done, you bastard?'

The bag struck Étienne a second time on his back as he tried to get up, holding his arms in front of him for protection. Blood was pouring from his eyebrow.

'Agnès! Stop it, for fuck's sake! Something in there weighs a ton!'

Éliette raced outside, wet-haired, toothbrush in hand.

'Whash going on out here? Have you losht your mind?'

'Who's this?'

'The owner of thish house.' (Éliette spat out her toothpaste.) 'I must ask you to calm down. As long as you're on my property, you'll sort out your quarrels with your boyfriend in a civilised manner!'

'My boyfriend? Please! He's my father, my fucking father!'

Open-mouthed, Éliette looked first at Étienne, who was holding both hands to his brow, and then at the girl, who was kicking at every piece of gravel and raising clouds of dust. Meanwhile, the taxi driver had heard all the shouting and got out of his car. Éliette knew him. He had taken her to Montélimar several times before she got her microcar.

'Is there a problem here, Madame Vélard?'

'No, it's fine. Just a family squabble.'

'All right, then. Either way, this little madam needs to pay my fare. I've got other jobs to get to.'

The girl took a note out of her bag and handed it to the driver without a word or a glance in his direction.

'Your bags?'

'Leave them by the door.'

The driver shrugged, waved goodbye to Éliette and drove off. The courtyard was filled with the chirping of crickets, accompanied by cymbal crashes of sunlight.

Éliette leaned over Étienne. 'Does it hurt?'

'It's OK. I'm sorry ...'

'I'll get a cold compress.'

The girl had sat down on the stone outside the door and lit a cigarette. Éliette almost had to climb over her to get inside the house. She heard Étienne mutter, 'Jesus, what the hell have you got in that bag?'

'My camera. Sorry. I hope it's not fucked ...'

While she searched the medicine cabinet for a dressing and antiseptic, Éliette heard them arguing in low voices on the doorstep. A name kept coming up, spoken by the girl with a note of panic: Théo. Who was this kid who had just parachuted into the middle of Éliette's dream? How had she got here? And why? So many unanswered questions colliding inside her head. The telephone rang out like a clarion call. As she passed the front door, she dropped off Étienne's dressing and ran back into the living room.

'Hello, Maman?'

'Yes, hello, Marc.'

'What's the matter? You're out of breath.'

'I was in the shower.'

'Oh, sorry. Do you want me to call back?'

'No, it's fine.'

'Who was the guy who answered the phone to me last night?'

'A friend. I was at the Jauberts'. Oh, Marc, I have to tell you something. Patrick was killed in a car crash yesterday. That's why I was at their house.'

'Patrick? ... Jesus!'

'It's hit them hard. I can't talk for long, I told them I'd pop round this morning. Serge is on his way.'

'Yes, I understand ...'

'Are you still coming on Friday?'

'That's the plan, yes.'

'OK, well, I'd better go, son. See you soon! Love you.'

Her hand was still on the receiver when the phone started ringing again.

'Madame Vélard, it's Serge ... Jaubert.'

'Hello, Serge, dear. How are your parents?'

'Not great. Maman would like to see you.'

'Of course. I was about to come round. I'll be there in ten minutes.'

'Thanks. See you soon.'

Éliette bounded up the stairs, threw on the clothes she had been wearing the day before, and hurtled back down again. Something akin to the blades of a food processor was mincing up her slightest thought. She was incapable of forming complete sentences, telling herself only: keys, glasses, bag ... Stepping from the gloom inside the house to the full sun of the garden was like walking into a shower of flames. For a few moments she saw nothing. Étienne and his daughter seemed to have disappeared. Then, shielding her eyes with her hand, she caught sight of them curled up like two cats in the darkness of her 'summer dining room'. They were leaning on the long wooden table and smoking silently, one's gaze concealed by dark glasses, the other's obscured by a thick bandage over his left eye.

'Better now? You've calmed down? Show me ... That's an impressive black eye you're going to have there!'

'What about this one? Impressive enough for you?' The girl lowered her glasses. Her right eye was a magnificent green, but the left was ringed bright purple.

'Étienne, did you ...?'

'No, he didn't, but it's *because of* him.'

'Agnès, please!'

'Look, I don't want to know. Let's just say it gives you a family resemblance. All I ask is that you avoid making a scene while you're under my roof. I have to go round to my neighbours'. You

309

know the situation, Étienne. Things are bad enough as they are. Can I trust you?'

'Absolutely, Éliette. I really am sorry. It was a misunderstanding.'

'All right. See you later, then.'

The one saving grace of the morning's dramas from Éliette's point of view was to have discovered that Agnès was Étienne's daughter and not his girlfriend, as she had first thought. The rest was as confusing as it was unsettling. In what kind of family did a daughter whack her father round the head with a camera while hurling abuse at him? She had been equally shocked by Étienne's completely passive response. Why had he phoned Agnès? After all, that was the only possible explanation: he had called her last night while Éliette was with the Jauberts ... And that bruise on Agnès's face: *It's because of him* ... Something was telling her to send the two of them packing, but the memory of the pleasure of Étienne's company the previous day put her off. She would wait and see. For now, she was coming up the Jauberts' drive as Serge came out to greet her, another young man of similar age hovering behind him. Both had very short hair and moustaches. Serge looked utterly crushed.

'Hello, Madame Vélard.'

'Come on, call me Éliette.'

'Yes, sorry. This is all so ... This is my friend Zep. He's German but he speaks very good French.'

'Pleased to meet you. So, how's your mother?'

'Still a bit woozy after those drugs you gave her, but ...'

'And your father?'

'He hasn't said a word. He's like a plank of wood.'

The three of them entered the house. It was cool inside and the smell of coffee vainly tried to cover that of aniseed. Paul hadn't budged from the position he had occupied the day before, sitting with both elbows on the table. Only the empty pastis bottle testified to the passage of time. Rose lifted her puffy face, broke into sobs and rushed over to throw herself on Éliette.

'My boy! My little boy!'

'There, there, Rose. I'm here ...'

Serge turned his watery eyes to the window and squeezed his friend's hand. Éliette noticed the gesture but made little of it, turning her attention back to Rose, who no longer even had the strength to cry.

'Come with me, Rose. Let's go outside and get some fresh air while we talk. It'll do you good. You too, Paul. You can't stay sitting at that table for ever. You've got to keep going.'

Serge leaned towards his father to help him up. Without moving, Paul said under his breath, 'Don't you touch me.'

Serge held out his hand.

'Papa ...'

'I said don't put your dirty queer hands on me!'

The slap aimed at his son met empty space. Carried by the momentum, Paul toppled over and fell onto the tiled floor. Rose was open-mouthed, frozen but for her chest which rose in quick shallow breaths, as if hiccuping. Serge and Zep knelt down beside the father.

'He's fine, he's snoring. He's pissed out of his head. Let's put him to bed.'

Éliette and Rose watched the two boys lift Paul's body and haul it up the stairs.

'Come on, Rose. Let's have a walk; it'll calm us down.'

'Yes ... Why did Paul say that?'

'Say what?'

'"Your dirty queer hands".'

'He's had too much to drink; he doesn't know what he's saying. Come on – show me how your geraniums are getting on.'

Agnès emerged from the kitchen carrying a bottle of pastis, a jug of water and two glasses on a tray.

'Agnès, you're going too far.'

'Why? She's cool, she won't mind. Anyway, I feel like a drink. If we weren't in the shit, I could imagine we were on holiday. OK, so when Théo's contact gave you the package, you got straight back on the train to Paris?'

'Yeah. But I'd been mulling it over since the day before. Six months back, when I finished my time in Morocco, I had so many good intentions. But you have no idea how hard it is to get used to life on the outside. I'm gonna be forty-five ...'

'But you'd have made ten thousand for a return train journey!'

'What the fuck did I care about ten thousand when I had that whole package under my seat! I kept thinking about Théo's face when he chucked me the five thousand upfront. Small change. All my life I've had nothing but small change from guys like Théo. You reach a point you can't take any more. The train stopped at Montélimar, and I got off.'

'You're crazy, my poor papa.'

'Don't call me Papa. It's ridiculous.'

'OK. So then what? How did you end up here?'

'I panicked a bit once I was on the platform. Everything was going too fast. I couldn't hang around; I stood out like a sore thumb. I went into the car park and stole a car. Once I got behind the wheel,

I calmed down. I headed out of town on back roads without much idea where I was going. I stopped in the middle of nowhere to stretch my legs and think things over. But I didn't regret it for a second! I found a little green meadow with clumps of white flowers. I lay on my back and watched the clouds drift past. It made me think of summer camp. I was eight years old in Le Chambon-sur-Lignon, one of the few good times in my life. The weather was always fine, even when it rained. It smelled clean; we were always hungry. We built tree houses. I thought to myself: if there's one safe place for the two of us in this shitty world, then that's it. I was picturing a little chalet in the forest, you coming to join me there ...'

'I'd have preferred the Caribbean.'

'I got back in the car and drove along this incredible little road that wound up the mountain ... Just my luck, I ran out of petrol halfway up. Couldn't leave the thing there, so I got out, started pushing and ... this guy comes roaring round the bend. It was so fast, I didn't see it happen. I just heard the screech of brakes, the crack of broken branches, the crunch of metal, and then nothing. I ran down into the ravine. The guy was dead. He was young ... What was I supposed to do? ... I went back up to the car, wiped everything down, the steering wheel, the seat, the door ... My head was on fire: anyone could turn up at any minute ... I grabbed the briefcase and legged it through the woods.'

'No way! You just dumped everything?'

'Yeah. Afterwards I walked for ages through fields and woods ... It was getting dark when I met Éliette. She'd broken down. You know the rest.'

'You're a magnet for trouble, aren't you?'

'Want to know the best part?'

'What?'

'The neighbours' son, the one who's just been killed in a car crash ...'

'Yeah? ... No! You mean he's ...'

'I'm almost certain. She was telling me how the accident happened last night.'

'Now that's the icing on the cake! Do excuse me, I think I'll serve myself another!'

Father and daughter locked eyes for a moment and burst out laughing. They were still in fits when Éliette's Aixam came bouncing up the dirt track.

'Looks like everyone's in a better mood. Have you made up?'

'Yes, Éliette, everything's fine. I hope you'll forgive us for the scene we made.'

'Let's put it behind us. I could do with a drink myself, actually.'

'I'll go. I'll fetch some ice as well.'

As Agnès was getting up, Éliette settled herself on the bench opposite Étienne. She closed her eyes for a second and a firework display went off inside her head, images flying around like meteors: Paul sitting at the kitchen table, Étienne changing the wheel, Rose's slipper in the mirror, Serge squeezing Zep's hand, Agnès hitting her father with her bag, Étienne doing the washing-up ...

'It's all a bit much, isn't it?'

'It is, rather. I'd been moaning that my life had become a bit monotonous of late. I can't complain about that any more!'

'Things have been a bit crazy for me lately too. I'd like the whole merry-go-round to stop. But we won't be under your feet for too long. Agnès lives in Lyon. I called her last night to come and get me. Unfortunately she had a little scrape in the car, hence the black eye and terrible mood. She was halfway here when it happened, so she had to get a train and then a taxi.'

'So long as there are no more fisticuffs in my garden, you're no trouble at all. In fact I don't know how I'd feel about being on my own at the moment.'

Agnès brought cold water and ice cubes.

'Y'know, Éliette – is it all right if I call you Éliette?'

'Yes.'

'There's a barbecue there, and sausages in the fridge. Do you think we could ...?'

'Agnès! You're overstepping the mark.'

'No, she's right.'

'Great! I'll sort it. I love making a fire!'

All tension disappeared once the barbecue was lit. They laughed easily and talked about everything and nothing, making the most of this momentary bright spell in the knowledge it was a temporary reprieve. Corroded by a sort of rust as they may have been, Agnès's twenty years added a spark to the conversation. Éliette watched in wonder. Agnès was nothing like she or even her daughter had been at twenty. She was both more mature and more carefree. She occasionally used a word or expression that Éliette didn't understand and Étienne would step in to translate for her. Éliette found Agnès's relationship with her father fascinating. Sylvie would never have spoken so freely to Charles, even though they were considered an open family. Some of the dubious situations father and daughter talked about planted a seed of doubt in her mind as to the true nature of their relationship to one another. And yet she found nothing distasteful about their stories, to the extent that she too began sharing things she had not told anyone in years. She was swooping into an unknown world and landing gently – aided, no doubt, by the nice cool rosé. And why not? There were so many other worlds ... Paul and Rose's, Serge and Zep's, Sylvie's, Marc's ... an infinite galaxy that could never be explored in a lifetime. It was as good as closing her eyes while being whirled around on a carousel.

'Are you all right, Éliette?'

'Yes. But I'm going to have a shower and get changed. I'm too hot in these clothes.'

Once Éliette had left the table, Agnès lay down on Étienne's side of the bench and rested her head on his thigh.

'What now?'

'Haven't got a clue. As long as we're here, nothing's going to happen. Are you sure you weren't followed?'

'Yes. Théo came round before you called. He could knock me around all he liked, I didn't know anything. Then you rang. I got the student across the hall to bring my bags down – you know, the one who's got a thing for me. I told him to take a taxi and wait for me at Gare de Lyon. I strolled out of the building a quarter of an hour later and took the métro.'

'I told Éliette you lived in Lyon, to explain why you're here. I said I called you last night to ask you to pick me up. Only, you had an accident somewhere between Vienne and Valence, which is how you got your shiner. Later on you need to pretend to call the garage where your car is, and then tell us it won't be ready until Thursday. As far as I can make out, her kids don't get here until Friday. That gives us two days' grace.'

'Right. Only trouble is I've never set foot in Lyon. Not that that makes much difference. Have you got cash?'

'A thousand, tops. Plus the briefcase.'

'Your two kilos of coke aren't worth shit around here. Who are you going to sell it to – the goats? The yokels?'

'I know! But we'll find a solution. We just need time to think. I need to stop for breath.'

'Poor Papa, you really know how to land yourself in the shit. To think I didn't even know you existed a month ago!'

'Please, can we not talk about that?'

'But it's not your fault! Stop with the guilt. How were you to know the girl you were about to cop off with was your daughter? Everyone calls me Lol at Théo's place, and I was only a year old when you left. If you hadn't found the photo of Maman, you'd

316

still be none the wiser. I might have got pregnant and given birth to a hideous monster! Bleurghhh!'

'Please, Agnès. It's not funny.'

'Fine! Whatever. So, this coke, have you tried it?'

'No.'

'Well, you should.'

'Now don't start poking your nose ...'

'Hang on a minute! You don't know how to be cool. The only person who can find you a buyer is me. So I want to know what it is I'm selling, OK? And I'll also need a sample. You don't just deal two kilos like that.'

'OK. The briefcase is upstairs, in the room I slept in. But just a sample!'

Birds were dabbling in the blue sky, the air hummed with the chirping of crickets, and plant smells mingled with wisps of smoke from the dying embers of the barbecue. Étienne was wondering what it would take to become a Trappist monk. Faith? Couldn't be that difficult. He had believed in a lot of things in his time, so why not a little guy nailed to a wooden cross? The truth was that freedom had never done him any good. Being locked up for the last few years had given him more of a taste for being inside than out. That was what he liked about this walled garden. We can only truly escape from within.

He would never have got mixed up in a crazy scheme like this if he hadn't found Agnès again. How had he landed up at Théo's place? ... Through a friend of a friend of a friend, most likely. Since getting out of prison, he had been knocking about around Paris. There was a big crowd that evening. The mirrors were covered in trails of powder. Tequila, beer, spliffs, wild Parisian nights. He didn't find it fun any more. He was there because he had to be somewhere after all. The girl with red hair had got up from Théo's lap and come to sit next to him.

'You look as bored shitless as I am.'

'Yep.'

'Shall we get out of here?'

'And go where?'

'Your place!'

'I'm in a hotel. Not a good one.'

'I don't give a shit.'

They made love all night and they did it well, very tenderly, pausing now and again for a line of coke or a drink. It was the first good thing to happen to him in months. He slept for the whole of the next day and she came back in the evening. They had dinner together at a little place near the hotel in the eighteenth arrondissement, and they picked up where they had left off the night before. It was like a fairy tale for little kids. In the morning, on his way to have a piss, he had used Lol's bag to shoot up. Among the objects that fell out of it were a photo of a woman he had known all too well and an identity card in the name of Agnès Doilet. He couldn't help letting out a cry, at which point the girl turned over in bed and opened one eye.

'What's going on?'

Étienne threw the identity card and photo onto the bed.

'What about it?'

'I'm your father, Agnès! I'm your father!'

Éliette had decided to be bold, and she did not regret it. The jeans and T-shirt she had bought the day before made her look ten years younger. She smiled blissfully into the mirror as though touched by a fairy's wand. On her own, she would never have taken these clothes out of their packaging. As a little girl, whenever she was given something new to wear, she would find an excuse to go straight out and show it off. But that was back on the busy streets of Paris ... What was the point in doing the same here? Today, though, she had an audience in the form of Étienne, and Agnès, whom she bumped into as she went from her bedroom into the corridor.

'Oh, Éliette, I wanted to ask: you don't have a set of kitchen scales, do you?'

'Kitchen scales?'

'Yes, I have some letters to post and I need to weigh them.'

'Um ... yes, I must do. Have a look on top of the kitchen cupboards.'

'Thanks. Ooh, love the T-shirt. The colour's great on you.'

Étienne had got out two sunloungers. He was stretched out on one of them with his head in the shade and his feet in the sun. He appeared to be asleep. Éliette sat down beside him. The heat trapped inside the garden walls made the air hum. She closed her eyes and every sound and smell became magnified. It was like dissolving in a kind of bouillon.

'Your house is lovely. It's like you.'

'I thought you were asleep.'

'No. I'm having such a good time, I don't want to miss a thing.'

'Are you ... are you thinking of leaving soon?'

'Agnès needs to call the garage to see when her car will be ready. Could be this evening.'

'I know we've only just met, but ... it's really nice having the two of you here.'

'The feeling's mutual, I think. An unexpected interlude, for all of us.'

'It's funny. Nothing happens for months and then it all comes in an avalanche!'

'It's like hunting. You spend more time lying in wait than you do shooting.'

'In two hours, we'll have known one another for twenty-four hours.'

'Long enough to have shared memories: the tyre, the storm, your neighbours' son's passing, Agnès's grand entrance this morning, a barbecue, your metamorphosis from widow in black to butterfly in blue. The colour really suits you.'

'Why didn't you tell me you had a daughter?'

'You didn't ask.'

'True. Come to think of it, I know nothing about you.'

'That's about all there is to know.'

Agnès appeared in the doorway. Her feet were bare and she was wearing a micro miniskirt and a men's shirt with barely a button done up.

'I've put the scales back, Éliette. I made a phone call as well; you'll have to let me know what I owe you. It was about my car.'

'Don't mention it.'

'It won't be ready until Thursday. Nightmare!'

Éliette could barely contain a sigh of relief. Agnès came to sit on the ground between the other two. She was sniffling, like a red-haired poodle.

'Do you have a cold?'

'It doesn't take much – a shower, a bit of a breeze and that's it! So, Étienne. What shall we do?'

'Éliette, would we be outstaying our welcome if ...?'

'Not at all. As I said, my children don't arrive until Friday, so it's no problem.'

'Thank you, Éliette. But we'll take care of the shopping and cooking. Agreed?'

'Agreed. We can sort that out tomorrow. We've got everything we need for tonight. Oh, looks like we've got a visitor ...'

The police van parked in front of the gate. Two gendarmes got out. They were red-faced, with rings of sweat under the arms of their shirts. Éliette went to greet them.

'Bonjour, Messieurs.'

'Bonjour, Madame Vélard ... Monsieur, Mademoiselle.'

Étienne and Agnès barely nodded.

'Have you come from the Jauberts'?'

'Yes. What a tragedy. No matter how many times you see these things happen, it's still a shock. And it makes you wonder what gets into these kids the minute they have a steering wheel in their hands. Twice we'd arrested Patrick! ... Though it's a bit different this time. Anyway, since we were just down the road and we know you like riding about in your little car on the back roads, we wondered if by any chance you might have come across anybody on foot who might have seemed a bit ... strange?'

'No. I went to Montélimar yesterday and then ...'

As she replayed the previous day's events, she instinctively turned to Étienne before going on.

'... and then I came home again. I didn't notice anything strange.'

'Just asking on the off-chance. And Monsieur, Madame, you didn't see anything either?'

'We arrived on the train this morning.'

Étienne's reply rolled straight off the tongue, as if he had learned the line by heart. Éliette was somewhat taken aback.

'Well, then ... We won't keep you.'

'Is it to do with the other car?'

'Yes, Madame Vélard. We've identified the owner. His vehicle was stolen around midday yesterday from the car park at Montélimar station. The fuel tank was empty. The thief must have panicked. Stupid. Right, we're off. Goodbye, Madame Vélard, Monsieur, Madame.'

Even after they had gone, a blue stain seemed to linger where they had stood. Étienne lay with his arm across his face and his head thrown back. Agnès was rolling pebbles through her fingers and Éliette was desperately trying to find the key to escape the heavy silence. The light was tinted copper and the house's stone-work was blushing pink. Agnès got up suddenly.

'I'm going to do the washing-up. I need to move.'

She disappeared, swallowed up in the shadows of the doorway.

'Éliette, why didn't you tell the gendarmes how we met?'

'Because ... because it's beside the point! You had an argument with your girlfriend and she left you in the middle of nowhere, isn't that right?'

'Yes, of course.'

'And the reason you told them you'd arrived on the train this morning was to avoid having to go into details like that.'

'Exactly. Why complicate things?'

'In the past, I always had to be in control, to understand and check everything. I couldn't feel at ease without answers and solutions. But since Charles died, I've tended to let things come and go as they please.'

'Did you love your husband very much?'

'Yes. The way we felt about one another was never in doubt. But ... how can I put it? It's as if that was another life. I think of it now as if it belonged to someone else. I've changed. I don't know if the life I had with him would suit me nowadays.'

Éliette got to her feet and began pulling up a few weeds around a scrawny rose bush. Étienne watched her through half-closed eyes. She was like a ripe fruit whose sugar was turning to honey. Certain people, like certain plants, flowered several times in one season. Others would never bear a single fruit: no sooner had they blossomed than they were already wilting. Étienne thought of himself as akin to an avocado stone: you kept its bottom wet in a mustard jar and it sprouted one measly stem, busting its guts to produce a single flower as pathetic as a flag at half mast. So much must come down to the soil the plant was grown in, the amount of water and sun it got. Above all, it rested on the great gardener on high knowing what he was doing ...

'You've got green fingers, then?'

'Let's just say I try.'

'Unlike me; I've managed to kill fake flowers before.'

'That's quite a feat!'

'I know. I'm quite proud of myself.'

Through the open kitchen window they could hear Agnès singing Gainsbourg: '*Inceste de citron, papa, papa* ...'

Agnès's sniffle did not appear to have cleared up, but strangely it had given her a burst of boundless energy. She had done the cooking and laid the table; now she was like a moth fluttering around the flickering light of the candles. All that was left of the daylight was a trace of purple at the bottom of the sky, with the rolling mountains starkly outlined against it. As at lunchtime, the conversation covered all kinds of topics, but everyone made a conscious effort to avoid talking about themselves. Hiding behind tales of other people's adventures was like swanning about at a masked ball. They had already polished off two bottles of rosé and Étienne was opening a third when a headlight swept like a brushstroke over the line of poplars at the entrance to the drive.

'That must be Serge and his friend. I rang earlier to see how they were. I told them to pop in for a drink, depending on how things were at home.'

The two young men appeared, their pale clothes almost phosphorescent against the dark mouth of the garden gate. Éliette did the introductions. Agnès made yet another excuse to slip inside the house, this time in order to fetch glasses. Éliette noticed that these comings and goings seemed to be getting on Étienne's nerves. Serge's face was drawn; Zep never took his eyes off him.

'So, how is everything?'

'Not great. Things are OK with Maman, but Papa's not speaking to me. My uncle and aunt came down from Aubenas this afternoon. They're staying a few days. I took the opportunity to get on with some of the formalities, going to the undertaker's and so on. Any excuse to get out of the house. The funeral's on Friday.'

'OK. I'll go and see them tomorrow. Try not to blame your father. He's having a hard time. It might not look like it, but he's more fragile than your mother.'

'I don't blame him. It just hurts, that's all. You saw how he was this morning when I tried to help him ...'

'He was drunk.'

'It's almost worse when he's sober. It's as if he thinks I'm the one who killed Patrick. I'm hurting too, even though Patrick and I didn't get on. I saw him two months ago in Grenoble; he wanted me to sign something. We had a row. You don't know at the time you're never going to see someone again; it's only afterwards ...'

Serge had tears in his eyes. Zep placed a hand on his shoulder. Étienne stood up, uncomfortable, made his excuses and went into the house.

Agnès was sitting on the bed tidying away her little kit: mirror, straw, razor blade.

'Don't you think you've had enough tonight?'

'This is the last one! You're so fucking tight! God, it's good though. What's your problem?'

'Nothing. I'm sick of hearing about that accident.'

'Chill out. Nothing's gonna happen. And anyway, Éliette has the hots for you, big time. I wouldn't mind having her as a step-mother. By the way, where am I sleeping tonight?'

'Don't know, don't care.'

'Thanks very much! OK, I'll stop pissing around. I think I've got an idea, a client.'

'Who's that, then?'

'A guy who works in the movies. I've sold to him before; there's never been a problem.'

'Nothing to do with Théo?'

'No, different network. Only thing is, if we want to get rid of the whole lot at once, we can't be too greedy.'

'And where is this guy?'

'Down on the Côte d'Azur at the moment, I think. I'd have to make a phone call.'

'I don't know … We don't want to rush things.'

'Rush things?! Do you have any idea of the shit you've got us into in the last twenty-four hours? D'you really think we have a choice? We're not on our holidays at Auntie Éliette's, dearest Daddykins. We've got two days at most before we need to get the hell out of here, as far away as we can get, because let me tell you, Théo's not going to let two kilos of good coke go without a fight, especially not to you. Don't forget you already pinched his woman – that would be me!'

'He didn't give a shit about you. That's why he gave the job to me!'

'How stupid are you? Do you really think you'd have got it if I hadn't made him give it to you?'

'You promised me you wouldn't see him again!'

'Oh, calm down … You didn't have two coins to rub together … Anyway, don't worry, nothing happened. So what do you think?'

Agnès was right. They had to make a move, try something. There was no use pretending, and yet …

The sound of Éliette's voice calling from the garden made him jump. He leaned out of the window.

'Étienne, when you come down, would you mind bringing the telescope with you? It's in my room, next to the wardrobe.'

'Yes, yes, of course.'

'There's a magnificent sky tonight and Zep's a bit of an astron-omer!'

'Righty-ho. On my way.'

How dumb the stars looked, as dull as the street lights lining the motorway. Agnès was lying on her back, knees bent, thighs bared, smoking a cigarette. The white triangle of her knickers was curved like a scallop shell.

'Well?'

'OK. But be careful.'

Agnès joined the other four in the garden a quarter of an hour later. They were drinking wine and staring up at the stars. Zep was pointing up at the sky, reeling off clever-sounding names that his accent made sound even more exotic. They took turns pressing their eye to the telescope and exclaiming, 'What a view!' All except Étienne, who passed on his go, preferring to keep a suitable distance between himself and the stars looking down on him in scorn.

'I prefer the bit in between, the darkness. The part you can't see.'

They all stopped talking after that. They let space seep inside them; the sky was reflected on earth. Serge and Zep had their arms round each other's necks; Agnès was lying on the grass, arms outstretched, Éliette on one of the loungers with her hands behind her head; and Étienne sat perched on the bench, chin in his hands, elbows on his knees. There was no movement, only a twinkling like an aura around each of them. They had become a kind of constellation, in a scenario brought about by what we call chance, for want of a better word. It lasted for a split second, or an hour … Serge and Zep whispered a few words in each other's ears and stood up.

'Éliette, it's getting late. We should head back up there.'

'Up there? Oh, yes! Come back whenever you want.'

'Thanks, Éliette. It's so nice to be able to … just be ourselves. Good night. Good night, Étienne. Lovely to meet you. Good night, Agnès.'

The three left behind watched the other two dissolving into the night, the same way they had come. Agnès stretched her limbs.

'Mmm! It's so pretty. You can see angels all over the place tonight … Éliette, where am I sleeping?'

'Wherever you want, love. The room next to your father's.'

'It's love, now, is it?'

'Oh, sorry, I …'

'It's fine. Love is all around. Good night!'

Neither Éliette nor Étienne knew how to take their leave. Perhaps they did not wish to. They both watched the light come on at Agnès's window. Earlier, Zep had explained to them how stars were dying and being born all the time. The sky was sparkling. The light bulb in the bedroom went out, but its image stayed imprinted on their retinas for a long time afterwards. All his life, Étienne had been in bars at closing time, among the last ones standing at the end of the party. He liked being around people who refused to accept it was over, who fought a losing battle against the inevitable.

'Éliette, how about a game of "Say what you're thinking"?'

'How does it work?'

'You don't think about it. You just say the first thing that comes into your head.'

'OK. Do we take it in turns?'

'Yes.'

'Right, then. Say what you're thinking.'

'I'm thinking it's too soon for everything.'

'I'm thinking we ought to get several lives.'

328

'I'm thinking my death will serve no purpose and that's a missed opportunity on God's part.'

'I'm thinking I don't want to make up my mind whether I'm too hot or too cold.'

'I'm thinking my family has a lot of dirty linen to air and it's getting out of hand.'

'I'm not thinking about my family, but I've got a big pile of dirty linen too.'

'I'm thinking that if I hadn't had a daughter, I wouldn't necessarily have had a dog.'

'I'm thinking we don't have to do anything, but everything is important.'

'I'm thinking no one is ever happy and that's our only source of satisfaction.'

'I'm thinking everyone else is better than me.'

'I'm thinking we shouldn't want to please everyone.'

'I'm thinking everyone else lies except me, and it's not a nice thought.'

'I'm thinking of all the times a lie has helped me to tell an unexpected truth.'

'I'm thinking of a quote of de Gaulle's: "I've spent a lot of time pretending, and usually it has worked."'

'I'm thinking we should have been warned the world was ending.'

'I'm thinking I'm dreading the sun rising in a few hours.'

'I'm thinking tomorrow is not another day.'

'I'm thinking by going too far you get back to where you started.'

Their fingers had become entwined; it wasn't a game any more.

Éliette had not taken in a word of the news, despite the fact the radio was droning in her ear. They could have told her the world had ended and still she would have carried on sipping her tea, staring into space, lost in thought. A fly was keeping her company, buzzing from one jar of jam to another, totally absorbed in its essential function: eating and washing its sticky feet in the tiny pool of tea beside the teapot. Éliette felt in perfect harmony with the fly. The minimalism of its existence suited her down to the ground. To aspire to more than eating jam and washing one's feet in tea seemed unnecessary. It had pretty eyes as well, this fly, and wings for which Éliette would have gladly swapped her feet. Agnès wafted into the kitchen wearing only her large men's shirt. She mumbled a hello as she sailed past without a glance in Éliette's direction. She sat down and poured herself a tea with such delicacy that she chipped the cup.

'Morning, Agnès. Sleep all right?'

'No. It's too quiet here; it keeps me awake. What about you two?'

'I slept very well. As for Étienne, you'll have to ask him your-self. I think he slept on the sofa in the living room. I heard snoring.'

'Oh!'

With her mass of wild red hair and big black eye she looked like a clown who had messed up his act.

'Shall I do you some toast?'

'Er …. OK.'

'It's always like this the first few nights when city people come to stay. The silence gets to them. But they get used to it.'

'You need time for that.'

'For what?'

'To get used to it. I've never had time to get used to anything. Just as well – I don't like habits. Why did he sleep in the lounge?'

'I don't know. He was still in the garden when I went up to bed. He was asleep on one of the loungers.'

'Pissed?'

'No, just tired, I think. Here's your toast.'

'Thanks. He's always tired. Some people have dogs for companions; he's got his tiredness. I'm heading off today; I'll be back tomorrow night.'

'Oh! OK, then.'

'I can't stay in one place. Gotta keep moving. I've got mates on the Côte. I'll visit them and then head back up.'

'Right, well, if you like ...'

'Can we borrow the limo? Étienne has some shopping to do. He'll drop me off at the station.'

'Yes, fine.'

'It'll give the two of you some space.'

'Honestly, you're no trouble, Agnès.'

'I know. But we should all be playing with friends our own age. I'll go and wake him up. My train's at eleven.'

Étienne was curled up on the sofa with Éliette's cardigan thrown over his shoulders. Certain pre-Columbian mummies had adopted the same foetal position for their last journey.

'Étienne! … Étienne!'

Agnès's face appeared just at the point in his dream when he was finishing setting up a cycle race.

'What the fuck are you doing here?'

'I could ask you the same question. Why aren't you in your room?'

'I fell asleep in the garden. In the middle of the night I got cold and came and flopped down here.'

'I thought you were in with Éliette.'

'And what if I was?'

'Nothing. My train's at eleven. Éliette's lending us her wheels. I'm going to see my mate in La Ciotat. I'll be back tomorrow night.'

'What are you talking about?'

'The buyer I told you about last night. He's up for it, but he needs to try it.'

'And then what?'

'How should I know? We'll see what happens. So are you gonna let me do my thing, or what?'

'Yes. I think I might have a shower and get changed. You've got a face like a slapped arse.'

'I just want to get out of here.'

It was the first time the Aixam had left without her. Éliette watched the little cream car disappear at the end of the road and, for want of anything else to do, decided to sort out her paperwork. It felt strange to be alone in the house again. The 'strangeness' came from already missing him. Étienne had not been gone five minutes and she was already eagerly awaiting his return. Being alone felt different now. Less serene, perhaps, but how delicious it was to be filled with uncertainty: 'Is he coming back?' Waiting for someone, having someone waiting for you ... No, nothing had happened besides their two hands pressed together between the sunloungers. Étienne had fallen asleep and she had left him in the care of the star-studded sky. It was important not to make any hasty moves. You didn't wake a sleepwalker standing on the edge of a roof. Agnès's departure this morning had not come as a surprise but seemed perfectly natural. She too must have felt that this Wednesday and Thursday were for them … only them. When she opened her eyes again, Éliette realised she had just torn her EDF bill into a thousand pieces of confetti.

Throughout the journey, Agnès had not stopped complaining about how fucking slow the piece of shit toy car was.

'I feel like I'm in a wheelchair. Put your foot down, damn it!'

'My foot's touching the floor!'

For the second time in Étienne's life, he found himself at Montélimar station. It was no worse than any other station, but he had no wish to hang around there. Agnès got out, slammed the door rather violently and went round to give her father a kiss through the open window.

'Don't do anything stupid, Étienne.'

'It's me who should be worried!'

'No. I'm going to do a deal: it's clear, straightforward; it's a certain amount per gram. As for you … you're putty in Éliette's hands.'

'What are you on about?'

'Watch out, Daddykins. The most dangerous thing about danger is that it comes where you least expect it.'

'Well, aren't you the philosopher?'

'I'm a wise old woman – older, even, than Éliette. I'll call you tonight.'

As she ran off into the station, bag slung over her shoulder, Étienne realised he had never seen her on the beach with a bucket and spade. One day they would go on holiday together. One day ...

Éliette had given up poring over paperwork and gone back to the Colette biography. She read the first line of the fourth chapter for the tenth time, and still took nothing in. Nothing can fill the gap of waiting, other than a swift blow to the head. She had reached the point of wondering whether to cut her toenails or fingernails when the sound of an engine swept away all such noble thoughts. It wasn't the Aixam, but Paul's diesel engine. She let out a curse that was absorbed into the hush of the house.

'Hello, Paul!'

'Hi ... Éliette. Gonna be a hot one.'

His speech was slurred, his step unsteady. His car was parked at an angle across the drive, its nose pointing into the ditch.

'Not disturbing you, am I?'

'Of course not. Fancy a coffee?'

'Not really the drink for this time of day, but if you like ...'

'A pastis, then?'

'I wouldn't say no.'

In the kitchen he instinctively sat at the table and took up the same position as he had the day before, elbows on the oilcloth, shoulders hunched.

'How's Rose?'

'All right. She's wilting.'

This unusual attempt at humour caught Éliette off guard.

'What about you?'

'Oh, just wonderful! One of my lads has just got himself killed and the other's about to marry a Kraut. May as well get the wedding and funeral done in one go!'

'You shouldn't be so hard on Serge. He's different, so what? He's hurting too. He loved his brother and he loves you.'

'Too much love, that's his problem! You can't go around loving everybody.'

'Why not?'

'Because ... Oh, I don't know. Because it all becomes a mess, one big orgy! There are men and there are women, and it's complicated enough as it is!'

He downed his pastis in one, ran a hand across his face and looked at his palm as though trying to find his reflection in a mirror.

'You can't have it all, is all I'm saying!' he continued.

'Why? It's not a crime! Serge is gay and you've known that for years. He and his boyfriend love each other. Where's the harm in that?'

'Well, let me tell you, if I feel like doing ... with anyone I like, I ... It's a bloody joke! It's not right!'

Paul had stood up. He had gripped the edge of the sink with both hands and was tugging on it as if he wanted to rip it out. He was sweating heavily and his ears were as red as a tobacconist's shop sign. He looked to Éliette like a wild boar being chased.

'So you understand everything, do you? Everything's normal to you, is it? And what if I told you I've wanted you for years? What would you say to that, eh? What would you say?' he asked insistently.

He was now standing close behind her, his rough hands clamped around her shoulders.

'You're hurting me, Paul. It's the alcohol talking, and the pain you're in. You should go home.'

'I'm not pissed. I could drink a whole tank of pastis and I still wouldn't be drunk. Why shouldn't I get to do what I want, the way everyone else does? I want you! You have no idea how much I want you!'

Trapped in his gnarly arms, Éliette could do nothing but squirm in her chair, saying over and over again, 'That's enough, Paul. You're hurting me!'

But the harder she fought back, the tighter he gripped. His stubble scratched her cheek. Stale sweat and the taste of aniseed made her retch. They fell to the floor together. Paul's left hand clasped Éliette's face, while his right hand groped under her dress. His fingers were like tools, hard and coarse. His breath whooshed in her ear like a pressure hose. The more Éliette squirmed, the more Paul bore down on her, a ton of long-suppressed desire. He was on the verge of penetrating her when a noise rang out like a gong.

Paul let out a groan and fell onto his side, clutching his head. Étienne was standing above them with a cast-iron casserole dish in his hand.

'Don't just lie there, Éliette. Run.'

'Is he ...?'

'No, just stunned. Get out of here.'

Éliette limped out of the kitchen.

Étienne pulled up a chair and placed the casserole dish on his lap. Paul was moaning and wriggling on the ground like a big flaccid worm. Blood was trickling from his ear. He stammered, 'I didn't do anything! ... I didn't do anything!' Étienne kicked him in the side.

'Get out.'

Paul propped himself up on his elbow and stared at Étienne, red-eyed.

'Bastard!'

'Get out, before I do your face in.'

Paul got up on all fours and ran his hand across his blotchy face. He coughed, spat, and eventually got to his feet.

'You ain't seen the last of me ...'

'I'm telling you, fuck off or you're gonna get it!'

'This isn't over ... No way ...'

Paul glared at Étienne, his blue eyes washed out by pastis, and left, cackling like the witch in a bad dream.

Éliette had retreated to the living-room sofa where she lay huddled, clutching her knees to her chest. She wasn't crying but was shivering uncontrollably. Étienne sat in an armchair facing her. He was incredibly pale.

'It's OK. He's gone.'

Éliette could not unclench her teeth. Her heart was beating like a banging shutter.

'What can I do to help?'

Éliette raised her eyebrows, but couldn't produce a sound. She felt a wave of nausea rising in her stomach. She just made it to the toilet in time to throw up her breakfast. It took a good half-hour in the shower to scrub off the smell of Paul which had seeped into her skin. She got changed and threw her soiled clothes into the bin. Étienne was waiting in the garden, smoking a cigarette.

'Are you OK?'

'Yes, I think so. It's just ... unbelievable! Thirty years we've known each other ... I don't know what got into him ... I would never have imagined he was capable of ... I don't know what to do, Étienne. I just don't know ...'

'He was drunk. Maybe he'll apologise when he's sobered up.'

'Maybe. But I won't ever forget what's happened. Things can't go back to the way they were. What on earth's been going on the last two days? I don't have a clue any more! It's as if the whole world's gone mad, me included!'

'That's life, Éliette, that's all. You think you're safe, like when you're on the motorway; it's a bit boring, you lose concentration and then ... a loose bit of gravel, an insect, and whoops! You've lost control, spun round, and find yourself facing the wrong way. But hey, if you're not dead, you'll still end up somewhere!'

I bought some tomatoes and lamb chops. Do you fancy some food?'

'I'm not all that hungry.'

'Leave it to me, I'll sort it out. You have nothing to be afraid of now. I'm here, and I'm glad I am.'

He looked like a kid with his black eye and his cowlick, but Éliette felt safe with him. She took the hand he held out to her, and pressed it against her cheek. He smelled of fresh bread.

The microcar carried them along the winding, practically empty roads that criss-crossed the region for the whole afternoon. They dipped their feet in the emerald-green pools of the Escoutay and lay on the warm flat stones beside the river. From time to time a fluffy little cloud drifted across the sky above them and they would watch until it thinned and disappeared as if by magic. The babbling water mingled with birdsong like an advert for paradise, a bucolic, pastel-painted scene extolling the virtues of the afterlife. They stopped off in Alba where, after wandering down unevenly paved alleys that seemed to be populated only with cats, they enjoyed an ice-cold drink at a café under the plane trees in the square. A pair of pensioners were getting some air, sitting in their front garden. Side by side in their deckchairs, they didn't say a word to one another, looking straight ahead at a future that already belonged to the past.

'It's fascinating how still they are, isn't it? It's as if they've been there for ever.'

'They probably have. Look at their hands and feet – they're like roots!'

'It would be nice to live like a pot plant.'

'What's stopping you?'

'I don't know. I always feel like there's someone prodding me on, as if I'm shuffling along in a queue.'

'Why not leave the queue, Étienne?'

'I've tried, but I'm scared shitless of breaking ranks. Fact is I'm just an average Joe.'

The sun was beginning to yawn above the Roman-tiled rooftops. A handful of people had emerged out of nowhere and were crossing the square, a baguette under their arm, a shopping basket in their hand, everyday people, life's walk-on parts; Étienne would have liked to swap roles. He sighed and his eyes met Éliette's lavender-blue gaze. She was smiling.

'What?'

'Nothing. You're sweet when you're sad. Shall we go?'

In the car, they heard on the news that a twelve-year-old English girl had just given birth. The father was thirteen. When the child reached the age of twenty, it would have a thirty-two-year-old mother. Éliette remarked that, given we were all living longer, it would soon be hard to tell grandfather from grandson in family albums. But another news item, this time from the United States, suggested the opposite: two twelve-year-old kids had just been shot dead by police after gunning down half a dozen of their classmates along with their teacher. Christ dying at thirty-three seemed like a doddery old man in comparison.

They said no more to each other but sat thinking how quickly our time on earth is up, all the way back to Éliette's house. A crow was nailed to the gate by its wing, its head smashed in. Éliette hid her face in her hands while Étienne pulled the bird free and sent it on one last flight before it landed beyond the bushes.

'He's mad! My God, what am I going to do? I can't stay here any longer! I'm calling the police.'

'Calm down, Éliette. I'm here. I'm sure we can find a way to sort this out without making a song and dance about it. Trust me.'

Étienne put his arms around her and kissed her on the forehead. Trembling from head to toe, she clutched him tightly. Their lips met. She kissed like a little girl, mouth barely open, the shy tip of her tongue flavoured with diabolo menthe. As they closed the door behind them, Étienne told himself there was no rest in this world until you were six feet under a marble slab.

The telephone rang for the first time while Étienne was making a tomato salad. Éliette went to pick it up. It was Serge. His father had not been seen since that morning and Serge wondered if he might by any chance have been by. After a brief pause, Éliette responded in the negative, then asked after Rose. She was doing OK. The cousins from Aubenas were plying her with sleeping pills, leaving themselves free to sniff around in cupboards, suss out what the land and buildings were worth, and do sums on the backs of envelopes. There was such an atmosphere up there, he wasn't sure he could stick it out until the funeral. On that note, he wished her a good evening. He would probably pop in to say hello in the morning, just to be around some normal people.

Next it was Agnès's turn to call. She sounded completely hyper. Étienne could barely make sense of half of it.

'I can't understand a thing you're saying. Speak clearly!'

'I'm on a boat! It's awesome! Loads of people and champagne and stuff!'

'Good for you. What about the rest of it?'

'It's all good. I'll be back tomorrow morning. Ben's giving me a ride – and man, wait till you see his car! It's Italian, red, a proper racing car. Nothing like Éliette's little toy!'

'Are you out of your mind? You're not seriously planning on bringing this guy here?'

'Why not? He's got the dough, he's cool. No problemo, Daddy-o. We'll be able to get moving.'

'Agnès! Do not bring that man here. Do you hear me? It's not a block of hash you're selling, for fuck's sake. These people could stick a gun under our noses and skin us like rabbits. You're off your head. You need to drop it and get out of there, Agnès ... Agnès?'

'I can't hear you! ... This phone is a piece of shit ... Hello?'

'Agnès!'

'I'll call you back tomorrow. Oh, and don't do anything silly with Éliette. You know I'm the jealous type!'

'Agnès ...'

'Love you, you funny old fart.'

Étienne remained in conversation with the dial tone for a few seconds before hanging up.

They picked at their supper of tomato salad and a slice of ham. The bird nailed to the door had cast the shadow of its withered wing over the sunny afternoon. They opened a bottle of rosé and sat on the front step, sipping their wine and waiting for shooting stars to make a wish on. Éliette wished that Paul would fall into a hole so deep and dark he might never have existed. And she had two other, more minor, wishes: that Sylvie's children be bedridden with measles, and that Marc be forced to cancel his visit because of work (which would hardly be a surprise, after all). As for Étienne, he wished only to go back forty-five years and for a big fat star to hang permanently above his head. But all these comets, most of which were actually Russian or American satellites, were so laden with the petty hopes of humans in disarray that they left nothing but calling cards in the sky, along with the false promise that things would soon return to normal.

Since they could expect nothing from these tin-plated stars, Étienne and Éliette held one another close and waited for desire to make them climb the flight of stairs to Éliette's room. It was more of a big cuddle than a night of torrid passion. Both of them were tired, moving about in the bed as if in an aquarium filled with thick blue jelly. Having become used to Agnès's matchstick body – so easily set alight – he struggled to find his way around Éliette's, made timid and awkward by abstinence. But it didn't really matter: their fond strokes and caresses were enough to make them feel that one day they would have time, all the time in the world. They fell peacefully asleep, like two prisoners on death row clinging to the tiny hope of a presidential pardon.

In her dream, Éliette was doing the washing-up, a huge great pile of it! She had barely finished one plate when someone handed her another. She could not tear her eyes from the foamy basin of clinking cutlery, glasses and saucers. She wanted to look up at the sky which she knew was so blue, but everything was going too quickly ... Still these anonymous hands were bringing piles and piles of dirty plates ... One of these went crashing to the floor, and she woke up.

'Étienne, I heard something!'

'Hmm?'

'I heard a noise. There's someone downstairs.'

'Stay here. I'll go.'

His dream had been filled with snow. Reach the summit and he would have won. But won what? ... He pulled on his trousers, wobbling in the dark, and left the room, coughing, his eyes still gummed up with sleep. It must have been around five in the morning; the pale light of dawn was creeping up the stairs like smoke. Outside, the birds were singing loudly, proud supporters of the breaking day. At the bottom of the stairs, Étienne hovered between the living room on his left and the kitchen on his right. He went for the kitchen, and the moment he stepped over the threshold, he knew what had been in store for the winner in his dream: a blow to the back of the head.

Pushing herself up on her elbows in bed, Éliette thought she heard a soft thud, like a pile of wet laundry being dumped on the floor, and then nothing.

'Étienne? ... ÉTIENNE?'

No answer. The light of dawn filtering through the slats in the shutters looked cold, like a grey shroud. She tried to cry out again but no sound escaped through the barrier of her gritted teeth. It was pointless. Someone was climbing the stairs, but it was not Étienne. Her fingers clutched the sheets while her eyes remained fastened on the half-open door, like an animal waiting for the butcher's axe to fall. We tell ourselves in books that we could jump out of the window, cry for help, lay our hands on a blunt object, do something. But it isn't true: fear paralyses you, makes an idiot out of you – the victim is suicidal, obediently waiting for the executioner to do his work. You know what's going to happen and you believe in it fervently, as though it were a form of deliverance. Perhaps it is all we have been waiting for, all our lives.

'Paul, why are you doing this?'

He had not yet pushed the door; only the barrel of his rifle pointed through the opening. He looked different, as though his profile had been etched on a bronze coin.

'Don't scream, Éliette. Don't scream or I'll kill you.'

The words were spoken calmly, as if to a restless child at bedtime. His gun was in his right hand, and with the handkerchief in his left he wiped the sweat from his brow. He surveyed the room and, having established there was no riot squad hiding behind the wardrobe, he sat down at the foot of the bed. He looked like a hunter returning home empty-handed.

'I know it's not right, all of that ... But all my life I've done the right thing and look where it's got me! I don't regret anything. I would have liked it to happen differently, but ... all those feelings ...'

He was beating his chest with the flat of his hand, and making the bed bounce. He had tears in his eyes, his gaze as clouded as his state of mind. Éliette let out a deep sigh. Perhaps there was a way out after all.

'Why don't you put down your gun?'

'I can't ... If you scream, I'll shoot you, obviously.'

'Why?'

'Because that's just the way it is! ... You spend your whole life trying to find a place there's no way back from. That's where I am.'

'What have you done to Étienne?'

'That stupid little bastard? He's not dead; I just gave him a good whack round the head. He's tied up downstairs. What the hell do you see in that idiot, anyway?'

'He's a friend, Paul. Just a friend!'

Paul was now standing again, the barrel of his gun chasing the shadows.

'He's no man, Éliette! No man at all. He'll hurt you, I'm telling you. I know what men are like – I was in Algeria! Up in the Aurès mountains, you soon sorted the men from the boys. I stood and watched the prisoners dig their own graves ... *Bang! Bang!* ... *He* is not a man, believe me.'

'You're scaring me. Put the gun down.'

He looked at her, dazed by his own rant, and began smiling as if he knew her game.

'I may not be the sharpest tool in the box, but I'm no fool, Éliette!'

'What do you want?'

'I don't know any more ... Good, evil, it's all the same ... Smashing that little bastard's head in was fun, just like nailing that crow to your door ... Doing wrong ... that's it, that's what I like.'

'You won't get anywhere with that attitude.'

'Who cares? I'm already there! I'm not afraid of anything any more! Anything at all!'

He banged his head against the door several times to demonstrate how pain made him numb. A trickle of blood ran down from his bandage, skirting his nose, to the corner of his mouth. He stuck out his tongue and licked it.

'It's nice. Tastes a bit like rust. I'm rusty, Éliette, just like you, just like everyone. We're all dead, only no one else knows it yet.'

Éliette shifted her weight on the bed. Paul stiffened.

'Don't move!'

'I need a wee.'

'Piss in the bed! Yeah, that's right, piss in front of me. I'd like that ... Go on, then!'

Using the tip of his rifle, he pulled back the sheets, exposing Éliette's bare abdomen.

'Well? Is it coming?'

'I can't ...'

'You'd do it for him, though, wouldn't you, slut? But not for me ... Well, from now on you're going to do all that filthy stuff in front of me. Even if I drop dead, you'll always have me there with you, in your dirty shitty little memories! No one's going to forget me!'

The barrel of the gun brushed against Éliette's nose. She could smell its acidic metal odour. Paul's eyes bored into hers, incandescent with rage. She didn't even have the strength to faint. Paul lowered his eyes first. The two black holes, set one on top of the other in the barrel of the gun, turned towards the window ledge, where a blackbird had just landed with much flapping of its wings. Paul let the weapon fall into his lap and burst into tears.

'Forgive me, Éliette. I'm not a bad person ... but what am I supposed to do with all the bad stuff that's happened? I want another life too! Do you think I chose to be a bloody yokel? To go to bed with bloody Rose every night? Of course I didn't! I've dreamed of going places, just like everyone else. I've just never been lucky enough to live my dreams. Maybe they've turned to nightmares now, but they're still my dreams, they're mine! It's all up to me! Damn, yes!'

Éliette was holding her breath. One false move and Paul could go up like a powder keg. In spite of her terror, she could not help feeling a little sorry for him. He was right: a nightmare was a dream that had gone wrong. Her bladder was straining. It was silly, but she was sure that if she could only go to the loo, everything would be better. Paul would calm down, everything would fall back into place, just like it was ...

'Do you remember when the kids used to play together? All laughing and shouting! Hmm? Do you remember, Éliette?'

'Yes, Paul. I remember.'

'We were happy back then. None of us could have imagined that one day ... Know what I think?'

'No, I don't, but I really need the toilet ...'

'Your friend, downstairs – I think it was him who killed my Patrick.'

'Why would he have done that? They didn't even know each other!'

'I don't know. But I'm sure it was him. Ever since he's been here, everything's changed. You're not the same, Éliette, nothing's the same. It's not just a coincidence!'

'Let me go to the loo and then we can talk about all this calmly ...'

Paul wasn't listening. He rubbed the trigger of his gun as if stroking a clitoris.

'I'll get rid of him. We've got to tackle him, like mildew.'

'Paul, please ...'

'Huh? Oh, all right, but I'm coming with you. You have to leave the door open. I can't trust you. It's not your fault; he's pulled the wool over your eyes, but I'm here. I respect you, Éliette. You can count on me.'

She got out of bed, naked, and Paul coyly averted his eyes while she put on her dressing gown. As she relieved herself, with Paul standing guard outside the door, the rifle over his shoulder, she could not help finding a modicum of truth in Paul's ramblings. Of course, he was raving mad, but there was no denying that since Étienne had appeared, everything had turned upside down. The abandoned car that had caused Patrick's death, Étienne strolling down the road, the way he had acted in front of the gendarmes, the story he had told about the girlfriend leaving him in the middle of nowhere, and Agnès, whose behaviour towards her father was so unlike what one would expect of a daughter ... There was nothing concrete or certain any more, as there had been in Charles's day; even the tiled floor of the bathroom seemed as treacherous as shifting sand.

'Done?'

'Yes.'

Paul had red eyes. He looked like one of those briar pipe bowls carved in the form of a sailor's head.

'Don't you think we could do with a nice cup of coffee?'

It may have been the sound of the flush upstairs, a waterfall in his dreams of mountains, that woke Étienne up, or perhaps it was the shooting pain behind his ear. It was only when he tried to lift a hand to his head that he realised he was tied up, his wrists and ankles so tightly bound he could feel them puffing up like rubber gloves filled with water. A filthy hanky had been shoved in his mouth. Inside his throbbing head, his thoughts were jostling together and pouring out like a bag of marbles in a schoolyard.

With his cheek pressed to the red floor tiles, he could see the undersides of the dining chairs with their battered straw seats and the table pocked with woodworm, along with a tiny mouse with round eyes, creeping the length of the skirting boards like a wind-up toy. He made an attempt to sit up, but the rope binding his limbs also went round his throat, preventing him from making any movement on pain of strangulation. He heard the door open and saw Éliette's bare feet (one of which had the beginnings of a bunion forming) rushing towards him, followed by Paul's heavy boots.

'What on earth have you done to him? Étienne, are you all right?'

The question struck him as somewhat absurd. He made do with rolling his eyes and grimacing.

'Paul, you're not going to …'

'Just make some coffee, Éliette. Don't worry about that …'

Éliette and Étienne exchanged a look punctuated with ellipses as Paul sat down heavily, mopping his brow.

'Gonna be a hot one today. Storm's on its way back in. No good this weather, coming and going; nature can't get its bearings.'

He sat with his rifle between his knees as if newly returned from a hunt, a good honest man full of concern for his land and ready and willing to discharge his weapon at the slightest move by Étienne. Éliette's hands were no longer hers; they moved of their own accord, putting coffee in the pot, rinsing two cups, taking the sugar out of the cupboard – they could easily have done without her. Éliette was working on autopilot. She didn't dare cast her eyes towards Étienne – taken the wrong way, a single glance could prove fatal to both of them. The sound of the birds chirruping outside made the situation all the more surreal. If Étienne had not been lying on the floor, it was just like countless other mornings when Paul had come round and she had made him coffee.

'Two sugars, yes, thanks, Éliette … Oh, I don't think I told you: the other night we were in Clément's car coming back from Privas and we hit a wild boar – eighty kilos, the thing was. We cut it up the same night and chucked the head and the skin down the old well – you know, behind the old rubbish dump. Quite handy that well – all you have to do is throw a few bits of scrap on top and the gendarmes are none the wiser! Bet people have got rid of some interesting stuff down there …'

As he said this, Paul turned to Étienne.

'Rose and I thought you might like a haunch to have with your kids. We put one in the freezer for you.'

'That's very kind of you, Paul, but if you want us to stay friends you need to untie Étienne and put your gun down.'

'You're having a laugh! You saw him whack me around the head with your pan! Four stitches I had to have!'

'Yes, but remember what you were doing to me!'

'I was drunk, Éliette. It doesn't count! And anyway, you know very well that's not the only thing. He's the one who sent Patrick into the ravine, no shadow of a doubt! Don't try to fool me you've known him ten years!'

Once again, doubts began rising in Éliette's heart like a corpse surfacing from a bog. Étienne's wide eyes pleaded with her.

'Let him explain himself, or let's call the police. You can't just go round accusing people without any proof!'

'Aha! You see – you've clicked something's not right too! I'm telling you, I know what men are like. You didn't call the police out in Algeria. You made them dig their hole and job done! Next!'

'But we're not at war any more, Paul, and even when we were, that wasn't …'

'Of course we're still at war! Thugs like him are roaming the streets. The towns are full of them and they're crawling all over the place here too, ruining things for everyone!'

'But for heaven's sake, Paul, what do you think you can do about it?'

'Some housekeeping! But not the kind women do. He knows exactly what I'm talking about. Isn't that right?'

The barrel of the gun lifted Étienne's chin; his face was pale.

'Paul, I know you're hurting, but this whole thing is ridiculous. I'm calling the police.'

'No, Éliette. These things are best sorted out man to man. Don't do anything stupid. Besides, I've cut the phone lines.'

'You what?'

'You're not on my side, Éliette. He's turned you. I don't want you to be angry but I just can't trust you. I'm going to have to shut you in the cellar while I finish the job. You'll thank me later.'

The sound of a car pulling up outside made Paul leap up and point his gun at Éliette.

'No funny business, OK? Or this is going to get nasty.'

There were footsteps on the gravel and then a knock came at the door. Serge's voice called: 'Éliette? ... Papa?'

The oak door creaked open and soon Serge and Zep stepped into the kitchen, dressed in shorts and white T-shirts.

'Papa? ... What the hell are you doing with that gun? ... We've been looking for you since ...' (Éliette discreetly drew his attention to Étienne curled up on the floor.) 'What the hell's going on here? ... Papa?'

'This has nothing to do with you! What's going on here does not involve queers!'

'You're insane!'

'Tell your Kraut not to move or I'll blow his skull to pieces.'

'Papa, please, put down the gun!'

'Think you can tell me what to do, you little shit? On your

knees! Everyone, on your knees! Even you, Éliette. Hands on your heads!'

Serge took a step forward. Zep moved away to the left, while Éliette pulled a chair in front of her. Paul stepped back.

'Fuck. The first person to make another move gets it!'

It was like a game of grandmother's footsteps. Everyone froze.

'Papa …'

'Shut up! You're all against me. I'm the only one who knows! That fucker there killed your brother but you don't give a shit! None of you do, because you never loved him, because Patrick was twice the person any of you will ever be!'

'Stop it, Papa! Let Éliette's friend go. We'll say nothing about this – it stays between us. If you won't untie him, I will. I loved Patrick just as much as you did.'

'Like hell you did!'

'I did, for fuck's sake! Even if I've known for years he wasn't yours!'

'Shut your mouth, Serge! Don't you ever say that again!'

'This has gone far enough! Let this man go. You're not the only one having a hard time. Have you forgotten Maman, back at home?'

'Your mother's a slag!'

'And Clément's your good friend – but what does it matter now? Look, I don't blame you for anything. Are you going to untie him or shall I?'

'Take one step and I'll kill you.'

'You know, Papa, I don't care if you don't love me, I still love you. Please, put the gun down …'

'Who told you? About your mother and Clément?'

'Everyone knows. Please, this is ridi—'

Serge didn't have a chance to finish his sentence. A sort of scarlet explosion speckled the wall in fragments of bone, brain and blood. The second shot hit Zep with full force, passing through his chest like a cannonball. The bang echoed around the kitchen for several seconds. Outside, not a bird was singing. They had all fled towards a boundless sky where human folly dissolved into wispy clouds that were munched like candyfloss between big blue teeth.

Éliette's ears seemed to be stuffed with cotton wool, and her lower jaw was practically touching her chest. Her eyes could not take in what they had seen and could still see now: the bodies of the two young men immobilised in grotesque poses, an arm here, a leg there, pouring with black blood that branched out into a complicated network of streams running between the floor tiles. Serge's right hand rested on Étienne's face; making short muffled cries as he moved his head from side to side, Étienne struggled to shake it off. There were unidentifiable splatters across his hair and forehead. Soon the stench of excrement mingled with that of gunpowder.

Paul let go of his gun and fell to his knees. His trembling lips muttered words that could not be made out. Éliette rushed to the sink and threw up the two coffees she had just swallowed. When she lifted her head two minutes later, Paul had not changed position. He was intoning words as though reciting a psalm, something along the lines of 'That's it, now, we're there ...' Étienne had finally managed to wriggle free of Serge's corpse and was resting his head against the wall. His throat was swollen – he was choking, the handkerchief sticking out of his mouth like a fat purple tongue, eyes rolled back. A ray of sunlight bounced off a kitchen knife on the draining board. Éliette slowly took hold of it, but as she did so, Paul let out a hoarse shout and did something incomprehensible. He undid his right shoe, took it off, yanked off his sock and took the rifle in his hand.

Éliette was clutching the knife tightly against her chest when he turned towards her.

'There's no need, Éliette. We're there, we're there.'

He thrust the barrel into his mouth and used his big toe to pull the trigger.

The minute Éliette had cut Étienne loose he had run into the bathroom with one thing on his mind: to strip off his soiled clothes and wash and wash and wash some more, from head to foot. But as the water ran and the soap lathered up, the bathtub filled with ever pinker liquid. Blood produced blood until the house was nothing but one huge open wound that seemed never to want to heal. He had brushed his teeth several times and still could not get rid of the indelible taste of rust and grease that the dirty hanky had left in his mouth. He needed to jet-wash his entire insides, his memory, his heart, wished he could watch it all disappearing down the plughole. Afterwards, Éliette helped him rinse the white enamel and the tiles. Étienne stared into the mirror, scrutinising his reflection in microscopic detail; every time he ran his hand through his hair, he was sure he could feel scraps of bone and brain under his nails.

'Jesus fucking Christ! I'm never going to get it out!'

'There's nothing left, Étienne. It's all gone.'

'No, it hasn't! Look, here! ... And here! It's still there!'

It took a very long time for Éliette to convince him to see reason. He could not bring himself to move away from the mirror; all the muscles in his body were so tight they could snap. As she draped her dressing gown over his shoulders, she felt as if she was dressing a wooden mannequin. She led him across the kitchen like a blind man, helping him to avoid the pools of blood and the bodies strewn here and there, with bluebottles already hovering above them. When they reached the sitting room she sat him on the sofa and poured him a shot which he downed through gritted teeth. And then, sitting with his head hanging, he told her everything: about the train, the coke, stealing the car, Patrick's accident, everything, except his relationship with Agnès.

He was sobbing now, his head still down. She had rarely felt so calm, so collected in all her life. Her hand stroked the lump at the nape of his neck; he could have confessed to the most sickening crimes and still she would not for one second have wavered in her love for him. It was a strange kind of love, both maternal and carnal, innocent and perverted, and it made her incredibly happy. For a few seconds, Charles's face came to her. He was smiling at her from the afterlife the way he smiled when she owned up to a minor sin, and he would shrug and open the paper, whose headlines were full of catastrophes and massacres from one end of the earth to the other.

'Étienne, you ought to go and get dressed and hide this briefcase of yours. Bury it under the compost heap. I'm going to have to go to the police station. You needn't worry about anything. Étienne, can you hear me?'

Étienne stood up. With his puffy eye, the lump on his neck and the too-tight dressing gown, he looked like a boxer approaching retirement.

'Yes, good plan. I feel better. I was so afraid it was going to be the end of me ... How on earth did he know it was me? His son, I mean ...'

'Instinct. He was a good huntsman. A good father too. Will you be all right?'

'I think so.'

'I'm off, then. Everything's going to be just fine – you'll see.'

'Éliette! ... Why?'

'I love you, and that's all you need to know.'

'But what do I …?'

'I'm asking nothing of you.'

Étienne made no reply. With all his body and soul he wished he could love like she did. He heard the unmistakable sound of the Aixam fading into the distance and went upstairs to change.

He had only black, grey and beige clothing. None of it suited him.

The sound of another car reached his ears as he was pulling on his trousers, a high-powered engine, out of place on this dirt track. Through the bedroom window he saw Agnès step out of the Ferrari, laughing, with a thickset guy – not very young, not very tall, not very attractive – following her. When she saw him, she waved up at him. Tangled in his trousers, he didn't have a chance to shout, 'No! Don't come in!'

'Come in, Ben, let's have a coffee …'

Agnès froze as she opened the kitchen door. Étienne had come hurtling down the stairs, and Benito was peering over Agnès's shoulder at the scene before him.

'Madonna!'

Étienne barged in front of them and tried to bar their way. Agnès stared at him, so pale she was almost transparent. She could not utter a single word. The Italian's eyebrows were practically touching the roots of his hair. He stepped backwards until he reached the front door, where he turned and ran. They heard quick footsteps on the gravel, the roar of the engine starting up again, and a screech of tyres. Agnès and Étienne stared hard at one another, as if meeting for the first time. Their gazes joined to form a bridge over the unspeakable. The multiple horsepower of the Ferrari gave way to the flies buzzing over the bodies. Open-mouthed and wide-eyed, Agnès looked like a Pompeii fresco.

'It wasn't me, Agnès! It wasn't me!'

Her sunglasses had fallen on the floor. Étienne trod on them; it was like walking on his daughter's eyes.

'I'm telling you, it wasn't me! Go up to your room and get undressed. You were asleep, you heard gunshots, that's it. Quick, the cops are on their way. I'll explain later. Run! I have to go and stash the case. Go!'

Agnès stared at him uncomprehendingly, as if trying to find a use for an unfamiliar tool. He had to push her up the stairs. The police van arrived a few minutes after he had buried the briefcase under the compost heap.

For the entire morning, the house was invaded by flies and police. More and more of both kept arriving. There were people taking photos, measuring things, scouring every corner. It sounded like a swarm of bees was nearby: no individual noise, only a worrying murmur. In the garden, in the shade of the summer dining room, an inspector whose slight squint made him always seem to be talking to someone else was taking statements from Éliette, Étienne and Agnès.

Éliette had not batted an eyelid when Agnès appeared dressed in the men's shirt she wore to bed. All three claimed to have spent the night at the house. In the morning, Éliette and Étienne had heard a noise in the kitchen. They came downstairs and found Paul in a state of extreme agitation. He threatened to shoot them. When Paul's son and his friend arrived, there had been a brief altercation over a family quarrel, and Paul had fired on them before turning the gun on himself. No, they didn't know why he had cut the phone lines, or how he had come by his head injury. Clearly he was aware of Serge's intention to visit Éliette, and he had ambushed him. This moment of madness could be put down to the pain of the loss of his son.

The three bodies were carried out by the men in white and shoved into the back of an ambulance which drove off, its wheels narrowly avoiding the ditch. It was like any of the countless petty stories that made it onto the front page of the local paper before being turned into fish-and-chip wrapping. The inspector with the wandering eye put his notepad away and sighed.

'Gonna be another hot one today. Right, then, we'll need you to stick around in case we require anything else from you, but it all seems tragically straightforward to me.'

'Inspector, we can't stay here … It's …'

'I understand, Madame. For the time being, nothing is to be touched. A cleaning company will be along when we finish. In the meantime, go and stay with friends or check into a hotel, somewhere we can get hold of you if need be.'

'In that case, we'll be at the Relais de l'Empereur in Montélimar.'

'Ah, yes, I know it well. The food's excellent!'

'Well, you know …'

'Of course, sorry. We'll be in touch with you there.'

'Would you be able to call us a taxi on your phone? Only my … car can only carry two people.'

'Oh, the little Aixam! My dad's got one … Yes, but I could give one of you a lift. Want to hop in, Monsieur?'

Étienne bit the inside of his cheek.

'That would be great, thanks.'

Two gendarmes remained at the scene. Éliette and Agnès saw Étienne disappear inside the inspector's car, holding himself upright, almost rigid.

'Air con all right for you back there?'

'Yes, fine.'

Étienne was suffocating in the back. The river they were driving alongside was nothing but a trickle of green water snaking between white pebbles, draining away.

'Always makes you feel guilty, sitting in a police car, doesn't it?'

'Not me, no. I'm just …'

'Of course, of course, sorry. I forgot myself. So what's the story with that black eye and the bump on the back of your head?'

'There isn't one. It was an accident. I fell off a ladder.'

'Just what you needed! You're not having much luck at the moment, are you?'

'Apparently not.'

'No, apparently not.'

They didn't exchange another word until they reached the hotel, where the inspector dropped him off and told him not to worry about anything.

In the microcar, Agnès and Éliette had barely more to say to one another.

'This car is a pile of crap.'

'It's a pile of crap.'

'How are we going to get anywhere in this?'

'We'll get as far as the Relais de l'Empereur.'

'And then what? Some adventure this is going to be.'

'Don't you think your father's had enough adventures recently?'

'Think he's ripe for retirement like you, do you?'

'Ripe for a bit of peace and quiet, I'd say.'

'I don't like you.'

'I don't hate you either.'

'You're making him old.'

'He wasn't expecting to meet me.'

'I was.'

They said nothing more.

As in all the places where Napoleon had left a strand of hair, the Relais de l'Empereur was decorated with golden bees, wall hangings and furniture of uncertain age, and peopled with staff so practised at bending and scraping that an avant-garde choreographer would have applauded them. Agnès smirked when offered a room adjoining that of 'her parents'.

'That'll be handy in case I have a nightmare, won't it, Papa?'

'You should go and have a shower. We'll meet back down here in half an hour.'

Éliette was already showering in her room. Agnès was starting to get on her nerves, along with all the other children in the world. What exactly did they have against their parents? What made them want to spoil what little future they had left? There was Agnès with her double-edged remarks; Patrick, who had, in a sense, caused his father's end and his mother's breakdown; even Serge and his provocative love life; even Sylvie, even Marc, who took her for an imbecile, as if she was incapable of leading her own life! Why couldn't they just leave their parents alone? Why were they still getting under their feet, just as they had when they were in nappies? She wouldn't be surprised if the younger members of society couldn't even pay towards their elders' pensions. Sick and tired of this unscrupulous generation that let the grass grow over the living corpses of their fathers and mothers.

There had been big scientific advances and it was now possible to live to a hundred. It was an old person's world – they had made it after all, and if it didn't suit the young, they could make one of their own. Marc and Sylvie were so far removed from her universe that it had not even crossed her mind to contact them. She had stopped being a mother in order to take a second chance at being a woman, barely living in the present moment. They no longer belonged with her. She would call them later. Recent events had provided an excellent excuse to put them off visiting. Afterwards, she would set things straight with Agnès. There was no way she was going to pass on the opportunity of the new life opening up to her like a long-awaited past. She returned to the bedroom with a towel wrapped around her hair.

'Étienne, I'm going to put the house on the market.'

'I understand.'

'Would you ... would you like to live with me?'

Étienne propped himself up on his elbow and blinked madly.

'Excuse me?'

'I'm not asking you to love me, just to be with me. I know there's something between us – I don't know what it is, but it's enough. You're at your wits' end; you can lean on me. We could be happy together, living in peace.'

'Éliette! We've known each other a matter of days and I've brought you nothing but trouble.'

'Exactly. That needs to change. You can't carry on living like this. Admit you're tempted?'

'I am, but it's impossible. There's the case, there's Agnès ...'

'Forget all that! You have a right to be happy!'

'I'd love to, honestly, Éliette, but I can't. I have to see this through.'

'Through to what? Prison? Death? Do you think that's what Agnès wants? I've a bit put away. If you want we can leave tomorrow. We can give Agnès some money. She's young ...'

'Éliette, please ... I need to think. My head hurts.'

It was true. His brain was being jolted inside his skull like the clapper in a bell. Agnès, Éliette, *ding-dong*! Left to his own devices, he probably would have gone to the police station and told the bog-eyed inspector everything just to get it over with. The slightest thought unleashed a wave of pain inside him, spreading from the tips of his toes to the top of his head.

'Knock, knock. Can I come in? ... Blimey, why the long faces? Trouble in paradise?'

Éliette shrugged and disappeared into the bathroom. Agnès stifled a giggle.

'Wipe your nose – it's covered in coke.'

'Oh, sorry! Right, well, I've got the munchies. See you down-stairs.'

Three o'clock in the afternoon. Montélimar was booming like a burst drum. A dreary pizzeria provided a place to sit, stale pizza and dry pasta. At the end of this dismal meal washed down with vinegary wine, Étienne, as if playing the tourist, had the absurd idea of asking what there was to see in the town. After several moments scratching his head with its shiny black mop, the sad Mickey Mouse-faced waiter suggested the Château des Adhémar. He had never been there himself, despite being a native of the town, but had heard it was worth a look. The view from up there was supposed to be amazing.

It was a painful slog up to these ruins, which had been spruced up by generous donors. The sun was not even out; it was just muggy. Agnès moaned at every step, like a child being dragged around beauty spots during the summer holidays.

'Where are you taking us? ... These alleys stink of dog shit ... My feet hurt ... I need to pee ... I've got indigestion.'

All three were suffering from heartburn, but they still made it to the foot of a pile of yellow stones. Your twenty-franc fee bought access to the castle's sad, empty keep and a few metres of rampart.

'Amazing view? Yeah, right! I get a better view every morning washing my arse. It's an utter hole!'

'Agnès!'

'What? Am I wrong? The whole town's like a cemetery. It's like a model someone forgot to finish.'

Below the fortifications, an old woman bent like the arch of the castle's portal was walking a dog whose hind legs were mounted on wheels.

'Let's get out of here, Étienne. There can't be many places worse than this.'

The wind had picked up. It blew under the Roman roof tiles, playing a monotonous chant as irritating as the songs of the Peruvian bands at Châtelet métro station. They would have liked to shoo it away.

'Come on. Let's go before you end up looking like that mutt.'

'I think your father's capable of making his own decisions.'

'Fuck off! He's not your lapdog.'

Leaving … it was all Étienne had done, his entire life. He envied the stone – or *molasse*, as it was known here – crumbling where it stood. Swallows punctuated the space between passing clouds like commas. A bell was ringing somewhere in the sky. Éliette leaned out to listen.

'A wedding …?'

Closer to the edge, Agnès replied, 'No, a funeral. Screw this, I'm off.'

She left them leaning out over the parapet. They watched as the red of her hair bounded down the dark alleyways like a glowing fag end.

Back at the hotel, Éliette called her children. Their voices sounded unreal, like those of air hostesses. Without going into detail, she informed them of the deaths of Paul and Serge. Given the circumstances, they probably shouldn't come. This was actually for the best all round because, as expected, Justine's measles had passed on to her brother; as for Marc, a meeting had come up which he couldn't get out of, and he would have had to cancel anyway. Although, if she wanted to come and stay with either of them … No, she would rather rest, perhaps even go and stay with friends near Marseille, clear her head, she didn't know, it was all so … She would let them know. They were thinking of her, of course, and she of them. These things happened. Speak soon.

As she hung up the phone, she felt a great weight lift off her. She had bought herself some time. It might only have been worth a few coins in a begging bowl, but at least it was something, like a cigarette and a glass of rum.

Étienne was sleeping, or pretending to sleep with an arm over his face and his legs crossed. While he was at her house, part of the furniture like an insect trapped in cut resin, anything was possible. But now, in the middle of this boundless freedom, she wasn't so sure. She felt like a young bride on her wedding night. She hardly recognised this man who had shut himself away in a semblance of sleep. Through the wall, a fuzzy noise was coming from Agnès's TV.

'Étienne, are you asleep?'

'No.'

'What are you going to do?'

'I don't know. I'm happy here, now.'

'Let's leave, Étienne. We'll go wherever you want, Morocco …'

'I was inside for a year there, there's no way I want to go back. Why are the pair of you so fixated on making me leave?'

'It's not the same with your daughter.'

'Listen, Éliette. I abandoned my daughter when she was a year old. I owe her. I can't have done all of this for nothing! I want to do something good for once in my life, for her. You can't imagine what it's like to have never had a chance in life. I want to give her that. And then, yes, we can do whatever you want. I like you a lot, Éliette, I really do.'

'Well, then, leave those filthy drugs with her and let's be happy! You'll not want for anything, you—'

The telephone rang. The inspector's voice on the line was as disconcerting as his cross-eyed gaze, but he had only good news to impart: everything had been put back in its proper place at her home and the case would soon be closed. There was no doubt over what had happened: a moment of madness that had ended in tragedy, and which they would do their best to keep out of the local papers. A cleaning company would be sent in to sort everything out the next morning, and her phone line would be reconnected as soon as possible.

Speaking of which, had she by any chance thought of any reason why Monsieur Jaubert had cut the line? ... No, never mind. Ah, one other thing: they had found a rope and a pair of blood-soaked trousers in the dustbin, ring any bells? ... No. Not to worry, they could talk about all that when they came to sign their statements the next morning. A formality. With that, he wished her a good evening and advised her to try the Relais de l'Empereur's excellent *côte de bœuf*.

Éliette could not decide whether to tell Étienne about the inspector's discovery. It was silly of them not to have told the truth, but when they had discussed doing so before she went to the police station, Étienne had been categorically against it. They would have asked why Paul had singled him out, and he was anxious to avoid having the spotlight turned on him, given his past. How could they have been so stupid? He had reacted as if he was guilty of something, out of habit, no doubt. By doing his best to stay out of it, he had achieved the exact opposite.

Tomorrow, the police would be bound to find this omission suspicious.

'So?'

'Everything's fine.'

'It doesn't look fine.'

'It is. But they found your trousers and the rope in the bin.'

'Shit!'

'We'll have to tell the truth when we go tomorrow. Just tell them you were in shock. You haven't done anything wrong – you saved me from being raped!'

'You don't know what they're like. Anyone who's done time is guilty in their eyes. I can see him coming at me with his wonky eye, asking "Why this?" and "Why that?" What if they find my fingerprints on the car? That fucker's sniffed me out like a dog. I'll get five years, at least!'

'You're behaving like a child. Trust me, for goodness' sake! It can't go on like this. You're innocent. You saved me!'

'I don't want to go back there, Éliette. I can't face it!'

'Then you have to do as I say, darling. Enough of all this, enough of being scared!'

Étienne lit a cigarette. It tasted like dust.

'But what about the briefcase? ... And Agnès?'

'I'll talk to her. I'll see to everything. You have a rest.'

'No, I should tell her. But yes, I agree with everything else. Let's do that.'

When Étienne had closed the door behind him, Éliette let her head fall back on the pillows, a faint smile on her lips. Cronus was devouring his children.

The section of McDonald's drinking straw and the razor blade lay across one another on the still powdery surface of the pocket mirror. Agnès ran her finger over it and rubbed the remnants into her gums. There was almost nothing left of what she had taken with her to the coast. The local anaesthetic did not produce the desired effect. It would have had to reach her heart for that, a heart as crumpled as Éliette's neck.

She grabbed the remote and cut off the dull stream of local news.

'What the fuck am I even doing here?'

Without admitting it to herself, she had spent almost the past two hours listening out for noises from the adjoining room. She had heard murmuring, then a phone ringing, and then nothing. It was the silence that was driving her mad. They were fucking, she was sure they were fucking. At that age, you didn't cry out or moan; you did it on the quiet, so Death didn't hear you.

'Idiot! I'm such a fucking idiot!'

Agnès had never been able to lay into anyone but herself. It was handy always to have your victim within arm's reach. She must have got this from her father. Him, in there! … The years had kept them apart, and now a miserable wall of brick and plaster stood between them. The old slag had won, with her wrinkles, her stupid little car, her horrible house and a future built on bus passes. It was quite funny when you thought about it. The pair of them could snuff it under a heap of cross-stitched cushions for all she cared! Let him suffocate while he pounded away at her ancient, hairless pussy.

She, on the other hand, had her whole life ahead of her, though it hardly looked like a happily ever after! She would fetch the damned case and get as far away from her shitty past as she possibly could. Her mother had died of an overdose when she was thirteen, and these days her father could barely keep his head above water. So let him die, let him suffer! Life had cheated her from the word go, made her think she'd be left with only the crumbs. Oh, no! She was going to gorge on it, and feed her left-overs to everyone at her feet. Bastard! Piece of shit! Father, why have you forsaken me? …

She spat out the nail of her right index finger at the same time as her 'yes' in reply to the tentative knocks at her door. Étienne's face looked like a mop that had not been wrung out properly.

'All right?'

'Better than you, by the looks of it.'

'We're going down for dinner.'

'I'm not hungry. Unless they have snails. I can't eat anything but snails.'

'Agnès … We've got a bit of a problem with the police. They found … Anyway, the point is, it's nothing to do with you. Tomorrow Éliette's going to give you some money and—'

'And I'll get married and have lots of children. Are you taking the piss? What about the briefcase?'

'We'd do best to forget about it. We can build new lives for ourselves.'

'Sure, crummy little lives, while two kilos of perfectly good coke sits under the compost heap … Do you think I'm a fucking idiot?'

'I swear I'll help you! We need to put an end to all this.'

'You're not exactly a walking advert for sex with the elderly. It's made you soft in the head. So you're trying to ditch me again?'

'Agnès …!'

'She's got you wrapped around her little finger, the old slapper! You've fucked around long enough, and now you want to leave me out in the cold! Well, you can't! Think about what you're going to get from her. A wheelchair and a little handjob at Christmas. You deserve better, Daddy dear, and so do I! I'll take your fucking case and cart it around with me wherever I go, cross borders with it, no problem. I'll take it to China if I have to! I won't let you leave me twice, you old bastard. We're joined together, you and me. Joined!'

'What are you suggesting?'

'We keep a low profile. You play along and keep your mouth shut. Later on, I'll go and get the case. We meet at the station. You buy two tickets to Rome – I know people there; the addresses are in my bag. Éliette will go back to being Éliette, and we … we'll carry on being what we are. You can't turn me down. You can't do anything except love me.'

'Do me a line.'

In a glass globe, everything is back to front. The snow always falls the right way.

'What? You haven't got snails?'

'No, Mademoiselle.'

'Even tinned ones?'

'Certainly not! Everything's freshly made here.'

'Fine, I'll have an ice cream, then.'

'For your starter?'

'An ice cream, I don't care what flavour but with Chantilly cream – and lots of it!'

'Very good, Mademoiselle.'

There were very few people in the hotel dining room, but those who overheard Agnès's order held their forks in mid-air. Éliette and Étienne hid behind their menus.

'What? I can order an ice cream if I want, can't I?'

'Don't you think you might be overdoing it a bit?'

'No, I don't, Daddykins. All I want is an ice cream and to get out of this hole as soon as possible. Don't you want that too, Éliette?'

'You read my mind. And you didn't even need to ask your mirror on the wall.'

'Oh, but I did ask. Mirror, mirror ... Mirrors covered in snow ... Whatever. The pair of you can do what you like, but I'm getting out of here, OK? I'm moving on. Éliette, if you'll take me back to fetch the case, I'll disappear. How does that sound?'

'What about your statement to the police tomorrow?'

'You can write me a sick note.'

Under the table, Éliette's hands were strangling her napkin. Étienne seemed unusually interested in the ceiling mouldings.

'Fine. Let's go straight away.'

'Great! I'll go and get my bag. Bye-bye, Daddykins, and don't worry, I'm kosher. As soon as the deal's done, you'll be getting your hands on your pension.'

The two women rose, as did the eyebrows of their fellow diners. When the waiter brought over a sorbet dripping with Chantilly and two vegetable terrines, there was no one left at the table.

'What's this factory?'

The Aixam's headlights swept over the towers of Cruas nuclear power station.

'A nuclear plant.'

'Why have they painted a naked kid playing with water on it?'

'Probably to make us all think the atom is perfectly safe.'

'It's dumb. Kids aren't afraid of atoms; they're all over the place.'

'What are they afraid of, then? The big bad wolf?'

'No. Their parents.'

The road slithered snake-like through the countryside. All they could see was blue or black, as if these were the only two colours left on earth. The journey seemed to go on for ever, the little car making painfully slow progress. Agnès never stopped crossing and uncrossing her legs, nervously drumming her fingers on the dashboard.

At last the house appeared at the end of the track. It looked like an abandoned dog. Éliette barely recognised it. In the space of a few hours, the haven of peace she had pampered like a pet all her life had become 'the murder house' that people would drive past quickly, crossing themselves, before it became derelict because nobody wanted to buy it. Despite the reassuringly thick walls, misfortune had found its way in and laid its cursed eggs.

She could not live here any more. For a split second, Éliette had a vision, blurred by the tears welling in her eyes, of Charles with his chest bared, mixing cement, and then of Sylvie and Marc spraying one another with the hose, and it all disappeared for ever when she cut the headlights.

'What's wrong?'

'Oh, nothing. I've just turned a page, that's all. Be quick. Go and find your filthy stuff and I'll drop you at the station. I never want to see you again.'

'No danger of that!'

Agnès got out of the car and disappeared into the porch. Éliette had lost her home, her memories, but she had gained Étienne. When he had returned to their room earlier, having seen reason, her heart had leaped in her chest. She was sure it would work out fine with the police. It was the memory of his prison days that had made him lose his head. He had stopped Paul from assaulting her. They would understand. It was all just an unfortunate combination of circumstances. Of course nothing would ever be the same again, but there were still so many pages of life to get through. Charles would have given her his blessing. As for Agnès's departure, taking the briefcase with her, she couldn't have wished for more. Oh, she didn't despise the poor girl, but truth be told she didn't give a damn what became of her. Sometimes, only selfishness can save you, even the good Lord knows that, He who condemns suicide.

Agnès reappeared, briefcase in hand.

'You haven't got a cloth, have you? This thing stinks! You country people are unbelievable. You want to grow flowers so you let a pile of crap sit rotting right under your windows!'

'That's exactly why the flowers smell good. Here's a cloth.'

Agnès rubbed it over the case, cursing filthy nature for being full of dead creatures, poison mushrooms, stinging nettles and insects that bite.

'Hey! Look at that! … A dead crow!'

Éliette jumped at the sight of the bird Paul had nailed to the door.

'Leave that! Let's go.'

The lights on the dashboard made it feel like they were inside an aquarium. They could have been at the bottom of a lake, were it not for the Aixam's throaty cough.

'Agnès?'

'Yes.'

'If you love your father, I think it would be best if you didn't see him again for a little while.'

'If I love my father? … And what if he loved me?'

'Of course he loves you, the same way any father loves his child …'

'The same way? Or … some other way?'

'What are you getting at?'

'Oh, poor Éliette! We've moved on from the days of steam engines. Know what we were doing when he came to my room earlier? … He was fucking me, and we were going for it like you've never gone for it in your life!'

'Agnès!'

'And not for the first time either! … Two months it's been going on. Well, that's shut you up, hasn't it, love? It's not our fault, you know; we didn't find out we were father and daughter till it was too late. Life's a bitch like that, isn't it? But at the end of the day, if we love each other, who's to judge us? Don't worry – we're not planning on having kids together.'

'You're lying. You're just saying it because …'

'Because it's true, just like the fact he's waiting for me at the station so we can fuck off together, somewhere, anywhere, who gives a shit?'

'I don't believe you!'

'You don't want to believe it, but it's the truth! 'Cos I've got something you ain't. So you've got your house and your little car, and you smile away like a happy little garden gnome, but I make him hard. HARD!'

The entire night sky burst out laughing in Éliette's face; the universe had creased up, the trees were in stitches, the river beneath them giggling between the rocks, and for good reason! Watching from his cloud, Charles himself was doubled up with laughter, slapping his thighs as the little car kept dead ahead while the road bent round.

'For Christ's sake, what the fuck are you doing?'

Just in time, Agnès grabbed the steering wheel and slammed her foot on the brake. The Aixam swerved, grazed one tree and came to a standstill against the trunk of another. The night sky had fallen silent. A red-faced moon tried to hide its shame behind the clouds.

'Jesus! You could have killed us! Éliette …?'

She was slumped over the steering wheel, her shoulders shaking. Agnès rubbed her elbow.

'Can't even kill yourself properly in this stupid fucking car.'

She got out. The ground swayed beneath her feet and she fell onto the grass. Never before had the silence seemed so full, an amalgam of thousands of tiny sounds: a falling leaf, a crawling insect, a passing breeze, a breaking bud, the water bubbling away below … It amounted to almost nothing, with darkness all around, but she was alive. Then came the sound of the car door slamming and the sight of Éliette, as she opened her eyes; Éliette lifting a rock above her head, a rock as big as the moon.

Montélimar station, unlike that of Perpignan, is less the beating heart of the city and more its back end. In a shady corner of the concourse, Étienne was beginning to regret not having sided with Éliette. A tramp with a mangy dog and a nasty stench had just squeezed ten francs and a cigarette out of him. The effect of the two lines of coke he had done in Agnès's bedroom had given way to a frightening sense of disarray. Inside his head was an incredibly complex maze which he weaved through frantically like a lab rat. The state he was in was not wholly down to what he had taken. Having spent three-quarters of his life high, until prison brought him down again, Étienne knew exactly what to expect from a hit. No, more worrying than drugs was the unbelievable addiction to life that paradoxically kept pushing him to get into deeper and deeper shit. His record was hard to top. He had become a kind of world champion of failure, a haggard wayfarer of the road of relationships. Éliette? ... Agnès? ... Queen of hearts? ... Queen of clubs? ... Though he knew it was stupid to dither at life's crossroads since the road taken must always be the right one, the others having become mere figments of the imagination, still he could not make up his mind. Escaping, anywhere, but on his own, seemed the wisest option. So what if some called that cowardice. No one but him was in his shoes ...

He stood up, threw his bag over his shoulder and began to laugh to himself, like a kid playing a prank. He was going to disappear, simple as that, walk through the night, and all the next day, and so on like the fool in a tarot set. He had barely stepped out of the station when the little Aixam pulled up in front of him.

'Éliette!'

'Get in ... Don't just stand there, get in!'

He obeyed, open-mouthed like any village idiot. The microcar's right eye wandered like the inspector's, and the wing was crumpled. No sooner had he taken his seat than Éliette put her foot down.

'What's happened? Have you had an accident?'

'Nothing serious. Agnès is dead.'

'What are you talking about? Are you mad?'

'Maybe!'

'Where are we going? This isn't the way to the hotel ... Tell me what's going on!'

'We're driving. It's seven minutes past eleven, and we're driving south.'

'I don't know what's gone on, but you're making a big mistake, Éliette.'

'No. I've done that already.'

Éliette's profile seemed to be carved in stone; she didn't so much as blink. She stared straight at the road ahead of her, oblivious to the honking of horns as she was repeatedly overtaken.

'Something's catching on the front right-hand wheel.'

'Yes, it is.'

As they drove out of town, the road sign with MONTÉLIMAR struck out looked like a funeral wreath with a red ribbon pinned across it.

'Why don't we stop and you can tell me all about it?'

'No. You've been doing your best to go nowhere all your life. Well, now you can.'

The sound of something rattling in the back made Étienne look over his shoulder. The handle of the briefcase was bumping against the window.

'You picked up the case?'

'When you're going nowhere, you have to take your baggage with you.'

'For fuck's sake, come on! Stop messing around. Where's Agnès?'

'Hey! Stop shouting! Agnès is nowhere, just like you, just like me, just like everyone.'

'Fine, be like that. You'll have to stop eventually to get petrol.'

Étienne reached for the handle of his door. The Aixam wasn't exactly speeding along, but it was going fast enough for a fall onto the tarmac to be fatal.

'What about our date with the law tomorrow?'

'They won't miss us.'

'No, of course not! This is ridiculous. You said yourself everything would work itself out.'

'I was wrong. I've killed your daughter, don't you get it? … Bashed her head in with a rock. It's just the two of us now.'

'You're not serious.'

'All the bridges are burnt now. The past is gone; now everything's in the headlights ahead of us …'

'I don't believe it. I don't believe it!'

'Me neither. I used to believe, but I don't any more.'

'But why? Why, damn it?'

'You're asking me why … Please. Take a holiday; stop acting like a bastard. It doesn't suit you.'

The lab rat in the maze suddenly came to a halt. The note of sincerity in Éliette's voice was crushing any vague hope of escape. If there had been a way into the labyrinth, there was surely no way out. It was pointless fighting it; all he could do was wait, and thank the heavens for the reprieve that had come in the shape of the Aixam's engine gasping for breath. The for and against had finally joined hands, slotting together like the pieces of a jigsaw whose picture you guessed long before it was finished. Going from one tragedy to the next, you eventually reached a nebulous nirvana, ending up more or less back where you started.

'You killed Agnès ...'

'Yes. She told me about you two. I could have understood, but I was so hurt ... You should have told me.'

'I couldn't even admit it to myself.'

'You know, it's not the incest that shocked me so much as the way you played me for a fool, or rather the way you played at life without me. I love you, Étienne – I would have understood; I could have been your ally. You needn't have been afraid of me. It's the fear of fear that did for us. I didn't hate her, you know; I could have accepted it. You don't try to compete when you're my age. If you like, I'll drop you at the next service station.'

Étienne's heart was like an Agen prune: shrivelled and black. Darkness was closing its fist around the ridiculous little beige car that no outlaw in his right mind would have used to make his getaway. In spite of everything, the kilometres of road kept coming, like parts of a never-ending telescope. They passed through villages with peculiar names. Chairs were being put away on café terraces, and soon the only light came from the street lamps looming over them like the eyes of a dinosaur. What they felt was more akin to the sensation of teetering on the edge of a vertical drop than of chasing the horizon. They shared the silence like a cell, without hope of escape.

As they rounded a wide bend in a sort of shadowy creek, the blinking pink and blue neon lights of a truckers' café, or a night-club, or something, made Éliette slow down.

'I'm thirsty. Let's stop.'

'OK.'

A dozen cars were parked outside, each sporting a white tulle bow. The puffed-out Aixam nestled in among them. The air was pulsing to the binary rhythm pumping out of the building. As soon as they stepped inside, they were confronted with a thundering rendition of 'Macarena'. A hundred or so people were writhing about on the dance floor, dripping with sweat and screaming along to the chorus. Waiters weaved their way through the crowd, hair slicked to their foreheads, carrying trays laden with glasses and bottles. Here and there children slipped under the tables and popped up to down the dregs of drinks. Just like in photos of family celebrations, everyone had red eyes – only here it was not the fault of the camera. The tang of sparkling Clairette de Die hung in the air. Éliette and Étienne gradually manoeuvred their way to the bar. Cupping his hands around his mouth, Étienne asked the glassy-eyed barman for a Coke and a beer which they drank while pinned to the wall. The bride – for a wedding was the cause of this bonanza of animal magnetism – was a tall, skinny brunette. A fine layer of bluish fuzz covered her upper lip, suggesting the rest of her body might be equally hirsute. Wearing the Barbie-doll outfit of her dreams, she swung on the arms of her guests, twisting her ankles on her high heels, a permanent smile slapped on her horsey face. As for the groom, he could have been any one of the prematurely aged, bleary-eyed young men singing at the tops of their voices, ties loosened, blue suits bursting at the seams, never to be worn again. The oldest and ugliest members of the party sat, deafened, eyelids heavy, around the edge of the room, their chins resting on ample chests or distended stomachs. A dishevelled-looking girl moving with difficulty in a tight lamé dress tried to make Étienne join a wild farandole around the room. Her sticky hand slipped between his fingers like a fat fish. There was no need to pay for anything. No one had fingers left to count on, or clear enough vision to keep an eye on things. In a few rare circumstances, the little people play rich. It takes them the rest of their lives to shake off the horrendous hangover, if not longer!

Neither the Coke nor the beer had quenched their thirst. But the fine spray from the night sky was now spitting in their faces. As he was about to get back into the Aixam, Étienne noticed that the keys to the car parked next to theirs had been left in the ignition. The car, which no doubt belonged to the wedding couple, was more laden with flowers than a hearse.

'Éliette, wait!'

'What?'

'Get the case and the bags out.'

'Why?'

'Just do it!'

The luggage was transferred from one vehicle to the other. Étienne got behind the wheel while Éliette sat in the passenger seat. An incredible racket like the sound of bins being emptied followed their departure. Étienne pulled over a hundred metres down the road to detach all the saucepans and chamber pots that had been tied to the bumper.

'We're not going nowhere any more; we're going everywhere.'

The tulle- and flower-adorned Citroën XM waited for a greengrocer's van to give way before rearing up and galloping into what remained of the night.

The speed, the real speed of a real car thrilled Étienne and made Éliette's legs stiffen plank-like in the footwell. The trucks and cars they overtook seemed to be treading water. Éliette stared goggle-eyed at the night's gaping mouth, as they steamed towards it. The heady scent of the bouquets heaped up on the back seats was getting to her.

'All these flowers are making me feel sick.'

'Open your window and chuck them out. It stinks of cheap happiness.'

The wind rushing at her head stopped her breath. One by one the sprays of roses were scattered on the tarmac in a firework display of multicoloured petals.

'Better?'

'Yes.'

'It's got the fire of God in it, this motor!'

'As if the Devil were biting at its heels. We'll get there quicker in this car.'

'I don't want to go anywhere any more. At this rate we'll be at the Italian border by daybreak.'

'And then?'

'We'll be Italian. This wedding car is worth all the passports in the world. They'll let us through in this, no question. No one will say a word. We're on honeymoon! Rome, Naples, here we come!'

Éliette burst out laughing despite herself. It was stronger than she was; she had just realised that for her entire life she had been two people and that the other Éliette who had played second fiddle for so long to the sweet version of herself – the good wife and mother, the dignified widow – had just taken charge. And she was capable of anything. With her head tipped back and a strange smile playing on her lips, she gave in to sleep. Étienne put the radio on. Bashung was singing '*Ma petite entreprise* ...'

A milky cloud was beginning to lighten the sky when Étienne pulled over. His eyes were prickly and his stiff jaws could no longer hold back the yawns. Éliette was still asleep. Soundlessly, he slipped out of the car. The dawn was thick with birdsong, as if this was the very first day on earth. He lay down with his arms spread wide, facing the horizon that rolled on as far as the eye could see. The sky was blushing like a girl's cheeks after a profession of love. The XM's bonnet was boiling hot. Through the windscreen, Éliette was dozing calmly, her head resting on her shoulder. For all Étienne repeated to himself that this lovely, gentle, peaceable lady had just killed his daughter, his mistress, by smashing her over the head with a rock, he could not bring himself to consider her guilty of anything. She was innocent, just like him, like the worst criminal, like the dog who kills the cat, the cat who kills the mouse, the mouse who … must kill something too. All around, in the bushes and the grass, prey and predators mingled in the same macabre dance. You could be one or the other, depending on the circumstances, all of which were extenuating. It was what they called life, the strongest of all excuses.

By way of breakfast, he took a sniff of coke off the point of the knife. Éliette opened her eyes at the same time as a streak of white powder shot across his brow.

'Where are we?'

'About sixty kilometres from Ventimiglia. How are you feeling?'

'Too early to say. What are you doing?'

'I took a sniff to wake myself up. Want some?'

'Why not?'

Étienne took a bit from the bag.

'You have to cover one nostril and breathe in very hard with the other.'

'You don't think—'

'Forget what you've read in the papers. If it wasn't good, no one would take it.'

Right nostril, left nostril, Éliette closed her eyes and slumped back in her seat. She expected to sink into a universe out of a Hieronymus Bosch painting, teeming with horned monsters and grimacing gargoyles, but instead of seeing infernal hallucinations, she found herself breathing fresh mountain air. It was like opening the window on the first day of springtime.

'Well?'

'It didn't do anything for me ... or maybe it did. I have the impression of being incredibly normal.'

'There you go, that's it.'

'I need to pee.'

The grass bounced beneath her feet like the fluffiest of carpets. Squatting behind a bush, she watched the sun rising above the patchwork of fields as if seeing the spectacle for the very first time. It was as if she had been myopic her entire life; never before had she seen so clearly and precisely. They ought to make bread with this strange flour, to give humanity its sight back. It made you wonder why the stuff was illegal. She was not unsteady on her feet, wasn't tripping over her words like a drunk, on the contrary! She had never been more alert in her life.

'Étienne, I'm hungry.'

'Me too.'

The little village they stopped in resembled a giant pot of geraniums. The flowers were bursting from every window sill, carpeting roundabouts, growing in between the bricks of the houses.

The light mist from the fountains made little rainbows form against the blue sky. Everything seemed clean and fresh, like a soft-boiled egg with its top cut off. The yellow yolk of the morning sun ran down the roads. The beribboned XM could not have parked against a better backdrop. The waiter in the nearest café greeted them with a flourish.

'My first customers of the day! And a pair of newlyweds to boot! I'll look after you. Sit back and make yourselves comfy!'

The nightmare was giving way to a dream. Everything that was happening seemed so totally natural and crystal clear that neither Éliette nor Étienne batted an eyelid. Life was regaining the upper hand because it was at home here. They ate a hearty breakfast of eggs and ham for Étienne and warm croissants with jam for Éliette. From the café terrace, they watched the growing crowd of people out walking with baskets on their arms and poodles on leashes, everyone polished, gleaming, almost metallic, as if they had all just left the same hair salon. The air smelled like something you could bottle.

'You know, Éliette, we should give ourselves a makeover. Newlyweds should have a bit of sparkle about them.'

The waiter gave them the coffees on the house – starting the day's business with newlyweds (even wrinkly ones) must bring luck!

Éliette bought herself a striped T-shirt dress that looked like a sailor's outfit, while Étienne picked up a pair of white jeans. They rounded off their purchases with a pair of sunglasses each and even a basket which they filled with a bottle of champagne and a jar of caviar, to really complete the newlywed look. The Italian customs officers welcomed them with open arms as if they had been waiting for them all their lives. It was such a relief that they took the risk of doing another little line in the car park next to the customs post. The sun showered them with laughter that no night could ever extinguish. Every Italian had a mandolin in his throat. They stopped in the first hotel they came to, with an ochre front and palm trees in the garden. There, as the daylight beat its drum against the shutters, they made love as if defying gravity.

It was very mild and the roads were filled with people casually strolling and taking the air, breathing in the blue pigment of the night sky. Étienne and Éliette were sitting on the terrace of a little restaurant overlooking the sea. By the glow of paper lanterns, they were tucking into a *fritto misto* accompanied by a bottle of Lacryma Christi. It was as lovely and as idiotic as a scene in a *fotonovela*. Yet Étienne seemed to have something on his mind. He looked like a sergeant major putting the finishing touches to a plan of attack.

'I think it would be safest to ditch the car tomorrow. We can take the train to Rome. Agnès left some addresses in her bag. I shouldn't have too much trouble shifting the case.'

'We'll keep a bit, though, won't we?'

'Éliette! … Yes, a bit. And then—'

The remainder of his sentence was carried away by the insect-like buzzing of a Vespa. Not that it mattered much; Éliette agreed to everything. She smiled as she sipped her drink, giving herself up entirely to this new-found happiness she had never dared imagine possible. She felt immortal, miraculously cured, even if she knew perfectly well that her state of mind was largely due to drugs. They had taken more in the bedroom before heading out for dinner. And so what, where was the harm in it? Forty years of yoga to achieve nirvana or a split second's inhalation, the result was the same. The hunger, this bulimic urge to live, justified the means.

'Why are you laughing?'

'If one of my children had told me last week that they were on drugs, I'd have been worried out of my mind.'

'Just be a bit careful. It's not a magic bullet. It comes at a price.'

'I think I've paid in advance. I've been retired; I deserve my final showdown. What do you think of this ashtray?'

'The ashtray? It's just like any other ashtray. Why do you ask?'

'I want to take it as a souvenir.'

'I'm going to ask for the bill. I'm tired.'

Étienne settled up, but as they left the restaurant they were stopped by the waiter.

'Excuse me, but please could the lady give back the ashtray she put in her bag?'

Étienne went green. He babbled muddled excuses until Éliette handed back the stolen goods.

Back on the road, he began almost running. The looks of passers-by seemed hostile; the Vespas were conspiring to run him over. The Devil had set foot in paradise.

'Étienne, what's come over you? ... Wait!'

'You're out of your mind! Do you think now is the time to get ourselves noticed?'

'Oh, please, there's no need to fuss! It must happen all the time. All right, sorry.'

Étienne didn't feel at ease until he had locked the door of their hotel room behind them. Lying on the bed with his eyes glued to the ceiling, he only unclenched his jaw to take a drag of his cigarette.

'Étienne, this is ridiculous! Everyone does silly things every once in a while.'

'You're not everyone! ... Draw the curtain, please.'

Éliette reluctantly did as she was asked. The night sky was so beautiful, like the one Van Gogh painted while wearing candles on his hat. She was sincerely sorry; how fragile their dream seemed to be.

'Will you forgive me, please? I'm going to order a bottle of champagne – do you want some?'

They were brought not champagne but Asti Spumante. Not that it really mattered; it was the lightness of the bubbles they needed. After two glasses and another line each, Étienne had reconciled himself to life, but a knot remained in his chest like a wrecking ball. They talked, both making extravagant plans and recalling fragments of fictitious or muddled memories. This blend of equally hypothetical pasts and futures was a kind of lifebelt that kept them afloat amid the treacherous waters of the present. Around four in the morning, exhausted, having run out of words, they let the night pull black wool over their eyes. Étienne woke with a start two hours later, his mouth apparently lined with blotting paper. In his dream, Agnès had been shaking something in her hand, something like a salad spinner. She was shouting, 'It's ready, Papa, it's ready!' It was a severed head, with blood spurting from the sawn neck onto virgin snow. In the fog, he could not see whose head it was.

He got up and went to drink as much water from the tap as he could manage. It was warm, and tasted of toothpaste. He splashed his face. Outside, daylight had come, a pearly-white sky like an oyster, the sun struggling to break through the clouds. A breeze lifted the curtain like a veil, but otherwise everything hung flat: the clothes on the backs of the chairs, the fake crystal chandelier, the seaweed-floppy terry towels, his cheeks, his arms, his balls. It was going to be muggy today.

Éliette groaned and rolled over as he lay back down next to her.

'Is it morning? What time is it?'

'Six thirty.'

'Can't you sleep, my love?'

'Yes, yes, I was just thirsty.'

'Is it nice out?'

'Grey.'

'Come here … closer …'

She felt for Étienne's body under the sheet. She found his thigh, the pelvic bone jutting out, his hand, his shoulder, but it was like stroking a statue. Not a shiver, not the slightest quivering muscle.

'Is something wrong, darling?'

'No, no, go back to sleep.'

She snuggled against his shoulder, murmuring something like, 'Everything's fine, everything's fine.' Étienne ran his hand through his hair as his gaze followed the grey light creeping in through the folds of the curtain like a toxic gas, and went back to sleep thinking to himself that the end of the world was not a big black hole, nor a multicoloured firework display, but, all the more stupidly, it was a day like any other, only a little overcast.

They left the hotel around ten o'clock, Étienne having barely touched his breakfast. He could not have said exactly what was wrong. He felt like the sky: a bit low. Despite her best efforts, Éliette could not instil her good mood in him, and this upset her.

'Won't you tell me what the matter is?'

'I don't know. I had strange dreams. It's left a weird taste in my mouth. It's this car; I'll feel better once we've got rid of it.'

They headed out of town on a coastal road. Étienne drove slowly as if seeking a picnic spot, looking out for tracks either side of the road where he could abandon the car, but found none suitable. Éliette was baffled. As far as she was concerned, any old parking space would have done the job, but Étienne pressed on, determined to find 'the right place'.

'Étienne, it doesn't matter. We're wasting time.'

'No, I know what I'm doing. We need to put it in a place where no one will find it for several days.'

'All right, fine.'

As they drove out of a village a kilometre or so further on, Étienne leaped out of his seat, pointing a finger skywards.

'There! That's the place – do you see it?'

A flight of gulls was circling in the air above a sort of truncated volcano with white gases rising up from its summit.

'Is it a landfill site?'

'Yes! That's the spot. It's as if I knew where I was going!'

'There might be people there.'

'No, we'll push the car in from up there. It'll soon be covered by tons of rubbish. It's perfect!'

Éliette remained unconvinced but, at the end of the day, whether it was here or somewhere else ... She just wanted him to stop obsessing about this and move on. They turned down a small bumpy track that ran through a pine forest. The further they went, the stronger the acrid stench of burnt rubbish became. They eventually came into a clearing that looked down over the landfill site. It was deserted but for the gulls scouring the rubbish, pecking here and there and letting out piercing squawks. Étienne seemed as happy as a little boy who has won a treasure hunt.

'It's brilliant, isn't it?'

'It smells horrible.'

'Let's take it up to the edge. You get out with the bags and all I'll have to do is give it a little shove. It's nice here, isn't it?'

'Uh ... There's a certain charm to it, but I don't know that I'd spend my holidays here.'

Étienne rolled slowly forward. With every turn of the wheels, worrying cracking noises could be heard – crates, cans, piles of boxes. A fridge wobbled in front of them, its door hanging wide open. Withered plastic bags flew up like sluggish hot-air balloons. The birds stirred up the air, which was thick with the stench of rotten cabbage. Étienne appeared fascinated, peering over the steering wheel. Soon there was nothing ahead but the void waiting to swallow them.

'Étienne! Don't go any further, we're right on the edge!'

'Huh? ... Oh, yes.'

The car came to a stop. Shielding her eyes to avoid looking down, Éliette got out, her legs trembling. Her feet sank into a pile of warm filth. Étienne was still clutching the wheel, dazzled by the emptiness before him.

'Étienne! ... Étienne!'

'Yes?'

'I'm getting the bags out. Let's push the car off and get out of here. It's making me dizzy.'

He had the same smile on his face as on the day she had met him by the little bridge, and the sight of it lifted her spirits. Wading through the nauseating sludge, she took out the bags and the briefcase and moved back a few metres. Étienne opened his door, took off the handbrake and turned towards her with his hands in the air, beaming.

'We did it!'

He leaned against the car and it started to wobble. As it began to tip, a gust of wind slammed the door closed, trapping Étienne's jacket. It happened before Éliette could even cry out. She heard the sound of crumpling metal as the car fell apart thirty metres below, and the thwack of the gulls' wings as they scattered, screeching off into the white sky. And then nothing but tumbling rubbish.

She stayed still for a moment, as if dazzled by a camera flash, before falling to her knees, her head in her hands. In the darkness between her palms she saw Étienne's face as he realised the trap had closed on him, his mouth opening to utter a word he would never speak, and his hands flailing in thin air. Click, clack!

She had no tears left, only spasms that shook her back. She stood up and with all her might threw Étienne's bag to the ends of the earth, where she now found herself. She opened the briefcase, tipping out the contents of one of the plastic bags which puffed out like a white cloud on the wind. She was about to move on to the next bag when she saw the gulls returning one by one, perching on broken mattresses and bicycle wheels. They were watching her with their beady little eyes and ruffling their feathers as if to say, 'No need to make a song and dance about it. If you're not dead, you must be alive.'

Éliette closed the briefcase, turned her back on the sky and began walking down the bumpy track.